Blood and Whispers

A.C. HASKINS

Blood AND WHISPERS

A.C. HASKINS

Blood and Whispers

This is a work of fiction. All the characters and events portrayed in this book are fictional, and any resemblance to real people or incidents is purely coincidental.

A Baen Books Original

Baen Publishing Enterprises
P.O. Box 1403
Riverdale, NY 10471
www.baen.com

ISBN: 978-1-9821-2523-3

Cover art by Todd Lockwood

First printing, March 2021

Distributed by Simon & Schuster
1230 Avenue of the Americas
New York, NY 10020

Library of Congress Cataloging-in-Publication Data

Names: Haskins, A. C., author.
Title: Blood and whispers / A.C. Haskins.
Description: Riverdale, NY : Baen, 2021.
Identifiers: LCCN 2020050086 | ISBN 9781982125233 (trade paperback)
Subjects: LCSH: Magic—Fiction. | Murder—Investigation—Fiction. | GSAFD: Fantasy fiction.
Classification: LCC PS3608.A8366 B48 2021 | DDC 813/.6—dc23
LC record available at https://lccn.loc.gov/2020050086

Pages by Joy Freeman (www.pagesbyjoy.com)
Printed in the United States of America
10 9 8 7 6 5 4 3 2 1

For my dad, Casey, who taught me to
love stories and storytelling.

For my mom, Esther, who first encouraged
me to write my stories down.

And for Mrs. Dawn Burnette,
my eleventh-grade English teacher,
who, more than anyone else, taught me how.

ACKNOWLEDGMENTS

WHILE THE AUTHOR TENDS TO GET ALL THE CREDIT, WRITING A novel is far more often than not a group endeavor, and there are many people who helped bring this book into reality.

First, thank you to my parents, for raising me to be a reader: for filling my life with books, for pretending not to notice when I thought I was being sneaky by reading under the covers after bedtime as a kid, and for everything else you did to help me become the man I am. I love you both dearly, and I am so very proud to be your son.

Next, thanks to those who directly contributed to the writing process, from giving me ideas to helping me with edits and rewrites. In no particular order, I'd like to thank Phil Bolger, Jack Clemons, Keith Finch, Esther Haskins, James Quigg, Eric Koske, Landis Ford, Kimmi Johnston, Jeff Ivie, Sam Stanfield, Emily Vick, Cathe Smith, and anyone else I'm forgetting (there are almost certainly at least a couple) who served as an Alpha or Beta Reader at any point and provided me notes, feedback, impressions, and suggestions for how I could make it a better book.

Chris Smith, I didn't forget about you. Your name didn't appear in that list because you get a special thanks, on two counts. First, for letting me crash your meeting with Toni, at which she invited me to send her the manuscript when I was ready—without that, this may never have happened at all. Second, for going above and beyond when I asked you to provide feedback on the completed first draft. Your notes and comments had more impact on the development of the final draft than anyone. Thank you, for everything.

I'd like to thank the entire team at Baen Books, but especially Toni Weisskopf, who graciously read my initial submission and, rather than rejecting it out of hand when she decided it didn't quite meet Baen's standards, gave me detailed feedback on the aspects of the story I needed to address to turn it into something she'd want to publish—and more than that, something for which I'm proud to have my name on the cover.

Thank you, also, to everyone who supported and encouraged me along the way. Many of you I've already named for your contributions to the editing and rewriting process, but all my friends and family deserve a second round of thanks, whether they helped with the actual writing or not, for helping keep me sane during the stress of writing, and rewriting, and submitting, and rewriting, and resubmitting. I wouldn't have gotten through any of it without you all.

And, of course, an especially big thank you to my lovely wife, Nora, for putting up with me locking myself in my office for hours at a time (and sometimes entire weekends) to hang out with Thomas Quinn and his supporting cast rather than spending that time with her. I love you!

Blood AND WHISPERS

A.C. HASKINS

Chapter 1

THEY SCREAMED. AS THE CLOUD OF FIRE AND GAS AND WHITE-HOT cinders bore down on their homes, as the world ended around them, as they and their children faced their last seconds of life, they screamed. A profoundly useless gesture.

I gripped my glass tightly, the tawny liquid within swirling as my hand trembled. An empty bottle sat on the table next to me, mocking me with its undelivered promises of relief. I'd been drinking for over two hours since the nightmare had woken me up, but the scenes continued to play through my memory, as clearly as when they'd unfolded more than a hundred years ago.

They'd screamed, and we'd done it to them. A god had gone insane, and my comrades and I had put him down like a mad dog. But it hadn't been easy. We'd had to destroy the entire island, and all those people in range of the eruption and the earthquakes and the tsunamis we unleashed. In killing him we'd made a conscious choice, sacrificed them all for the sake of millions of others.

Thousands. Tens of thousands, even. Tens of thousands of pitiful, desperate, futile screams.

I'd stood there watching the demise of Krakatoa with my fellow sorcerers from a safe distance. We'd done nothing to save them. There was nothing we could have done to save them. But knowing that didn't make living with it any easier. It had been almost a century and a half since that day, and the screams still ruined my sleep on a regular basis.

That wasn't the only memory that haunted me, of course. Between the things I'd seen and the things I'd done over a very long lifetime as a professional sorcerer, I had no shortage of nightmares to keep me company. Half a bottle of whisky before bed, give or take, and I could usually manage to sleep through them. But not always.

As I finished the last sips in the glass, I looked at the clock. Just after four in the morning. No point trying to get back to sleep. With a resigned sigh, I threw the bottle in the trash and headed back upstairs to brush my teeth and get ready to face the day.

At least I didn't have much of a commute. After getting dressed and a quick breakfast, I made my way back downstairs, flipped the lights on, and glanced around the small shop I owned and operated below my small apartment.

Floor to ceiling shelves packed with books on every occult subject under the sun lined the walls of the cramped main area, and the rest of the floor was occupied by shorter shelves stocked with the sorts of arcane supplies and tools one might expect to find in such a store. One corner was set up as a reading nook, with a couple of armchairs and a small table. The register sat on a narrow counter toward the back. It wasn't much to look at, but it was mine—I'd been running Quinn's Esoterica for almost sixty years now, since I'd settled into my present semi-retirement. I could have lived comfortably without a job, but the shop gave me something to do. Sometimes it was even enough to distract myself from the memories.

It was still far too early to open up for the day, so I headed through the door behind the counter into the back room and turned on the light. This was both my office and where I stored the good stuff. One complete wall of the room was a wrought-iron cage, locked with a half dozen padlocks of varying ages and materials, its shelves filled with ancient tomes, jars and vials, boxes, and bags full of the rare, valuable, or powerful supplies and tools that drew my primary clientele to my door—every sorcerer, Fae creature, or other magical being within a two-hour drive of Philadelphia knew Quinn's was the place to go for hard-to-find items.

Two of the remaining walls of the room were lined with uncaged shelves, full of various books I kept for myself and my own research, as well as various small statues, knickknacks, and other mementos of a long magical career. From the ceiling hung the taxidermied remains of a tentacled creature vaguely resembling an octopus. Along the back wall there was a small desk, covered in papers and books and an old laptop. Next to it, a coffeemaker sat on a small filing cabinet, yesterday's cold leftovers still in the pot. Sighing again, I grabbed it and headed for the sink in the customer bathroom.

Once I had a full cup, I wearily sat at the desk and contemplated the documents in front of me: a large map of greater Philadelphia which I'd been steadily covering with markings, along with a handful of scattered sheets of paper with notes scribbled on them in my near-illegible handwriting. There was also an old book, opened to a page on ley-lines, the currents of magical energy which fuel advanced sorcery for those of us with the knowledge and skill to use them.

The global ley-line network is a living thing, constantly shifting around in vast and complex—but generally predictable—patterns. But a few days ago, I'd noticed the ley-lines in the area moving unexpectedly, resulting in nodes hundreds or even thousands of yards from where my experience told me they ought to be. Normally one of the largest in the city hovered under Fairmount Park, shifting slowly only from about Strawberry Mansion to The Cliffs between the summer and winter solstices. But now it was all the way down below the Museum of Art, almost a mile from where it should be this time of year. I'd spent most of yesterday mapping out the movements and trying to figure out what was going on.

I sipped my coffee, willing my brain to wake up, then set back to my task. Focusing for a second to bring my magical senses to the front, I mentally reached out to the nearest ley-line. I followed it along to a node where it intersected another line, feeling the tingling hum of its energy in the back of my mind. Once I reached the node, I felt back to my start point to figure out how far and in what direction it was from me, and carefully marked its location down on the map. Then I returned my attention to the node and followed another line, and repeated the process for node after node, line after line.

Tracing ley-lines like this is done by feel, not sight, so I couldn't exactly look up addresses—I had to figure out the distance and direction between each node as I went along and mark it on the map so I'd be able to compare the magical geography to the physical later. The work wasn't terribly difficult, but it was tedious and time consuming. I had to be meticulous, triple-checking each step; any error would throw off everything I calculated after that point.

At some point my gray tabby, Roxana, wandered down from the apartment upstairs to curl up in the bed I kept for her behind the desk chair. By the time I'd finished mapping out the changes in Center City and the surrounding neighborhoods, I looked up to realize it was time to open up shop for the day. I threw back the rest of my coffee and steeled myself to interact with people.

I needn't have bothered, as I had no customers that morning anyway. Could have been the rain. *That's it,* I told myself, *it's the rain. Definitely not my customer service skills.*

I didn't dislike people, necessarily. But I had a reputation in the magical underworld as a recluse, practically a hermit, who only dealt with others when necessary. Aside from customers and the occasional conversation at Bran's Pub, my interactions with other people were largely limited to some important professional contacts, visits to the Market, and attending the Grand Conclave every thirteen years as my rank obliged me to do. I'd long since stopped bothering with social pleasantries. It had been a couple decades since the last time I'd been on a date, and it had not ended well—Samantha was a nice girl, but I wasn't suited for dating anymore. The only woman I'd ever really loved had died seventy years ago. Her death was among the more prominent of the many memories which haunted my dreams.

In the absence of customers, I stayed in the back, idly reading through whatever I could find on ley-line movements in my personal collection, and had a few glasses of whisky to tide me over and keep the whispers in the back of my mind at bay. I had nightmares enough in my sleep; I didn't need them disturbing me during the daylight hours. I tried to put other thoughts out of my mind and to focus on my research.

The problem appeared to be that no matter how carefully I mapped the ley-lines or how many old books in long-forgotten languages I strained my eyes to read, the simple truth was that none of the authors on my shelves really seemed to know much about the nature of the ley-line network and its shifts. I'd looked—there were no historical records tracing the movements of the lines or the nodes anywhere that I could find. Plenty about using the energy contained within them, but little to nothing about their nature. It was a puzzle. Was this recent change something unique and unusual? Or was it merely part of a longer cycle?

I'd studied ley-lines in more depth than most—one of my mentors, an immortal sorcerer named Johannes, was something of an expert on them. But I hadn't spoken to him in three-quarters of century. Calling him for help on my ley-line curiosity wasn't really an option. There was far too much baggage, too much history. I just wasn't up to dealing with it. I put Johannes out of my mind, settled in with my survey notes and my map and my Scotch, and tried to look for patterns in the chaos.

Eventually I noticed that closing time had come and gone without the bell over the shop door ringing even once. I set aside my reading and stood up with a groan, then headed out to lock up. As I turned the deadbolt and set the magical wards, I noticed my hand was starting to tremble. Whether it was from the booze, the constant struggle to ignore the little voice whispering in the back of my mind of things I'd rather not think about, or simply that I'd forgotten to eat lunch, I couldn't say. Maybe all three. Regardless, I knew it was a sign I needed to eat something and get as much sleep as I could manage.

I didn't feel up to cooking, however. I grabbed the holstered Smith & Wesson J-frame revolver from my desk drawer and clipped it inside my waistband just to the right of the belt buckle, then unlocked the door I'd just locked so I could venture forth for dinner.

The gun was just one of my many eccentricities. Sorcerers tend to have enemies, even those of us who keep to ourselves, so we always need to be prepared to defend ourselves when outside the relative safety of our wards. But most of my brethren prefer to stick to magic. To my knowledge, I was the only ranked sorcerer in the world who had ever even considered a gun as more than a novelty.

There was a time—back when I was a dedicated soldier of the Arcanum—when I would have agreed with the rest of the magical community that guns were pointless for someone like me, who could throw fireballs and lightning from the tips of his fingers, who had fought demigods and demons and Fae monsters. The destructive power of a bullet paled in comparison to the things I could do.

But those days were long past. I hadn't conjured battle magic since the Shadow War. After what I'd done, what I'd seen on the Fields of Fire, I couldn't stomach the thought of doing so again. Defensive magic was fine, but the idea of burning my enemies down with the power I'd drawn on that day revolted me to my very core. I knew I could still do it, should I be driven to that level of anger again. I also knew now what it would cost me to lose control like I had that day and I had no desire to add to my existing collection of torturous memories.

No, if I were forced to defend myself these days, I'd rather put my faith in firearms than in magic. Besides, even if I were willing to consider using such powers, I'd realized a while ago that guns often make a lot more sense for self-defense. Fireballs are slow and cause a lot of collateral damage, and mages tend to prepare for spells and magical weapons anyway. Faeries—or most anyone else who might hold a grudge against me—don't often wear Kevlar.

I relocked the door behind me, double-checked the wards, and slowly walked the three blocks to Bran's, my knees protesting at every step. The pub was dim when I entered. It was always dim. The place was indistinguishable from the hundreds of other dingy Irish pubs in Philly: low lighting, dark wood paneling, faded Guinness ads on the walls, and a general feeling that the place hadn't been properly cleaned in years. It was mostly empty, unsurprising on a Tuesday. One elderly man in a trucker hat sat down at the end of the bar, there was an unattended drink covered with a napkin to indicate its owner had gone to the restroom and would be returning, and a couple of middle-aged women chatted at a booth in the back, but otherwise I had the place to myself. That was the way I liked it.

Behind the bar was a short man with thin bones, little muscle, and striking golden eyes, wiping down a pint glass. He noted my entrance and cocked his head.

"Mr. Quinn," he greeted me with a lilting Irish brogue. "Been a few weeks since ye set foot in here."

I took a seat at the bar, my joints thanking me for the respite, and gave a short nod. "Aye, Bran. I've been busy. What news?" My own brogue was softer, more of a background accent that lent some character to a voice gone gravelly from years of hard drinking. I'd dropped most of the typical Irish speaking mannerisms of my youth, but I'd never been able to divest myself of the lingering accent no matter how long I lived on this side of the Atlantic.

He shrugged. "Not much at all, to be sure. Things have been quiet since I saw ye last. I heard a rumor that a pair o' city detectives were asking around the community about some sorcerer this afternoon, Ethan or Eric or summat like tha', but they have not visited here, and I do not know what the questions were."

I grunted. "Well, let me know if you hear anything more about it."

He nodded, and I waved towards the whisky. He gave a slight smile and turned to get me a drink, his movements sharp and precise, like those of a bird. That wasn't a coincidence. The bartender—and proprietor—was a type of lesser Faerie known as a púca, a shape-shifter. Bran here could take on the form of a hawk at will, and his eyes, thin bones, and movement all reflected his other shape. That made him an excellent contact for a reclusive sorcerer who still liked to stay informed about the goings-on of the Philadelphia magical underworld: between the rumor mill in his pub and the things he saw and heard while hunting, he was generally better informed than most anyone else I knew in the area.

But the police asking about a sorcerer barely even counted as news. There were all sorts of mundane reasons cops want to talk to people. He might have witnessed a crime in progress or just happened to be friends with a suspected criminal. I filed the information in the back of my mind as something to worry about if and when it turned out to be cause for concern.

"So what can I do for ye, young Quinn?" he asked as he set a dram of Oban down in front of me. "You need some of me feathers again? I can give ye a good price."

I frowned. He called me young because he knew it annoyed me. And because he was entitled, being several millennia old. Damned Fae. To them, we're all young. I'm ancient by normal human standards, and finally coming into a respectable age in sorcerer terms, so it was annoying to be reminded that I was still a child compared to a huge portion of the magical world. I could remember when England's great sail-powered warships ruled the seas, but Bran could recall when men were still struggling to domesticate wolves. And he wasn't even a major player, just a minor Faerie whose feathers were useful for binding enchantments.

I shook my head. "Not buying today, Bran," I said curtly, "just had a craving for shepherd's pie."

Directness is generally best in conversations with the Fae. It helps keep them from dissembling. You start small talk and ten minutes later discover you've accidentally given away your first-born or some such. They're always looking for the advantage in a conversation, and they've had a long time to practice. I locked my eyes onto Bran's, letting him know I was in no mood for his games.

Regardless of our relative ages, I was still one of the highest-ranking sorcerers of the Arcanum, and that commanded respect from even the oldest of the Fae. The púca might remember when the first man set foot on Irish soil, but his own personal power paled beside mine, and he knew it. That's why he gave me information without demanding something in return—the Fae normally ask a price for anything, even minor rumors, but Bran had decided a while back that it was wiser to stay in my good graces in the long term rather than maximize his profit every time we spoke.

He returned my gaze for a few seconds, before nodding and looking away.

"No need to get testy," he muttered as he turned toward the kitchen. "I was only asking."

I said nothing in reply, just taking a sip of my drink while he headed to get my order.

"Thomas Quinn!" I heard someone call my name. I turned and saw a tall, pretty, blonde woman walking back to the bar from the restrooms.

"Sam," I acknowledged politely, while internally grimacing. Samantha Carr was a fellow sorcerer who lived somewhere in the Philly area. She'd been a frequent customer of my shop when she'd first moved here in the '90s, but I hadn't seen her in a while. She also happened to be the woman with whom I'd gone on that ill-fated date, over two decades ago. I already wasn't in a mood for conversation, let alone with her of all people.

"I haven't seen you in ages!" she continued as she took a seat. "When was the last time?" Her voice was silky, as if seduction were her default state. I remembered why I'd agreed to go on that date despite my reservations. I also remembered how I'd ruined it and forced my attention back to the present.

"The last Grand Conclave, I think. Where have you been?"

She smiled broadly, ignoring my gruff tone. "Travelling a lot, mostly. Just came back to the area a few months ago. How about yourself?"

"Same as ever," I mumbled.

"Still a surly curmudgeon?"

I shrugged. "I suppose. Where were you travelling?"

"Oh, all over," she replied. "Europe, Asia, Africa. Six months in South America. Just trying to experience things, you know? I realized I hadn't gotten to see anything worth seeing, and after the Trials, there wasn't any reason not to anymore."

I nodded silently.

It takes a long time to become a ranked Sorcerer of the Arcanum. By ancient tradition, those apprentices deemed powerful enough to face the Trials must first study under three Masters, each for a period of nine years. Then the Trials themselves can often take another three years of preparation and testing, as the Master of the Trials and his staff devise individualized tests across a wide spectrum of magical skills to determine how powerful the candidate is. Sam had still been finishing up her Trials when we met. Now that she was a fully-fledged Sorcerer of the Third Rank, I didn't blame her for choosing to enjoy her newfound freedom. I'd certainly done so when I passed my Trials. But that was a long time ago.

She continued telling me about her travels, but I only half listened. I didn't want to be overtly rude, given our past history, but I also had little interest in small talk tonight. I just wanted to eat and be on my way. I nodded at the appropriate points, threw in the occasional "Oh, really?" and thought about ley-lines.

Was it any wonder our date hadn't ended well?

After a few minutes Bran brought out a steaming plate of shepherd's pie and I turned my attention to the food.

Sam chuckled. "I can see you have higher priorities, and I need to get going anyway. I have some things to take care of," she said, tossing back the last of her drink. She reached out and touched my arm. "Speaking of which, take care of yourself, Tom. I'll see you around. Maybe I'll swing by the shop sometime."

I nodded as I swallowed a bite.

"You know where it is," I mumbled in way of goodbye. I focused on eating as she left, trying to forget about everything else for at least a few minutes.

Chapter 2

DREAMS OF DEATH AND DESTRUCTION PARADED THROUGH MY mind in jumbled scenes and images, as they did most nights. Mangled bodies in a nineteenth-century London apartment. An ancient temple beset by demons, my friends and comrades being torn to shreds around me while I was helpless to stop it. Another trip down memory lane to Krakatoa. But none of them woke me before light came through my window. It seemed the bottle of whisky I'd grabbed upon my arrival home had done its job.

The following morning, I actually had customers. Not many, but a handful—enough to keep me distracted. The weather was clear and sunny, so that probably had something to do with it. No regulars, however, until almost lunchtime.

"Quinn!" a familiar German-accented voice greeted me just as the bell rang to mark the opening door. "Good morning!"

I looked up to see a short, ugly dwarf with a huge nose and a bushy beard, wearing an oversized mustard yellow hoodie which did nothing to improve his looks. He was smiling merrily at me as he entered the shop and approached the counter.

"My, you look like shit," he said with the same jolly tone. "Bad dreams?"

I scowled. "Mannfred," I muttered gruffly in reply.

He was a klabautermann, a variety of kobold known for their

mastery of sailing, their love of music, and their irrepressible—and incredibly irritating—cheerfulness. Most magical beings hid their natural form when living among humans, but Mannfred had once told me that he figured he just looked like a particularly unattractive little person, so he didn't bother with a glamour. Sneers and looks of disgust didn't concern him in the least. Few people looked closely enough to notice the slight point to his ears, and those who did likely thought nothing of it given his deformed appearance.

"Just here to pick up my new hammer," he said, charging on with his insistent joviality.

I nodded and went into the back room to get it from the cage. His kind used special mallets to focus their magic, but Mannfred had lost his a few weeks ago in a boating accident. He probably could have replaced it himself—hell, he could have made himself a new one if he'd wanted—but he figured I'd be quicker and it would give him a bit of a vacation in the meantime. That kind of artifact is hard to come by in the New World, and while kobolds have been known to travel, once they settle in an area they tend to prefer to stay near home.

I'd asked a German contact to pick one up from the Faerie Market in Hamburg, and he'd dropped it off a couple days ago. Middleman transactions like this were my primary source of income. People will often pay a premium just to have someone else do all the work for them; Faeries and magical beings are no exception. A single such exchange could keep the bills paid for months, even when business was otherwise slow. I didn't really need the money, but it was nice not to have to dip into my savings to keep the lights on. I preferred to use my personal funds for more important things, like whisky.

"Stay safe," he said after he paid and tucked his new mallet into the pocket of his hoodie. "Apparently life is getting dangerous for sorcerers in these parts." He turned to leave, but I stopped him.

"Wait. What do you mean?"

"Have you not heard?" he replied, raising an eyebrow. "Everyone is talking about it this morning."

I shook my head. "Heard what?"

"Someone killed a sorcerer two nights ago. Nasty business."

"Oh? Bran mentioned the police had been asking around, but he didn't know what about."

Mannfred nodded. "I just heard it myself this morning, down at the docks."

"Who?" I knew most of the sorcerers in the city.

"Evan Townes. Nice kid. Damn shame, this sort of thing. Stay safe, my friend."

I didn't bother answering as he left. Evan was dead. That was certainly news worth knowing. So much for mundane police inquiries.

Evan had been one of my regular customers, like virtually every practicing mage in the area. He was just a kid, a grad student at Penn. More importantly, he was Arcanum-trained. Not a particularly powerful mage, certainly never a candidate for rank or voting membership in the society. But a talented kid who had been identified in his youth and given training in his power.

There were lots of such unranked sorcerers scattered around the world, who were never enrolled in a true apprenticeship, but were trained enough not to hurt themselves or others as their power developed, and were taught about the realities of the world like the Arcanum's customs and treaties and the consequences for breaking them. I'd identified him as talented in his early teens when he first started shopping at my place and ensured the Master of the Trials had taken him for instruction. We weren't close, but I didn't care for people murdering my customers.

There wasn't much I could do about it, however. We sorcerers are a hardy bunch—even the least powerful among us generally live well over a century before aging catches up—but we can be killed just like anyone else. If we see it coming we have more capacity to defend ourselves than most, and we heal from wounds a lot faster than other people, but there's little anyone can do about a bullet in the brain or a stab wound to the heart. The news bothered me, but people get murdered sometimes, especially in a city the size of Philadelphia. It was a matter for the police, and it sounded like they were already on the case.

Later that afternoon, when the shop was temporarily free of customers, I ducked into the back room to see what the news had to say about it. After pouring myself some Scotch, I cleared my ley-line research aside and logged onto the old laptop, searching for anything I could find on Evan's murder. It didn't take much detective work: right on the front page of the *Philadelphia Inquirer*, "Police Investigating Satanic Murder in Mill Creek." That could be problematic. I continued reading.

According to the article, Evan had been found dead in his own apartment. He'd been the victim of what appeared to be an elaborate occult ritual of some kind, though the reporter didn't go into any detail of the crime scene. It quoted the reactions of some community members, which varied from "He was such a nice young man, a model student," to "This is just further proof of the toxic influence TV and video games have on impressionable youths." And it ended with a contact number and a request that anyone with any information please report it to the police.

Not much useful in there, but it was worrying. If it had in fact been an occult ritual, this probably wasn't just an ordinary murder. Evan was a sorcerer. A ritual sacrifice meant either he'd gotten himself tied up in some bad business, or he'd been targeted for some other reason. Either way, I highly doubted it was a coincidence that the victim was an Arcanum-trained sorcerer.

I sighed. I was the only Sorcerer of the First Rank in the area. Which meant that, if someone were running around doing death rites in Philly, it would fall on me to deal with it. At the very least I needed to figure out whether it was anything the Arcanum at large needed to worry about. There was no getting around that, no matter how much I might prefer otherwise. My city, my responsibility. It was the way things had been done for a thousand years. Short of formally renouncing my rank, I had to check it out.

Just then I heard the bell over the shop door, and I set my whisky down next to the laptop before heading out to see who'd come in.

There were two of them, a man and a woman. The man looked familiar—tall, muscular, with ink-black skin and a shaved head—but I couldn't place him immediately. That wasn't terribly surprising; I'd met an awful lot of people over the last two centuries. I couldn't be expected to recognize every one of them by name.

The woman with him was new to me. She was a petite, fairly attractive brunette, wearing an irritated expression on her face. She glared around the room as if the shop somehow offended her.

The man stood idly thumbing through books in the African Animism section. I assumed it was out of default rather than anything to do with his own ancestry—alphabetically it was the closest section to the front door. I wasn't sure why, but I got the feeling neither of them were here as customers. That piqued my interest, as there were few other reasons anyone visited my shop.

I cleared my throat to alert them to my presence.

Both of them reacted immediately, their eyes snapping over to me, slightly widened in surprise—I have a lot of practice being near silent when I want to, and they'd clearly missed my entrance into the room. They both considered me for a quick moment. It felt like they were scanning me as a potential threat, further reinforcing my suspicion they weren't looking to buy books.

I must not have seemed that threatening. Apart from a faded tattoo on the back of my left hand, there was nothing outwardly distinguishing about me at all. I was just another skinny white guy in a predominantly Irish neighborhood. My shaggy brown hair, just starting to go grey, revealed nothing of my true age. I was wholly unremarkable. Of course, if it weren't for the long sleeves of my rumpled button-down shirt, the rest of my many tattoos and scars might have given them a second's pause. Then again, in this day and age, maybe not.

The man replaced the book he was thumbing through, exchanged a measured look with the woman, and approached me while she watched from her position near the door.

"Good morning, sir," he said evenly, displaying a badge. "I'm Detective Henri Lajoie, Philadelphia PD." He gestured at the woman. "This is my partner, Detective Adrienne Connors."

His voice was deep and melodious, with the faint hint of an accent from long ago, as if he'd moved here when he was a child and never quite lost the language of his youth. Haitian, if I were to guess, based on his dark skin and French name. I still couldn't figure out where I'd seen him before. I hadn't had any run-ins with the police in ages.

"Are you Thomas Quinn?" he asked.

I looked at him without a word for a long moment. I didn't exactly scowl, but my expression wasn't especially welcoming. I was disgruntled. It wasn't anything in particular—I was just usually disgruntled these days. And if my intuition were correct, they weren't here to give me money in exchange for goods, so there was no need for me to pretend to be polite.

"Yes, I'm Quinn," I eventually replied, begrudgingly.

"I thought so," the big detective answered. "You fit the description we got to a T."

"Oh?" I raised an eyebrow.

"Yeah," he nodded, "we were told to look for a guy who looks like he just got out of bed and reeks of booze, with a voice that sounds like Liam Neeson."

That was fair, I supposed. I hadn't showered in a couple days, I hadn't shaved in a week, and I'd been drinking whisky just before they'd arrived. The dark circles under my eyes weren't doing me any favors, either. I wasn't sure who Liam Neeson was—a cinema actor, probably—but it was an Irish name, so it probably wasn't too far off either.

"Well, you found me. What do you want?"

"My partner and I are working a case, and we're trying to clear some things up. We've visited several occult and new age shops around the city, as well as a couple college professors. No one's been able to help us so far, but the general consensus seems to be that this is the best place in the area to go for information on the occult, especially obscure topics. John Rafferty over at Penn, in particular, spoke very highly of you."

I scoffed and rolled my eyes. Rafferty was a professor of philosophy and religious studies, and self-styled occult expert, who occasionally ordered books through my shop. Personally, I thought he was a hack, someone who picked evidence to support his theories rather than developing theories to explain the evidence. But he wasn't an idiot, and while he wasn't part of the magical underworld himself, he likely knew enough from his studies and his tangential contact with it to figure out that I was more than a simple entrepreneur.

Detective Lajoie glanced back at his partner. She didn't say anything, but her eyes were narrowed in irritation and she was absentmindedly—or perhaps intentionally—tapping her foot in impatience. I didn't know what her problem was, but she clearly didn't want to be here. That was fine. I didn't want her here either. And I certainly had no interest in getting involved with a police investigation.

"I sell books. I'm not a consultant," I said curtly and turned back toward the back room.

"It's a murder investigation, Mr. Quinn," he entreated. "Please, just a few minutes of your time."

I stopped but didn't turn to face him. "Evan Townes, I assume?"

"That's the one. What do you know about it?"

"Aside from the fact I know the victim was one of Rafferty's teaching assistants at Penn, not much," I gave a slight shake of my head. "I read about it in the *Inquirer*, and I've heard rumors that some detectives have been asking around. It's a small community."

"Fair enough, Mr. Quinn. Will you help us catch his killer?"

I thought about it for a few seconds. I was already going to have to investigate Evan's death. I saw no sense in complicating that investigation by getting tied up with the police. If it were a genuine magical ritual, their investigation would go nowhere—the police had no hope of catching a rogue sorcerer. And if it were just a mundane murder with occult trappings, my expertise would be pointless. It was a waste of my time either way.

"No," I finally answered. "Ring the bell if you decide to buy anything." I again started toward the door to the back room.

"We just need help identifying some symbols found at the crime scene. Google has come up short. Everyone else we spoke with mentioned you're some kind of an expert with esoteric languages and symbols."

I stopped again and reconsidered. That was truer than they would believe. While some aspect of the Fae's magic allows them to speak any human language they choose without ever having to study it, I'd had to work hard for two centuries to gain fluency in several dozen tongues. But that effort meant I was probably the foremost human scholar in obscure languages alive. Maybe I could help their investigation after all.

I turned around.

"Fine. You get two minutes. Show me."

He pulled a yellow envelope from an inside pocket of his jacket. As he laid out several pictures on the counter in front of me, I quickly realized two things.

I immediately recognized the symbols in question as Faen glyphs, the characters used to write a variety of Otherworld languages, including a couple with which I was familiar. That was probably why they'd been directed to me; a handful of other occultists in the city might recognize it as Fae writing, but that would be about the extent of their knowledge. Even among trained sorcerers, it was the rare specialist who bothered to learn the languages of the Otherworld—there were no Barron's courses in Faerie tongues; I'd had to study the few I knew the hard way, over many years. Unless the detectives happened to stumble across a Faerie willing to cooperate with mortal authorities, which was unlikely to say the least, I was probably the only person within a few hours' drive who might actually be able to help them.

Right after identifying the glyphs, however, I also noticed that they appeared to be scrawled on the walls in blood.

I looked back up at the detective, one eyebrow cocked.

He nodded at the unvoiced question on my face. "Yes, Mr. Quinn, the symbols were drawn in the victim's blood after his death. Do you recognize them?"

"Erm," I grunted as I gave them a few seconds consideration. "Yes. They're genuine glyphs, characters from an obscure ancient language not many alive have ever encountered." No need to go into details about their origin.

"Can you read them?"

I looked back down at the photos and studied them carefully.

"No," I replied after a moment, furrowing my brow. "I know the writing system, but not the dialect. Some of the words are somewhat familiar, but not enough so that I can piece it together. It's like if I were trying to read German, but only spoke English. I don't know if I could translate it in any reasonable amount of time."

Of course, I also had a few Fae contacts who could almost certainly translate it faster. But I wasn't about to volunteer that information to the police, for the same reason no Faeries were likely to cooperate with the detectives of their own volition.

Immortal beings have long memories, and many of the Fae haven't gotten over the wars and persecutions they suffered during the rise of Christianity and Islam, displacing them from their ancient territories in this world and forcing them into hiding. A lot of them still don't trust humans, especially authority figures. The Treaty of Tara, the peace accord that ended the Faerie Wars a thousand years ago, includes a mutual commitment between the Arcanum and the Fae to keep the existence of Otherworldly beings—and that of the magical community in general, for that matter—a secret from ordinary humanity. Non-sorcerers don't get to know about how the world really works except in only the direst of circumstances. Potential blood rites were bad, but not enough to justify risking a treaty violation, even if I'd thought the police would believe me.

"Hm," Detective Lajoie mused, but then Detective Connors rolled her eyes and stomped over from her spot by the door.

"Come on, Henri. I told you this was a waste of our time. He's just another crazy occultist with delusions of magical grandeur. We should be letting the lab guys find someone who can translate it for us."

"Excuse me?" I looked over at her with a scowl, struggling to remain somewhat professional in the face of her insult.

She ignored me and continued addressing her partner. "We have more useful things to do with our time, like following up on the skinning angle."

He turned to face her. "You heard what Professor Rafferty said, along with everyone else we talked to. You think the lab guys are going to hear anything different?"

She looked as if she was about to object further, but then thought better of it. She looked over at me, glaring as if I were somehow at fault for her partner's decision to come here.

"Whether or not I'm deluded, Detective Connors," I growled, "you and your partner came to me, not the other way around. And I won't be insulted by people who came to ask my help, police or not. Get the hell out of my shop. Your two minutes are up. We're done here."

"Wha..." she began to say, but her partner cut her off.

"Adrienne, go have a smoke," he muttered. "I'll meet you outside."

She looked at him and saw the expression on his face. He was clearly in no mood for further discussion. I assumed they'd been having a similar argument before they even got here, which at least explained why she'd looked irritated since they'd arrived. After shooting me another glare, she spun on her heel and walked outside in silence.

The bell over the door rang quietly after she left, and Detective Lajoie turned back to me.

"I'm sorry about that, Mr. Quinn. I understand your anger, but I'd appreciate if you reconsidered. This is still a murder investigation. Your assistance could help catch a killer."

I closed my eyes and breathed deeply for a moment, trying to recover my composure. My hands were shaking. I knew full well what I was capable of when angry enough, so I had worked for many years on my ability to keep that particular emotion in check. The quiet voice whispering in the back of my mind to let it free slowly faded into silence as I calmed down.

I opened my eyes and looked at the big Haitian detective.

"No, Detective Lajoie," I shook my head. "I gave you two minutes. I told you what I know. Now I have to be getting back to work."

He glanced around the empty shop and turned back to me with a raised eyebrow.

"Really? This place keeps you that busy?"

I scowled. "That's no concern of yours."

"It's a concern of mine," he replied, "because right now you're the only person to look at these photographs and recognize the symbols at all. Which means you may well be the only person who can help us catch a brutal murderer, Mr. Quinn. I hope you'll do the right thing."

I took a deep breath and thought it over. I had little desire to get involved—I much preferred to stick with my ley-line research and ignore the world around me. Plus, his partner's behavior further disinclined me to assist them. She had made me angrier than I'd been in a very long time. I didn't like having to silence that voice in the back of my mind, the one that was always ready to act if only I'd give in to its urging. Anything that gave it an excuse was something I would rather avoid.

But the victim was a sorcerer, the newspaper had described it as a satanic ritual, and the glyphs had been written in the victim's blood. While I hadn't been on good terms with most of the Arcanum for the better part of a century, I had never renounced my rank and actually left the society. And since all signs were pointing to a sacrificial blood rite of some kind, that rank meant I was obliged to investigate. I couldn't just ignore those responsibilities, no matter how much I might want to.

And if I were going to have to translate the writing anyway, it couldn't really hurt to pass that information on to Detective Lajoie, as long as I left out anything which might lead to him learning things he was better off not knowing.

I finally grunted affirmatively. "Okay, Detective. I can't promise it will be quick. But if I can translate them at all, I'll let you know. Should I keep the photos, then?"

He shook his head as he started to gather them up and return them to the envelope. "No, that would be against policy, sorry.

Can't risk them getting into the newspaper. But I can have the writing transcribed for you."

I narrowed my eyes slightly at the implication I might leak details to the press. But I brushed it off—he didn't know me, so that one wasn't a personal insult, just a general precaution.

"Do you have an email address I can send the transcription to when it's done?"

I silently handed him a business card from the counter next to the register, and he tucked it into his jacket. He then pulled out one of his own and laid it on the counter.

"Thanks for your time," he said as he turned toward the door. I briefly heard him saying something to his partner outside, but they walked off before I could make out anything clearly.

I put it out of my mind—Detective Connors wasn't my problem anymore and thinking about her would only make me angry.

Instead, I went into the back office and downed the remainder of the whisky I'd been working on when the detectives arrived, then poured myself another.

Chapter 3

THAT NIGHT, WELL AFTER DARK, I LOCKED UP THE SHOP AND caught a cab to Mills Creek. I'd found Evan's address in my records, from an invoice for a book he'd ordered last year. I needed to check out the crime scene, to determine if his murder had in fact been a magical working, and if so to look for clues the police wouldn't be able to find.

All magic leaves residual energy behind, like ripples and stains in the fabric of reality, which fades over time in proportion to the amount of power used. Those of us with the gift can see such energy patterns. Back in the late nineteenth century, back when I'd still been young and naïve enough to believe in the Arcanum, I'd volunteered for a team tasked with investigating and stopping what turned out to be a mad djinn rampaging across Europe. We'd tracked it from Istanbul to London via the residual energy it left behind as it tore its victims apart.

A major blood rite like human sacrifice would leave plenty of evidence, which would last days, maybe even weeks, past the original event. Hopefully I'd be able to reconstruct the ritual's structure and technique enough to start figuring out who—or what—had killed Evan. Complex rituals tend to be fairly unique to whoever designed them, like an artist's signature style. If I could identify specific themes or aspects of the working's construction,

I might be able to identify a suspect. Or at least figure out what *kind* of mage was behind it.

Assuming it was a genuine magical working at all, of course. With any luck, it would turn out to be just some kind of Satanic cult that happened to get their hands on an ancient book written in a forgotten Faen dialect. In that case, I could safely leave it in the hands of Detective Lajoie and his partner, and crawl back into my whisky bottles and ley-line research.

As I approached the door of Evan's somewhat shabby building, I focused for a second and whispered a phrase in Aramaic. Nothing happened from my perspective apart from a slight tingle on my skin, but I knew that if anyone were watching me, I had just faded from their sight and they'd forgotten I'd ever been there. It was a handy glamour I'd picked up many years ago from one of John Dee's journals, one which he'd attributed to the medieval Syrian sect called the hashashin. It wouldn't stand up to any amount of magical scrutiny, but it was useful to avoid the police knowing I was sneaking into their crime scene.

I unlocked the front door of the walk-up almost absentmindedly with a wave of my hand and headed upstairs to Evan's apartment. Locks are easy.

Before I even got to his front door, I knew for certain that whatever had happened here, it was definitely real magic. The whole third floor stank of blood, urine, and human defecate. But the hallway radiated terror and desperation, far beyond a mere smell. It wasn't subtle. It was the kind of energy that even the non-magical pick up on, though they don't realize it—the kind that gives people a shiver down their spine, a desire to leave a place despite not knowing what happened there. Something truly evil had occurred here, leaving its mark in everything around it.

There was a uniformed guard sitting in a chair outside the police-taped door to Evan's apartment. He looked distinctly uncomfortable. I couldn't blame him. But I needed him to act on that discomfort, long enough for me to get past the door.

The Arcanum is more a loose cooperative organization of individualistic sorcerers than a true government, so we don't exactly have laws about the use of magic beyond upholding the terms of our treaties with other factions in the magical world. But we have numerous ancient customs and traditions that are broken only at one's peril. Among those is a strong taboo against using magic directly to subvert the free will of another sentient being, meaning I couldn't just psychically order the officer to stand up and walk away. I didn't even know how to do so if I'd wanted—the taboo extended to the mere study of such skills, not just their application.

However, it did not extend to the use of magic to induce physical sensations. While I couldn't take control of the man's thoughts, I could certainly influence him in other ways, to prod him just enough for him to give in to his already-strong desire to leave, at least temporarily. With a silent apology, I focused briefly on making him feel like his bladder was uncomfortably full. He squirmed in his seat for a few seconds, then abruptly stood up and rushed down the hallway past me toward the stairs, desperately seeking somewhere to relieve himself.

I didn't want to touch anything here if I could avoid it, so once he was gone, I willed the door to open and stepped into the apartment, ducking under the police tape. I didn't bother to turn on the lights; my eyes saw just fine in the dark. But as soon as I crossed the threshold, I stopped just inside the doorway, stunned.

The photos Detective Lajoie had shown me were just of the walls. I hadn't seen the rest. I hadn't seen the blood on the floor. There was so much of it. It's easy to forget how much blood a human body contains, even when you've seen it before. The furniture had all been removed from the living room, and blood pooled on the bare hardwood floor like a layer of spilled paint. Evan hadn't just been killed, he'd been drained like a slaughtered animal.

But it wasn't the blood that had stopped me in my tracks. The energy I'd felt in the hallway was almost overwhelming once across the threshold. A tidal wave of misery and hopelessness pressed against my mind, trying to push me away. I struggled to fight off its influence.

This wasn't just the residual energy of an evil act. It was an active, malevolent force. It was purposeful. Setting something up like this required intent—the deliberate desire to cause terror and anguish to all who encountered it. Why would anyone, even an evil being, put the additional effort into leaving this dark energy behind? I'd never encountered such a thing before.

But malicious residual energy or not, I was here for a reason.

Even for those with the right natural gifts, it takes decades of intense training to master high-level sorcery, and a large part of that training consists of learning to control one's mind. Trying to tap into the energy of a ley-line is a little like trying to fly a kite in a tornado—every emotion and instinct says to stay away, that it's too dangerous, too overwhelming. Anyone seeking to wield that kind of awesome power, then, must first learn to quiet their subconscious emotions and instincts, to push their clouding effects to the side.

By itself, it's not magic. It simply requires a disciplined mind, a strong will, and many years of practice. Your emotions don't go away; they are exactly as strong as ever. They're just pushed aside into their own little compartment of your brain. The thinking, rational part of your mind can work free of distractions like fear or anger. It considers your emotions, catalogues them with interest, and proceeds without being bothered by them.

But while sorcerers learn this skill to help us work with ley-lines, it's fantastically useful in a variety of other situations, too. Such as when you're overcome with revulsion, but still need to be able to think clearly.

I closed my eyes and took a deep breath in through my nose, fought through the overpowering stench of blood and death, and I focused. My emotions and preconceptions fell to the side, and my rational mind noted their intensity as one might consider a particularly grotesque piece of art in a museum. I opened my eyes and looked around with absolute calm and clarity.

I again noticed the volume of blood spread throughout the room, but rather than recoil in horror, I observed the stains and tried to understand what they were telling me.

I'd seen plenty of bloodstains before—that djinn had left an awful lot of its victims' blood behind, alongside its residual energy. So had the Shadows. I'd learned to read the stories left in dried blood through long experience.

I noticed that the main pool of blood, which had turned black as it dried, had an unusual surface shape. Blood is a liquid when inside the body, but it holds various solids that do weird things as it dries: when pooled outside the body, it clots and separates. The main clot in the center forms a bumpy, uneven sheet, the edges develop radial cracks as they dry faster than the viscous portion in the middle, and the liquid serum which separates during the clotting process forms a yellowish-red stain around the solid black main pool. But in this case, the bumpy, uneven center wasn't quite right. On closer inspection, I saw it had a fine ridge, clearly tracing the outline of something heavy which had been laid atop the blood as it dried.

There was the telltale brownish-red spatter of arterial spray a few feet away, and another smaller pool of blood off to the side.

I looked up and saw a bloody hook in the ceiling. When livestock is slaughtered, the carcass is often hung from a hook so gravity can help drain the blood before the meat is butchered. I realized that was what must have happened here: Evan had been hung from the hook, probably upside down, and his throat opened. That accounted for the initial arterial spray pattern, with the rest of his blood pouring out from the wound to the floor below. Then his body had apparently been removed from the hook and laid on top of the blood pool, where it dried around him into its present pattern. I could see the footprints where the killer had moved the body after the blood was drained. In fact, from the footprints I identified there were at least two killers, one with significantly smaller feet than the other.

I next noticed holes in the hardwood filled with pooled blood that could only have come from stakes driven through his hands and feet, pinning his body in place. But he had to have already been dead by that point, his blood drained beforehand. Had he been executed while pinned to the floor, most of it would have pooled in his body, contained by his skin.

On close inspection, the shape of the outline was odd, not quite right. My detached mind quickly realized that he hadn't merely been killed and drained of blood, but also dismembered. Human bodies aren't proportioned the way this outline indicated—it looked like his arms and legs had been removed and swapped, so his legs extended from his armpits and his arms from his hips. Then they'd been staked in that position. I didn't know why anyone would do such a thing, but that was clearly what the physical evidence indicated. The why would have to wait until I could get back to my books and start researching sacrificial blood rites. It wasn't exactly my area of expertise.

That also might explain the smaller bloodstain: if Evan had been wearing clothing at the time, the killers would most likely have removed it before dismembering him. A pile of bloody clothes may well account for the stain pattern in question, though they would have had to get a lot of blood on them before being cast aside like that.

I then turned my attention to the writing on the wall, which I had already seen in Detective Lajoie's photographs. I could now see that they had been inscribed with two fingers from the same hand, written in an orderly, unhurried pattern. The hand in question had been calm and steady. From the red footprints below, I could identify the starting point and follow the order in which the glyphs had been written, which would be useful for deciphering their meaning.

I slowly looked all around the room, up at the ceiling, down at the floor, storing everything in photographic detail. The blood patterns, the footprints, the writing, everything. It's amazing what the mind can do when you manage to cut through all the clutter.

Now for the unpleasant bit—the actual magic. Focusing might be a skill anyone can master with the will and the patience to learn, but it's only the first step. The next part was a bit trickier.

It's sometimes referred to as opening the "third eye," but only by people who have never done it. It's nothing like opening an eye. It's more like tasting than seeing and involves opening your whole body to the magical energy around you, letting it pass through you.

And goddamn was the magic in this room foul.

Not exactly painful, but certainly not pleasant, it played along the energy channels of my body. I knew the emotional side of my mind was shuddering, revolted by the touch of this energy. It tasted of dead, rotting flesh, of desolation. It felt of all things rancid and putrid and decomposing. That was my first impression. I didn't get a second, because it was also aware. And angry.

What happened next was something I'd never experienced before. Unlike actively probing around me, tasting was a passive form of magic. It didn't require acting upon anything, just letting it act upon your senses. Much like seeing something with your eyes or hearing it with your ears, there was no way tasting would alert anything to your presence in itself.

But somehow, a fraction of a second after I began tasting it, the energy in the room changed. It coalesced in a spot directly above the site of Evan's death, the lights in the room flickered once, the temperature dropped to freezing, and it lunged at me. It was like someone expected a sorcerer to show up and set a trap.

How interesting, my detached mind remarked.

But focusing doesn't shut down the subconscious, just pushes it to the side. Recognizing the threat, my instincts kicked in before my rational mind had a chance to process what was happening and decide on a course of action. I instantly slammed shut my energy channels and threw up a shield. Just in time, as I felt the impact of the dark energy a fraction of a second later, the cold of it washing over me, trying to penetrate. I was surprised, but I had it handled. Then I heard an unexpected sound.

"What the hell? How did this door get opened . . . ? Goddammit, is someone in there?!"

It seemed the officer on crime scene guard duty had returned from his urgent bathroom break. And in my initial shock after walking into the apartment, I must have forgotten to close the door behind me. He still couldn't see me through my glamour, but if he came in to investigate, there was a good chance he'd walk right into my back.

To make matters worse, a fraction of a second later I realized I had a bigger problem than being discovered. Maintaining active spells like glamours and shields takes energy. If I'd had time to bind the shield to a physical object like a piece of jewelry or a wand, the focus would have acted as a conduit, letting me power the spell with the surging energy of the ley-line node I felt in the earth directly below us. But since I'd been caught off-guard, I was instead drawing on my own reserves, limiting how big a shield I could maintain while also holding the glamour. I felt the attacking spell starting to seep over the top of my defenses. Directly toward the police officer who was about to investigate the open door.

He wasn't going to walk into my back, he was going to walk right into the path of whatever the hell this spell was. I didn't know what that would do to him, but I could hazard a guess that it would probably be very, very bad.

Shit. I didn't have much choice here. I had enough on my conscience already. I wasn't going to let an innocent bystander pay the price for my miscalculation.

"What the f . . ." I heard the officer start to exclaim behind me as I dropped the glamour and suddenly materialized a few feet in front of him. But I would have to deal with him in a minute; right at this very second, I had a more pressing concern.

No longer maintaining two spells at once, I was able to expand my shield to block the spell's advance. I flooded it with energy, and it flared into a bright blue wall of light, from floor to ceiling directly in front of my outstretched left hand, and the faded tattoo on the back of the hand glowed a matching color. I was already starting to shake with the exertion, but fortunately I didn't have to hold the shield long. After a couple seconds, I felt the attacking spell dissipate as it wasted itself on the effort to get through my shield.

I let the shield fade back into nonexistence and stood there for another second, just breathing heavily as the trembling got worse.

"Hands up, pal! You've got a lot of explaining to do!"

I turned to see the officer aiming his sidearm at me, his eyes wide with confusion and shock. I slowly raised my hands, palms out towards him. It wouldn't do to get myself shot by the man whose life I'd probably just saved.

"What the fuck just happened?!" he barked. "Who are you?!"

"I..."

I started to answer, but between my exhaustion and my efforts to process what had just happened, combined with my need to figure out what to do about this particular situation, my focus slipped. Before I could get any more words out, the emotional part of my mind slammed back into the rational part like a locomotive.

Focusing comes almost instinctively to me at this point, my emotions separating from my rational mind in a fraction of a second. But no matter how easy it gets to slip into, no matter how practiced one gets with it, coming out of it never changes. The two halves of the mind have both just experienced the exact same situations, seen the same things, and registered their individual reactions. Once they're reunited, the conscious mind gets to experience every emotion that had been pushed aside.

I had just witnessed a couple horrors back to back. My emotions had ranged from revulsion and despair to fear. And I got the full impact of all of it at the same time, while already exhausted.

My mouth opened and closed a couple times, no words escaping.

Then I passed out.

I came to on the floor, where I'd collapsed. I heard the officer requesting backup on his radio, so I couldn't have been out for more than a few seconds. I was shivering violently—drawing on my own energy reserves the way I'd done to power that shield had chilled my core body temperature several degrees.

I was also in handcuffs, and I no longer felt the weight of my firearm in its holster. Evidently the officer had decided to secure the "suspect" before calling it in. Maybe I'd been out a little longer than I initially thought.

With a groan, I struggled to sit myself up. The shivering was rapidly subsiding now that I'd stopped expending energy and the magical fields around me were able to restore my power reservoirs, but the wave of nausea I had to fight off from the simple effort to sit up told me I'd be feeling the lingering effects for a couple hours at least.

"Okay, buddy," the police officer addressed me, "if you could go ahead and start talking, that would be great."

I shook my head. There wasn't really anything I could tell him that would get me out of this. I knew that if I stuck around, I was going to spend the rest of the night in a holding cell. I wasn't worried about going to prison or anything: even if trespassing on a crime scene were a felony, humans hadn't built a prison which could hold a sorcerer who didn't want to be there. But I had more pressing matters to attend to. First, I needed a good night's sleep to recover from what had just happened. But then I needed to start following up on what I'd found in Evan's apartment.

In blood magic, the blood itself is a conduit along which the mage can funnel power. Blood is an extremely effective channel for magical energy, much like gold is for electricity. It's one of the most easily accessible material bases of life, and life is energy. Blood magic, by itself, isn't a big deal. Plenty of people use it for minor things, like finding people, healing minor illnesses, or binding oaths. Such small workings only require a few drops of blood, usually voluntarily given, and are generally harmless.

But Evan's death was something else entirely. Major blood sacrifice went out of fashion centuries ago, for the simple reason that it usually requires murdering someone, or at the very least slaughtering an animal. People are more effective than animals because they're more aware of what's going on. The fear and pain magnify the power gained through the blood—the more pain and terror, the more energy in the victim's blood.

Evan's murderers were building power for something. I didn't know what yet—that would require a deeper understanding of the ritual's construction and might require that translation Detective Lajoie had asked me for. But between the scale of the working itself, the deliberate malevolent energy left behind to deter people from the location, and the trap left behind for any sorcerer who might come along to investigate—sophisticated magic in itself—I could virtually guarantee that Evan wasn't the end of it. I was probably looking at the beginning of a serial murder spree, and if the first victim were anything to go on, they were probably targeting sorcerers specifically, or maybe magical beings in general.

All of which meant I couldn't afford a few days in holding. Whether I wanted to or not, I needed to deal with this before it got worse. Which in turn meant I needed to get out of there before this officer's backup arrived.

"Hey, pal," he said, "this'll be a lot easier for both of us if you tell me what's going on."

"Sorry, son," I groaned, looking wearily up at him, "but you wouldn't believe me even if I told you."

"What's that supposed to mean?" he asked, but I ignored him. Instead of answering, I closed my eyes, calmed my breathing, and focused. With a slight whisper, my handcuffs popped open.

"What the fu . . ." he started to react, but I was way ahead of him. He didn't have time to process what was happening before I was already on my feet. I stretched my hand toward him and lightly tapped his forehead.

"Somnum," I said under my breath, and he fell asleep at my touch. I caught him as he started to collapse to the ground, and laid him down as gently as I could manage—he'd been through a lot in the past few minutes, and I didn't mean him any harm, but I needed to get out of there. Preferably with no solid evidence I'd ever been present in the first place. I knew I didn't have the energy to maintain the glamour spell I'd used to sneak in, so I couldn't make him forget I'd been there. But I could at least make his description the only thing I left behind. Hopefully his story would be crazy enough that no one would believe it.

I put my hand on the body camera on his chest and directed my will into it. With a slight pop, faint tendrils of smoke issued from the plastic casing, confirming that it was destroyed, erasing the video proof I'd been at the scene.

I used the bottom edge of my shirt to wipe my fingerprints from the camera casing, then glanced around. Spotting my J-frame and wallet in an evidence bag next to the officer's chair, I grabbed the bag and his notebook, and walked toward the stairwell.

I was three blocks away, turning the corner, by the time I saw the red and blue lights of his requested backup drive past in the other direction.

Chapter 4

I WOKE UP THE FOLLOWING MORNING FEELING WELL RESTED FOR the first time in ages. It had been a long time since I'd used that much magic, especially without the assistance of a ley-line, and it had left me exhausted enough to sleep dreamlessly. It was a novel experience—I'd forgotten what it felt like for my joints not to ache. I even felt up to showering and shaving before opening up the shop.

Then, having no customers to immediately deal with, I headed into the back room and started going through my books, pulling anything I could find on blood magic and ritual sacrifices, especially involving the Fae, off the shelf into a stack by the desk.

I didn't have a particularly extensive background in the subject—mages who can access the power of ley-lines don't generally have to resort to crude alternatives like blood and elaborate rituals—but I had been given a well-rounded education. Between what I'd learned from my Arcanum masters and what I'd encountered dealing with rogue sorcerers over the years, I knew enough about the basics to recognize that something was off about this particular ritual setup.

It wasn't just the unusual trap spell, which was something I'd never seen before—as best I could figure, that had to have been set to attack as soon as the magical energy in the room was disturbed in any way, like a sorcerer allowing it to flow through him so he could taste its patterns. That alone was interesting, because I wasn't even sure how one would set such a trigger. Whoever had been behind the trap was highly skilled and likely extremely powerful. Which raised the question, if they were that good, why did they need the ritual and the blood sacrifice in the first place?

Furthermore, the actual construction of the ritual itself just didn't make sense. Why lay the body down on top of the blood? Why the apparent dismemberment? Why stake the limbs down *after* the victim was already dead? I couldn't put my finger on it, but there was something weirdly familiar about all of it—it reminded me of something I'd heard about before. I didn't think it was anything from my personal experience, but it felt like I'd read about a ritual similar to this before, or maybe been told about it by someone else. Unfortunately, this was where my long memory became a liability: I had read about so very many things, and heard so very many stories, that I had no idea where to start narrowing it down.

And so, without a better plan, I cracked open the first book and started skimming, hoping something would spark that little hint of recognition in the back of my mind.

By midafternoon, I'd made my way through a half dozen books, but was no closer to an answer when a quiet voice rose up from the dark recesses of my mind. *The Immortal would know. Johannes could help you, if you let him.*

I froze.

This was the second time in three days I'd thought about my old mentor, someone I'd successfully avoided thinking about for years. This is exactly why I tried so hard not to get involved with anything beyond my shop and my own research. Getting involved meant having to think about things, having to face memories I didn't want to confront.

My relationship with my old mentor had not ended on good terms. It had been shortly after the first reports of the Shadows, mysterious creatures from another universe which had begun preying on humans and Fae alike. That was the last time I'd answered the Arcanum's call. The last time I'd been foolish enough to think I could save the world.

I'd been in a bad place when I met Johannes. By the time he found me, I was already halfway towards being a drunk, in large part because of the things I'd done in the service of the Arcane Court over the century before. Krakatoa. The Tear. Tunguska. That last one had been the final straw. What had happened in Siberia that morning had left me angry and resentful and cynical.

He'd tried to save me from myself. The Immortal wasn't affiliated with the Arcanum—he was much older than it; to my knowledge no one else in the society was even aware of his existence—and he'd done his best to rescue me from what they'd done to me, what they'd turned me into.

But he may have done too good a job. Over the two decades I'd spent learning from him, I'd rediscovered myself, and even regained some of my ideals. I'd learned to hope again.

Then the call came. The Shadows appeared out of nowhere, and the Arcanum needed everyone they could get. In my newly restored idealism, I'd seen it as my duty to answer the call, to serve humanity once again.

Johannes had begged me not to go. He reminded me of what I'd been when we'd met, what my service to the Arcanum had done to me once before. He warned me that if I followed that path again, this time it might well destroy me.

I went anyway. He'd been right.

I hadn't spoken with the Immortal since I'd left his house three quarters of a century ago. I hadn't been able to face him. I had too many regrets, too much shame about the things I'd done in the Shadow War, the things I'd done with the gifts he'd taught me.

I opened a new bottle of whisky and stamped that whispering voice back down into the darkness.

I'd found nothing useful in my books on blood magic, so I decided to try a different tack. I pulled out my copies of the Annals of the Arcanum, the society's records of every major event in its long history. I knew something was familiar about the ritual that had killed Evan. Maybe I'd read about it in the Annals at some point.

An hour later I found it.

It was a description of a series of blood rites the Lord Marshal of the Arcane Court and his men had discovered in thirteenth century Brittany. I'd read it before, a long time ago, and as I skimmed it now something about it jumped out at me. I reread it, carefully, then again, making sure I understood the archaic

Latin properly. The description wasn't straightforward, but after my third reading it still seemed like it was exactly what I was hoping to find, the memory that had been teasing me all day.

There had been a series of four murders. In each case, the victim had been tortured, flayed, and dismembered. The description wasn't clear on how exactly the ritual had been arranged, but it did say their blood had been used to write words of power around the body in Fae tongues.

Thinking back to what I'd seen the night before, I realized that if Evan had been flayed before being dismembered, his discarded skin would perfectly account for the secondary blood stain, the one I'd initially guessed was from bloody clothing cast aside. And hadn't Detective Connors mentioned something about skinning when she was arguing with her partner that they had better things on which to spend their time? It all fit.

And it named the people the Arcanum had executed for being involved. A rogue sorcerer, two apprentices, and . . . *oh, that's problematic.*

I grabbed another book off my shelf and laid it on the desk. Unlike most of the books I'd been reading through for the past several hours, this one wasn't dusty at all, nor was it written in Latin. It was still huge and leather-bound, but it was written in Elizabethan English, and was less than five hundred years old. It was a compendium of every kind of magical creature in the world for which the author could find a name, and I regularly used it as a go-to source when I needed fast information about a specific being.

I found what I was looking for where I knew it would be but had greatly hoped it wouldn't. The Avartagh, he was called in Irish.

Legends claimed he was a powerful example of the walking dead, who tormented his human subjects and drank their blood. Legends are told by someone who heard something from someone else. The reality is rarely even close, often to the point that it's impossible to tell how the truth became the myth. But according to the compendium's author, in this case it was clear where the stories came from.

He was a monster, an insane Faerie who hated humans for the perceived crimes of the Christians, mostly stealing his territories in Ireland and depriving him of worshipful followers.

Apparently, the part about drinking the blood of the humans in his territory was true. He hadn't been killed, despite the stories which credited druids or the hero Fionn mac Cumhaill for doing so, just banished back to the Otherworld.

Evidently, he'd returned at some point, if the annals' account of the blood rites in Brittany were accurate. And the annalist may have said the Arcanum executed him, but he'd been executed before. At least three times. Clearly it didn't take very easily.

I finished my whisky, thinking over what this meant.

It was not good. It was very not good. If the Avartagh were active once again, things could get out of hand rapidly. I might not be able to contain this alone.

Just then I heard the bell over the front door ring for the first time all day. I took a deep breath to calm down and slow my heart rate back to normal levels, then headed out to greet my customer.

Except it wasn't a customer: I stepped out of the back office to discover Detective Lajoie had returned. A quick glance around showed no sign of his partner.

"Mr. Quinn," he greeted me as he walked over toward the counter where I stood.

I grunted in annoyance. I didn't care for the interruption.

"What can I help you with today, Detective?" I asked in a tone suggesting I had no desire to help him with anything right now. "I haven't had enough time to translate those glyphs yet." They'd arrived in my inbox this morning; knowing what I now knew, I wasn't going to waste time. I'd have one of my Fae contacts translate it for me as soon as I got the chance.

"No, I know," he shook his head, "that's not what I'm here about."

"Oh?" I cocked my head in feigned interest. My thoughts were still on the Avartagh. I didn't have time for this.

"What does the word Arcanum mean to you, Mr. Quinn?"

My heart skipped a beat, and I hesitated for a fraction of a second. That was a dangerous question. Detective Lajoie suddenly had my full attention.

"Literally," I answered carefully, acting nonchalant, "it's a Latin word meaning 'the secret,' or 'the mystery.' Why do you ask?"

"My grandpapa died when I was young boy," he told me, putting his hands on the counter and looking me in the eye. "My mama kept a small box of some of his personal things when we left Haiti. In a couple of his letters, he mentioned 'the Arcanum' like it was some kind of secret occult society. I think he was a member. Have you ever heard of it?"

That gave me pause.

"No," I shook my head after a second's thought. "Doesn't ring a bell, sorry."

"Bullshit," he said frankly, looking me in the eye.

"Excuse me?"

"Let's stop fucking around, Mr. Quinn."

"What?" My voice grew dangerously quiet.

"There was a second murder last night, virtually identical to Evan's. We're now officially looking for a serial killer. Two of them, actually, but you probably noticed the footprints last night when you were in Evan's apartment."

That took me aback. I'd covered my tracks. How did he know I'd been there?

"I wasn't..."

Before I finished my protest, he wordlessly pulled a smartphone out of his pocket, turned it to face me, and tapped the screen. My voice trailed off as a video began to play.

It was security camera footage of the hallway outside Evan's apartment. The video began right as the police officer I'd encountered last night returned from his bathroom break to discover the open apartment door. I watched as he froze at the opening, then a flash of bright blue light illuminated the doorway, blinding the camera for a few seconds. When the light levels readjusted, I saw myself lying unconscious on the ground in the doorway, my face clearly visible, the tattoo on the back of my left hand still glowing blue, though dimming rapidly. The officer handcuffed me, frisked me and found my gun.

I watched in silence as the events unfolded from there exactly as I remembered them. My voice was clear as I told the officer he wouldn't believe me even if I told him the truth. The video cut out after I put him to sleep, destroyed his bodycam, retrieved my revolver, and left the frame toward the stairwell.

I looked up to see the detective watching my face, his expression carefully neutral.

"I guess you didn't see the other camera, huh?"

I was silent for a few seconds, processing this turn of events.

"Who all has seen this footage?" I asked quietly as I met his eyes.

"As of right now, just me," he replied. "This was my camera, not the department's—I set it up just in case someone turned up. I wanted to see what happened. But before you get any ideas, I have an automated email scheduled to forward a copy to Detective Connors and Captain Paulson, along with a couple friends at the *Inquirer* and some other news outlets, at midnight. Anything happens to me before then, and your secret gets out. Now, Mr. Quinn, how about you start telling me the truth? I know you're not one of the killers, because our timeline for the second murder puts it almost exactly when you were busy trespassing on the first crime scene and destroying police property. What I don't know is who or what the hell you are, or what you were doing there."

He was smart. And just then, as I looked into his eyes, recognition dawned. I suddenly realized why Detective Lajoie had looked familiar since I'd met him the day prior.

"Antoine Richelieu," I whispered in recognition, "You're Antoine's grandson."

I hadn't put two and two together immediately because of the different surnames, but he was the spitting image of his grandfather. A fellow First Ranked Sorcerer of the Arcanum, and a renowned master of Vodou, I'd known Antoine for most of my life. He'd died in the late eighties under mysterious circumstances, but that was long after I'd withdrawn from the magical world at large, and I didn't know any details.

He nodded. "I am. Now what the fuck is going on?"

I looked away for a few long seconds, thinking things over.

This changed the situation dramatically. It meant I would have to cooperate with Detective Lajoie whether I liked it or not. I certainly wasn't going to kill innocents to keep that video from getting out, and even if I had some other way to keep them quiet, there was no way of knowing who he'd addressed on that email. The video alone wasn't damning proof of magic, but it would lead to a lot of awkward questions I didn't have the time to deal with. At the very least I'd probably have to face charges of obstruction of justice, tampering with evidence, and maybe even assaulting a police officer, which was a hassle for which I didn't have time. My only real option was to convince him to cancel it, which meant giving him what he wanted.

The Avartagh's involvement also changed things. If he were behind Evan's death, and right now all signs pointed in that direction, this could escalate rather quickly. The truth, which I already knew, was that the Arcanum wouldn't be able to contain things rapidly enough to keep the human world unaffected, even if I could convince them of the threat and they responded immediately. The local authorities needed to be able to help protect the people of Philadelphia.

Furthermore, Detective Lajoie was personally in danger. The magical world is a perilous place—if I let him continue investigating this case uninformed of those hazards, he faced a very real risk of injury or death, far beyond the normal dangers of police work. What if he encountered the Avartagh or a rogue sorcerer and I wasn't there to protect him? And given what he already knew, even if I somehow managed to destroy his video and stop his email he was likely going to keep searching for the truth. In which case his blood would be on my hands.

However, I also realized I could now answer his questions without risking a treaty violation: as Antoine's grandson, the Treaty of Tara no longer bound me to keep magic secret from him. Close kin of Arcanum members, even those in whom the gift never manifested, were traditionally allowed to know their family history. Admittedly, that was mostly because they inevitably saw magic around them growing up, so this case was somewhat unusual. But it was still within the bounds of the customs.

I made a decision. I didn't know if any Lord Marshal had ever condoned actively working with law enforcement in the history of the Arcanum. And despite my long-standing relationship with the current Lord Marshal, and my many past services to the Arcane Court, I had no idea how she'd react when she found out I'd chosen to do so. But this wasn't her city. It was mine, and it was Detective Lajoie's. He had a right to know what was going on, and a right to help protect its citizens. And he damn well had a right to know about his own grandfather.

"We're going to need this," I announced, as I pulled a bottle of Scotch and a pair of glasses out from under the counter.

Chapter 5

I SAT DOWN HEAVILY IN ONE OF THE ARMCHAIRS IN THE READing nook, gesturing for the detective to take the other, and I poured us each a generous amount of dark whisky.

"Alright, son," I began, "let's talk." I took a large sip and savored the fruity, leathery flavor, letting it roll over my tongue for a second or two before swallowing and feeling the warmth spread down my throat and into my gut. This was the good stuff, twenty-five-year-old Glengoyne. It seemed appropriate.

The detective didn't touch his. He just cocked one eyebrow and waited expectantly.

I closed my eyes and thought back to my memories of his grandfather. "Where to begin? At the beginning, I suppose." I took another sip, then nodded to myself. "Yes, at the beginning. The Arcanum. That's the first thing you asked me when you came in, so let's begin there." I opened my eyes and looked over at him. "How old were you when Antoine died?"

He shrugged. "Three, maybe? Four?"

I nodded. "That would explain why he never told you about the Arcanum. Did you ever ask your mother?"

"I did, but she wouldn't talk about her papa. When I found the letters, she said it was just some club he'd been involved in back in Haiti, like the Freemasons."

"That's not technically incorrect," I chuckled. "The Arcanum is an ancient global society of human sorcerers. I am a sorcerer. Antoine was, as well."

Detective Lajoie was silent for a few seconds. Then he grabbed his glass of Scotch and took a big sip.

"Fuck," he whispered, looking away and thinking to himself for a long moment. He closed his eyes and just breathed, his hands shaking as he held the glass. Finally, he opened them and looked back at me.

"I've believed there was something more to the Arcanum for decades, but I could never find out anything about it. Do you think my mother knew?"

I nodded again. "She did. I met Antoine's daughter once, at a Grand Conclave—an assembly of all the voting members of the society. Isabelle, right? She must have been, oh, ten or eleven years old. Old enough that she certainly knew what was going on, at least."

"Wait," he furrowed his brow in evident confusion. "How could you have met my mama back then? You're what, forty-five? Fifty? She'd have been almost twenty years older than you."

I snorted. "I'm far older than I look, my boy. Sorcerers age well."

"How old are you?"

"Two-hundred and thirty-seven as of this past May."

"No shit? Huh." He sat back and took another sip, apparently processing that revelation. "Let's say I believe you," he said after a moment. "Then why would my mama never tell me that my grandpapa was a sorcerer?"

I shrugged. "That I can't speak to. She must have had her reasons. You'll have to ask her, I suppose."

"She's dead," he told me flatly.

"Oh," I replied quietly. "I'm sorry, son, I didn't know."

"This Arcanum," he asked, changing the subject, "what does it do?"

"Argue and get in people's way, mostly," I waved a hand dismissively, "but occasionally it saves the world. It was founded a thousand years ago, in theory to protect humanity from the dangers of the magical world and to keep the peace between humans and other magical beings."

"And that's what my grandpapa did?"

I nodded. "Sometimes. Most of the time we sorcerers keep to ourselves. We have plenty of our own politics, but we don't involve ourselves with everyone else's. One of the Arcanum's most sacred traditions is that we don't interfere in normal human affairs. But when there's some kind of threat, we respond as necessary. Antoine and I fought alongside each other for many years, against various forces that threatened the human race. I knew him well. I was sorry to hear that he'd passed."

"I take it that's what you were doing at Evan's apartment, with that blue flash and putting my officer to sleep. Responding as necessary."

I grunted affirmatively. "Well, I was seeing if there was anything worth responding to, at least. Evan was a sorcerer, too, so I had to check. Putting your officer to sleep afterwards was just to avoid going to lockup for trespassing when he discovered me there."

"And was there?"

"Was there what?" I raised an eyebrow.

"Anything worth responding to."

"Oh yes," I answered somberly, looking him in the eye as seriously as I could. "Yes, son, there most certainly was. We have a pair of magical serial killers on our hands, Detective Henri Lajoie. One who set a trap for sorcerers. That's what the flash of light you saw was: I was defending myself, and your officer, from a magical booby trap I'd accidentally set off. Whoever killed Evan was a mage—a powerful one, at that. I believe at least one of the killers is a Faerie."

"Faeries are real, too?" he asked, his eyebrows raised.

"Yes," I nodded. "But they aren't cute little winged pixies out of a children's book. Faeries are powerful magical beings from an alternate plane of existence called the Otherworld. Most of the pagan gods of ancient myths were Fae creatures of one kind or another. What I'd just found in my books, a few minutes before you got here, was a description of what sounded remarkably like the ritual for which Evan was sacrificed, and the name of the Faerie who designed it."

"So you have a suspect?"

I shook my head. "In a manner of speaking, but not one the police can go after. Not only are you not going to be able to find the Avartagh without magic, if you do happen to encounter him, he'll just kill you without a second thought. You don't have the tools to defend yourself from something like him. You aren't a sorcerer."

"But you are. You can find this Avartagh and deal with him." It was a statement, not a question.

"Yes, I am," I answered, nodding. "And a Faerie killing an Arcanum-trained sorcerer like Evan Townes is a violation of a thousand-year-old treaty between humans and the Fae, which means I'm obligated to do so—to find the killer and bring him to justice. But I'm qualified. In this particular case, you aren't. So I'm asking you to leave the heavy work of this investigation to me. No need for you to be in danger."

"Mr. Quinn," he began to answer, but I put up a hand and interrupted him.

"You can just call me Quinn, son. Most people do. No need for the Mister every time."

"Fine. Quinn. I hear what you're saying. And even if every word of it is true—and given how long I've been looking for answers about my family, not to mention what I saw in that video, I do want to believe you—that doesn't mean I can just stop investigating. It's a murder case, and I'm a homicide detective. Faeries or not, magic or not, my partner and I have a duty here."

I didn't answer for a second, just taking another sip of whisky and savoring it for a long moment.

"That's what I was afraid you'd say." I set down my glass. "So where do we go from here?"

"Well, given that I can't magically stop you from investigating—"

"You can't?" he interrupted.

"No, mind control is taboo within the Arcanum. We believe in free will, even when it's inconvenient. Which means that you're going to investigate, and you're going to get yourself hurt unless I make sure you don't. Plus, I think I could actually use your help—I can't be in more than one place at a time, and you're better suited to follow physical evidence and forensics anyway. Who knows? We might get lucky. So we need to figure out how to work together."

"And how do you suggest we do that?"

"Well," I replied picking my glass back up and draining it, "I propose a partnership." I looked him in the eyes. "We investigate together. You take care of things like physical evidence and victim background and so forth. I'll handle the magical aspects and deal with the Faerie, and any sorcerer accomplices, if and when we find them."

"By deal with him..."

"I mean kill him if necessary, or if possible, capture him and hand him over to the Faerie Court for justice."

"Leaving no one for Philly PD to arrest."

I shrugged. "That's the way it goes, Detective. Humans haven't built a prison that can hold either Faeries or sorcerers."

He thought it over for a long few minutes, sipping his whisky while I poured myself another and waiting for him to process all of this. Finally, he looked back over at me.

"I've been chasing answers for so long that I really want to believe you, Quinn. But I'm going to need more evidence to go on than your word. How do I know you're not just playing me?"

"Why on Earth would I do that?"

"I don't know. Maybe you're just a crazy occult enthusiast playing out your fantasies. Maybe you're hiding something. But regardless, I can't just operate on the assumption magic is real and you're a sorcerer based on your word and the fact you knew my grandpapa's name. Can you prove you're a sorcerer somehow?"

"How about the video on your phone? Or the fact I knew your mother's name, too?"

"That's not conclusive of anything. A flash of light, an officer fainting, it's all very suspicious, but it doesn't prove you're a sorcerer, let alone any of what you've said about the Arcanum or Faeries. You could have found my family background in public records if you looked hard enough."

I thought about it for a minute. "I can. At least, I can give you some stronger evidence you can see with your own eyes."

He got visibly excited—eyes wide, nostril flared, leaning forward in his chair slightly. "You mean you can do some magic?"

"No," I answered brusquely and shook my head. "Not right now, anyway. I don't perform on command, Detective, regardless of the reason. Magic is serious business."

"Then what evidence are you suggesting?"

"You said there's a second crime scene."

His eyes narrowed. "Yes, there is. The killers struck again last night, and a neighbor discovered the scene this morning. It's still being processed. Almost the same as the first one, except this time there were other victims."

"Other victims?" I raised my eyebrows in question.

"Yes. The family who lived in the house were all killed, but they don't seem to have been used for the ritual at all."

"Hm," I replied. I wasn't sure what to make of that. "Take me there. If the killers set another trap, you'll get all the proof you need. You can see exactly what happened at Evan's apartment last night. If not, I'll find some other way to prove that I'm telling the truth."

"Okay," he nodded, visibly disappointed I wouldn't be conjuring a fireball for his entertainment. "That I can do."

Chapter 6

THIRTY MINUTES LATER, AS THE SUN WAS STARTING TO SET, WE pulled up to a public housing project, rows of two- and three-story townhouses around a common area. I could see a playground in a little park through the buildings as I got out of the detective's car.

The townhouse we'd stopped at was blocked off with police barriers and a couple uniformed officers standing guard, along with a pair of crime scene investigators looking somewhat annoyed. Detective Lajoie had radioed ahead and told them to clear out of the building, so they'd had to stop processing the scene and wait for us.

The detective led the way, and the uniforms held up the crime scene tape for us to pass through. One of them handed each of us a pair of nitrile gloves to put on before we went inside. I felt the same sense of despair that had emanated from the previous crime scene, which would have driven off anyone but the police, who got paid to be in such places. No wonder the crime scene guys were irritable—they clearly didn't want to be here any longer than necessary.

"The victim's a woman," Detective Lajoie told me as we approached the front door. "We're not sure who yet. Jane Doe at the moment. Definitely not any of the people who actually lived here. The coroner will have to figure it out through DNA or dental records, if he can."

I nodded. There were a few dozen unranked sorcerers in the city. If the killer was sticking with them, I probably knew the victim again. I tried not to wonder who it was.

"Are you ready?" I asked him.

He looked me in the eye as he put his gloved hand on the knob. "Are you?"

I nodded. Expecting an ambush this time, I'd prepared a counterspell ahead of time: a spherical shield to contain the trap, using a ring I'd slipped onto my left index finger as a focus. I felt a powerful ley-line node below my feet and tapped into its energy to fuel the spell before I stepped inside.

The detective led the way in through the front door, down the hallway, and into the living room.

The smell hit me first. The furniture had been removed from the living room, drying blood covered the floor, reddish-brown glyphs on all four walls. Apart from carpet instead of hardwood, it looked almost exactly like Evan's apartment. But this time, arriving at a fresh crime scene that was still being processed, the body was still present. I could clearly see what I'd only deduced from the bloodstains at Evan's apartment: the victims hadn't merely been killed; they'd been violated. Defiled.

The corpse was flayed, the skin piled on the floor a few feet away. Her arms and legs had been severed and rearranged, with her legs extending from her shoulders and her arms from her hips. The elbows and knees bent at right angles, her hands and feet staked to the ground. Without eyelids her eyes bulged out, her mouth opened as if in an eternal, silent scream.

Despite her skin having been peeled off and cast aside, she was still recognizably a woman. Somehow that made it worse.

I tried not to breathe too deep. Just do what I had to do and get out, so we could let the crime scene unit guys do their work. I turned to the detective next to me.

"Stand behind me," I instructed curtly.

Despite his best efforts to remain professional, he looked awful. Given the energy of the place, I didn't blame him at all. But he nodded and stepped back into the hallway.

"Alright, you son of a bitch," I muttered to the malevolent energy in the room, "give me your best shot." I closed my eyes and calmed my mind, focused on pushing my emotions to the back, then opened myself to the magical energy in the room.

Once again, I tasted desolation and horror and terror and pain. And once again, that malevolent force rose and lunged for me. But this time I was ready. Without even a whisper or a conscious thought, I released the spell I'd bound to my ring.

The shield sprung closed around the attack, a translucent blue-tinged sphere of pure energy trapping the magic within, mere inches from my face. The spell was strong, but I was stronger, and I'd been expecting it. To my magic-enhanced eyes, it appeared as a writhing mass of darkness, streaked with shifting veins of angry crimson and violet within the bubble of power around it.

As quickly as it had appeared, it began to dissipate, but I bared my teeth and hissed, "Oh, no, you don't. Let's see what you are."

I directed my will into the sphere, into that foul cloud, and forced it to stay in place. I worked my way through the structure of the underlying spell and neutralized it, but rather than letting it evaporate into nothingness, I stabilized it. I pushed some of the ley-line node's energy into it, making it visible to the naked eye.

I heard the big man gasp behind me as he could suddenly see the dark cloud shifting around within the floating sphere.

"There's your evidence, Detective."

"It's . . . that's . . ." he trailed off, evidently at a loss for words.

"It's evil made manifest, that's what it is," I finished for him. "Now, this next part is going to be a lot more boring to watch. But it's a great deal trickier, so I'm going to need a few minutes to work."

Hearing nothing in response, I nodded and turned my attention back to the room in front of me.

I focused first on everything but the ambush spell, carefully studying every aspect of the magic in the room, starting from the outside and working my way in. There were subtle layers of energy throughout the space, and peeling them back, I confirmed the hints of Fae magic I'd expected. Faerie magic tastes differently to that used by humans or other magical creatures from our world—the Otherworld is so steeped in magic that it's part of its residents' very being. No other creatures can replicate that energy, and I've never encountered a Fae who could disguise those traces in its workings. There was definitely a Faerie present at this sacrifice.

I turned my attention to the corpse, noting without surprise that she had been a sorcerer as well, probably of about the same level of talent as Evan. That made sense—no logic in stepping back and targeting ordinary humans once you've started harvesting mages. That would just take longer to build up the required energy for the final working, whatever it was.

Convinced there were no further secrets to pry from the rest of the room, I finally turned my attention to the malignant ambush spell held captive in my trap. I wanted to study it, to see what I could find out about its creator.

The first surprise was that there were no counterspells to prevent such an investigation—anyone skilled enough to develop such an ambush should have known enough to incorporate such defenses. Either they had major gaps in their skillset, which was always a possibility with a rogue sorcerer, or they hadn't planned on anyone examining their work. Such things were child's play for someone like me. I'd learned how to study the structure of another's spell when I was an apprentice—my first master had taught me how to craft my own spells by having me dissect his workings. And given the ley-line node right under my feet, I could easily overpower the spell and make it reveal its secrets.

Slowly, cautiously, I teased it apart, working my way through it with care. Every sorcerer develops patterns in creating his or her workings, almost as reliable as a fingerprint. More like a signature, really, as the patterns change over time, but they remain true to the practitioner's character and mind. I soon realized that the malevolence and anger emanating from the spell weren't natural to the sorcerer who created it; they had been added after the basic structure was in place. Whoever had built this trap was cold and calculating, and definitely wasn't Fae. But I couldn't tell with any certainty what kind of creature it was. Humans aren't the only species that use magic and don't call the Otherworld home.

Finished with my examination, I let the spell dissipate and closed myself to the energy around me. Detective Lajoie and I were once again alone in the room, with just the unnamed victim's remains for company. But I sensed more death toward the back bedroom.

"I'd like to see the other victims," I said quietly, turning to the detective.

He looked shaken, far beyond the simple effects of the residual energy in the house. He'd just seen, firsthand, genuine magic. Something wondrous and terrible and inexplicable, undeniably right in front of him. He could no longer comfort himself with the possibility that all of this was a lie or a trick or a fantasy. He now knew the truth, that this really was a world beyond Horatio's philosophic dreams. It was a hard thing to accept, even for those who already suspected it. Even for those who hoped for it.

He swallowed. "This way." He stepped past me to take the lead.

There were four bodies, as I'd been told. A woman lying on her back, limbs askew, the expression on her face one of surprise, not fear. Her neck was clearly broken, but otherwise she hadn't been hurt at all—no signs of the torture that had been inflicted on the poor victim in the living room. Her three children were lying haphazardly around the room, looking for all the world as if they'd just been thrown in there without a second thought. From the skin lying next to her, the woman in the living room had been Caucasian, but this family were black, like most in this part of Philly. I wasn't sure what the connection was. Maybe they were friends who'd been in the wrong place at the wrong time. The detective had said they were the ones who lived in the house, but clearly they hadn't been the target of the ritual. No blood spilled at all, in fact. Just four necks broken, then the bodies casually discarded.

I didn't believe in a single omnipotent God. Not after having met so many purported gods in my life and having helped kill at least one. But I'd seen a crucifix hanging in the hallway. If Jesus and his purported Father were real, they definitely weren't Fae, of that I was certain. But just in case, for the sake of this woman and her children, I closed my eyes and asked her God, if he were listening, to take care of them.

"We can go," I told the detective, and he gratefully nodded and led the way out of the house. The cloying smell of blood in the living room was almost overpowering since I'd stopped focusing, and I just tried to keep it together before the emotional impact could knock me on my ass again. At least it wasn't as much of a shock this time.

We stepped outside, and we both closed our eyes and took several deep breaths of fresh air.

"Alright," Detective Lajoie told the crime scene guys. "We're done. You can finish processing it now."

He looked over at me. "Are you okay, Quinn?"

I nodded, my eyes still closed. "I'm fine. Just need a few minutes. If you thought that was rough, you should try it with full magical senses."

"I can't imagine," he said quietly. "We were in there almost twenty minutes. Did you get anything?"

"Yes, I definitely did. Let's go somewhere else to talk about it, though. I need something to warm me up after that."

We headed to a cafe down the block from the housing project, where I ordered a black coffee. Sitting in there, about to take a sip, I only then noticed that my hands were shaking. I took a few deep breaths. The detective politely didn't say anything, just waiting for me to begin.

"We already knew there were at least two attackers from the footprints. And I confirmed the presence of a Faerie. But it wasn't the one who set up the trap spell you saw. There was no hint of Fae magic in its construction."

"A human accomplice, then?" Detective Lajoie asked.

"Not necessarily," I replied, taking another sip of my coffee. "Humans and the Fae aren't the only magical beings around. There are dozens of magical species native to Earth. Most people just assume they're folk tales, like Faeries. Humans spend so much time asking if we're alone in the universe, while we aren't even alone on our own planet—but that's a conversation for another time. I couldn't narrow down what type of creature cast this spell. Odds are it was a human, but no way to confirm that just from the energy itself."

"Okay," the big man mused, "whoever was working with this Faerie, why are they killing people?"

"A ritual like this, a blood sacrifice on this scale, serves to build power. In both cases the victims were low-level sorcerers—I know Evan was, and I sensed the second victim's power at the scene of her death. Which means they're not just harvesting the raw energy from their victims' deaths, they're also likely channeling magical power through the release of the blood."

"Two sorcerers, huh?" the detective considered this, then paused for a second. "What about the others?"

"Others?" I asked, slightly confused.

"The other victims, Quinn. The family."

"Oh," I replied. "Them. I don't know. They weren't used in the ritual."

"Then why were they killed?" he asked. "That wasn't random. Four cleanly snapped necks. They were targeted."

I shook my head. "I honestly don't know. Maybe they're

connected to the victim somehow. Or the killers. That's more your line of work than mine."

"My partner is already following up on that, trying to see if there was any connection between them and Evan Townes, or the second victim when we get her identified."

"Good. Magical or not, the killers are probably staying in the general area, which means there might be something that connects them to the victims."

"You said the local magical community is pretty small, right? Is it possible someone knows who they are?"

I shook my head. "I doubt it. The Avartagh's definitely not local, at least." I paused and gave it a few seconds thought. "And he'd be unlikely to recruit any accomplices from the community around here. It's too tightknit. Too much chance someone would catch on and alert the Arcanum or the Faerie Court before they managed to finish their work. This isn't the kind of thing one does close to home. If I were going to hunt down low-level sorcerers somewhere, I'd find somewhere with plenty to choose from, but also where no one knew me."

"Alright, then. Where does that leave us? Where do we go from here?"

"The glyphs," I answered. "The glyphs focus the power released from the victim's death, channeling it for some purpose. We need to get those glyphs translated to figure out what the killers are building power toward."

"Have you made any progress on that front, then?"

I shook my head. "No, I haven't had time. But that's not a problem. I know someone who should be able to tell us what they mean."

"Who?"

"A Faerie. More specifically, a Faerie prince. The language in question is some dialect of High Taranic, spoken by the Aes Sidhe—the gods and goddesses of the ancient Celts. I'm on friendly terms with one of them. There are other Fae I know who might be able to translate, but Aengus will also be able to tell us about the Avartagh."

Bran was a good source of general information, but I doubted he'd have in-depth knowledge of someone like that. For this, I needed someone closer to the Faerie Court. Aengus would do. Besides, I liked him more than Bran anyway.

"Alright, can we go see him now, or do Faerie princes have visiting hours?" The detective was taking this all remarkably well, considering he'd only seen his first spell less than an hour ago.

I pursed my lips in thought. "I'm not sure where he is right now. But I know where he'll be tomorrow evening. We'll have to go see him at the Faerie Market."

"And what, exactly, is the Faerie Market?"

"It's what it sounds like, Detective. A gathering of the magical community for the exchange of goods and services. Think a flea market, but with Faeries and sorcerers."

"Okay, that seems straightforward enough," he replied. "Detective Connors should come, too."

I paused for a second.

"No," I responded quietly. "I don't think that's a good idea."

"Look, I know you two got off on the wrong foot the other day," he said, holding his hands up in a conciliatory gesture, "but she's my partner. She needs to be involved in the case, too. And she's a damn fine investigator in her own right, as well as one of the smartest people I know."

"That's not what I'm worried about," I shook my head, my voice low, my tone serious. "I got angry the other day because she caught me off guard. While I don't exactly relish the idea of spending more time with her, I can deal with it if necessary. But in this particular case, it isn't necessary, because it's not possible that we bring her."

"Excuse me? What do you mean it isn't possible?"

"There are rules, son." I paused. "Not many, but the ones that exist are taken very seriously. Video or no video, the only reason I've been able to tell you as much as I have, and to show you what I've shown you, is because of your grandfather. Antoine was a full member of the Arcanum, and members' kinfolk are allowed—expected, even—to know the truth. But your partner has no such dispensation. And even if she did, even if I were willing to take the risk of bending the rules and introducing her to the world as it really is, Detective Connors is a skeptic who I know from personal experience is liable to insult people who we can't afford to insult."

"I'll keep an eye on her, and make sure she keeps her opinions to herself."

I shook my head again. "Not good enough. You only learned

the truth this afternoon. You don't know what you're doing, how to interact with Faeries and sorcerers and other magical beings. I'm going to need you to follow my lead so as not to offend any sensitivities. A single misstep could potentially put both our lives on the line. I can't very well babysit your outspoken skeptic of a partner, too."

Hell, I thought, *that wasn't the half of it.* While I could explain the situation with Detective Lajoie, if I brought his partner to meet with the Fae and Aengus decided that decision unnecessarily risked the safety of the magical world at large, he could cause me serious problems. He was as close to a friend as I had among the High Fae, but he had his own obligations and people to consider—and the Treaty of Tara would be against me in any such disagreement. If we were to get the answers we needed, I didn't just need to avoid offending Aengus, I needed him on my side. The odds of that went down dramatically if Detective Connors were to come with us.

But Detective Lajoie took a hard line. "Quinn, look at this from my perspective. You're asking me for a lot of trust from someone I barely know. You've proved to my satisfaction that magic exists and that you're a sorcerer, sure. That doesn't mean you're on the level about everything else, no matter how much I want to believe it. So this doesn't go any further unless I have my partner to watch my back."

"Feel free to stay at home, Detective Lajoie. I'll get you that translation when I have it."

He shook his head. "I still have that video, Quinn. You're taking us with you."

"Knowing what you now know, you'd take that risk? I think you're bluffing, son."

"Maybe," he retorted. "But maybe not. Either way, I'm coming with you. So let's imagine what happens if I come with, we investigate this case on our own, and we leave Connors out of it. Sooner or later she's going to realize I'm up to something. And then she's going to try to figure out what I'm up to, and when she does so, she's liable to catch you doing magic—the way I did—or witness something else equally damning. And then your secrets, your rules, are a hell of a lot more at risk than if you get to control how she learns about all of this. She may be skeptical of the occult in general, but she's not stupid. She's got an engineering degree and both her parents are scientists; she'll believe the evidence if it's right in front of her and there's no other explanation for it. And when that happens, it's probably going to be a lot more awkward than a quiet conversation in your shop. She comes with. It's better for both of us."

I looked him in the eye for a long moment, then looked away. Damn it. He was right. Leaving her out would cause its own kind of trouble, with at least as much potential harm as bringing her along. Plus, if I were in his position, I'd want someone I trusted to watch my back, too.

I closed my eyes and breathed for a couple seconds, trying to calm myself as I thought all this through. In and out. If I were going to bring both of them with me, I needed to be very careful how I did so. Taking a risk was one thing. Being stupid about it was another entirely.

I finished my coffee.

"Okay, Detective. Your partner can come, but you two need to do this my way, or not at all. I need you not to tell her what's going on beforehand. You said she'll believe it when she sees it. Well, she'll get plenty of evidence to convince her. But don't raise her skepticism ahead of time; that'll make it a lot harder for everyone."

"Okay, Quinn. I'll just tell her you're taking us to meet a potentially useful contact. Where should I tell Connors to meet us?"

"Tomorrow night at my shop. Around ten. We'll head to the Market from there."

"Alright. Anything in particular we should bring?"

"No," I shook my head. "But you should make sure to eat dinner first. And probably take a nap. We're going to be meeting the Fae, and you don't want to be sleepy or hungry in their territory."

"Get some sleep yourself, Quinn. You need a ride back to your shop?"

"No," I waved a hand in a vague dismissive gesture. "I'll take a cab. I think I'm going to sit here and have another cup of coffee first."

"Okay then. We'll see you tomorrow evening."

Chapter 7

I DRANK MYSELF TO SLEEP THAT NIGHT. I NEEDED TO BE WELL rested, and short of burning out my magical power reserves again, that was the only way I knew I would get a full night's rest. And thanks to magically enhanced healing, I didn't even have to suffer through a hangover after. Though the tradeoff was that it took me an awful lot of whisky to get drunk, let alone to pass out—and that was true even before the tolerance I'd built up over the past decades.

Sure, that much even halfway decent whisky was expensive. But the shop mostly paid for itself, and it's not as if I had a whole lot else to spend my money on. Besides, I had plenty of reserves before I needed to worry about my budget. I'd lived a long time. Compound interest adds up. I wasn't sure how much I still had across my various accounts, but I knew the safe downstairs had at least five million in cash and precious metals even if my checks started unexpectedly bouncing.

The morning was uneventful. A handful of customers wandered in and out, and a few even bought things. It almost felt like the past two days hadn't happened at all, that things were back to normal. But I knew that wasn't true. In the evening, I'd be taking two Philly PD detectives to meet with a member of the Tuatha Dé Danann, the de facto royalty of the Aes Sidhe, the single most powerful of the Fae nations. And I knew that if

Aengus weren't convinced my decision was the correct one, I'd have to face a formal inquiry from the Arcanum's Master of the Seal, which could lead to all manner of unpleasantness.

I hoped the gamble paid off.

Just in case, however, I decided to get out ahead of potential trouble as much as I could. Later in the morning, when someone on the West Coast was more likely to be awake, I picked up the landline on my office desk and dialed from memory.

The woman on the other end picked up on the second ring. "Hello?"

"Rachel," I said.

"Thomas Quinn. What do you want?" She sounded irritated. Maybe I'd interrupted something. Maybe I'd just woken her up.

"Watch the tone, Rachel, you know I don't call for no reason," I snapped.

"Jesus fucking Christ, Quinn. I'm not in the mood. Just get to it. What's going on?"

"Someone in Philadelphia is committing ritual blood sacrifices. They've already killed two unranked sorcerers, and I doubt they're stopping there."

There were a few seconds of silence on the other end of the line as she processed that blunt statement.

"So," she eventually answered, speaking slowly, "the rumors are true?" The irritation had faded. It seemed she agreed that sort of news was worth a call.

"True enough. And I'm near certain there's a Faerie involved. Ever hear of the Avartagh?"

"Um," she paused, presumably trying to think, "not to my recollection, no. Unseelie, I presume?"

The Unseelie were the faction of the Aes Sidhe who'd refused to recognize the peace after the Treaty of Tara and continued to lash out at humanity for our supposed sins against the Fae. Most of them had given up their campaign after a few centuries, but there were always a few troublemakers who refused to admit defeat. Of course, for many of them it was just a convenient excuse to act on their natural sociopathic tendencies.

"Very much so. The last time the Arcanum dealt with him was in Brittany in the thirteenth century—there's an entry in the Annals if you want the details. It seems he's back. The crime scenes bear a remarkable resemblance to the description."

"Fucking hell," she swore. "Thanks for the heads up, but can you handle this? Philly's your city, and I need to go investigate reports of a wechuge up in British Columbia. It apparently killed a couple hikers yesterday, and there's no one local to deal with it. I was planning on heading that way in the morning."

Rachel Liu was a Rector, one of the Arcane Court's official regional representatives, which meant that she acted as an all-purpose deputy to the various elected officers of the Arcanum. She dealt with magical threats to humanity on behalf of the Lord Marshal, investigated potential Treaty violations on behalf of the Master of the Seal, arbitrated in disputes among Arcanum members on behalf of the Lord Justice, and evaluated potential sorcerers for training on behalf of the Master of the Trials.

Technically she had jurisdiction over her entire assigned region, which covered most of North America, but in practice there was always too much for the local Rector to do personally. Instead, by long tradition, ranked sorcerers like myself were responsible for dealing with such issues within our own declared territories, while the Rectors handled whatever happened outside those areas and left us mostly alone. Greater Philadelphia was my declared territory and had been since I'd settled here in the sixties. In theory I could refuse to deal with the issue, forcing her to step in and take over the investigation, but doing so would also forsake all future claim to autonomy in my home territory—it would be akin to telling the Arcanum that I was no longer the Ranking Sorcerer of Philadelphia, that the Court and their Rectors were free to meddle in the local magical community all they wanted. That was an even worse prospect than the hassle of dealing with the Avartagh myself.

"I wasn't calling to pass this on to the Rectors," I growled, annoyed. "This is my home. But I needed to let you know that the police are already involved."

"Of course, they are," she replied. "It's a pair of ritual murders in a major American city. Are they going to cause problems?"

"Do you remember Antoine Richelieu?"

That caught her off guard. "What? Yes, I knew Antoine. He died, what, almost forty years ago? What the hell does that have to do with anything?"

"It turns out the lead detective on the case is his grandson. Henri Lajoie."

Another long pause.

"Oh. Does he know?"

"He does."

Rachel didn't need to know that the reason Detective Lajoie knew about magic was because I'd made a mistake and let myself be caught on camera. As long as I'd clearly established that he already knew before I brought him to the Market, that would go a long way toward heading off potential trouble with the Arcane Court. Which had been the main reason for calling her in the first place: I'd wanted to establish through official channels that I was already working with Philly PD, and that my main contact there was kin to a deceased Arcanum member.

I didn't mention that his partner would also be tagging along. It would be a lot easier to beg forgiveness than ask permission on that issue, especially if I could convince Aengus it was the right decision. And by making sure Rachel knew ahead of time that at least one of the detectives was legitimately allowed to be there, it was a lot more likely the court would forgive me bending the rules for his partner.

She sighed. "Okay, there's not much we can do about that. If he knows, he knows. Keep an eye on him to make sure nothing gets out where it shouldn't."

"Anything else you need to tell me that I already know, Rachel?"

She ignored my sarcasm. "Thanks for the call, Quinn. I trust you're more than capable of cleaning up your own backyard but call me if you need backup. If you, of all people, can't handle it . . . well, let me know if that's the case."

"If I can't handle it, I'll probably be dead. But I'll give Detective Lajoie your number in case that happens."

"Fair enough. Try not to let it get to that." She paused. "Oh, Quinn, one more thing. Call your mother. She asks about you every time we talk."

I scowled again.

"Mind your own damn business, Rachel."

"Cheers, Quinn." She hung up before I could respond.

I replaced the phone on its hook, fuming. At least I'd achieved my purpose with the call.

I put it out of my mind. At six in the evening, I locked up the shop for the night, then prepared for a trip to the Faerie Market.

I wasn't terribly concerned about the Market itself. I attended it several times a year, generally to buy or sell some rare item or another that I couldn't find elsewhere. But old hat or not, one can never be too careful when dealing with the Fae. A lot of the stories about them are bullshit, but many are also based in truth. It takes a bit of experience before you start to know which is which. Take iron, for example: many people—of the relatively few who think about such things at all—believe that iron is anathema to all Faeries, either painful or poisonous, even corrosive to their very being. But really it depends on the type of Fae in question: some are pained by it, some merely find it distasteful, and some actually use iron tools themselves.

This evening, however, I was far more concerned with the tales about consuming Fae food and sleeping in their territory. Gift-exchange is taken very seriously among them. Guest and host, giver and recipient, both parties have mutual obligations. Sometimes it's simple, like the host granting hospitality and the guest agreeing to keep the peace of the house. Most often it's not. Eating a Faerie's food without first ensuring it's a gift freely given can magically link you to that Faerie, obligating you to return the favor in a manner of their choosing, regardless of your own opinions on the matter.

The Otherworld may be a magic land, full of wonder. But it's also full of danger—not knowing the rules and making even the slightest misstep can have huge consequences. No human could possibly know all the rules and all the dangers, even after a sorcerer's lifetime of study. That's the main reason why I was concerned about Detective Connors coming along. But there was nothing to do about that now except hope she would follow my instructions. In the meantime, I prepared as best I could.

Eating and sleeping were critical, to ensure I wasn't hungry or tired. When I woke up from my nap, I cooked and ate a steak in my tiny kitchen. I shared a bit of it with Roxana, who graciously accepted my offering as her just due. Then I showered and shaved for the first time in days. My eyes were still bloodshot—not much I could do about that. But I combed my hair and put on clean clothes. Nothing fancy, just some old jeans and a plain black T-shirt, untucked. At least it wasn't wrinkled. I completed the outfit with a pair of comfortable hiking boots.

Then I armed myself for battle. I didn't expect to be fighting, but after my unpleasant ambush the other night, I preferred to be ready.

I first put on a necklace, a simple chain with a golden pendant in the shape of a tree within a circle. This had been a gift from my father many years ago, and had a spell tied to it which would warn me of magical attack by heating up the metal. I tucked it under my shirt, against my skin, where it would be most effective.

The silver ring on my left index finger, engraved with Celtic knotwork, was the same I'd worn to the second crime scene. It would once again serve as a focus for defensive spells, anchoring the power of the nearest ley-line so I wouldn't have to burn through my own stores.

Into my left pocket went a small dagger with a bronze blade, its surface etched with runes of power binding a couple of useful minor spells to the metal. The sheath was secured to a pocket shield, a handy plastic contraption specifically designed to conceal the distinctive outlines of tools or weapons in pockets.

I also pulled out my gun. Not the J-frame, this time. I decided to bring a bit more firepower, just in case: a customized Glock 20, carrying fifteen rounds of ammunition plus one in the chamber. I pulled the slide back a quarter of an inch to confirm there was, in fact, a round in the chamber—when you actually need to use a gun is a bad time to discover it isn't ready to fire. Once I was satisfied, it went into a holster inside my waistband just to the right of my belt buckle. A carrier on my belt, behind my left hip, held two spare magazines.

Over it all I put on a thin wool overcoat. It was a little warm for the early August night, but the coat was the most important part of my outfit.

Traditionally, sorcerers are depicted wearing robes and funny hats. The funny hats are meaningless: everyone wore funny hats in medieval Europe. But the robes, like those of monks and priests, are a mark of station. They set us apart from society at large, proclaim us to be members of an order above that of the secular world. However, unlike priests and monks, it's a lot more hassle for sorcerers to go around wearing robes or cloaks every day in the modern world. To keep a low profile, we've taken to coats in keeping with relatively modern fashion norms.

Mine was a simple charcoal-colored wool overcoat, but the spells woven into the fabric proclaimed my Arcanum membership and rank, clearly visible to anyone attuned to magic. When visiting the Fae it didn't exactly give me diplomatic immunity, but it did oblige my hosts to abide by the treaties they had with the Arcane Court. That could well mean the difference between walking out with the information I needed and not walking out at all.

I looked myself over in the mirror, spinning around in a complete circle, and nodded in satisfaction. No telltale bulges of concealed weapons. I had a license to carry in Pennsylvania, but I preferred to avoid the subject entirely unless I actually needed it, and the easiest way to do that was to make sure it stayed concealed. Detective Lajoie already knew I carried, of course—he'd seen the crime scene guard take the revolver off me on his video. But there was no sense making an issue of it, especially given that Detective Connors didn't know me at all.

Ten minutes before ten o'clock, Detectives Lajoie and Connors knocked on the front door of the shop. Time to meet a Faerie prince.

Chapter 8

"NICE COAT," DETECTIVE LAJOIE COMMENTED AS I LET THEM IN.

I grunted. "Did you both eat and sleep?" I asked.

"We had dinner after work, and I took a nap," he replied. He looked at his partner.

She nodded. "Yeah, an hour or so."

"Hmph," I muttered. "Give me a second." I headed into the back office, unlocked the cage, and grabbed two bracelets off a shelf. Relocking the cage, I took them back out to where the detectives stood waiting.

"Wear these," I instructed, holding one out to each of them.

They each took them from my hands and looked at them curiously. They didn't look like anything special, just plain silver bands.

Detective Connors arched an eyebrow at me. "Jewelry? Really?"

"Yes," I answered, my tone flat. "You two will be my guests tonight. The bracelets identify you as under my protection, and that's important where we're going."

"Under your protection?" she asked. "Who do we need protecting from, and how do you propose to provide it?"

I shook my head. "Not like a bodyguard. It's an older form. Hospitality is very big in this community. When you're wearing those, any guest-right I can claim automatically extends to you.

Just wear the bracelets. Your partner agreed you two would do this my way."

I didn't bother trying to explain that the bracelets would also let them see any magical beings which happened to be invisible to the naked eye. That could wait until later, if it were relevant.

She glanced at the big man, who just shrugged. She shook her head but put on the bracelet.

"Detective Connors," I looked at her with a serious expression, "your partner here has told me you're skeptical of the occult."

"You might say that, yeah," she nodded, rolling her eyes. "I believe in the laws of physics, and nothing I've ever seen in my studies or in the real world has led me to believe they allow for magic. I prefer evidence to folk tales."

I could actually respect that, even if it were dead wrong. Most people don't believe in magic these days. TV, their science teachers, their books all tell them it doesn't exist, that it was just a primitive way of explaining things unknown to science. I remembered when people were still afraid of demons and changelings and would literally move their house if they believed it had been built in the way of a Faerie path. I don't much care what the general public believes either way. Back then, if you told them you were a sorcerer, they feared you. Now they laugh. I've never decided which reaction is more annoying. But I could at least respect someone who preferred evidence to stories.

However, given her lack of tact at our last meeting, the chance of that behavior again was problematic.

"Detective," I addressed her quietly, "it doesn't matter to me whether you believe in the occult or not. But the person I'm taking you to meet will be extremely offended if you express your feelings on the subject the way you did when we first met. So unless you want to sabotage your investigation, I'd advise you try to keep such opinions to yourself for the rest of the evening."

"Understood," she said, though she practically rolled her eyes as she did so. "I'll keep my feelings to myself."

That was probably the best I was going to get. I hoped it was enough.

"Let's go, then." I led the way out of the shop, making sure to lock the door and check my security wards behind me once Detectives Lajoie and Connors were outside.

Then I whistled, a loud birdcall that sounded like a deep trill, for several seconds, changing pitch a couple times. If either of the detectives were bird enthusiasts, they may have recognized the song of the European nightjar. But from their quizzical expressions I guessed they weren't.

"What on earth are you doing?" Detective Connors asked, one eyebrow arched.

"Calling our ride," I replied.

"We have a car, you know."

I shook my head. "It won't get us where we need to go."

"Oh? Where exactly is this Market, anyway?" Detective Lajoie asked.

"The Magic Gardens. Where else would you hold a Faerie Market?"

Detective Connors snorted. "The Magic Gardens are on South Street. It's a twenty-minute drive. My car could get us there just fine."

I reminded myself to be patient. "Yes, physically, it could get us to the address. But it wouldn't get us where we need to go. Not tonight."

Before either of them could respond, a taxi pulled up, a spotless Mercedes-Benz C-class sedan, driven by a bearded dwarf. I opened the back door and gestured for the two detectives to get in, then ducked through the door in time to see the look of confusion on their faces.

The interior of the taxi did not match its exterior. This was no ordinary cab, with its cheap plexiglass divider and credit card reader. The interior wasn't even the right size: the vehicle was enchanted to be larger on the inside, so upon passing through the door, we found ourselves sitting in a luxurious stretch limousine.

The customers and proprietors of this particular taxi service were of an older world and insisted on keeping up appearances. They would make no concessions to modernity beyond the bare minimum. The interior décor of the Market Taxi was inspired by a private Pullman luxury train car from the early twentieth century: mahogany and cherry wood trim, rich leather upholstery, with deep blue carpeting on the floor. Not to mention a fully stocked wet bar.

I'd been expecting it, so I took a seat next to the bar and started selecting a whisky. When I'd poured myself a couple fingers of eighteen-year-old Macallan, I looked up to see Detective

Lajoie smiling like a child—he'd gotten over his confusion quickly, and was apparently excited to see further clear and undeniable proof that magic was real. His partner, on the other hand, looked dazed, cognitive dissonance plainly written across her features.

That was understandable: two minutes ago, she'd declared that she didn't believe in magic, only now to be confronted by an impossible truth. She was sitting in a limousine, when she'd stepped into a taxi. Her brain was still insisting that what her eyes were telling her couldn't be real, that it was some kind of trick or illusion. And this was just the cab ride. We were in for a long night.

"What is this? Where are we?" she asked, as she looked around her. "What did you do to us?"

I looked at her. "I did nothing to you. We're in the taxi you stepped into thirty seconds ago."

She shook her head. "That's impossible. This is a limo."

"Minor distinctions," I shrugged. "Clearly, this is a special taxi. Specifically, it's the Market Taxi, and due to some rather complex spells, it's the only way to get where we're going."

She looked at her partner in desperation. "Henri, what the hell is going on?"

He put his hand on her shoulder and met her eyes. "Adrienne, calm down. Quinn can probably explain better than I can." He glanced over at me.

I took a sip of my whisky and then shrugged. "Detective Connors, your partner is already aware of this, but you should know that magic is real, whether you choose to believe in it or not. You're sitting in proof of that fact—a limousine that cannot exist, hidden inside a taxi too small to hold it—and I'm sure you'll get plenty more evidence before this is over. But I don't really give a damn whether or not you believe me, so long as you don't offend Aengus."

She stared at me, eyes wide, for a moment, before turning back to her partner.

"What the fuck is he talking about?"

He looked almost apologetic. "It's true. Magic is real. Quinn isn't crazy. I insisted you come with us tonight, over his objections, even knowing it was going to be a lot for you to swallow—not only do you need to know what's going on with the case, but I need you. You're my partner; I need someone to watch my back."

"And the fact that you're so very wrong about magic," I growled, "is why I need you to do exactly what I say tonight. This investigation, and possibly all three of our lives, depends on it."

Detective Lajoie leaned in close and whispered something in her ear. She whispered back, furiously. I could have listened if I'd cared to, but I didn't bother.

A few minutes later, just as I was finishing my drink, the taxi pulled to a stop and I got out, just outside the front gate of Philadelphia's Magic Gardens. The detectives silently followed, looking behind them to see that, from the outside at least, it was again just a Mercedes sedan.

Once Detective Lajoie closed the door the driver pulled away, presumably to pick up more marketgoers. The local Nibelungen community operated the Market Taxis, and by an elaborate enchantment, a ride in one of the half dozen or so such vehicles was the only way to enter the Market without going through the Otherworld. If you arrived at the same spot by any other means, the Faerie Market was closed to you. It may as well not even exist to your senses.

I opened the gate and looked back at my companions.

"Don't wander off. Stay close to me, and don't touch anything. I mean that. This is a dangerous place."

Without waiting for reply, I ushered them inside.

Back in the mid-1990s, a local artist bought an old, abandoned building and a couple empty lots, and started covering them in wild, crazy murals, many made from junk and garbage. He called it Philadelphia's Magic Gardens. It's a fascinating artistic experiment. It was also the obvious choice when the city's magical community were looking for a fitting new venue for the Faerie Market about a decade ago. What could be more apropos?

Of course, no one had ever told the owners that a bunch of Faeries and sorcerers and so forth were using their building every few weeks for a secret gathering after hours. What they didn't know wouldn't hurt them. And unless they somehow showed up via Market Taxi, they'd never find out.

On Market nights, the winding, multilevel, almost maze-like space was filled with stalls, vendors, and even some tents against the walls and back in the corners, with a clear path for marketgoers throughout. It was a fairly small venue, just a few thousand square feet—it felt crowded with only a dozen or so dedicated vendors and fewer than a hundred customers. Groups moved together from stall to stall, individuals darted through the crowds from somewhere to somewhere else, and here and there old friends, seeing each other again and catching up, stood in everyone else's way. Clouds of colored smoke issued from both stalls and groups of customers. I heard at least five languages being spoken besides English, three of which I could name. The vendors sold everything from books and tools to bottles of strange beverages and non-beverages and even liquid sunshine. In the Faerie Market one could buy potions and poisons and enchanted objects of all kinds. Or information, one of the most valuable commodities in the magical world.

The most common people seemed to be tall, beautiful men and women: the Aes Sidhe, the High Faeries of Ireland, Scotland, and the Isle of Man. Dozens of them lived in Philadelphia; any city with a large Irish diaspora community tended to have plenty of Irish Faeries as well. But there were others who appeared to be normal humans except for their eyes—flashing iridescently or glowing violet or golden or solid black—and their slightly pointed ears. There were impossibly short people and a couple of impossibly large people—giants, most likely, as trolls tend to avoid humans—and a half-dozen or so individuals in cloaks hiding their identities.

Detective Connors gasped as a couple walked past with curling ram horns sprouting from their temples and cloven hooves in place of feet.

"What the hell?" I heard her exclaim softly, and the pair looked sharply in our direction. Noticing my coat, they hurriedly turned away and minded their own business.

I looked over at the detectives. "Satyrs. Don't be rude, don't draw attention to yourselves, and try not to touch anything. Now come on." I strode into the crowd, looking for Aengus or someone who might know where he was.

Like the satyrs, everyone here could recognize my coat for what it was and gave me a fairly wide berth; Detectives Connors and Lajoie trailed in the clear space immediately behind me before the crowd closed back up in the wake of my passage. I wasn't sure where I was headed, because I had no idea where Aengus would be. But as the ranking member of the Fae community in the northeastern U.S., he almost never missed a Market night.

Unlike most of the Tuatha Dé Danann, Aengus had remained in this world when his kin had withdrawn to Tír na nÓg centuries ago. He'd wound up living in New York for a while when the Irish started flooding in during the Famine years, though to my knowledge he'd never established a permanent home on this side of the Atlantic. I'd met him there, at a Market up in Manhattan when I was in the city on Arcanum business, and he was one of my best contacts among the Fae. If he didn't know about the Avartagh, he'd know who I needed to talk to. But first I had to find him and convince him to help me.

I strolled through the Market, keeping an eye on the detectives behind me to make sure they hadn't wandered off. A group of small ugly creatures walked past, smoking pipes and chattering excitedly in some dialect I didn't recognize. Kobolds, distant cousins of Mannfred, though of a more land-based variety. I wondered what was running through the skeptical Detective Connors's head right now. Was she open to changing her mind? Or was she instead convincing herself this was all some sort of elaborate charade?

"Quinn!"

I turned to see the striking, Amazonian figure of Samantha Carr walking my way from over by one of the stalls, her own Sorcerer's coat much more stylishly cut than mine.

"Sam," I acknowledged her approach.

"I hoped I might run into you here," she said, smiling broadly. "Imagine, seeing you twice in less than a week! Lucky me!" But she stopped in her tracks as she noticed the detectives. I saw her eyes take note of their bracelets. "Friends of yours?"

I nodded but didn't make any introductions. "Have you seen Aengus Óg anywhere? I need to talk to him."

Sam frowned. "No, don't think I have. But it's good running into you again—I have something I want to talk to you about. I don't want to take your time if you're busy, though, and I was just about to head home anyway. I'll just come by the shop sometime. If I see Aengus on my way out, I'll let him know you're looking for him."

"Sounds good, thanks. See you around, Sam," I nodded curtly and moved on, the detectives close behind.

A few stalls on, I recognized a vendor who might know where Aengus was.

"Zoya," I greeted her as I approached her stall.

"Ah, Sorcerer!" she answered as she turned towards me.

She appeared to be a slender young woman with pale, greenish hair and wide blue eyes. She was pretty at first glance, but there was something off-putting on closer inspection. Her skin was clammy, and her features were oddly distorted, as if she were made of wax that had ever so slightly melted in the sun's heat.

Zoya was a rusalka, a type of lesser Faerie which had once been common in Slavic areas, known as fickle nature spirits—sometimes they helped ensure a good harvest, other times they lured young men to their deaths. That was the way with the Fae.

"I'm looking for Aengus. Do you know where he is?"

As with Bran, I knew the best route was always to get directly to the point. No sense giving Faeries an opening to play their word games.

She smiled, but rather than answer, she looked past me at the detectives, her eyes shifting from one to the other.

"Oh hello there, dear children. You look lost."

"Zoya." I snapped my fingers, bringing her attention back to me. Her serene expression faltered and she looked annoyed. "I'll have none of that. They're under my protection. Now where's Aengus? If anyone's seen him it's you. I know how you like to look."

The rusalka's eyes narrowed in anger. That had been downright unkind—like many in the Faerie world, she'd been hopelessly in love with Aengus for centuries. While he was never impolite and never led anyone on, she wasn't his type. She knew it, yet that didn't stop her from pining.

But my rudeness had been calculated—it succeeded in getting her attention off the detectives and back on to me.

"That will cost you, Sorcerer," she snarled. "I have seen the Óg, yes. But for your discourtesy, my price for the location is your blood. Two drops."

A gift freely given is a rarity among the Fae. Even something as inconsequential as the whereabouts of a mutual acquaintance had its price; they haggle as naturally as they breathe. But ill manners or not, her price was far too high—there plenty of others I could ask, and there were too many dangerous things an offended Faerie could do with fresh blood.

I shook my head. "No. Absolutely not."

"In that case, five drops from each of your companions." Her gaze shifted back to the detectives, and her expression looked almost hungry. "Less potent, perhaps, but still valuable. How about it, darlings? Just a pinprick, a few drops, and you shall be off to see Aengus."

"Why do I get the feeling that would be a bad idea?" Detective Lajoie responded.

I again shook my head, putting up a hand to stop him saying anything more.

"No, Zoya," I growled, my eyes narrowed in irritation. "I already told you they're under my protection, and I don't appreciate you making me repeat myself."

She looked back at me, her own eyes widening. She clearly realized she'd overstepped—she'd seen the bracelets, but her annoyance at my remark about her unrequited love for Aengus had led her to go too far. She knew exactly who—and what—I was, and knew she was outclassed. The rusalka was proud and haughty, but not stupid.

"I of course meant no offense, Sorcerer," she backpedaled. "Forgive my anger. We have known each other a long time. For the sake of our past dealings and in the light of my mistake, I will give you the information you seek at no charge. But remember this favor next time I am in need."

I nodded, my lips firmly pressed together. It wasn't the same as giving her a favor in exchange, but it was a promise to bear this courtesy in mind in future transactions. That I could tolerate. It was essentially the same deal I had with Bran for his news.

"I saw the Óg on the lower level, in the company of Tylwyth Teg. Two of them. You will likely still find him there."

That made sense—several legends about Aengus dealt with his love of fair women, and those of the Tylwyth Teg were some of the most beautiful in Faerie. They weren't uncommon in this area, so close to the Welsh Tract. That might also explain Zoya's sensitivity about my earlier comment—the Tylwyth Teg were exactly Aengus's type, wild and lovely dryads of the wood.

I grunted in acknowledgement and led the detectives toward the lower level, where I spotted Aengus as she'd said, chatting with two stunningly beautiful redheads. They were short, barely reaching his chest, and very slender, but with curves in all the right places. By custom, glamours were dropped at the market, so neither exuded the mind-ensnaring splendor they might normally project, but their natural beauty was literally Otherworldly anyway.

I approached, but politely waited a few paces from the conversing group, just at the corner of Aengus's vision. It would be rude to interrupt, and I needed him to be in a good mood.

While waiting, I noticed that Detective Lajoie didn't seem especially interested in the two extremely attractive Faeries a few feet from him, instead continuing to look around the market with barely suppressed wonder and excitement. I understood the excitement—after a lifetime of believing and hoping, he was finally getting to experience the magical world in the open. But it was still a bit odd that he didn't spare them a second glace. Even without glamours, the Tylwyth Teg were exquisite. He wore a wedding ring, yet even for a happily married man that was an unusual level of personal discipline. I mentally shrugged.

After a few minutes, the three of them laughed—the two dryads prettily, Aengus with a deeper reverberating chortle. And with that, the girls smilingly walked away and Aengus turned to face me.

"Thomas Quinn!" he greeted me with a broad smile. "How are you this evening, my old friend?"

"Aengus," I nodded. "I need a word."

He chuckled. "All business, every time we meet. You could stand to lighten up some, you know that? I remember a time when you still told jokes. I miss that Thomas Quinn sometimes."

He paused and looked at the two detectives behind me. Connors had regained her composure, though she hadn't said a word since we'd seen the satyrs shortly after our arrival. Lajoie still looked like wanted to wander off on his own, like a child in a candy shop, but was fighting the urge. Aengus looked them up and down and noted their bracelets.

"And who are your companions, Sorcerer?"

This was where things could get tricky. I hesitated for a second, and Aengus's eyes narrowed slightly as he noticed.

"Allow me to introduce Henri Lajoie and Adrienne Connors," I began carefully. "They're detectives with the Philadelphia police who brought something very unusual to my attention."

Aengus's eyes snapped to mine, examining my face for any sign I was joking or lying or misleading. He had a couple thousand years of practice spotting lies. He dropped his voice to a sotto voce.

"You are serious? You brought the police to the Market? And under your protection, no less? Does the Court know of this?"

I shook my head and replied in that same undertone. "No, they do not, and if I have my way, they're going to remain ignorant until I'm sure what's going on. We need to talk, you and I. In private."

"We do at that," he replied, a hard edge creeping into his voice. "I hope you have a very good reason for this breach of custom, Sorcerer. Or I will notify the Court myself. Follow me, all of you."

Chapter 9

AENGUS LED THE WAY TO A TENT TUCKED BACK INTO A DARK corner of the Gardens. It wasn't very large, but it was comfortably appointed, with carpets and several overstuffed armchairs around a small coffee table. Aengus gestured to the chairs.

"Please, have a seat."

He offered tea, which I politely rejected—Aengus may have been my friend, but rules are rules among the Fae.

Once we were all seated, he met my eyes. "Now, Sorcerer Quinn. Explain yourself."

I gazed back at him and raised an eyebrow. "You know me well enough that I'm almost insulted, Aengus."

He didn't even flinch. "I am sorry to hear that. I have always been fond of you, my friend. But this is too serious a matter to let our personal relationship affect my judgment. So how about you tell me what you thought was so important that you would violate sacred custom."

"I have evidence the Avartagh is active again. Here. In Philadelphia."

His sharp intake of breath was revealing. He knew exactly what that meant.

"And," he replied, "presumably, these two detectives are investigating whatever crime led you to that conclusion?" The old Faerie wasn't stupid.

I nodded. "They brought the murder to my attention. And while I probably could have come up with a way to keep them out of this meeting, the truth is I think they have a right to know what they're dealing with. And to be honest, we will need their help if I'm right. The Arcanum is still spread too thin—we haven't recovered from our losses to the Shadows. The Fae can't operate openly. The police have the resources, just not the know-how. They can be a useful asset. But that means the detectives here need to know the truth."

I paused, then added, "Detective Lajoie here is also the Sorcerer Antoine Richelieu's grandson. He has a natural-born right to be here any way you look at it. And he insisted on his partner coming, too, and pointed out that leaving her ignorant was inviting more trouble than initiating her in the first place. And I agreed with that assessment."

Aengus's brow was furrowed in thought for a long moment. Then he turned to the detectives.

"Do you know who I am?" The question was directed at both of them. Both shook their heads. He looked back at me.

"Very well, Sorcerer. They are under your protection, and you have earned my attention, if not my countenance just yet. Complete the formal introductions, then tell me what makes you think the Avartagh has returned to this world."

I didn't let it show, but internally I breathed an enormous sigh of relief. We'd made it past the first hurdle. He'd stopped short of granting his approval of my decision to bring the detectives, but at least he was willing to listen.

Since I'd already introduced the detectives to the Faerie, it just remained to present him in return.

"Detectives Lajoie and Connors," I said, turning to acknowledge them for the first time since we'd sat down in the tent, "It's my pleasure to introduce you to Aengus Óg, son of the Dagda, of the Tuatha Dé Danann, a warrior and poet without equal." I paused. "Also somewhat of a cheeky trickster," I added as an afterthought.

Aengus snorted. Good, that meant he had relaxed. Even the Fae could have a sense of humor. Maybe that's why he and I got along—he counterbalanced my generally sour disposition.

The Faerie princeling nodded to the two of them. "A friend of the Sorcerer Quinn is a friend of mine. I am honored to meet you both. May the road rise with you."

The detectives didn't know it, but for the first time since

we'd entered the Market we were safe. The blessing meant he'd officially acknowledged my guest right in his tent, and that it extended to them. He now had a responsibility to protect us until we violated his hospitality or left his domain. That's why he'd insisted I complete the formalities and introduce him to the detectives, rather than introducing himself. Custom and ritual were a big part of the magical world.

Much to my surprise, Detective Connors inclined her head in response, straightened, and extended her hand toward him across the table.

"May the wind always be at your back."

I was slightly taken aback—I hadn't expected her to know the traditional response to Aengus's blessing. Aengus, however, just laughed heartily and clasped her hand.

"Well said. At least someone," he paused and glanced meaningfully, if playfully, my way, "respects traditions."

Her partner mutely extended his hand as well, and Aengus shook it.

Detective Connors saw me looking at her, my eyebrows raised, and shrugged.

"My grandmother was born and raised in a village in Connacht," she explained. "She taught me some Irish greetings when I was a kid, back when she was still telling me stories about the Tuatha Dé."

I was less interested in how she'd learned Irish blessings, and more curious about her apparent change of heart in regard to the Fae. She'd been so dismissive of the idea of anything supernatural less than an hour ago, and now she just accepted it when I introduced her to a man out of the Faerie tales her grandmother told her when she was a little girl? Even given the taxi ride and the Market itself, that struck me as an oddly rapid change of her fundamental beliefs about how the world works. Most people put up more resistance. I was waiting for the other shoe to drop, but there was little I could do about it at that exact second. Maybe her partner had been right, and she was just open to changing her mind in the face of clear evidence.

I shook my head slightly and looked back at Aengus, who was still grinning at Detective Connors, his head cocked slightly as if he were trying to figure her out the same as I was. I cleared my throat, getting his attention.

"Okay," he nodded, and his grin disappeared, back to being

all business. "Now that introductions are complete, tell me about this crime, and why you believe it was the Avartagh's doing."

His eyes narrowed as I started to tell him the details of the two murders.

"Were there words of power written in blood?"

I nodded.

"What did they say?"

"I don't know. I recognized the glyphs as Faen, but I didn't know the dialect."

He pursed his lips and thought. After a moment, he looked at the detectives. "Do you have pictures of the crime scene?"

Detective Lajoie nodded, then reached into his coat and pulled out a folded manila envelope containing smaller versions of the same pictures I'd seen. He removed the pictures from the envelope and handed them to Aengus.

He skimmed through the photos, his lips tightening. "I understand," he said, looking back up at me, "why you concluded this was the Avartagh's work, Sorcerer. The ritual is the same as I have heard it described, as well. It appears to be the same working, but this was not his doing."

I raised my eyebrows. "How can you be sure? He's always done what he felt like, and he likes causing pain."

"Because," his expression became frank, "the Avartagh has been imprisoned in the Dún Dubh for five hundred years."

Well, damn. I hadn't expected that at all. My theory was completely trashed. But before I could recover, Detective Connors spoke up.

"What the hell is a 'dune dove'?"

Aengus turned to her. "Dún Dubh," he gently corrected her pronunciation. "It means 'Black Fortress.' And it is the prison of the Tuatha Dé."

"Why haven't I heard any stories about it?"

"Because your grandmother probably only knew the stories the monks wrote down for posterity," I told her. "The Tuatha Dé were a popular subject because they were seen as the heathen gods Christ supplanted. The Christian monks focused on the common stories or those that made them look bad—look how the Dagda is described as fat and ridiculous when he meets with the Fir Bolg. They weren't interested in literal accuracy but spreading their own propaganda. Most of the stories you know bear very little resemblance to the truth of things, I promise you. You've never heard of the Faerie prison because the monks either never heard the stories of Dún Dubh or, more likely, deliberately chose not to record them. Even talking about the place was taboo among those who knew. The tales were rarely told, and only then in broad daylight. There was too great a fear that the Fae would take vengeance on those who told the secrets of their prison."

Aengus was nodding in agreement. "The monks heard the stories. Everyone heard the stories. Some even dared to write them down, with their conviction that they were merely myths. But those manuscripts didn't survive into the modern era. The Morrigan keep their secrets. There are many things about the Tuatha Dé and the Aes Sidhe your grandmother did not know, and many things she likely thought she knew that are wrong."

"I've never been there," I told her. "I've never had reason to go. Very few humans have. But nothing I've heard has been nice. And no one has ever escaped the fortress. If the Avartagh has been there for centuries, he wasn't involved in Evan's murder."

She rolled her eyes. "Of course he wasn't involved in Evan's murder. He's not real. You guys know that, right?"

My eyebrows shot up. I glanced at Aengus, who had cocked his head in confusion, and Detective Lajoie, who shrugged.

"I thought we'd gone over that," I replied.

She laughed. "What, you mean the tricks with the limo and the people in costume? I've been to sci-fi conventions before, Quinn. I was happy to roll with it if it actually helped us get some answers, but I think we've indulged your fantasies long enough if you're seriously suggesting a mythical creature locked in Faerie prison might be involved in our case." She looked over at her partner. "This has been fun, but I think enough's enough, don't you?"

There was the other shoe, after all. I was almost impressed at her ability to rationalize the wonders she'd seen that evening. But I'd specifically requested she keep such opinions to herself for a reason. The Fae are proud. Aengus had lived in the human world for a long time, but if he were to take umbrage at her condescension, her implication that he—and everything around us—was nothing more than an elaborate charade, we could be in a great deal of trouble.

"Adrienne," Detective Lajoie began, almost pleadingly, but I interrupted.

"None of this is a trick or a game, Detective Connors." My

voice was deadly serious. "Aengus here is a Faerie, as was Zoya. I'm a sorcerer. Those satyrs you saw, and the giants and kobolds and all the rest, aren't wearing costumes and playing pretend. The Market Taxi was not an illusion. It's all very real."

She looked at me with a frank expression. "Fine, then. If you're a sorcerer, prove it. Do some magic."

"No."

Aengus looked alarmed. He knew how I felt about this subject.

"Why not, O mighty sorcerer?"

I closed my eyes, took a long, slow breath, let it out through my nose.

As it turned out, Aengus's potential reaction to her behavior wasn't the only cause of concern this evening. I thought I'd be better able to ignore her insults, but my knuckles were white as I struggled to control my rising wrath. I could hear that little voice growing louder and louder in its insistence I let it loose.

I fought it back down, refusing its demands. I had faced far worse than Detective Connors's skepticism. It would take a lot more to make me lose the control I'd struggled so hard to achieve over the past decades. But it wasn't easy. That voice was seductive. It would be so simple to let it have its way...

"Because," I said quietly, meeting her eyes, "I am not an exhibitionist." I bit off each word distinctly. I had suppressed my flash of rage, but it was still near the surface, and I focused on calming down.

"I am not a cheap stage magician," I continued, "and I do not perform on command. Magic is a serious matter, and I will not demean myself with tawdry acts for your amusement, Detective Connors. I have done things in my life that you cannot imagine. I have seen things you have not dreamt. I am an old man, and I do not live for your approval. You and your partner asked for my help, and I have given it. In return, you have twice now insulted me to my face. If you choose not to believe me, after everything you have seen tonight, very well, that is your prerogative. But I will not be your dancing monkey just to make an ignorant child feel more comfortable with the truth."

"Child?! Why..." she began, but Aengus stopped her with a voice like a whip crack.

"Enough!" he declared, glaring around. He wasn't speaking loudly, but his tone brooked no dissent.

"Detective Connors," he addressed her, "you are very lucky I am not so quick to take offense as many of my kin. I understand you are skeptical of magic's existence, so I will let your breach of my hospitality pass." He paused for a moment as she sat back, her expression unconvinced.

"Do you share your partner's concerns?" he asked, turning to Detective Lajoie.

"No," he answered. "Quinn has shown me the truth."

At this, she frowned and opened her mouth to speak, but he shot her a glance and raised a hand to stop her interrupting. She closed her mouth tightly and sat back, her armed crossed.

"As Quinn said," he continued, "my grandfather was a part of this world, and the sorcerer here and I spoke about it at length yesterday. Then he showed me proof, the ambush spell the killers left at the second crime scene, which he trapped in a sphere of energy not three feet from me. I saw it with my own eyes, and it was no illusion. But frankly, all of that matters a lot less at this exact moment than solving this case." He looked meaningfully at his partner, who looked away at the implied reproach. "So if there's anything you can do to help us with that, I'm listening."

"Good enough," Aengus replied, then looked back at Detective Connors. "It is a great deal to accept all at once," he said with a softer tone. "But before this night is through, I am certain both of you will have seen enough to believe."

She rolled her eyes, but kept her mouth shut. Maybe her partner's reminder that solving the case was what really mattered had gotten through to her.

"What do you mean?" Detective Lajoie asked. "What more is there to see?"

Aengus smiled at him without a trace of humor, then shifted his gaze to me.

"The Avartagh is in the Dún Dubh, so he cannot be a party to the crime. Where does that leave you?"

"If someone else is copying his ritual," I mused, "we need to know why. That might help us figure out who. You can read the focusing glyphs—what do they say?"

He frowned. "They focus the energy released in the ritual toward something called 'Tamesis,' which is not a Fae word. But that's what the glyphs spell out."

I cocked my head. "It's Old Brythonic." Being a bookworm

with an ear for obscure languages was sometimes useful. "It means 'darkness.' Which, while somewhat ominous, doesn't tell us much about the goal of the rite."

Aengus bared his teeth in what might charitably be called a smile, by someone who had only read descriptions of them and never seen the real thing.

"No, it does not. But we do know someone who could answer that question. And we know where to find him."

"Are you saying," Detective Lajoie sat up straighter in his chair, "we could go visit this Avartagh guy in that Faerie prison you mentioned?"

"Yes. That is precisely what I am saying." This time Aengus's smile was genuine. "But we shall have to get permission. Very few sorcerers have ever visited the Dún Dubh, and I do not think an uninitiated human has ever done so. This is a treaty matter. It will require a special dispensation."

"From whom?" Detective Connors asked, her tone still skeptical.

"The High King. We shall have to go see Lugh."

She rolled her eyes once again but didn't say anything else.

I spoke up. "There's one other thing you should know, Aengus. I sampled the residual magic at the second ritual site. It may not have been the Avartagh, but there was a Faerie present when he died. And it took an active part in the ritual. Whoever flayed the victims was inhumanly skilled with a blade."

Aengus frowned for a moment, but then nodded. "All the more reason to speak with him." He looked thoughtful, then stood up and looked me in the eye. "Alright, Sorcerer, you and your companions have my countenance. Let us go meet Lugh."

He walked to the far end of the tent, the side that was up against the mural-covered wall. He opened a flap like a door, through which light shone, revealing a grassy plain and a single small, gnarled tree. He gestured for us to precede him through the doorway.

I stood up and looked at Detective Connors.

"Are you coming? Or do you need proof first?" I asked scornfully.

She glared at me, but stood up when her partner did, and nodded.

"Lead on, then," she said.

With a scowl of my own, I stepped through into the Otherworld.

Chapter 10

AFTER THE RELATIVELY DIM LIGHTING INSIDE THE TENT, THE blazing sun overhead made me squint. Everything was too bright and vivid: the grass was greener than it should have been, the sky a deeper blue. Colors seem to have more substance in the Otherworld.

The air was noticeably warmer, as well. I wanted to shrug off my overcoat, but the protection it gave me as a declared member of the Arcanum was worth the discomfort. I was glad I was wearing just a T-shirt underneath.

The two detectives stepped through behind me, and I heard Detective Connors gasp. I guessed she'd seen the twenty-foot stone archway the door led through, reminiscent of its cousins on Salisbury Plain. Such structures weren't the only gates into the Otherworld, but they were permanently bound and required a lot less energy to open and maintain compared to opening a portal. Someone like Aengus could open most any of them from anywhere on Earth, with no more effort than opening a physical door. I couldn't make use of them as easily, but there were a few I knew well.

Looking around, I realized this wasn't one of them. I didn't recognize where we'd arrived, though the tree was familiar. Hawthorn. They grew in places where the boundary between our world and the Otherworld were thin, on both sides of the veil.

I heard the faint whisper of the gateway closing after Aengus stepped through.

"This isn't Rath Nechtan," I muttered. I'd expected we'd be heading to the great fortress of the High Kings of the Tuatha. I'd been there many times, but I wasn't sure where Aengus had taken us instead.

"No," Aengus replied from behind me. "It is Lughnasadh."

That explained it. For me, at least.

"What's Lughnasadh?" Detective Lajoie was looking around in wonder, much as he had when we'd first entered the Market.

"A festival celebrating the High King," I explained. "Kind of like a month-long royal birthday party. And it means Lugh's court isn't at his fortress—the festival takes place in the Plain of Delight. One of the nicer parts of the Otherworld."

Detective Connors was stubbornly silent as I looked over at her. "Still don't believe in magic?"

She shot another glare at me, the reaction I'd expected. But then something changed, a sudden realization struck her. I could practically see the acceptance of this new reality enter her eyes.

Adrienne Connors might be stubbornly cynical, but she couldn't just dismiss what all her senses were telling her. Her expression transmuted into something almost heartbreaking, as I watched her struggle to accept the truth that the world she knew was, well, not exactly a lie, but certainly only a small part of the universe.

I felt almost ashamed at causing that pain. The Taxi, the Market, meeting Aengus, none of that had been enough to push her over that edge. She'd been able to tell herself it was an elaborate game, illusions, costumes, that there was a perfectly rational explanation for it all.

But this—stepping through a magical door into a world that couldn't possibly exist—sent her tumbling into the wild, terrifying awareness that she was beyond the edge of the map. And the old cartographers had gotten it right: "Here there be monsters."

She had to realize this more than most in modern society, as the tales her grandmother had told her were undoubtedly the real Faerie tales, the ones Walt Disney didn't show. The stories of violence and betrayal, of great love and greater loss, of blood and whispers in the darkness, right alongside the songs of mighty heroes and their glorious deeds. She might not know exactly what the Otherworld held in store, but she had a good idea of how dangerous it could be.

It wasn't the first time I'd seen such a realization hit someone, but it was the first time with an adult. Children are more accepting of such a huge shift in their worldviews. They haven't grown comfortable with the world as they know it yet. It was different with a grown woman. It was tragic.

But it was necessary. She wasn't in Kansas anymore.

The whole process took a few seconds, but her eyes remained locked on mine the whole time. Before she could answer the question verbally, I just nodded. She looked away, at Aengus, her eyes growing wide as she realized he really was a Fae creature from her grandmother's tales. For a few seconds I was afraid she would have a full-blown panic attack, as her breathing sped up and she looked off into the distance.

Then her partner put his hand on her shoulder and leaned in close, whispering to her. I could see her calm down, regain control. Her breathing returned to normal and she shut her eyes, rubbing her temples with both hands. After a moment she opened them again and met his concerned gaze, nodding and muttering that she was alright. That she would be alright.

I found I no longer needed an apology before I could forgive her most recent insult.

She took a deep breath and held it for a second, then looked over at me.

"Fuck," she said quietly. "It's all real?"

I nodded. "I'm afraid so, my dear. And there's no going back now. Can you handle that?"

She looked away again, biting her lip.

Detective Lajoie nodded at me. "She'll be okay. Just give her a few minutes to come to terms with it. In the meantime, we've got work to do."

Aengus had seen the whole process and kept a respectful silence, letting it play out. He caught my eye and gave a sad smile. But he nodded at the big Haitian detective's comment and began walking up the long, shallow grassy hill to our right, talking as he went. We followed, listening silently.

"A story you probably never heard from your grandmother, Detective Connors," he began, "is how my parents met and how I was born. You may know that my father is the Dagda, as he was known among the people of Ireland after our conquest."

His tone was matter of fact, as if she'd believed he was the

Dagda's son all along, instead of just coming to terms with that reality a minute before. That was kind of him.

"But what you may not know," he continued, "is that another name for him is Eochaid Ollathair—it means 'All-Father' in English. Some human scholars suppose this just to be a common title for major deities. But the truth is simpler. The All-Father of the Celts is the same as the All-Father of the Norse. The Dagda is just another name for Odin."

I could see the detectives listening intently, the look of wonder on Adrienne Connors's face. It wasn't every day that a being out of myth takes the time to explain the truth behind those myths for your edification. And now she recognized that he was in fact such a being, not some crazed occult enthusiast role-playing in an open-air art gallery. She was paying attention. How often do you get the chance to hear a Faerie tale from the lips of a Faerie?

"At that time, long before the rise of the Christians, the Tuatha Dé did not yet even exist. The various Fae peoples spread across the surface of the Earth, where they intermingled with humans, whom they considered their lessers, but still useful allies in their constant wars for territory and power. The humans, in turn, treated the Fae as the gods and protectors of their tribes.

"The Fir Bolg and Fomor lived in the Celtic isles. The territory of the Aesir and their cousins the Vanir stretched from Scandinavia through the Germanic forests of northern Europe. By the time Rome rose to prominence, the Olympians controlled everything around the Mediterranean Sea. And in Iberia and throughout the Alps were the people of Taranis and Danu."

Aengus was simplifying a great deal, but it was still far more accurate than what either of them would know from the mythology they studied in school.

"You have heard, I am sure, that Odin wished above all else for wisdom, and gained it by giving up an eye for a chance to drink from the Well of Wisdom. Well," he said with a wry smile, "that is not quite how it happened. The Well was owned by Nechtan, also called Nuada, a great warrior prince, leader of a tribe of the people of Taranis. His lands were in the north of Iberia, and were disputed with other tribes, but he managed to hold them through the power his Well gave him. He jealously guarded it, as any who drank from the waters would gain knowledge of the nature of time itself, one of the most powerful magics even among the Fae.

"Even Nuada's wife was not permitted to drink of the well's waters, and over time she grew to resent her husband over this. So when Odin came seeking a drink, she coupled with him—sex does not hold the same taboos among the Fae as among humans—and then snuck him past Nuada, where he drank from the well.

"Nuada knew what had happened as soon as Odin's lips touched the water. Because the magic was so precious, Nuada could not risk its secrets spreading among the Fae, and he tried to kill the All-Father rather than let him leave in peace. Odin was dazed by the onset of his new wisdom, and Nuada got the better of him, cutting out his left eye. But before he could strike the killing blow, his wife rushed in and stayed his hand for the sake of the child she bore in her womb.

"Instead, he made the All-Father three times swear an oath to safeguard his newfound wisdom and not share its power with anyone, nor to reveal the location of the Well, and to always ally himself with Nuada when called upon to do so. In turn, Nuada would raise the child as his foster-son, train him in the ways of the warrior and the poet and lead him in war. Which is what he did, for I was that child.

"When I was a man, he called upon the All-Father to honor the final part of the oath, and together they went to war with their common enemies to carve out a kingdom for Nuada and his kin outside of the rule of Taranis. The Dagda helped him defeat his enemies, and he became king over the Isles."

Aengus paused in his story, another sad smile on his face, this one of remembrance, of nostalgia. He had been there on the glorious day when Nuada of the Silver Hand had triumphed and won the crown.

"But he died in battle many years later." Aengus added, with a melancholy hint to his voice. "My cousin Lugh was our war chief, and avenged Nuada's death. He was acclaimed the new King of the Tuatha and has ruled since that day. But that is another tale for another time."

The Faerie princeling lapsed back into silence. By now we were near the crest of the hill, and the final moments of the walk passed in reflection—Aengus in remembrance of days long past and the two detectives in consideration of what they had just heard.

It was a precious gift for one of the Fae to tell such a story without obligation. I hoped they appreciated how valuable such a thing was, and the import of the story. It was one of the least-known tales of the Fae even among sorcerers. I could only guess at Aengus's motive in telling it now. As well as he and I got along, and as friendly as we were, I could never forget that he was an alien creature who had walked two worlds for thousands of years.

I found myself remembering how we'd met, at the Faerie Market in New York. It was my first trip to that city. It was already a bustling metropolis, the entrance for immigrants to the United States, which were then engaged in their Civil War. Thousands of Irish refugees were stepping on shore and immediately being pressed into service in the Union Army. But not all of those refugees were human.

The Treaty of Tara forbids Faeries from fighting in wars between human powers—humans are allowed to kill each other all they want, and Faeries are allowed to kill each other all they want, but no Faeries killing humans or vice versa. Aengus was in the city to make certain none of the local or newly arriving Fae were scooped into the Union war effort. He wasn't an official representative of the Tuatha Dé, but as one of their princes he'd assumed responsibility for enforcing that Treaty provision.

I, on the other hand, had been formally dispatched by the Arcane Court to observe and ensure the Fae were keeping up their end of the bargain. Aengus and I had hit it off from the start. Of course, back then I'd been a lot friendlier. I didn't know then what I knew now, hadn't yet done any of the monstrous things I'd done since—my first atrocity was two full decades in the future. I was young and naïve, still shy of my first centennial.

Aengus and I hadn't stayed close over the years, but we ran into each other every so often, usually at one of the Faerie Markets on the east coast. He'd witnessed my descent over the past decades into what I was today. Every time he saw me, he was the same, and I was further gone. Less cheerful, more withdrawn, more prone to anger. He was too polite to say it, but I knew he worried about me, about my drinking and my isolation. He remembered when I used to laugh.

Before I got further drawn into my own reminiscing and self-pity, we crested the hill and saw the Court of the High King of the Faeries spread out before us. It was a sight straight out of myth, a sprawling camp set up inside a great earthen ring, spiraling outward from a circular wooden hall at the center. I wasn't familiar enough with court protocol to recognize from a distance how the camp was actually organized, but I could clearly see a crowded market, an open area for riding and games and competitions of skill, several vast piles of wood that could only be bonfires in the making, a stage of some sort, and tents of all colors and shapes. The gate into the ring was wide open, with Fae streaming in and out. It was a small city.

I had never seen so many Faeries at once. The detectives were staring in amazement, far more openly than they had at the Market. It had been an interesting day for the pair of them, I supposed, so I couldn't begrudge them their bewilderment. They were well and truly through the looking glass.

"Detectives," I addressed them quietly, "before we meet Lugh, you should have a basic understanding of some concepts Aengus and I have mentioned but haven't really explained. First, where we are right now is called the Otherworld. Specifically, we're at the edge of the Plain of Delight, which stands at the heart of Tír na nÓg, the territory ruled directly by Lugh. Around that is the rest of Sidhe, the region loyal to him as their High King.

"The word Faerie describes any being native to the Otherworld. This includes most of the 'gods' you've heard about in myths—most of the various historical pantheons are just different nations of the same Fae race, commonly called the High Fae. There are also the Low Fae, which includes the Djinn and various nature spirits, as well as much darker creatures: goblins, ghouls, trolls, giants, and many far lesser known things that stalk the Otherworld's darker forests and caves. This is a dangerous place. Never forget that."

I looked over at the detectives. Their faces were both solemn. Good. That suggested they took my warning seriously.

I looked over at Aengus, who was waiting patiently with a small smile. "Anything you want to add?"

He considered for a moment, then turned to the detectives. "We should speak about the consequences should you attempt to reveal the existence of the Otherworld, and the truth of magic, to humanity at large. Do you understand what would happen should you speak out to the human authorities about what you have seen here?"

"You mean apart from mandatory psychiatric evaluations?" Detective Connors asked.

Aengus scowled. "This is not a matter for jest."

"I wasn't joking," she said, shaking her head. "If we tried to explain to the captain that we had spent the evening at a party with Faeries in the Otherworld, we'd be suspended pending psych evals."

"That," I growled, "would be the least of your problems. While I'm certain it's enough deterrence, and I relied on it when your partner insisted you come with us this evening, Aengus is right. You should know what would happen if you revealed the existence of this world." I paused.

"Should you pass those evals," I continued, "and somehow manage to get yourselves taken seriously, it would be bad for everyone. First, the Arcane Court's closest Rector would step in and do everything in her power—which is a lot—to ensure you were silenced and ignored. She'd probably also arrest the both of you, and you'd spend the rest of your lives in a prison you have no desire to be in. I might well be in prison alongside you, should the combined power of the Arcanum manage to take me against my will, for having brought you in the first place.

"The Treaty of Tara ended centuries of war between the Fae and humanity a thousand years ago, and no one wants to risk that peace falling apart. If word got out to the rest of the human race that there's a whole other world out there, that's almost certainly what would happen. Some people would panic and make stupid decisions. Others would try to take advantage of the magical community, which may well include efforts to enslave the Fae as happened in ages past. Both courses of action would likely lead to an all-out war between humanity and the magical races, with the Arcanum—the primary faction of human sorcerers—caught in the middle. A war which the magical world would lose, but it would be very messy in the process. Even if it weren't enshrined in the Treaty of Tara, there's general agreement in the magical underworld that it's better we continue to live in the shadows."

Detective Lajoie frowned. "If you're all as powerful as legends would have us believe, there's no way humans would win that war. I just don't see it."

"There are just too many humans," I explained, "and the Fae have never been numerous, nor any of the other magical races. It doesn't much matter if each of your warriors can kill a hundred men when you're outnumbered by three times that ratio or more.

And the odds have only gotten worse—there are a lot more people on Earth now than there were in the Dark Ages. Maybe the magical races could have won the Faerie Wars back then, but it would have required basically annihilating the entire human race, and the Arcanum was formed to ensure that didn't happen. Nowadays, they couldn't win even if we'd let them go that far: a Fae army is a dangerous threat, but not one equipped to defeat machine guns and tanks and close air support. Let alone nuclear weapons." I paused for a second to contemplate that terrifying thought.

"I'm a very powerful sorcerer. Among the top few dozen most powerful magic-using humans on the planet. That's not a brag; there's a ranking system, and I'm near the top. Aengus here is at least as powerful, if not more so, and there are Faeries and demigods out there who make both of us look like children. But no one could possibly maintain a shield strong enough to stop an actual nuclear explosion. Humans can't cross into the Otherworld without magic, so the Fae would be able to retreat to safety, but that doesn't do much good for those magical beings who live on Earth. It's better not to risk it, to live in the shadows and keep everyone thinking we're just children's stories."

Apparently, the walk had been enough for Detective Connors to process and come to terms with all of this. She nodded thoughtfully.

"That makes sense, I guess. I wasn't planning on even trying to explain this to someone who couldn't see for themselves, but I understand the logic, too."

"We're here to do a job," Detective Lajoie added, nodding in agreement. "We won't try to expose anything to anyone. We just want to talk to a potentially relevant witness to our investigation and get back home in one piece. In our report, this will just be listed as a 'private gathering of the occult community in an undisclosed location.' You both have my word on that."

I looked over at Aengus with an eyebrow raised. "Good enough?"

He looked silently at Detective Connors, and then her partner, for a long moment. Finally, he nodded. "Yes."

I looked back at the two of them. "Any questions before we continue, then?"

"I thought the Faeries were supposed to be ruled by a queen," Detective Lajoie mused.

Aengus snorted. "That was a poem, nothing more. It was an allegory for Queen Elizabeth. Edmund Spenser never met a Faerie in his life, to my knowledge."

"And this Lugh is the King of the Faeries?"

He shook his head. "Many call him that, but it is not a true title. There are dozens of Fae nations, great and small. In days long past, they all vied for supremacy, competing in this world and in yours for territory and power. Now most keep to themselves in their respective parts of the Otherworld—the Olympians, for example, have not been seen off their mountain for centuries. Lugh rules the Tuatha Dé directly and is High King of the various tribes of the people called the Aes Sidhe. Between the warriors of Sidhe and his court's ancient alliance with Odin, he is by far the most powerful ruler in the Otherworld."

"But there are those who don't recognize his authority?" Detective Connors asked.

"Many," Aengus nodded. "But few who would dare challenge him directly."

The detectives looked thoughtful.

"If there are no further questions . . . ?" I asked after a moment.

Both of them shook their heads. I started walking down the hill.

"Then let's go meet a Faerie king."

Chapter 11

WE HUMANS GOT SOME STRANGE LOOKS AS WE ENTERED THE camp, and I got a few polite nods of welcome from Faeries who noticed the overcoat marking my station, but no one spoke to us. Aengus, on the other hand, was a favorite son of the Tuatha Dé, and acknowledged cheerful greetings from his kin and friends as we walked along the spiraling path from the gate toward the central hall—he rarely visited Tír na nÓg these days. He wasn't here to make small talk, however, and we continued down the path, the bustling fair atmosphere quieting down and growing more orderly as we approached the royal seat.

Then a woman stepped from a tent up ahead of us, and my heart skipped a beat as I recognized her.

Her pale skin contrasted with her jet-black feathered hair, while her gray dress matched her granite eyes. She towered over me, as tall as Aengus and Detective Lajoie. And she was stunning, with that unearthly beauty that can only be found among the Fae, that ensnared even the worldliest man's mind and inspired him to write bad poetry. Unlike that of the Tylwyth Teg, however, hers was clearly a dangerous beauty—like a great wild cat, she could be appreciated from a safe distance, but the terror of being close to her far outweighed the chance to bask in her glory.

Despite it being a bright, sunny day, in a land where most

everything seemed to exude its own light to supplement that of the sun above, this creature absorbed the ambient light around her, wreathing her in a tiny space of darkness. She smiled in warm greeting, but the coldness of her presence prompted the opposite reflex—to run and hide. I forced that instinct down.

"My favorite cousin, and his pet sorcerer! The prodigal son returns to us, at the hour of our celebration!" She spoke in the old Fae language of High Taranic, which in human throats had over the centuries become the Celtic tongues of ancient Europe. Her voice was melodious and intoxicating, totally at odds with her reputation as the original banshee, whose wailing marked the death of warriors on the field of battle.

Aengus's matching smile was wide and genuine.

"Old Crow!" he replied in the same language, before switching to English for the detectives' sake. "It has been too long. But you dishonor my friend," he reproached. "The Sorcerer Quinn is no one's pet, even in jest."

Her smile didn't even flicker at the rebuke or the change of language. "Of course not, as I well know," she replied, then turned to address me. "Accept my humble apologies, Sorcerer. My words were only teasing and meant no offense."

I nodded, my face solemn. "And none was taken, Lady Badb. No apology is needed."

"That is well," she nodded acceptance. "And who are your friends?"

I hesitated. Telling Aengus what was going on was one thing. But this was Badb. One of the three sisters who comprised the Morrigan, the three-faced war goddess of ancient Ireland. The Battle-Crow of the Tuatha Dé, a death-prophet and a warrior upon whom the ancient Celtic tribesmen called for aid on the field of battle. She reveled in fear and death and blood, in the glory of combat. She was no insane monster like the Avartagh, but she was also no one to take lightly—her legendary wrath made that of Achilles look like a child's tantrum. Fortunately, Aengus had a lot more experience dealing with her, and he stepped in.

"These are colleagues of the Sorcerer Quinn in a task for which he sought my aid, and in pursuit of which we now seek audience with Lugh. They are under his protection and have my countenance, but they are also warriors of their people, sworn to protect the innocent from those who would do them harm."

"Truly?" Her predatory smile widened. "It is rare I meet honest warriors in this era." She turned to directly address the two detectives. "To whom are you sworn to protect, warriors?"

They seemed put off in the presence of Badb. That was understandable, especially for people who had only met real Fae for the first time an hour ago.

"We serve the people of the city of Philadelphia," Detective Lajoie answered, humbly and quietly.

"Bah," she replied. "I prefer my warriors with more pride and boastfulness. But few enough are willing to fight for their people in your world, in this age. That alone inclines me toward you."

Both nodded, and Detective Connors replied, "We are honored, Lady Badb."

I heard a catch in her voice. She had heard the tales of Badb and the Morrigan. She knew what kind of creature she was addressing. But Badb either didn't hear it or, more likely given her long history of terrifying even the most hardened human warriors, chose politely to ignore it.

She turned her attention back to me.

"You, Sorcerer, have been absent from our world for quite some time. What has kept you so busy these past many years?"

I shrugged. "I'm retired, I suppose. Since Canada."

"But you were superb in Canada." She frowned. "So much potential. I had my eye on you. And you are yet young. Why would you step back just as you were coming into your own?"

"That's personal, Badb." I closed my eyes as memories I had no desire to revisit rose to the forefront of my mind. Fire. Screams. Blood. I fought them back down like bile in my throat. "I didn't want to be a soldier anymore. I run a bookstore now."

She looked as confused as the detectives, although for a different reason. They had no clue what we were talking about. Badb just couldn't grasp the idea of anyone not enjoying war.

But before she could pursue it further, Aengus interrupted.

"Is Lugh in the hall, cousin?"

She looked back at him with an expression of mild irritation at the intrusion, which softened after a second.

"Lugh? Our King is not Nuada, spending all his time in a cold chair while others entertain him. You will likely find him riding in the field or showing off with his spear, or possibly reciting poetry."

Aengus chuckled. “Thank you, cousin. We must be on our way, for our task is of pressing importance.”

She inclined her head. “I shall bid you farewell, then. Do come visit us more often, cousin. We miss your wit around the Court.”

She then turned to me. “Sorcerer, I do not understand your race. But I have long watched it, and I warn you against rejecting your potential and turning your back on your way. What is meant to be shall be, whether we wish it or not, and our doom is far more painful when we fight what we are.”

With that she turned on her heel and walked toward the central hall.

My human companions were visibly relieved at her departure.

In a very small voice, Detective Connors asked, “That was Badb? The Crow?”

Aengus nodded. “Aye, she is. One of the three sisters of the Morrigan. We shall meet her sister Nemain as well, should Lugh grant the permission we seek. She is warden at the Dún Dubh.”

I considered her for a moment, my expression pitying. “You’re down the rabbit-hole, Alice,” I told her softly. “Try not to get lost.”

Her partner looked confused, but Detective Connors looked almost desperate.

“Don’t lose that bracelet,” I told her, “and don’t do anything without asking me first, and you’ll come out of this just fine.”

I saw her clutch her wrist as if to reassure herself the bracelet was still there.

I turned to Aengus. “The riding field?”

He smiled slightly and nodded his head to the left. I followed where he led, and the detectives continued to trail behind. We followed the spiraling pathway around to the far side of the camp to a broad clearing amid the tents, where we spotted the King of the Faeries.

He didn’t look very royal. The four of us joined a quiet crowd of observers ringed around the field. Three Faeries of the Tuatha Dé stood armed with spears near the edge of the circular space about fifty feet to our left; a target made of canvas mounted on a wicker frame stood by in the open about fifty feet to our right. I had met Lugh before, so I recognized him even from a distance—the tallest of the three spear throwers, with wavy golden hair falling to his shoulders. He wore no crown or regalia; his clothing, in several shades of blue, wasn’t markedly different from what any of the other Tuatha Dé were wearing. But even from this distance the intensity of his alien beauty stood out from the rest. In more ancient days, he had been worshipped as a sun god by the Celts, and it wasn't difficult to see why.

One of the Faeries with him, a black-haired woman almost as tall as he, lifted her spear to her shoulder, took aim, and gracefully let fly with a step toward the target. It silently sailed through the air and struck the man-shaped wicker target with a crack, quivering through the center of its breast. There was a round of polite applause from the crowd, like one might hear at a golf tournament.

The next competitor was a shorter, broadly muscled Faerie with a neatly trimmed red beard. He squinted an eye, stepped forward, and hurled his spear with a great deal more force than his compatriot. It thudded home in the left side of the target's breast, where its heart would be were it a living man. He stepped back and grinned, his arms open wide as he faced the applauding crowd. The woman who had gone before him scowled, but she nodded curtly in acknowledgement of the superior throw.

Even before the applause had quieted, Lugh stepped forward and lightly, almost nonchalantly, tossed his spear, then turned to chat with his fellow competitors while it was still in flight. The sharp crack of the impact brought everyone's gaze to the target, where Lugh's spear protruded through its head, precisely where its left eye would be in life. The watching crowd went wild. The two Faeries who had competed with their King laughed and clapped him on the back; obviously neither had actually expected to prevail against Lugh's prowess.

This was competition merely for the sake of competition, rather than for the glory of victory. It was Lughnasadh, a time of celebration, and while many Faerie contests could end in bloodshed and anger, especially among the proud Tuatha Dé, such behavior was taboo in this camp. Besides, Lugh's skills with a spear were renowned among all the races of the magical world, along with his talents with a sword, a sling, a harp, and many others. He was called Ildánach, "skilled in many arts," and he'd won that title fair and square long before he'd won the throne.

As the contest broke up with laughs and smiles, and the audience milled into the open area between the contestants and their target, Aengus led us toward the High King.

Lugh saw our approach and turned to face us, the good humor fading from his fair face and his eyebrows rising in interest.

"Friend cousin," he called out to Aengus in an even tone, speaking High Taranic, *"you return to our court after all these centuries of absence?"*

"Aye, my King," Aengus replied with a slight nod of his head. The Tuatha Dé do not bow to anyone. *"But only briefly, on an errand which requires your assent."*

A puzzled look crossed Lugh's features, but before he could speak Aengus continued in English.

"You have previously met my companion, the Sorcerer Quinn, in the ruins of the forest where he and his comrades battled the Last Dragon. He came to me for assistance on behalf of these two," he gestured at the detectives, who looked relieved the conversation had switched to a language they could understand, "and the people they are sworn to protect."

There was a long pause while Lugh absorbed this statement.

"Welcome," he said after a moment, nodding to my companions in turn. He faced me and smiled faintly. "Sorcerer Quinn, son of William and Bridget. It has been some time since you have graced my Court with your presence. Not quite as long as some," he paused, glancing at Aengus, "but a long time for a human. What is this pressing errand that could compel you and my cousin to bring human warriors to Lughnasadh?"

"You are not angry that I've brought fellow humans to your realm without your leave?"

"Whatever your reason is," he answered, shaking his head, "which I am sure you will explain momentarily, it was enough to bring Aengus Óg back through the veil after all this time away. That tells me it is no trifling matter."

I relaxed a bit. Lugh was no fool. He couldn't have ruled the Aes Sidhe for millennia had he been. This might not be the uphill battle I'd feared.

"Lord Lugh," I began, "two days ago, Detectives Connors and Lajoie here brought to my attention a murder within the city of Philadelphia..." I summarized the details of the two crime scenes and what I'd found in the residual energy—the ambush spells, and the traces of Fae magic.

Lugh's eyes widened, then narrowed, his nostrils flared as he sharply sucked in a breath. "The Tamesis rites."

Aengus nodded. "That is what the glyphs spoke of, and I know of the Avartagh's rituals well enough to recognize this is the same working, but I am unfamiliar with this Tamesis."

"You would be," his king replied. "You were newly gone from our ranks during the Avartagh's rampage." He paused, as if thinking, then his eyes narrowed. "You are here to speak with him, to learn what you can of the ritual and why another would imitate his efforts, to determine their future course of action. Yes?"

I nodded. "Yes, exactly. If we can learn what the ritual is and what the next steps are, we may be able to stop the culprit before there are further killings. Also, I am certain one of the Fae took part in this ritual, and the Avartagh may know who it was."

"But you need my consent to speak with a prisoner in the Dún Dubh." That wasn't a question; I recognized he was just working through the implications rather than asking clarification. "And time is of the essence. Which is why you and Aengus Óg thought it sufficiently important to break ancient standing custom and bring human lawkeepers to Lughnasadh without my leave or the consent of King and Council." He paused again.

Lugh looked directly into my eyes. For a long moment, I saw the depth of him, the ancient and terrible knowledge of a Faerie warrior king, a being who had walked the Earth before the founding of Troy. It was not the first time I had been reminded of the awesome power of the Fae, but the impact never lessened. I felt drained from that contact, that awareness, though the moment couldn't have lasted more than a few seconds. This was a creature worshipped as a god for millennia, with good reason.

Finally, Lugh looked away. "Sorcerer, I will grant leave for you and your companions to enter the Dún Dubh and speak with the creature known as the Avartagh. But it will cost you a favor, to be collected at any time in the future that I deem fit. Agreed?"

I sighed. Of course. This was the Otherworld. Everything had its price. Everything. I bit my lip and thought it over.

"So long as nothing you ask of me conflicts with my loyalty to King and Court, nor to any oath I have sworn or obligation I have undertaken prior to your redeeming of the favor, and is not likely to result in my own death or dismemberment, I will agree."

"I accept the stipulations." Lugh smiled warmly. "The favor I ask in return for granting your audience with the Avartagh will not in any way require you to be disloyal to King and Court, nor break any oath nor forswear any obligation freely undertaken before I collect, nor will it knowingly require the sacrifice of your life or health. This I swear, and I swear again, and I swear a third time." He held out his hand. "As is the custom of your people, let us grasp hands and seal our bargain."

I hesitated. I thought it over deeply, making sure I hadn't missed anything in the wording of his oath. It's a myth that the Fae can only tell the truth—they can lie all they like unless they're under a geas, a powerful enchantment that binds them to obey specific terms under pain of severe magical consequences. There were only two ways to impose such an enchantment: invoking a true name, which they really don't like, and having them swear an oath three times. If we shook on his thrice-sworn oath and then Lugh went back on his word, he would suffer serious ill-effects, from physical pain to losing much of his power, potentially even his own death. And only the person who imposes a geas can lift it, meaning I could trust he'd keep to his promises. But only in the exact wording of the oath, so I was trying to spot loopholes in his phrasing. Faeries don't recognize anything like the "spirit of the law." They're worse than lawyers when it comes to wording.

Not seeing any, I shrugged and took his hand.

Aengus chuckled. I glanced, irritated, in his direction.

"What's so funny?"

He smiled a toothy grin. "You just agreed to owe a favor to a Faerie King, my friend. I know not what Lugh will ask of you, but I guarantee it will not involve reading books in the backroom of a dusty old shop."

I sighed again. He was right, and I'd known that before I shook Lugh's hand. But I'd had to do it. It was a low price for the prize gained, and we needed that permission. At least Lugh wasn't grinning or laughing. He was merely smiling serenely, much like a wolf might gaze at a passing fawn when it wasn't hungry, as if to say, "Your time will come soon, little one."

I shrugged. "What's done is done. We have business elsewhere."

Aengus nodded, more soberly. "I can take you to the Fortress. The way is not far. By the King's leave?" He looked at Lugh, who merely nodded and waved a hand, granting permission to depart his presence.

We walked out of the clearing, leaving Lugh to laugh and be merry with his friends and retainers as we continued our mission to meet the monster who had terrorized the humans of Brittany centuries ago, and of Ireland before that. As we followed the spiral path out of the camp, I was deep in thought about the favor I now owed Lugh and what it might mean for my future. The detectives trailed just behind me, in silence, presumably processing everything they'd been through so far this evening.

Aengus led the way out of the encampment and up the hill to the west, opposite the direction we had come from. Just over the crest of the hill, there was a single large standing stone covered in worn carvings of stylized animals, spirals, and rows of short straight lines that looked reminiscent of Ogham stones I had seen in Ireland. I tried to read them as we approached, but they were too faded to be legible without close study. Time takes its toll even in the Otherworld. Aengus stopped by the stone and waited for we three humans to catch up.

When we were all gathered around the standing stone, Aengus had us all hold hands, then touched a spiral carving. Without fanfare, the scenery changed.

Chapter 12

WE WERE STILL STANDING NEAR A STONE LIKE THAT IN THE Plain of Delight, but the sky above was now the deep blue and purple of late twilight, and the ground below our feet was rocky and covered in a light layer of snow. The air was noticeably chillier, and I was glad of my coat for the first time since leaving my shop. The detectives looked uncomfortably cold.

Huge mountains reared up from the rocks near us, with no foothills to break the transition from the plain. Through the evening gloom I could make out the shape of a massive dark stone fortification looming partway up the mountain nearest us, its outer curtain wall squat and imposing. There was a narrow stair cut into the rock leading to a gate high above us. I had never before seen the Black Fortress of the Tuatha, but there could be no doubt about the nature of that structure. It oozed menace from its perch on the stony slope.

Detective Connors craned her neck to look up at the fortress. "That's where we're going?" I heard a dubious note in her voice.

"Aye," Aengus answered, his voice rumbling in the cold air. "The stair is treacherous, as befits the only approach to an impregnable fortress. Many of those imprisoned within the walls have friends who would free them. The Morrigan do what they can to ensure such efforts remain impossible."

With that he led the way to the base of the stair and began the ascent. I gestured for the detectives to follow, then took up the rearguard to ensure they did not slip or falter, and to protect us from attack from behind. We were still within Sidhe, but there is no such thing as a safe place for humans in the Otherworld. I kept a watch out for anything out of place, as I trusted Aengus to do up front.

The climb took about forty-five minutes, just putting one foot in front of the other. The snow got deeper as we climbed higher, making the rocky steps more treacherous. Detective Lajoie slipped once, but caught himself before falling, and from then on everyone set their feet down carefully. We made it to the top without further incident and rested for a moment on the narrow flat plaza before the great bronze gate. My legs were burning. It had been a long time since I'd walked up stairs for forty-five minutes straight. At least I didn't look as cold and miserable as my companions. The petite Detective Connors's lips were turning blue.

Once we humans had caught our breath, Aengus picked up a small hammer hanging beside the gate and struck the brass bell next to it once. It rang out with a high even tone that split the otherwise silent evening. As the echoes faded away, the gate swung open and a tall figure in a black-feathered cloak strode slowly out toward us. Nemain had a mass of wild dark curls framing her pale face. Like her sister, her beauty was cold and treacherous—she had a reputation for driving men mad. Her lips curled in a faint smile as she greeted Aengus.

"Welcome, dearest cousin. It is a pleasure to see you return to this world." She spoke in English, presumably for our benefit. Her voice was deeper than I'd expected from her slight frame.

He nodded, but she turned to me before he could reply, and her smile was replaced by seriousness.

"Sorcerer Quinn. You have been granted access to the Dún Dubh by bargain with the High King. Few sorcerers have been within these walls, and no ordinary humans have ever been granted that privilege. Your bargain grants you an audience with the being known as the Avartagh, who has been imprisoned for crimes committed in violation of the Treaty of Tara and for experimentations with forbidden magic. Once you are within the Fortress, you and your fellow mortals are to speak with no one other than myself, your companions, or the Avartagh himself. You are to remain only within the audience chamber to which I lead you. I will remain in the chamber during your audience—should you require anything, simply ask and it shall be provided. Do not, however, attempt to leave the chamber or venture into any other part of the Fortress. Any such action will be construed as an attempt to free the prisoners and shall be dealt with accordingly. Your safe passage is guaranteed by the countenance of Lugh, provided you obey these rules exactly as I have specified them to you. Do you have any questions?"

I looked at my companions, one eyebrow raised. Both shook their heads.

"No," Detective Lajoie answered, "that's pretty straightforward. Just like any other prison interview. But with Faeries."

His partner smiled wryly at that, her amusement warring with her obvious discomfort at being so close to a second sister of the Morrigan in the space of an hour.

I turned back to her. "No, Lady Nemain. We will obey your instructions and depart as soon as we have the information we need."

Her faint smile returned as she nodded, then turned without another word and led the way into the fortress. With a shrug of my shoulders, my companions and I followed her into the darkness.

She led us through winding halls dimly lit by evenly spaced lamps. The only sound was the echo of our footsteps. We came to a stop before a solid wooden door, unadorned with any marking, exactly like dozens of others we had passed.

"Within here is the Avartagh," she said facing the door. "His cell is separated from the audience chamber by bonds he cannot break—some you can see plainly; others you, Sorcerer, may be able to sense; and still others that only the Fae may know. You have no need to fear his power while in these walls. But he is a trickster. Listen carefully to what he says. Pay attention to the words as well as their intent. And do not trust anything that issues from his lips, for his mind is twisted and devious, and his entire being is malevolent." She paused. "Are you ready to enter?"

I looked at the detectives again. The fortress was heated, so they seemed far less miserable than they had outside the gate. Detective Connors looked nervous, but she met my gaze evenly and I saw the strength of her purpose. Next to her, her partner's expression was determined. This was their first chance to interview a potentially relevant witness in the case. Even if it wouldn't go in the file, we had come all this way because it was our only real chance at a lead before the killer struck again.

They were as ready as they would ever be. I nodded, then remembered Nemain was facing the door and couldn't see me. I started to answer aloud, but before I even opened my mouth, she touched the door and the wood melted away into nothingness. She stepped back and gestured for us to enter.

The room was lit by lamps identical to those in the corridor. There was no place to sit, no table, nothing but an open space between the doorway and a golden line etched in the floor. On the far side of that line, there was another open space and a stone shelf about four feet deep running the width of the room, upon which a figure lay sleeping. Once all five of us were inside the room, the door faded back into existence behind us. The only other decoration in the room was a small brass bell mounted on the wall next to the door, with a matching hammer hanging next to it. I guessed that was to get Nemain's attention were she not with us. Or perhaps for her to summon assistance if necessary. I certainly hoped it wouldn't be.

For a minute or two, nobody spoke. Nemain just stood near the door with her arms crossed. The silence was finally broken not by us, but by the figure lying on the shelf.

"Aren't you going to say hello, Sorcerer?" he said in High Taranic, his voice raspy as if it hadn't been used in a long time. He hadn't moved beyond speaking, still stretched out on the shelf with his hands on his chest.

"Do you know who I am?" I replied after a moment's consideration.

"English, then? Very well. A boring language."

I wasn't surprised he spoke with a perfect Oxford accent despite having been in prison since well before Shakespeare's time. Those were quite probably the first English words this particular creature had ever spoken—modern English, at least—but he would be fluent anyway. Considering the effort I'd put into learning languages over the past two centuries, it was annoying that he could speak English with nary a second thought. But it was convenient at the moment, at least, because it meant I wouldn't have to translate for the detectives.

As for the accent, that just seemed like the kind of pretentious affectation a being such as this would take.

"Boring, perhaps, but it's the one everyone present speaks. Do you know who I am?"

"Yes," he replied, still without moving. "You are the Sorcerer Thomas Quinn. Your father is the reigning King of the Arcane Court. Your mother is his Lord Marshal. You participated in the Shattering of Krakatoa and witnessed both the Predations of the Djinn and the Tear of the Gods. You killed the Last Dragon at Tunguska. You bathed the Fields of Fire in the blood of your enemies during the Shadow War, so much blood that Lord Kigatilik himself recoiled in fear."

At this he finally moved, swinging his legs off the shelf and sitting up, looking straight into my eyes. Thin silver chains lightly rattled at his wrists and ankles as he moved. They led back to a small ring set in the stone.

"A creature after my own heart, you. You've killed at least as many innocents as I. Probably more. Of course, it has been disappointing since, wasting your time in your ridiculous shop, trying to drink yourself and your shame into oblivion. That will not work, you know. You are who you are, and no amount of shame or whisky will change that."

My blood ran cold. All of that had occurred in the centuries he had been sitting in this cell, which meant either he was somehow in contact with the world outside, or he had reached into my mind and extracted the deepest, darkest secrets of my memory in the few minutes since I'd entered the room. Either possibility I hadn't counted on beforehand, and both were troubling.

The detectives were looking at me funny. I hadn't told them any specifics of my past. This was all very interesting to them, I was sure, but I didn't like that they'd found out this way. Even Nemain was looking at me differently, more measuringly. Before I could respond, however, the prisoner had already moved on, switching his gaze to Detective Lajoie.

"As for the police officers, I know you, too. Henri Lajoie, from Haiti, a land of dark magic. Your grandfather was a powerful necromancer, a man I would have respected. But you? I have no respect for cowards and sexual deviants. And that is what you are, you know. You became a police officer because of what happened to your family, but that's just paper over the wound. When the actual moment came, you froze in terror, doing nothing. Your family died because deep down in your heart of hearts you're a coward, and no medal, no valor commendation, will ever change that fact. You know that, don't you? That's probably the reason for your perversions, too. Disgusting." The Avartagh's face was now twisted in a cruel smile, like a boy pulling the wings off a butterfly as it struggled in his hand.

I saw the big man's expression. I saw the pain and the fear and the anger all warring for supremacy on his features. I hadn't known any of that. But it was petty and sick, what the Avartagh was doing. I was certain now he was reading our memories, extracting our greatest shames and fears and playing them out for the group as a twisted game.

Nemain had warned us he was malevolent and insane. She'd also claimed that his power would not extend into the audience chamber—apparently there was something she'd forgotten to mention. Although it was possible this particular skill just didn't apply to the Fae, so she honestly didn't know. Whichever it was, the bastard focused on Detective Connors next. I wanted to stop him, but I had no power here, and I knew he would just ignore my interruption.

"And last—and most certainly least—we have Adrienne Connors. Connors, who bears the name of one of the greatest kings of men, a man who was a worthy enemy, but herself is nobody. Nothing special has ever happened to you, has it, Adrienne? Your partner may be a coward, but at least he seeks to right his wrongs. You have no wrongs to right, because your life has been pointless and sheltered and completely void of meaning. You'll make no mark on your world. Would anyone even notice if you'd never existed? I'm honestly impressed by the depth of your insignificance, my dear. It is—" He would have continued, I was sure, but he was interrupted.

"Enough." Nemain's clear voice chopped across the line of the Avartagh's spiteful taunting like an axe. That's all she said. She hadn't moved, her facial expression had returned to the stony nonexpression she'd shown before the taunting had begun. But it shut the creature up. He sat there with that same sadistic smile, but at least he was no longer talking.

"Of course, Lady of War," he replied with a pleasant tone. "As it pleases you."

He didn't look evil, at least not at first glance. He looked almost like any of the hundreds of Aes Sidhe we had seen at Lughnasadh: tall and fair-skinned, with dark hair down to his shoulders. His eyes were different, though. They were black, all the way through. No whites, no pupils. Just black. With his thin lips curled into his sneering smile, I could see his teeth were filed into points. He wore a simple linen tunic and breeches. Prison garb, I supposed, as he certainly seemed the ostentatious type given his druthers.

After a long, tense few minutes, I spoke again, quietly. "Do you know why we have come here?"

He cocked his head and stared at me intently. "Do you?"

Detective Lajoie stepped in before I could reply. "What do you know about a ritual murder in Philadelphia five nights ago, and a second last night?"

"Five nights?" The Avartagh turned to him and grinned. "Five of whose nights? You are in the Otherworld. The revolutions of the mortal world have little meaning here."

He was right. Time passed differently in the mortal world than in the Otherworld—that's why so many fairy tales included time jumps, like Rip Van Winkle's twenty-year nap. I'd already considered that for our current visit; since we'd be returning to the city the same way we came, almost no time at all would have passed on my clocks back home.

"Five human nights," Detective Connors stepped in. "Five nights ago in Philadelphia, someone or something skinned a man alive and butchered him, using his blood to write all over the walls. Last night, the same happened again. What do you know about it?"

He looked down and laughed, a slightly hysterical giggle.

"What would I know about that? I have been stuck in here for more than five hundred years in your world. Sounds delightful, though." He giggled again.

"It sounds like one of your greatest hits, you mean," she replied.

I had to give it to her, even though she and her partner had been following me for the past couple hours like scared lost puppies, once they got into the interview, they were holding their own. She wasn't backing down an inch. Maybe she just had something to prove, after the Avartagh's fucked-up little game.

He looked up, locking onto her eyes. The laughter and the sick smile were gone. He radiated hatred.

"Yes," he hissed. "Armorica. I came so close to ending your race's dominance over my people, breaking the pathetic humans' power, restoring the glory of the Fae. If the Arcanum had remained ignorant only another week, I would have completed the rite and ridded the Fae of humanity's scourge entire." He almost snarled the last words.

"What is the Tamesis?" I asked, quietly.

The Avartagh snorted. "Do you think it is that easy? You come to my cell, you irritate me, and this one" he nodded at Nemain, "orders me around in my own mind, then I am supposed to answer every one of your questions like a good little boy? What do you think I am, Sorcerer? It is you who are the child here, not I."

"What is the Tamesis?" I repeated.

He shook his head. "No, Sorcerer, it is not that easy. Even were I inclined to tell you, which I am most certainly not when that will give you ever so much more grief, I could not. The Tamesis is nothing that can be explained. It must be experienced. It is visceral, primal. Words can only be a hollow reflection of its power. Shall I try to explain? No, I think not. Certainly not so long as you keep asking the wrong questions."

We had him. I could sense it. He wanted to explain, in his arrogance he was dying to brag about his accomplishments, how close he was to success. He wanted to taunt us. He wasn't stupid; he knew revealing such details would give us an advantage. And while he may not be involved in this case at all, he certainly had no desire to help us. But he was also unstable, and if pushed just right...

"Very well," I said. "What is the relationship of the ritual killing to the Tamesis?"

"Bah," he snorted. "You already know the answer to that."

Detective Lajoie looked at me with a question in his face.

"Yes," I nodded. "I do. It's to build power, to channel energy for the final rite. That's why there must be pain and terror, why there must be blood."

The Avartagh smiled grimly, showing all of his sharpened teeth. "Very good, Sorcerer. You are not completely stupid after all."

I tried a slightly different tack. "How much power is required for the Tamesis?"

"Lots." He scowled. "Lots and lots. More than you can dream.

But you have never killed a sorcerer for his power, so you do not realize how much energy that represents. It is a moot question if you do not know the measuring units."

Detective Connors jumped in with the obvious response. "How many sorcerers would one have to kill to have enough power for the Tamesis?"

He smiled again, like a schoolboy showing off an achievement to his parents. "Not many, child. Not many at all. I was almost there before the Arcanum arrived." He looked away, as if remembering. He looked very pleased with himself.

"Does that power have to be collected in a specific manner?" Detective Lajoie asked.

The monster nodded. "Yes, yes, of course. Complicated. Very complicated. Patterns within patterns, hidden within the cycles of the two worlds. That is the most difficult part. Everything must be just so, all the variables accounted for to keep the balance just right."

"What is the Tamesis?" Detective Connors pressed. I mentally smiled, though my face remained expressionless. Keeping up the pressure. This was their element, and Faeries and gods be damned—they had a job to do.

"The Darkness, of course." The Avartagh was scowling again. "It's right there in the name."

Aengus spoke up, for the first time since we'd entered the room. "How did you develop the rituals?"

"Dear cousin!" Those pointed teeth gleamed in an evil smile once again. "I thought you would never ask!" He giggled. "It was difficult. Most difficult. I cannot take all the credit—I needed a push to see the critical point in the Great Cycle. But even with such assistance, it required a lot of experimenting over the centuries. A lot of very enjoyable experimenting. Enjoyable for me, at least. I do not think the subjects enjoyed it very much at all. But does the master of the slaughterhouse worry about the feelings of the cattle?" He paused, another hysterical giggle escaping.

"It was rather annoying, being constantly interrupted in my research by damned sorcerers and you lot of Tuatha Dé. They thought they killed me. Twelve times. Twelve times they thought they killed me. It was easy getting away, but every time set me back centuries of effort. That made me mad."

His face twisted into a sneer. "But I figured it out, despite the setbacks, despite the interruptions. I figured out how to summon the Tamesis. How to breach the walls. How to bring the Darkness that would destroy the power of the Arcanum and rid our people of their meddling forever." He slipped into a fit of high-pitched giggling for a long moment, as if remembering something funny, before trailing off and scowling angrily.

"But before I could finish the rites the Arcanum came to kill me yet again. They failed, of course. They always failed. But they killed my assistants and spoiled the blood channels. All of that energy, wasted." He was breathing heavily, his nostrils flared, his eyes wide and insane. "And then you damned Tuatha Dé and your pet Fianna gave me no rest, no chance to begin again. And here I am, in chains and a stone room, sealed in by unbroken gold and the dreams of a sleeping giant. And there you are, worried about the Tamesis anyway." He stopped, controlled his breath. He pressed his lips together and looked away.

"Why did you need a sorcerer to help you?" Aengus asked calmly, his eyebrows raised.

He looked angry. "Now you just want all the answers?"

"If it was so complicated and took so long to figure out, how could someone else know of your rituals?" I asked.

He didn't answer at first. He lay back down, exactly as he was when we first entered the room, supine on the shelf with his hands on his chest, fingers interlocked, and his eyes closed. Finally, after a long moment, he spoke. "That, Sorcerer, is a very good question."

"Who is the Faerie involved in the current ritual?" I asked. No answer.

"Who helped you find this critical point in the Great Cycle?" I tried again.

I waited, but he said no more.

Aengus sighed. "He is tired of the game. We shall get nothing further from him."

He looked to Nemain, who nodded and waved a hand, the door fading back into existence. She gestured for us to precede her out into the corridor.

Chapter 13

NEMAIN LED US OUT TO THE MAIN GATE, THEN TURNED TOWARD the fortress and started to walk back in. But Henri Lajoie's softly accented voice split the quiet evening before she opened the door.

"Excuse me, ma'am."

She stopped and straightened, turned back to face us, one eyebrow raised in question.

"When we first got here," the detective continued, "you mentioned that the Avartagh was imprisoned for experimenting with forbidden magic. Do you know anything about those experiments?"

My heart caught in my chest, and Aengus stiffened next to me—I heard him draw in a sharp breath. It was a dangerous gamble, and one Detective Lajoie probably didn't even realize he was taking. He was merely seizing the chance to clarify some information which might be relevant, as any experienced investigator would do.

But if she felt the question constituted undue interest in forbidden magic, she might well decide he was a possible ally or spy of the Avartagh and immediately act to eliminate that potential threat, just in case. And Nemain was the most unpredictable of the Morrigan—to the Irish tribesmen who worshipped the Tuatha, she'd personified the havoc and chaos of war and combat. Legend said her battle cry could kill a hundred men. I couldn't guess how she'd react.

I'd wanted the detectives to direct such questions through me specifically to avoid situations of this sort. But mere moments ago they'd been asking similar questions in the Avartagh's audience chamber, and he must not have realized that very different rules were at play out here.

As she silently regarded the detective for a long moment, my hand inched closer to the hem of my shirt and the Glock underneath.

I wondered whose side Aengus would take if it came to that—he'd given us his countenance on this trip to the Otherworld, and until he formally withdrew it, honor demanded he protect us while we were here. But this was the Dún Dubh, and I didn't know if the standard rules of Faerie hospitality applied to this situation. Protecting the prison against any potential threat may well outweigh such prior commitments.

To my great relief, I didn't have to find out.

"Yes," she replied, breaking the tension. "He was experimenting with the veil, the boundary between this world and the rest of creation. This is forbidden."

I let out a breath I hadn't realized I was holding. The energy I'd called up on a mental hair-trigger dissipated harmlessly into the mountain. I looked over at Aengus, who met my eye and nodded slightly in shared relief—he'd known exactly what had come close to happening.

"Why is it forbidden?" Detective Connors asked. Her partner had initiated the line of questioning, but she was jumping on it, refusing to let go until they'd gotten every bit of information out of it possible. From what I'd seen this evening, that was the difference between them, the complementary roles that made them an effective team. Lajoie was the deep thinker, the chess player, tracing all the possibilities in his mind and making the initial forays. Connors was the fighter, the determined and driven investigator who'd follow the rabbit down the hole as far as she could while Lajoie moved on and thought about the next angle for them to explore. It was a good partnership.

"Because any disruption to the veil may well doom us all," Nemain replied somberly. "Whether hubris or madness, the Avartagh's belief he could control it is folly."

"Do you know what the Tamesis is, exactly?" Detective Connors followed up immediately.

She shook her head. "I do not. Others may—Lugh, the Dagda,

the sons of Lir, perhaps. But the secrets of the veil are not of my domain, nor those of my sisters."

Detective Lajoie opened his mouth to ask another question, but she held up a hand to stop him.

"I will answer no further questions about the Tamesis or the Avartagh's experiments. That is all I am at liberty to say about this. But perhaps," she said, her voice becoming thoughtful, "I can help you in another way."

She looked each of the detectives in the eye in turn, then smiled, broadly and sincerely. For the first time since our arrival, her beauty outshone her menace.

"My sisters and I admire boldness and determination, and you have shown both: you have come across the veil to fulfill your oaths, you faced the Avartagh's cruelty, you met two of the Morrigan without showing fear—yes, I know of your earlier encounter with my sister Badb, for what one of us knows, all of us know." She paused and thought for a moment, then nodded.

"Great risk, taken boldly, should by right lead to great reward or great catastrophe. This is the way of the Fae, and we of the Morrigan honor the old ways. You warriors have taken such a risk and acquitted yourselves well. Therefore, we offer you a just reward, earned by your own actions. Once only, without obligation, either of you may call upon the name of the Morrigan in your hour of need, and we shall strike fear and confusion into the hearts of your enemies, whosoever they may be."

I took in a sharp breath. That was a hell of a gift. To my knowledge, the Morrigan hadn't directly helped a human in battle like that for centuries. Likely not since the days of Fionn mac Cumhaill, almost seventeen hundred years ago.

"Our thanks, Lady Nemain," Detective Connors replied after a few seconds, in a very, very quiet voice. "You honor us."

Nemain nodded solemnly, again meeting each of their eyes.

"This is a mighty weapon. Wield it with care, only in the direst of circumstances, for you are unlikely to earn another in your lifetimes."

That was quite the understatement.

She then bid Aengus farewell before returning inside the fortress, and the four of us began to descend the stairway.

"Hey, Quinn?" Detective Lajoie's voice broke the silence a while later, when we were about halfway down the mountainside.

"Yes, Detective Lajoie?"

"You heard what the Avartagh said about my... perversions?"

I snorted. "Has that been bothering you, son? He was just trying to get under your skin."

"Well..." he began but trailed off.

We continued our careful descent for several more steps before I figured he wasn't sure how to express what he wanted to say.

"I already gathered that you're homosexual, Detective. Is that what you're worried about?"

"That was enough of a clue?" he sounded surprised.

"Well," I answered, "that and your lack of reaction to the Tylwyth Teg earlier, when we first met up with Aengus. I originally thought you might simply be exceptionally professional, but after the Avartagh's comments, I made an educated guess."

"Given what that asshole said, I thought there might be some stigma against it. If it makes you uncomfortable, we should have that discussion sooner rather than later."

"No, not at all." I shook my head, though he couldn't see me as I was once again in the rear of the line on the stairs. "In fact, the magical community is probably more welcoming to alternative lifestyles than most. No one really cares. When you live in this world, you learn to recognize there are a lot more versions of 'normal' than most people believe."

"How enlightened," Detective Connors remarked.

"At some point, somewhere, most varieties of romantic and sexual partnerships have been not only accepted but commonplace," I explained. "Homophobia tends to be more commonly associated with monotheism, not paganism, and you've spent the evening in the company of beings that ancient pagans worshipped as their gods. The Avartagh might genuinely care, but probably not. More likely, he just figured it would get under your skin, same as everything else he said to the three of us."

"That is correct," Aengus added from the front. "The Fae do not normally consider homosexuality a perversion of any form. As I mentioned earlier this evening, sex does not hold the same taboos among my people as it does among humans."

"I'm glad to hear that, then," Detective Lajoie replied. "I was just afraid it might cause some tension in our working relationship. Happy that's not the case."

"There may well be tension in our working relationship in the future, Detective. You certainly wouldn't be the first to find me difficult to work alongside. But your taste in romantic partners will not be the cause."

He didn't respond to that, and we lapsed back into silence for the rest of the walk down. When we reached the plain at the bottom of the stair, we huddled together for a moment before heading back to the stone by which we'd travelled here.

"So what did we actually learn?" The big Haitian man's voice chattered slightly—the detectives were once again miserably chilled.

I'd been pondering just that since we left the Avartagh's chamber.

"We still don't know who is responsible," I answered, "and haven't even narrowed down the list of suspects. We still don't know what the end goal of the ritual is, beyond somehow destroying the power of the Arcanum, and that it has something to do with the veil between Earth and the Otherworld.

"What we do know," I continued, "is that the ritual is extremely complex and requires everything to be absolutely perfect. And that there will be at least three more victims before it's over, unless we can stop it."

"Three?" Detective Connors asked, her brow furrowed in confusion. "How do you figure?"

"The Avartagh said he was almost there before the Arcanum stopped him, and he'd sacrificed four sorcerers by that point. That means five victims seems to be the bare minimum, maybe even more if the strength of the sorcerers matters. Evan was one. The Jane Doe in North Philadelphia was two. Ergo, at least three more."

"What about the four others in North Philly, the mom and her kids?"

I shook my head. "They weren't used in the ritual. I don't know why they were killed, but they weren't part of the Tamesis rites."

Her partner nodded. "That all makes sense. But do we know how to stop the next murder?"

"No," Aengus replied before I could. "The Avartagh said 'patterns within patterns.' We have the basic pattern of each ritual itself, but we do not know how the sacrifices are connected to each other and to the 'cycles of the two worlds' he mentioned. Like Nemain, I have little understanding of the nature of the veil and know nothing of any Great Cycle. We cannot guess where the next sacrifice will be without more information."

"That's a good point," Detective Connors added. "Does it even have to be in Philly? Are we going to have to start coordinating with other departments? Feds? We don't know anything yet that could help us narrow it down." She looked over at me. "Unless you're still holding out on us, Quinn."

"I'm not," I shook my head. "At this point you know basically everything I do about the Tamesis rites, except some technical magic details about the ritual construction and the ambush spell left behind. Nothing that would be useful to either of you. But it's possible that I could come up with something on that front by extrapolating from the ritual itself. I'll work on it tonight once we get home. It might be pointless without more information, but it's worth trying."

"There's something else," Detective Lajoie mused. "You asked him, at the end there, about who helped him develop the ritual in the first place. Do either of you have an idea who that may have been?"

"I do not," Aengus shook his head, "for as Lugh said, I had left the Faerie Court before the Avartagh's experiments. I heard of them after, and have seen the depictions of the rites themselves, but I know not the details of the events surrounding the rampage."

The three of them looked at me, but I had to shrug. "No, sorry. It was at least eight hundred years ago. It wasn't mentioned in the annals, and the Rectors didn't exactly keep detailed investigation records at that time. I'll check whatever I can find and let you know, but don't get your hopes up. There are a lot of magical beings who might have that kind of knowledge. Too many to narrow down without more to go on."

"Okay," Detective Lajoie began, but then a thought struck him. "That bastard said something about time being different here than in our world. What time will it be when we get back?"

"We left at about eleven, so it will be around a quarter past eleven when we get back," I responded.

"Fifteen minutes?" Detective Connors laughed. "All of this, in less than fifteen minutes?"

"Yes," I replied, "although your watch has been running steady since we got here, so you'll have to reset it. But it means I'll have plenty of time to work on figuring out the pattern of the rite, and you two can get some sleep before you have to be at the office in the morning. The three of us can meet up at lunch tomorrow and compare notes."

"What about you?" Detective Lajoie asked Aengus.

"I am happy to help with anything involving the Fae, but I cannot directly participate in the investigation of sorcerer matters on Earth. The Treaty of Tara forbids my interference in the Arcane Court's jurisdiction without formal sanction from the Council or a duly appointed representative such as a Rector."

"And the fact that Quinn is pretty sure a Faerie is involved doesn't change that?" Detective Connors raised an eyebrow.

"Not without proof." He shrugged. "My hands are tied, unfortunately. I, like the rest of the Tuatha Dé Danann, swore a threefold oath upon the exact wording of the Treaty. I cannot break it."

"That's alright," I replied. That's why I'd gone to him for information rather than asking him to help investigate. "You've done what you can, and for that we thank you."

"Is there anything else to do in the Otherworld before we go home?" Detective Lajoie asked.

"No," Aengus answered. "Even if the sons of Lir know of the nature of the Tamesis as Nemain suggests, we would not get that information from them. They are the protectors of the veil and would not reveal its mysteries to anyone. And Quinn here has already entered into one bargain with Lugh. Another would be foolishly dangerous."

"What about the Dagda?" Detective Connors asked. "Nemain said he may know, as well."

Aengus shook his head vehemently and looked away. "No. I will not—I cannot—take you to my father." His tone brooked no argument.

I remembered the tales I'd heard about him and his father: how Aengus felt he had been slighted and responded by stealing the Dagda's house, how the son had saved the father at the Battle of Moytura, how the Dagda had disapproved of his son's love for a mortal Christian girl. I didn't know what had happened between them when Aengus had left Ireland and the Otherworld, but I'd heard rumors that he hadn't spoken to his father since. I'd never asked about their history—it wasn't my place. But clearly something remained unresolved.

"In that case," I broke the tension after several awkward seconds, "let's head home."

Aengus nodded and led the way to the carved stone. We returned to the Plain of Delight, then walked past the camp back to the gate from which we'd initially arrived in the Otherworld.

Chapter 14

THE TRANSITION FROM QUIET FIELD IN MIDAFTERNOON TO DIM tent in the confined and noisy market was mildly disorienting, despite having undergone multiple such trips that evening. But everyone got back through without any problems, and Aengus closed the gateway behind us.

"I hope you got what you needed out of that trip, Quinn," Aengus said quietly, still facing the muraled concrete wall where he'd just closed the passageway into the Otherworld. "The price may have been far steeper than you yet realize." After a moment, he closed the flap in the tent, covering the masonry, and turned around. "I was not jesting when I stated your life will likely never be the same. It is no small thing to owe a favor to a Faerie. Especially when that Faerie is Lugh."

Didn't I know it. I wasn't at all pleased with the direction my life had taken recently. Over the past three days, I'd been drawn into investigating a serial killer, introduced two uninitiated humans to the reality of magic, and promised a favor to a Faerie king. Not to mention being reminded of all my sins—everything I'd spent so long desperately striving to forget—by an insane monster locked in a magical prison. It had not been a very good week so far. But if I did nothing, the killing would continue, and things would likely get far worse.

"It'll have to be enough," I replied. "I don't know what I can do to repay you for your help, Aengus."

He laughed, his first sign of amusement since Detective Connors had brought up his father. "Go on, get out of here before you end up owing favors to another Faerie. If you need me, you know how to find me."

I looked at him for a long minute, contemplating.

Aengus hadn't been home in centuries, if the rumors were true, avoiding the Otherworld almost entirely after whatever had happened between him and his father. But when I asked for help, on behalf of people he'd never met and a species that had shunned him and his race a thousand years before, he hadn't even hesitated. And unlike virtually every other Faerie I'd ever met, he'd asked for nothing in return—he'd done it all, as best I could tell, simply because we were friends. What did it say about me that the only real friend I had left in the world was a four-millennia-old Faerie?

What did it say about him?

I nodded to him, then ducked out of the tent without another word, back into the swirling madness of the Faerie Market. It was just as busy as when we'd left, which made sense given how little time had passed in this world. But the time had certainly passed for us—I was exhausted. I tilted my head in the direction of the front gate.

"Are you two ready to go?"

Detective Lajoie nodded. "Unless there's anyone else material for us to talk to, I think we're good for the night."

I led the way to the front gate. While humans generally needed to arrive at the Gardens via magical taxi in order to gain entrance to the Market, there was nothing special required to leave. We stepped outside and joined a small group of other market customers who had apparently decided to call it a night, including the pair of Tylwyth Teg who had been flirting with Aengus earlier.

"Can one of you call a taxi?" I asked. "Just a regular old cab is fine. But I don't have a cell phone."

It wasn't an aversion to technology. I was perfectly comfortable using computers and other modern electronics—I had even installed cloud-based digital security cameras in the shop a few years back once I'd figured out how to magically ward the servers against unwanted access. But I'd never had need of a cell phone, especially of the "smart" variety. I rarely traveled, and I had a perfectly serviceable landline at home for phone calls and a laptop for the internet. A cell would just be a waste of money.

"Uber work?" Detective Connors replied.

"Whatever," I shrugged. I'd never ridden in an Uber before, but I'd heard about the concept. It would do.

Detective Connors pulled out a smartphone and started messing around with it, presumably ordering us a ride.

"Hey, Quinn, do you mind if I ask what the Avartagh meant about your parents?" she asked as she dealt with her phone. "Something about a king?"

I thought about it for a moment. There was now a good chance we'd have to deal with the Arcane Court and its official representatives at some point during this case, so it was probably best the detectives know the basics.

"Sorcerers are an individualistic bunch," I explained. "There aren't very many of us. Most of the time we keep to ourselves, and dislike anyone meddling in our affairs—Tolkien got that one right. But sometimes something comes up that requires cooperation. In ancient days, sorcerers would cooperate as necessary, then disband after. But about fifteen hundred years ago, the spread of Christianity through traditionally Faerie-controlled lands caused too much trouble, lasting too long, for an ad hoc alliance to deal with.

"As the religion spread out among the peoples of Europe, its practitioners taught that beings of magic were demons, minions of Satan. People who had for thousands of years peacefully coexisted with the magical races, and even worshipped them as gods, turned on them. The sorcerers of the time banded together to prevent the Fae from retaliating, to keep them from wiping out the human race in response. Eventually, it became a more permanent society, called the Arcanum, with the mission of keeping the peace between the Fae and humanity, and protecting humanity from other magical threats.

"The Arcanum isn't really a government. There are no laws sorcerers must follow beyond upholding the various treaties the Arcanum has signed with the magical races, such as the Treaty of Tara—the pact between humanity and the Tuatha Dé which Aengus mentioned. Not every sorcerer is a member of the Arcanum, of course, though most of them at least get their initial training from the society. But even nonmembers have to abide by the treaties. That's how we keep the peace. Ranked members are responsible for upholding those treaties and protecting the populace from magical threats within their respective territories, as well as a couple obligations like mustering in the event of war and attending the Grand Conclave every thirteen years."

I paused for a second. "The Grand Conclave is where the ranked members of the Arcanum vote on major matters like treaties. It's also where we elect the Arcane Court—the King and Council—who govern the Arcanum and conduct any necessary diplomacy between Conclaves. My father is the current King. It's his third term. My mother is his Lord Marshal, the member of the Council responsible for the apprehension of rogue sorcerers and Fae and other magical threats to humanity."

She'd been Lord Marshal during the Shadow War, too. Back when I'd been one of her loyal soldiers. But I didn't mention that part.

"But," Detective Lajoie frowned, "if the Lord Marshal—your mom—is responsible for stopping magical people from doing bad things in the human world, why didn't you just call her when you realized that the Townes murder was a blood rite?"

"I did, actually. Well, I called one of the Council's Rectors, their regional deputies, earlier today. But she isn't taking responsibility for it. As a ranked member, I'm generally considered responsible for my own territory—she'll only step in if it turns out I can't handle it." I chewed on my lower lip for a couple seconds. "Anyway, I haven't really spoken with my parents in a long time."

We lapsed back into an uneasy silence, the two detectives clearly unsure what to say to that last bit, and me intently not thinking about my parents.

"Uber's nearly here," Detective Connors announced. "Less than a minute. Keep an eye out for a white Toyota Camry."

We turned to look for the car. But when I'd gotten dressed for the evening, I'd made sure to wear my amulet under my shirt, the one with an enchantment bound into it so it would heat up if anyone used offensive magic in my immediate area. And as the detectives expectantly watched the corner of the street for our approaching ride, it flared into heat against my chest.

I instinctively threw up my left hand and released the shield spell tied to my ring. Because we were standing at the right end of the group waiting for rides, and I didn't know where the attack was coming from, I just blocked that entire side off as I shouted a warning to the detectives to get down.

As the shield blazed into bright blue life, forming a wall between the three of us and the rest of the group, I was slammed back by an impact against it and heard the surprised yells and screams of those who had been minding their own business waiting on the sidewalk. The glow of the magical barrier meant I couldn't see who the attack had come from. But while I was throwing up the shield, I was also reaching my right hand under my coat.

I quickly cleared the covering T-shirt and drew the Glock one-handed, silently thanking myself for all the practice I'd put in over the years. I rapidly switched my stance to bring my right side, and the gun, toward the threat. As soon as I was in a decent one-handed firing position, I dropped the shield and scanned for the attacker.

Fortunately, most denizens of the magical world have the sense to drop to the ground when people start throwing magic around. Until you've seen the effects of a particular spell, only the practitioner who cast it knows exactly what it will do, so most people wisely try to get out of the way, just in case. That meant those who had innocently been waiting for taxis or rideshares were all prostrate on the sidewalk—no one was running around hysterically, though a couple were still screaming. I could see exactly who had attacked us as soon as I dropped the barrier: a tall figure in a cloak was the only one still standing, and he had his hand outstretched, a dagger pointed directly at me.

Unfortunately, dropping the shield also gave him a perfect shot at me, and while I saw him quickly, I still had to bring my gun to bear. He, on the other hand, knew where I was going to be when the barrier fell, so he got his shot off first, a silvery pulse of energy that seemed to burst from the tip of his knife. It flew at me quickly, but not so fast that I couldn't dodge—my instinct kicked in and allowed me to sidestep out of the way, if only barely. I felt the white-hot energy as it flew past, maybe an inch from my still outstretched left arm. It was so hot that I felt my skin blister despite the protective spells of my overcoat.

But it seemed to be a spell that took a second's effort, and that was enough. Even while I moved, I continued bringing my gun to aim at my attacker.

As soon as the sights lined up with his torso, I squeezed the trigger. Bullets travel quite a bit faster than his spell. He didn't have time to dodge, or to throw up any active defenses. And as soon as the sights dropped back into alignment, before I even saw if I'd hit him, I squeezed the trigger again, and a third time. A lot of creatures in the magical world have superhuman reflexes, but few can react quicker than I can get off three or four shots, even shooting one-handed.

Now, gun enthusiasts will debate for hours at a time the merits of the ten-millimeter, and even its supporters would likely be horrified to know what metals I used in my bullets. But no one doubts that it packs a punch. Contrary to popular belief, there is no handgun round that will knock down a person by virtue of its own kinetic energy; the only way to guarantee an instant stop is to hit something vital in the central nervous system, and that tends to result in death in short order. But one-shot stop or not, anyone who gets hit in the chest with three ten-mil bullets in rapid succession is going to notice.

And notice he did, though not as much as I would have preferred. He grunted as the bullets hit, but he absorbed the impacts like a boxer taking a combination of punches, rolling with the blows but shrugging them off. The knife dropped, and he threw up a translucent red shield of his own before I could resume firing.

I maintained my aim at the hazy outline I could see through his shield, but rather than resuming the fight, he kept the barrier up, took three steps, and jumped into the middle of the street. Directly into the path of an oncoming city bus.

Chapter 15

THE BUS CAME TO A STOP. AFTER A FEW SECONDS I DECIDED there was no further immediate threat, so I pulled my T-shirt back up with my left hand and safely returned the Glock to its holster. Everyone else was still on the ground, but at least the screaming had stopped.

It had been maybe fifteen seconds from the surprise attack to the mystery sorcerer's escape. That's the thing about gunfights in the real world as opposed to the cinema: there's no script or choreographer, and they tend to be a lot shorter than one would expect.

By the time I'd pulled my shirt back down over my holstered gun, the detectives were on their feet.

"Did that guy... did he just jump in front of a bus?" Detective Connors looked shocked.

"Yes," I answered, shaking my head, "but I doubt it had much effect. Sorcerers tend not to shuffle off their mortal coil from minor things like that. It was probably his escape plan all along if things didn't go as he wanted. He timed the attack so he could use the bus to cover his retreat."

"How...?" She asked, the confusion obvious in her voice.

"You saw the shield I used to stop his first shot? He threw up something like that after I started returning fire. When he jumped in front of the bus, it would have protected him from the impact, and he was likely pushed down the street unharmed, far enough away we wouldn't be able to catch him if we gave chase."

Detective Lajoie frowned. "I saw you hit him. Three times."

"Yes," I replied. "I don't know how much damage it did, but I learned one thing: whoever he was, he was almost certainly human."

"How do you figure?"

"Most any kind of magical creature would have been a lot more affected by the rounds I use than our attacker seemed to be. Unless it were wearing a bulletproof vest, which is pretty unlikely among nonhumans. Meaning a high probability of human."

By this point everyone had seemed to realize that bullets and spells were no longer flying, and they were getting up and dusting themselves off. No one seemed to have been hurt in the fight. The bus had come from the wrong direction to be in the line of fire, and none of my shots had gone wide, so at least there was no collateral damage to deal with. But gunshots are extremely loud, so count on some of the neighbors to call the police anyway. I heard the sound of approaching sirens.

"We'll handle the responding officers," Detective Lajoie offered. "You figure out what the hell happened."

"Nice shooting, by the way," his partner said. "What kind of gun was that you were using?"

"Glock 20. Why?"

"Do you have a concealed carry permit for it?"

I scowled. That was her primary concern right now?

"I do, as a matter of fact. Have since eighty-eight. Do you want to see it?" I started to reach for my wallet in my back pocket.

She shook her head as a police cruiser came screaming up the block, sirens blaring loudly. "Maybe later. Let's deal with this first."

She and Detective Lajoie held their badges high as they approached the driver's side. The sirens cut off, but the lights stayed on.

"What happened, detectives?" the uniformed officer at the wheel asked through a rolled-down window. They engaged him in muted conversation for a minute, then Detective Connors went to talk with the bus driver while her partner stayed at the patrol car. I saw the cop reach for his radio, hopefully to pass the word that no other units needed to respond. While they obviously wouldn't be able to enter the Market itself, the fewer police officers who arrived to see something happening after hours at the Magic Gardens, the better.

After the commotion and gunshots, people were milling around the front gate to see what had happened. Aengus pushed his way through the crowd of rubberneckers.

"What is going on?" he demanded, looking around to see me standing, helping up the last of the small group who had been waiting with us. He also saw Detective Lajoie in conversation with the uniformed officers in the squad car, and his eyebrows went up.

"Everyone back inside. Now," he commanded.

I caught the detectives' attention and jerked my head back to indicate the crowd re-entering the Magic Gardens. Lajoie finished up the conversation and, after the officer turned off his lights and drove off, he joined me. Connors returned a few seconds later, the bus resuming its route for the night.

"I convinced the driver it was just kids messing around," she told us. "No one was hurt and the bus wasn't damaged, so no need to worry about it." I nodded.

"So what's up?" Detective Lajoie asked.

"The Treaty of Tara guarantees a general truce at any sanctioned Faerie Market, which makes what just happened the magical equivalent of an international incident. And as the ranking member of the Tuatha Dé present, enforcing the Market Truce falls on Aengus. He needs to talk to us and figure out what happened. He'd rather do that away from prying eyes and ears, so we need to go back inside." I led the way.

"Sorcerer Quinn," Aengus called out to me once we'd re-entered the Market, "explain to me what happened. Why was the Truce breached?"

"My companions and I were waiting for a ride home," I explained in a careful, measured tone, my eyes on his. "We were attacked without provocation by an unknown cloaked assailant. I defended myself. The assailant fled into the night as the bus arrived."

"That is the truth!" I heard someone speak up. Aengus and I both turned. It was one of the Tylwyth Teg from earlier. "He was doing nothing and was ambushed by an assassin! The Market Truce was breached, but it was not the doing of this sorcerer or his friends."

I gave her a slight nod of thanks for speaking up. Aengus stared hard at her for a long moment, as if deciding whether she was telling the truth or had an ulterior motive. She had tears in her eyes—the Tylwyth Teg are highly emotional creatures. But before she actually burst into hysterics, he nodded too.

"Very well, Child of the Forest. I believe you."

He turned back to me. "Nevertheless, as you are the ranking sorcerer in this region, I am bound to summon a Rector to confirm that the breach of the Truce was not initiated by a member of the Arcanum. And I shall have to insist you remain here until then."

I nodded.

The closest Rector to us was Rachel Liu, with whom I'd spoken earlier that day. She was a decent sort, as far as they go. She could be a bit stuck-up sometimes, but not a bad person. But it would be some time before she could get here, even through the Otherworld—last I'd checked, she lived in San Francisco. And she'd mentioned a trip to hunt down a Wechuge, a type of demon found in cold mountain regions like the Canadian Rockies, so she might not even be available.

Aengus told the crowd to disperse, and they did so slowly and reluctantly. I needed fresh air, so I stepped back outside and found a seat on the floor against the wall while he returned to his tent to summon Rachel.

The detectives followed me out, and Lajoie moved over to the exterior wall where the attacker's heat spell had struck the muraled façade. From what I could see, it had melted a hole into the underlying concrete. He wasn't likely to find any clues from the damage, but maybe he was just curious.

His partner, on the other hand, approached our attacker's knife where it still lay on the sidewalk, exactly as he had dropped it before he fled. She knelt next to it, examining it minutely, then stretched a hand out towards it.

"Don't touch that," I snapped.

She looked up at me, her hand only a couple inches from the knife. "Why not?"

I looked at her like one might regard a small child wondering why you were telling her not to touch the lit burner on the stove.

"Because," I explained, reminding myself to be patient, that she honestly couldn't know the potential danger, "that athame was just used as a focus for extremely dangerous offensive magic, and it was dropped in place by someone who clearly both meant me harm and had a plan in the event of an unsuccessful assassination. We have no idea what residual effects could linger on the blade, and there's a good chance it wasn't dropped by accident."

She looked at me, then dubiously back at the knife, and withdrew her hand. "Contact poison?"

"Very possibly," I murmured. "Or worse. Leave it be until the Rector gets here."

I pulled up the sleeve of my coat and saw that the spell had left a nasty burn on my forearm. I sighed. Reaching into my left pocket, I drew my dagger. I focused briefly on it and whispered a word, and the blade chilled until it covered in a fine layer of frost. I pressed it against the burn on my left forearm, to cool the flesh and reduce the blistering. Not really my original intention in binding that particular spell to the blade, but it would suffice until I got home and could treat it properly.

Connors walked over and sat down next to me. She looked tired. It had been an eventful day for her, too, I supposed. Learning that her grandmother's stories were true—or at least based on truth—and being taunted with her worst fear by one of the monsters from them was enough to wear anyone out.

"So that was magic? I mean, I know we visited Faeries in the Otherworld, but the only part of it that felt like real magic was the portal. But your shield, that was magic."

I smiled politely, without much feeling, looking out over the tracks at the far wall. "Yes. That was the type of magic I wouldn't do for you in the tent. The showy stuff. The type of magic that convinces otherwise completely rational and scientific people that magic does exist."

"So why did you use a gun at all, if you can do things like that?"

"Because . . ." I faltered. It was harder to explain than I'd thought it would be. "Because this isn't the cinema. Magic doesn't consist of 'wave a wand and say some Latin words.' It's a lot harder than that. If you don't have a spell prepared, it's not very easy to come up with one on the fly, even when you've practiced."

That wasn't the whole story. It wasn't even the main part of it. The truth was that magic has to come from the heart and the mind and the soul of the sorcerer, and I didn't have fire and lightning in me anymore. I'd burned it all out. But that was too hard and too personal to explain, so I took the coward's route and lied through half-truths.

"A gun is more reliable, faster, easier, and a lot less tiring than combat magic. And causes significantly less collateral damage if you can hit what you're aiming at. I practice hard to make sure I can."

"Fair enough," she replied. "But the Glock 20's a ten-mil, right? Kind of an odd choice."

That wasn't really a question, but I answered anyway. It's not like I had anything better to do while we waited.

"It's a niche caliber," I shrugged. "But when I first started shooting back in the early eighties, it had just come out. I experimented with some and realized they worked better for my purposes than any other round I'd tried—they're large enough for my custom anti-magical bullet design, the flat surface makes it easier to engrave counterspell glyphs to help them slip through magical defenses, and their added penetration is useful for someone who might find himself fighting demons and Fae monsters. I started out on a Colt Delta Elite; I switched to Glock about a decade back."

"Wait, the early eighties? And you said you've had a license since eighty-eight. That would make you at least in your early fifties. You don't look it. I'd have guessed around forty, maybe forty-five at the most."

I snorted. "Thank you, my dear, but I'm considerably older than that. Sorcerers age slowly. I was born in 1783."

Her eyes went wide. "Wait, for real?"

I nodded. "Your partner had a similar reaction when he learned that yesterday, too. I started my training in sorcery before Napoleon ruled France. I've known Aengus since the American Civil War."

"Christ," she whispered. Then chuckled lightly. "You don't seem like it. You grumble enough for someone in his seventies, but you don't talk like you're in your two-hundred-thirties."

"And how should someone in his two-hundred-thirties talk?" I raised an eyebrow.

"I don't know. More formally? More flowery language? You said you met Aengus during the Civil War—I've read letters from back then. You don't talk like that."

"Spoken language has always been more casual than the written word—every generation has had its slang. But even so, the point is taken." I shrugged and thought about it for a few seconds.

"Sorcerers learn to blend in from an early age," I explained. "We live in the shadows and try not to draw attention to ourselves. Speech patterns, fashion—the mannerisms and behaviors people consider normal—change over time, and most of us manage to keep up. I've never been able to get rid of my accent despite living in this country for almost a hundred years, but the rest of my speech mannerisms I've managed to adapt. I try to match my speech to my audience. With Lugh, or Badb, or Nemain, it makes sense to be formal, to use more traditional forms of address, to sound like I'm in my two-hundred-thirties as you put it. But with you and your partner and most other humans, that would just sound wrong."

She nodded. "That makes sense. You do speak a bit stuffier and more properly than most people I meet, I suppose. When you aren't just mumbling and grunting in annoyance, that is. I assumed it was from education, not age. No wonder you don't have a cell phone. But then, how'd you get started with guns at the ripe age of two hundred? I can't imagine someone who can throw fireballs gets excited by gunfire."

I shook my head. "No, that's true. I'm probably the only ranked sorcerer alive who has ever used a gun, at least as more than a curiosity. The early eighties were a pretty bad time here in Philadelphia, especially in a working-class neighborhood like Fishtown. A lot of crime and violence and drugs. Before your time, but I'm sure you've heard stories."

She nodded. She was a cop, and old-timers in any police or military force I'd ever encountered loved to tell war stories about the "bad old days."

"After a string of robberies in the neighborhood," I continued, "one of my nonmagical customers recommended I get a gun to protect the shop. I thought about it and realized that being able to defend myself without magic could be useful." *Especially to a burned-out sorcerer who'd grown sick of combat magic.*

"It started as a mere novelty, a hobby to take my mind off things. But the more I studied and practiced, the more I realized how practical it really was as an alternative. I may be old, but I'd be an idiot not to take advantage of technology and stay stuck in old ways of doing things just because they're old. Plus, at this point range time is almost therapeutic."

She nodded again. "I get that. It takes a lot of discipline and focus to shoot well. It can be almost Zenlike."

"Exactly," I answered. "Zenlike is a good way to put it."

"You looked like you don't just stand at the range plinking targets at seven yards, though," she added.

"Because I don't," I shrugged. "I actually make an effort not just to know how to shoot, but how to fight with a gun. It's different than fighting with magic or a blade, which is what basically all of my previous training and experience was. So I go to classes. Defensive handgun, combat shotgun, fighting in buildings, that sort of thing. I try to make it to at least one or two good training courses a year, and I keep up with developments in the field. There's been a great deal of innovation in technique over the past couple decades. Technology, too—my gun, for example. About a decade ago I realized that some of the aftermarket developments available for Glocks made them perfect for the types of threats I might face."

I set the cool blade down next to me, then reached under my shirt and drew the Glock with my right hand. I dropped the magazine and worked the slide with my left, then checked the chamber before handing the gun to Connors for her to inspect. I wasn't worried about witnesses—this close to the gate, the Market illusion spells would obscure the views of any nosy neighbors who might still be peering out of their windows after the earlier excitement.

"Reshaped and stippled grip for improved ergonomics. Aftermarket trigger for a smoother action. Night sights, because a lot of magical threats appear around dusk and dawn. And a Cerakote finish, to help prevent corrosion from salt, manticore blood, that sort of thing."

I picked up the round that had ejected from the chamber during the clearing process and held it up to show her, as she passed the gun back to me.

"Silver core, jacketed in copper with inlays of gold and iron, etched with glyphs against basic magical shields and Faerie armor. I have variations on the design in a couple other calibers, including nine-mil and thirty-eight special, as well as shotgun shells with a similar concept and a lot more punch. But the ten-mil works the best in a concealable package. The Glock carries fifteen, plus one in the chamber. Almost twice as many as my old Colt." I passed her the round to see more closely.

She looked at it silently for a moment, turning it over in her hand and holding it up to see the inlays and etchings. Then she handed the bullet back to me. "You said you have these in nine-mil?"

"Yes," I answered as I put the round back in the magazine, loaded the mag into the Glock, worked the action to chamber the round, then returned the gun to my holster. I picked my knife back up and resumed cooling the burn on my left arm. "But it's not as effective. Less penetration. Smaller silver core, and a lot less iron and gold. Plus less room for glyphs, so it won't go through as many types of magical defenses."

"Still," she said, "if we're going to be working with you, and maybe going up against people who can shrug off three of your ten-mil rounds and jump in front of a bus, Lajoie and I might want something a bit more suited to the task than department-issued hollow points."

I grunted. "That's fair, Detective. You're both in this, now. I'll get you a couple boxes of nine-mil tomorrow. They're definitely better than nothing."

She smiled. "You know, Quinn, this is the most I've heard you speak about one subject since we met the other day."

I just shrugged. "You and I haven't spent much time together before now, Detective. And you seemed intent on making a habit of insulting me."

She looked away, her expression almost ashamed. I hadn't intended to chastise her. Sometimes things just came out that way. We lapsed into mutual silence for a few moments.

She broke the tension. "I owe you an apology, Quinn."

I looked over at her, my eyebrows raised in question.

"For my behavior towards you before . . . before the Otherworld, I suppose. I'm sorry. I was rude, and condescending, and dismissive. I find myself having to confront a new normal that includes magic being real, humans not being alone in the world, a whole other world full of magical beings and gods. Things that I was rude to you for believing in, because I couldn't grasp the idea that there might be more to the universe than what I already knew about."

I thought for a second, then shook my head. "No apology

necessary, Detective. It angered me in the moment, but I understand. It's a hard truth, and one most people aren't equipped to confront at all, let alone as quickly as you have."

"My grandmother believed. I don't know if she knew anything for certain like I do now, but she definitely believed. She told me the stories like they were things that actually happened, real history, even with the Faeries and Tuatha and Fianna and magic and druids. To her it was as natural and plausible as anything she heard in Church, and no one thinks twice about someone believing in Jesus walking on water." She paused for a second.

"But my parents were both scientists. They were skeptics who taught me that the Faerie tales she told us were just myths and legends, that science could explain everything. It got bad, to the point where my father stopped letting my sister and me visit her, because he didn't want our heads filled with superstitious nonsense."

"I'm sorry to hear that," I said. "I suspect I would have enjoyed speaking with your grandmother."

"She'd have liked you, I think," Connors chuckled. "She always got along with surly grumps."

I raised my eyebrow at that but didn't respond. One should never be insulted by the truth, and I was undoubtedly a surly grump.

"But anyway, I'm sorry. Even if none of it had been true, you were right to call me a child. I was acting like one. You didn't deserve it. Even if you'd just been a crazy old man, I should've been more professional. I didn't treat you with the respect you deserved, as someone trying to help us when we asked. And I'm sorry for that."

She held out a hand, and I took it, accepting her apology. No sense pressing the issue further and making things uncomfortable for both of us.

"Also, you don't have to keep calling me 'Detective' every time, you know," she said, as the handshake ended. "My name's Adrienne. Or Connors, if you prefer. It just seems silly to be so formal at this point, after everything that's happened tonight."

I nodded. "I'll keep that in mind, Det—Adrienne." I reminded myself to stop mentally adding the "detective" in front of their names. If I stopped thinking of them as Detectives Lajoie and Connors, it would be easier to stop calling them such out loud.

Her partner apparently grew tired of examining the hole in the wall and came to join us, sitting on the other side of Connors.

"I was looking at the damage from whatever he attacked us with," he explained. "The wall was literally melted. What could do that?" he asked me.

I was still cooling my arm with the chilled silver blade. I shrugged.

"I've never seen it before, but it was some kind of pure heat given form."

"Does that tell us anything we didn't know before?" he asked.

I shook my head. "Not really. It reinforces my initial thought that our attacker was a mortal of some sort. It didn't feel like Faerie magic. It felt like it came from this world."

"That means human, right?" Connors interjected.

I pursed my lips. "No. Humans aren't the only magical creatures from this side of the veil."

I thought back to the attack. "He was much taller than pretty much all the magical races of Earth, at least those likely to be in Philadelphia, which does point to human as the most likely culprit. And again, if he weren't human, he had to have been wearing some kind of armor, or those bullets would have had more of an immediate effect."

My musing was cut short when a small Asian woman with spiked hair, wearing a long coat and carrying a staff in her left hand, stepped out of the Magic Gardens front entrance onto the sidewalk. Rachel Liu. Time to face the music.

Chapter 16

RACHEL HADN'T ARRIVED BY NIBELUNGEN TAXI, WHICH MEANT she had travelled here via the Otherworld, through the gateway in Aengus's tent. She stood at the Gardens entrance and looked both ways before spotting me sitting against the wall. She walked over, her face stern. I looked up nonchalantly as she stood in front of me, her staff planted firmly on the ground.

"Sorcerer Thomas Quinn."

"Rachel," I sighed, "I've known you for over a century, and we spoke on the phone just this morning. Is the formality really necessary?"

She didn't answer. Instead she regarded my companions.

"Who are these people under your protection?" From her lips, "people" sounded like a racial slur. Some in the magical world have a tendency to look down on the rest of the human race.

I put away my knife and rolled my coat sleeve back down, then climbed slowly to my feet before I answered. I'm not a tall man, but I stood head and shoulders above her. Lajoie and Connors got up as well—the big man towered over her. I smiled politely as she was forced to look up at me to maintain eye contact.

"Detectives Connors and Lajoie, may I present the Sorceress Rachel Liu of San Francisco, Rector of North America for the Arcane Court." If she wanted to be formal, so be it. "Rector, may I introduce Detective Henri Lajoie and Detective Adrienne Connors," I said, indicating each in turn with nods of my head, "of the Philadelphia Police Department. Detective Lajoie is the grandson of Antoine Richelieu, Sorcerer of the First Rank of the Arcanum. You may remember when I mentioned him on our phone call this morning. They are the investigators assigned to the case which I called you to discuss."

She sniffed. "You mentioned nothing of a second detective on that call. Has she been initiated as well?"

I nodded. "She has, with the full knowledge and consent of Aengus Óg. There has been no Treaty breach."

"Apart from the one for which I was summoned."

I rolled my eyes. "Yes, Rachel. There has been no Treaty breach apart from the violation of the Market Truce. But neither I nor the detectives were responsible for that. Feel free to interview the witnesses. The attacker's athame is still lying over there," I pointed to it, "where he dropped it after I shot him. No one has touched it, and I didn't even inspect it, to avoid accusations of tampering."

Her right eyebrow arched up. "You shot him?"

"Yes. With my gun."

Shaking her head, she sighed. "Quinn, you're the only ranked sorcerer in history who would even consider responding to an attack with bullets. You know that, right?"

It seemed that piece of information had been enough to cut through the formality of her office and get her back to speaking like a normal person.

"I'm the eccentric one." I groaned and rubbed my temples. "Would you mind getting this over with, so I can get some goddamn sleep tonight?"

She raised an eyebrow. "Doesn't look like you're getting much sleep at night anyway. You look terrible."

I scowled. "Just investigate and confirm I didn't violate any treaty terms."

She smirked. "Fine, Quinn. Wait here." She walked over to the athame and began examining it much as Connors had. The difference, I knew, was that she was examining not only with her eyes, but with her magical senses. She'd be able to tell what residual effects and potential traps remained on the blade before she touched it.

Lajoie muttered, "What's got a stick up her ass?"

I shrugged. "Being a Rector is a hard job in general, and she got called out fairly late to deal with this even considering the time difference. She has the right to be a bit prickly."

I sat back down. Connors followed suit, but Lajoie remained standing, his arms crossed over his chest. I could see Rachel talking to the witnesses. It didn't take long. She came back over to where I sat.

"So, Quinn," she said, in a much friendlier tone than earlier, "what have you found out about the Avartagh?"

I looked back up at her. "He's not involved. At least not directly."

"How did you figure that out?" she cocked her head.

"The detectives and I paid a visit to the Otherworld this evening, courtesy of Aengus Óg. We interviewed the Avartagh in his cell in the Dún Dubh, where he's been imprisoned for five hundred years." I spoke casually, as if describing my morning walk.

The blood drained from her face. Her voice dropped to a near whisper. "You took police officers to the Otherworld to speak with a prisoner in the Black Fortress, and didn't even run it past the King or the Lord Marshal first? Quinn, what have you done?"

My voice got hard and cold. "I've done as I saw fit given the circumstances, Rector. As is my prerogative. These murders occurred in my declared territory. I don't need the King's leave to deal with this affair in any manner I deem necessary, so long as I violate no treaty."

She took a deep breath and looked at me for a long moment, as if considering me carefully. "You are correct, of course. Legally speaking, you haven't broken any treaties. But there will be plenty who don't like it anyway. Maybe even enough that the King will be forced to act. You should come with me and explain your actions to the Court voluntarily, before they summon you. Or worse, before they summon an Emergency Conclave."

I looked at her calmly. "Rachel, the King is free to do what he must. If he or the Lord Marshal, or any of the rest of the Court, wish to speak to me about my actions, they know exactly where to find me." I paused. "And as you've acknowledged I did not break the Market Truce, I am free to go."

She chewed her lip as I stood back up. "You know the letter of the law, yes. But you've always been terrible at politics, Tom."

She met my eyes. "I'll have to report this, you know. All of it. Including this conversation."

"Report what you wish," I replied. "I'm leaving."

I walked away, leaving her standing there thinking. The detectives followed me.

"Where are we going?" Lajoie asked.

"You're free to head home. I need a drink first."

I found a bar a few blocks away. The detectives stayed for one round, which we all sipped quietly, pondering the events of the evening. I suppose both of them saw the mood I was in and decided any questions they had could wait. Connors eventually called an Uber, we agreed to meet the following afternoon, and then they left me there drinking and feeling irritable.

Growing tired of paying too much for mediocre whisky, I got the bartender to call me a cab and headed home. I'd originally planned on trying to figure out what the Avartagh had been hinting at that night, but that had been before the assassination attempt. Now I just wanted to go to bed. I'd do my thinking in the morning.

I got out of the cab in front of my store after paying the fare and tasted the magical fields around me. I didn't sense anything beyond the standard protective spells on the shop, so I unlocked the door and went in, locking it again right behind me. Roxana was sleeping on the counter, but she looked up when I entered, blinked lazily at me, and returned to sleep. Such is the devoted affection of a cat.

I picked her up, to her not very strenuous protest, and carried her upstairs. I locked the door at the top of the stairs and, setting Roxana down, double checked the wards on the door and both windows while she curled up on my bed. Someone had attacked me, so I was being extra careful.

I smeared some antibiotic ointment and aloe gel on my arm from the first-aid kit under the bathroom sink. It was still tender, but at least I'd kept the blisters down. I'd hate to have seen the effects of a direct hit from that heat spell.

First aid complete, I decided I was too tired even to make a snack, though I hadn't eaten in hours. Instead I undressed, slowly and creakily, then changed out the Glock's magazine and set it on the small table next to the bed, within easy reach should anyone come knocking. Finally, I collapsed into bed, causing a distressed squawk from Roxana as the bed bounced under her, and fell asleep instantly.

But I didn't rest as easy as I'd hoped. Tired as I was, the nightmares came like they always did.

The vast forest of Siberia, still with a light layer of frost from the night before that hadn't yet burned off in the summer morning. A dragon, her green and gold scales shimmering in the early morning summer sun as she flew overhead. Thirteen sorcerers of the Arcanum waiting for her. The battle challenge, the ensuing fight. Screams, blood, and fire. A massive explosion. More screams. Blackness.

I woke up with a gasp, drenched in sweat, momentarily confused about where I was. From my watch on the table next to the gun, I saw it was four in the morning. I took a few seconds to collect myself, slowing my heavy breathing. Roxana looked up at me and held my eyes for a long moment, until I swung my legs out of the bed. I knew from experience that I wouldn't be returning to sleep any time soon, so I put on some clothes that didn't smell too dirty, then my way downstairs, followed by Roxana. She liked to keep an eye on me when I was distressed.

I went into the back room and grabbed a bottle of Oban and a glass, and wearily sat in the desk chair. I poured myself a large glass, drained it in one long gulp, and poured another. One of the statues on the shelf opposite me caught my eye: a dragon masterfully carved in marble, seated with her wings folded, looking nearly as regal in stone facsimile as the genuine article had been in life. I stared at it for a long moment, my mind a confusing jumble of shame and anger and pain and regret, then forced myself to look away. No magic would let me change the past.

The images of my dream kept flashing through my mind as I drank, mixed with scenes from all the others. They didn't tell a coherent story, there was no chronological order. It was just a parade of memories, discontinuous and jumbled and all of them painful.

The whisky helped, eventually. Far more than it had the other night, at least. It didn't stop the mental slideshow, but it dulled the edges, making the colors less vibrant, the smells less pungent. After that first glass, I sipped at it and slowly felt the alcohol take effect. Several glasses in, the memories no longer felt like mine, as if they'd happened to someone else and I was just watching them unfold. Roxana lounged on the filing cabinet next to the coffee pot, keeping an eye on me to make sure I didn't do anything stupid. She was a good friend like that.

The bottle was half empty when I was pulled out of my reverie by forceful knocking on the front door. Looking around, I realized that I'd left the Glock upstairs. Under the circumstances, I didn't think answering the door without a gun in my hand was a wise plan, intoxicated or not. Normally I wouldn't advocate handling firearms while drunk, but in this case it was my only option for a weapon—I'd used the alcohol specifically to reduce my ability to focus, so I would be unable to cast any spells very effectively.

So I grabbed the J-frame revolver I kept in a desk drawer. It was loaded with regular jacketed hollow-points, so it wouldn't do me much good against a non-human threat. But if my suspicions were correct, it would work fine against the person knocking. I then stood up, realized that walking in a straight line was going to be a challenge, and carefully made my way out toward the front.

Holding the gun aimed at the center of the door, as steadily as I could manage in my current state, I asked loudly, "Who is it?"

"Open the damn door, Thomas," I heard in loud reply. A low-pitched woman's voice with a thick Highlands Scottish accent.

I sighed and laid the gun back on the counter, then unlocked the bolt and swung open the door. The dim light coming from the back room revealed a short feminine figure in a long coat, with her arms crossed in front of her and her legs spread wide. I couldn't see her facial features very well, but I could tell she had one eyebrow raised and she was unhappy.

"Well? Are you going to invite me in?"

I sighed again. "Come in."

She walked in and I closed the door behind her and relocked the bolt. She stood there inside the threshold, her eyes casting around the shop as she took it all in. She spotted the revolver on the counter and looked back at me, this time with both eyebrows raised.

"Honestly, Thomas. A gun? Were you going to shoot me?"

I shrugged and walked back into the office, retrieved my glass and bottle, then reemerged and made my way to the reading corner. The lights were still off in the main room, the dim glow from the back room the only illumination in the place aside from some streetlights filtering in through the windows. As I settled myself into one of the chairs, my visitor followed and sat down in the other chair. I could feel her judging eyes following my hand as I poured another glass of whisky and sipped.

Her eyes narrowed. "You're drunk."

"Erm," I grunted in reply, then took another sip. "Yes, I suppose I am. It's my store and my home. It's five in the morning. I'm allowed to be as drunk as I want." The slight slur in my speech emphasized my point.

She shook her head slowly. "What happened to you?" she asked quietly.

"Whatever could you mean?" I muttered and drained the glass.

She didn't answer, just watching me pour another glass and sip at it. For a long few minutes, she just watched me get more inebriated. Finally, I couldn't take any more of it. "Why are you here, Mother?"

She cocked her head to the side. "You told Rachel Liu that if the King or the Lord Marshal wanted to speak with you about your actions, we knew where to find you."

I paused and thought back. "I did say that, yes." I shrugged. "I didn't really mean at five in the morning, though."

Her lips tightened. My mother, the Sorceress Bridget MacDonald, Lord Marshal of the Arcanum, was a wonderful mom, honestly. I'd experienced nothing but love and care as a child. She'd even been willing to live on what she saw as the wrong side of the Irish Sea so I could grow up in my father's childhood home, the farm his family had maintained for generations. She'd hated it, and she and my father had returned to her native Scotland almost immediately after I had moved out. But she'd made the sacrifice for her family, because she loved us.

But she didn't approve at all of my life choices for the past century or so, and she had no problems making that clear at our every meeting. I hadn't seen her in several decades except for Grand Conclaves, because I got tired of her incessant badgering to get my life together.

"Well, it's mid-morning in Glasgow, and this is when I need to talk to you." She bit each word off carefully as if to prevent herself from saying something she'd regret later. "The matter at hand is rather pressing."

I took a big sip, savored the flavor, then swallowed. I swished the remaining ounces of whisky around my glass, staring at the swirling golden liquid.

"Yes," I eventually replied. "Of that I couldn't be more aware."

"And yet," she said, "here you are, drunk."

"That has nothing to do with the matter at hand. Nothing whatsoever."

"I know." She looked at me frankly. "That's what worries me about it now. The fact that even something this important, which clearly requires clear faculties, can't inspire you to stop your insistence on drinking yourself to death."

"I can think as well as anyone while drunk," I replied, my voice getting hard and sullen. "What I can't afford right now is to be drowning in memories."

"And if someone else attacks you? How exactly do you expect to be able to defend yourself or those police officers Rachel mentioned, when you can barely stand?"

I scowled. "I'm drunk in the safety of my wards. I'll not step out of them before I'm sober. Now what exactly is it you wanted to talk about, besides berating me for my life choices over the past hundred-odd years?"

"Rachel reported to me your actions and subsequent conversation at the Faerie Market. Why were you attacked?"

I raised my eyebrows. "I don't know. I suppose someone doesn't much care for me."

"Do you know who attacked you?"

This time I smiled and took another sip. "No, Mother, I do not."

She frowned. "But you have theories." That one wasn't a question, so I didn't answer. Her eyes narrowed in annoyance.

"Why did you take two police officers to the Otherworld? And why did Aengus Óg assist you in your efforts?"

"Because those two police officers are working on a murder case." I sipped again at my whisky. "They asked me for some expert assistance in translating glyphs written in blood at the scene of the crime. I had to investigate, whereupon I determined that the crime in question was a genuine magical working built around human sacrifice, forcing me to involve myself in the case whether I wanted to or not. And because one of those two police officers is the grandson of Antoine Richelieu. And because at least one of the responsible parties is of the Fae races."

"You thought a Faerie may have killed someone in Philadelphia and your choice was to go to the Fae for help rather than Rachel or myself?"

I shrugged. "I notified Rachel, and she requested I handle it while she was busy chasing demons in the Canadian Rockies. I was handling it as I saw fit, which is my right. Besides, you know full well that my relationship with the rest of my own species has been strained for quite some time. You also know my opinion of your fucking Court, and the Arcanum as a whole."

"It's not that simple," she shook her head, "regardless of what you think of us. Faeries murdering humans in our own world is a Treaty matter. Even ignoring your breach of the customs—which most of the Arcanum won't ignore or forget, by the way—by going straight to the Óg, and through him to Lugh, you've bypassed the Arcanum entirely and left us to get blindsided by a fait-accompli. There are some muttering that you've gone rogue yourself."

I started to protest, but she held up a hand and continued, "I know that's ridiculous, Thomas. You called the Rector and she requested you handle it informally; obviously you haven't gone rogue. I've already spoken with Rachel about the foolishness of not bringing this matter to my attention immediately. But be that as it may, perception is as important as reality in politics. You've never understood that. Right now, the voices calling for your censure are a tiny minority, but if you were to continue breaking customs without an official dispensation, they would grow. And you, my dear idiot son, are exceptionally powerful, and you made a lot of sorcerers very wary of you on the Fields of Fire, but even you can't take them all on."

I nodded and set down my glass. I'd known the possible repercussions, but I hadn't counted on word getting out so quickly. I'd hoped to have the problem solved by the time the rest of the Arcanum caught on to my decision to take the detectives to see Aengus. The attack had put me in a bit of a bind.

"What do you advise?"

"First, you tell me everything that you know about this case. Then we'll figure out a way forward together."

I covered my lips with my right hand as I thought. After a moment I nodded. "I'll summarize. The police discovered a murder scene that appeared to be related to the occult. Looking for an expert on the subject, they were referred to me. I told them what I could, then investigated the crime scene for myself..."

I filled her in on the rest of the events of the past days: the ambush spell at Evan's apartment, Detective Lajoie confronting me about the Arcanum, what I'd found at the second crime scene, the Faerie Market and the Otherworld, the attack earlier that night. I concentrated through the fuzziness I felt from the whisky and did my best to leave nothing out, especially about the Avartagh's words during our interrogation—she was right that this was a serious matter, and I could certainly use her help if she were willing to give it.

She listened through it all without comment or even changing her facial expression. When I finished and picked up my drink again, she closed her eyes in thought. After working through it in her mind, she opened them again and looked at me.

"Son of mine, this is a right mess you've gotten yourself involved in. I hope that bargain with Lugh doesn't come back to haunt you. But in the meantime, all we can do is move forward." She stood up and looked down at me for a moment, then smiled.

"As Lord Marshal of the Arcane Court, I, Bridget MacDonald, do formally charge you, Thomas Quinn, to investigate the matter of the so-called Tamesis rites in Philadelphia, in any manner you deem appropriate in accordance with standing Treaties, to determine who is the responsible party for this violation of the Treaties, and to eliminate the threat to the peaceful coexistence of the races of this world and the Otherworld."

I raised an eyebrow. "I was already doing that."

"Aye," she nodded, "and nothing I could have done would have stopped you from doing so. Once you get on something, you don't let go. Just look at how you've been beating yourself up for all these years about that dragon, about Charlotte, about Canada. But now I've officially tasked you with it. This way no one can reasonably claim you have gone against the will of the Arcanum. Do try to avoid breaking further customs, please?"

I smiled without a trace of humor. "Yes, Mother." I paused. "So that's it? When you said we'd figure a way forward, you meant that you'd figure out a way to get me out of trouble with the Arcanum, but not a way to help me with the slightly more pressing matter at hand?"

She nodded. "That's exactly what I meant. You can figure out the other part on your own. It'll do you good to be back in the world again, instead of hiding in a whisky bottle, blaming your woes on everyone and everything but yourself." She walked over to the door and unlocked the bolt, glancing once more at the gun on the counter and then back to me. "I do love you, you know," she said.

She walked out before I could reply and shut the door behind her. I waited a minute, thinking. Then I got up, stumbled my way over to the door and relocked the bolt.

I debated trying to return to bed, but I figured that, despite all the whisky I'd drunk, I was too awake at the moment. Instead, I returned to my chair and poured another glass, while Roxana sprang on to the other armchair.

"Blaming my woes on everyone and everything but myself?" I directed the indignant question at the cat, but she just looked irritated with the entire sequence of events and curled up in a ball.

That was the problem, though—I didn't blame my woes on anyone or anything but myself. I knew exactly how I'd gotten where I was.

My mother thought I drank because I blamed the things I'd done, the atrocities I'd committed, and the long list of horrors I'd experienced on the Arcanum. No, I drank because I knew full well that my choices, and every awful thing I'd ever done in their name, were my own.

Chapter 17

I WOKE UP IN THE SAME CHAIR, HOURS LATER, TO SUNLIGHT streaming through the cracks in the window blinds. I looked around, momentarily disoriented. Seeing Roxana in the other chair and an empty Oban bottle on the floor near me, I realized I must have passed out in the reading nook sometime after my mother's visit.

At least I didn't have a hangover. Benefits of high-level sorcery: aging five or six times slower than the normal population, immunity to most diseases, and healing extremely quickly from anything short of death. No matter how drunk I got, I generally recovered from the hangover before I woke up.

That did not, however, protect me from being somewhat sore and creaky after sleeping in an awkward sitting position. I stood up and stretched with a groan, and slowly walked over to the counter. I wasn't sure what time it was, but I was definitely late opening the shop. I dragged myself upstairs to brush my teeth and wipe the sleep gunk out of my eyes.

By the time I got back downstairs and opened the shop up for business, I was feeling mostly human again. Unsurprisingly no one had lined up outside waiting for me to open the doors, so I headed to the back office to begin puzzling over the Avartagh's words.

I went through my bookshelves—both my personal collection and the rare tomes in the cage—and pulled out anything that might shed any light on the Avartagh, his reign of terror in Ireland, his blood rites in Brittany, or whatever the hell he meant about the cycles of the two worlds. I ended up with a stack of books about a foot and a half high, most leather-bound, all old. Then I sat down, poured myself a breakfast glass of Lagavulin, and opened the first one.

I couldn't find much detail on the Avartagh or the blood rites beyond what we already knew. But after a great deal of skimming various books, interrupted a couple times by customers, I finally found something useful.

It was a three-hundred-year-old monograph on comparative metaphysics by an Italian sorcerer, Giuseppi Bertoni, which had been in my cage for a while, but I hadn't yet gotten around to reading. Now that I did so, I realized it was precisely what I needed.

Bertoni analyzed more than a dozen different metaphysical theories from various religious and mystical traditions across the world and discovered some interesting commonalities. He postulated that each of these systems was a distorted view of a part of the whole, much like the ancient parable of the blind men and the elephant. This alone wasn't particularly groundbreaking, as plenty of magical scholars would agree with him. But where he went further was in his effort to put the parts together to develop a tentative metaphysics of the universe, based on a nested series of cycles.

Bertoni theorized that our world and the Otherworld were locked together in a metaphysical orbit, which he called Il Grande Ciclo—"the Great Cycle." This resulted in the periodic patterns seen in things like magical fields and ley-lines. It also caused smaller nested cycles, such as the waxing and waning of the veil throughout the year, with the quarters and cross-quarters of the seasons being fixed points in the calendars of both worlds, and time in the Otherworld being more fluid in between.

There wasn't anything terribly specific in Bertoni's text, but that was enough to get me thinking. The old scholar had struggled to build his theory based on myths and legends from over a dozen different cultures across thousands of years of history, many passed down through oral tradition for generations. He freely admitted he had little more vision than the metaphorical blind men who'd first told the myths he used, and only had the advantage of being able to compare their various accounts and put them together like a puzzle, as well as some firsthand evidence about the relationship between our time and Otherworld time.

But the more I thought about it, the more his theory fit what I already knew about the interactions between our world and the Otherworld. This had to be the same Great Cycle to which the Avartagh had referenced, the cycles of the two worlds in which his patterns were hidden. And he'd mentioned that the rites he'd developed were aimed at some critical point in the cycle. But what that point was, how the Tamesis rites affected it, what would happen if it did, those were questions I couldn't yet answer.

While I had a fairly impressive library of obscure esoterica, I didn't have many books that delved into the nature of the veil or the relationship between the worlds on either side of it. Fortunately, I knew where to go to find more. And with Bertoni's theory as a starting point, I had some idea of what I was looking for, a direction to explore.

I knocked back the rest of my Lagavulin and headed upstairs to pack an overnight bag. When I got back downstairs, I called the number on Detective Lajoie's business card.

"Hello?"

"It's Quinn," I said gruffly.

"What's up?"

"I've found something on the Avartagh's comment about the cycles of the two worlds. It might be the key to figuring out the larger pattern of the ritual, and where the remaining sacrifices will occur."

"I'm sensing a 'but' coming," he prompted.

"But," I replied, "I don't have enough information in my own books. I need to go to a library."

"Okay, should Connors and I meet you there?" he asked.

"No, not the New York Public Library. It isn't anywhere you can meet me. I'm just letting you know that I'm going to be out of town for a few days."

"I see," he said, then paused. "Can you at least tell me where it is you'll be going?"

"Egypt," I answered.

"Alexandria?"

"No, the Great Library of Alexandria is no more, in any form. This one is in the Sinai. In the meantime, you and Connors should continue investigating what you can. See if there's some connection between the victims besides them both being sorcerers."

"Yeah, we're already going through all the physical evidence from both apartments looking for connections or anything else that might be useful. Hurry up and get back as soon as you can. And let's hope we don't have another murder before then."

On that gentle reminder of the ticking clock, I made sure Roxana had enough food and water for a few days, then locked up and caught a cab to Philadelphia International Airport.

One might assume that travel in the magical world is simple—just open a gate to the Otherworld, make your way to a point corresponding with where you want to go in the physical world, and open a gate back, nice and easy. But it isn't like that.

For starters, you have to know where the corresponding points are. The Fae can tell to where any point in one realm connects in the other as a matter of course, but the rest of us have to look it up or find out for ourselves. Then you have to consider the political realities of the parts of the Otherworld you need to cross—not everywhere in the Otherworld is quite so hospitable to sorcerers as Sidhe. And even if you know where you're going and a safe route to get there, odds are there isn't a direct gate between your entry and exit points, so you're still going to have to do a lot of walking.

Rachel had managed so easily the night before because she'd had an escort, courtesy of being summoned by Aengus for a treaty matter. I wouldn't have any such advantage in making my way to the Sinai, so the Otherworld route was a tricky option. It might save some time, but it wouldn't be worth the extra effort required.

Instead, I used a reloadable prepaid Visa card to purchase an extremely expensive first-class ticket to Egypt. Fifteen hours and a brief layover in Cairo later, I was in Sharm El-Sheikh, a coastal city on the Red Sea and the capital of Egypt's South Sinai Governorate. I even managed to sleep on the flight, after enough "free" drinks. It wasn't high-quality sleep, and I still had nightmares, but it was better than what I'd gotten the night prior.

Sometimes the easiest answer is to forego magical means entirely. Well, not quite entirely—I'd used a concealing spell on my Glock and knife to get them through airport security. I'd be damned if I were going anywhere without ready protection after that attack at the Market.

I found a taxi at the Sharm El-Sheikh airport to take me up into the mountains. A three-hour drive later, I was standing in front of the Monastery of Saint Catherine, an ancient Greek Orthodox complex built around what is purported to be the very bush which burned without being consumed when Moses first spoke to his God. It's nestled in a small valley at the foot of the Mount of the Decalogue, the summit of which is believed to be where Moses later received the Ten Commandments. The monastery is one of the holiest sites in Christian tradition, a sacred pilgrimage destination for almost two millennia. It also happens to be home to one of the world's most ancient libraries, known to scholars and historians for its importance in Christian scholarship—only the Vatican has a more extensive collection of ancient codices and manuscripts, and some of the oldest handwritten copies of the Bible ever found were discovered in the Saint Catherine archives. But my visit had nothing to do with the library known to the public.

The taxi driver dropped me off outside the thick fortress wall of the monastery proper, protesting in Arabic that the monks wouldn't grant me entrance this late in the evening, that I should find a guesthouse for the night in the nearby village and return in the morning. I told him not to worry about me and paid him, and he sped off back onto the road.

After I brushed the dust his tires kicked up off my coat, I walked up to the steel-coated door in the north side of the monastery's curtain wall and knocked loudly. The inner doors creaked as someone passed through them, then the outer door cracked open and a black-robed monk with a long beard split into two forks, wearing the black flat-topped hat of an Orthodox clergyman, peered out at me in the twilight gloom.

"*I'm sorry, my son, but the monastery is closed to visitors for the night. Please come back in the morning if you wish to enter,*" he said in Greek.

"*I am not a tourist,*" I replied in the same tongue. "*Fetch Father Andreas. I have urgent business that cannot wait until the morning.*"

"*Very well. Wait here, please.*" He stepped back and the door creaked shut.

The Arcanum had no central headquarters, and thus no equivalent to the Library of Congress or the Vatican Archives. Instead, there were a handful of archives hidden throughout the world, generally attached to a university or other scholarly collections. Oxford University in England, the University of Salamanca in

Spain, al-Qarawiyyin University in Morocco, and Yuelu Academy in China, along with several other venerable institutions, all had such secret athenaeums nested within their libraries, only accessible to those who knew the right spells to unlock their secret gates. But the first was right here, hidden within the walls of the Sacred Monastery of the God-Trodden Mount Sinai, more commonly known as Saint Catherine's.

I knew from my own studies many years before that this particular athenaeum was home to the most extensive collection of works on Hermes Trismegistus, the greatest sorcerer of the ancient world, books that could be found nowhere else. They even had a copy of what was reported to be Hermes's own grimoire, though to my knowledge no one had delved into its mysteries in the entire existence of the Arcanum, and likely many centuries before. Few sorcerers spoke Middle Egyptian or could read the hieratic script in which Hermes and his contemporaries had written.

Fortunately, thanks to my affinity for learning esoteric languages, I was likely the only human alive with the knowledge to read both his original writings and the commentaries of his followers. If any human sorcerer had ever unlocked the mysteries of the veil, had ever achieved any level of understanding of a purported Great Cycle, it had been Hermes Trismegistus. I needed to know what he had learned.

The door creaked back open and I saw the face of a wizened old man, his snowy beard forked like that of his fellow monk.

"Father Andreas?" I asked, still speaking Greek. I had never met the man before; I knew who he was through reputation alone.

"Yes," he answered. His eyes ran me up and down, then he met my gaze. *"A Sorcerer of the Arcanum, I see."*

The Athenaeum at Saint Catherine's dated from long before the establishment of the Arcanum. Local sorcerers had spirited the writings of Hermes and his followers from the Great Library of Alexandria before its final destruction and they had ended up in the monks' hands over the ensuing centuries. Sorcerers had come to the Sinai to study Hermetic magic for generations before the Arcanum was formed a thousand years ago; they had formed a partnership with the monks in residence. By ancient tradition, one of the monks was always appointed as Caretaker of the Sinai Athenaeum, and he was trained in the basic magical skills necessary for the task, including recognizing the signs of a sorcerer's robe. In exchange for this continuing service, the sorcerers had crafted powerful, complex spells of protection over the monastery, which had helped it survive the many centuries of conquests, despots, and wars which had destroyed most other Christian houses of worship in the region.

The previous caretaker chose his own successor, as it had to be someone with enough latent magical talent to meet the requirements of the position—on many occasions, there was no one suitable within the brothers of the monastery, and someone had to be sent from other monasteries in Greece. Father Andreas had been the Caretaker of the Sinai Athenaeum for over fifty years. From the looks of it, if he weren't already training a successor, he should probably start soon.

I nodded. *"I need to access the Athenaeum. Time is of the essence."*

"Very well, Sorcerer. You may follow me."

He opened the door wide enough for me to pass through, then securely closed it behind me. He led the way in silence through the two inner doors in the curtain wall, the third at a right angle to the others. We emerged into a small courtyard, facing the side of the Catholicon of the Transfiguration, the main church within the walls. Behind its bell tower peeked the minaret of a medieval mosque. All Abrahamic faiths were welcome here.

I didn't have much opportunity to look around, however, as Father Andreas led me to the left around the Catholicon toward the southeast courtyard. I knew from my last visit here, almost two hundred years ago, that the library was located against the curtain wall on the far side from the entrance, just past the monks' dormitory.

He opened the door and gestured for me to enter, then followed me in and hit a light switch. Electrical lighting was a pleasant upgrade from my last visit, but otherwise little had changed. It was a long room with bookshelves along both walls, metal staircases leading up to a gallery lined with yet more books. But we ignored all that as Father Andreas led me down the central aisle, then stopped at a pillar in the center of the room. Wordlessly, he reached out and touched the pillar and closed his eyes.

A second later, a section of the floor beside the pillar faded away to reveal a hidden staircase down into the ground below us, disappearing into darkness. The stairs and the walls around them were rough-hewn stone, the same as the walls of the monastery itself.

"Come, Sorcerer," Father Andreas said quietly, leading the way into the blackness below. As his feet reached the sharp line where the light from above seemed simply to cut off and give way to dark, he touched a small bronze fixture on the wall next to him, and the space below filled with a glow which seemed to come from the stone itself.

Below us I could now see a long room, its outline the mirror of the one above it. Here, however, the bookshelves were cut into the rocky walls themselves, and the books were all chained to their shelves. I knew the chains were reinforced with magic, to ensure no one could steal the tomes they secured. The circumference of the room was lined with a waist-high reading table, with a handful of chairs along its length, to allow scholars to read the books by the shelves to which they were locked.

"Welcome to the Athenaeum of Sinai, Sorcerer. Have you been here before?" Father Andreas asked.

"Many years ago. Long before your time." I nodded as I walked over to the shelves and began looking through books.

"Is there anything I can help you to find?" the Caretaker asked.

"I seek information about the veil, and the cycles between the two worlds. Where might I find the works of Hermes Trismegistus?"

He nodded and headed to the other end of the room. *"I believe these shelves here will contain most of what you seek. Do you need anything else?"*

"You don't happen to have any whisky on hand, do you?" One could hope.

He shook his head. *"I'm afraid not, Sorcerer. We have wine, if that will suffice."*

I shrugged. *"It will do, I suppose."*

It had been a while since I'd had wine, but anything was better than nothing.

"I will fetch you some wine from the rectory, and then leave you to your work. When you are finished, or if you need anything else before you are finished—food, drink, sleep—simply ring the bell beside the stairs."

With that, he climbed the stairs and sealed the floor again behind him, closing me in to the secret library. I started pulling books down off the shelf he'd indicated and got to work.

Chapter 18

A DAY AND A HALF LATER, I WAS ON A FLIGHT BACK TO PHILADELPHIA, in a first-class seat, carefully pondering what I'd learned over a glass of Glenlivet.

Hermes Trismegistus may well have been the greatest sorcerer to have ever walked the face of the Earth. His grimoire, and the personal journals of several of his students, had been treasure troves of information about the nature of the veil, the structure of the magical universe, even the ley-line network.

The grimoire had laid out in detail the relationship between Earth and the Otherworld, far beyond Bertoni's simplistic hypothesis despite having lived thousands of years before Bertoni had been born. He'd compared the waxing and waning of the veil throughout the year to the tides, a phenomenon driven by the cycles in the connection between the Earth and its moon, but not the connection itself. The wheel of the year, pinning the quarters and cross-quarters between time in the two worlds, was more like the monthly lunar cycle. The Great Cycle, on the other hand, was akin to the actual orbits of the Earth and the moon and all the other planets and their moons whirling through the heavens: just as the solar system spun in a great interconnected dance driven by the force of gravity, so our world and the Otherworld, and likely still others besides, spun in an immensely vast and complex cycle. Furthermore, according to the teachings of Hermes Trismegistus at least, magic itself was a product of this Great Cycle of the Worlds.

As I flew over the Atlantic in comfort, whisky in hand, I contemplated all that I knew so far, trying to understand how it all fit together.

First, I needed to know what the Tamesis rite was supposed to do to the Great Cycle. It was possible the Avartagh was trying to destroy the Cycle completely, but I doubted it. He wanted to restore the glory of his people, not annihilate them. He'd spent centuries carefully experimenting to find the proper balance in his rites, which suggested to me that destruction wasn't the end goal. Besides, the Great Cycle was vast and complex—it would be virtually impossible to destroy, especially from the inside. But what if the critical point he'd identified would enable him, if pushed just right, to throw the Cycle off balance enough that it would settle into a new equilibrium?

Trismegistus believed the Cycle to be the source of magic—such a shift could change the nature of magic as we knew it. The right force, at the right point, might be enough to do so. That would explain why everything needed to be so carefully balanced: too much force, or applied to the wrong spot in the cycle, could easily lead to the wrong equilibrium, with unwanted effects.

As for determining what he hoped to achieve with such a change in the Cycle, I had only his own words. To break the Arcanum's power and end humanity's dominance over the Fae, to restore their glory. To rid them of "humanity's scourge entire." How would shifting the Great Cycle do so?

I only saw one way. If the Cycle were the source of magic as Trismegistus hypothesized, moving it to a new equilibrium could potentially neutralize the source of the Arcanum's power: the ley-line network which gave humans such potent magic on this side of the veil. The Fae didn't power their own magic with the ley-lines; they drew directly from the veil itself—that was a large part of what made their magic unique. If the Avartagh's supposed critical point would shift the Great Cycle such that it maintained the veil but disrupted the ley-line network, it would greatly weaken the Arcanum—along with the other magical races of this side of the veil—while leaving the Fae's source of power untouched.

The Tamesis, if successful as the Avartagh intended, could be the end of a thousand years of peaceful coexistence between the magical races. While what I'd said to Connors and Lajoie about their inability to win a full-scale war with humanity at large would still be true, the Fae would become almost unchecked in the magical world, free to interfere with human affairs to their hearts' content once the Arcanum no longer had the strength to challenge them.

But, as Nemain had mentioned, any disruption to the veil could be catastrophic. If the Avartagh's calculations were off, or if something went wrong in the execution, it might not just disrupt the ley-line network. It could disrupt the veil itself—the bridge between the two realms and the source of the Fae's power. It could break the connection between the Earth and the Otherworld, leaving those Faeries trapped on this side defenseless and unable to hide, possibly even killing them outright given how much magic was woven into their very being. I couldn't even speculate what the consequences of such an error would be for the Otherworld and its inhabitants, but Nemain had suggested it might be the doom of all Fae. That was a hell of a gamble, even for an insane monster. The Avartagh must have been exceptionally confident that his rites would work as intended.

And the Avartagh was locked in the Dún Dubh, while someone else was trying to enact the Tamesis now. Whoever it was, what did they want? I knew there was a Faerie involved, so perhaps it was simply another Unseelie seeking to right perceived wrongs from ages past. Though that left open the question of how this Faerie had learned the details of the rites so long after the Avartagh was imprisoned.

It was possible, I supposed, that whoever it was had no idea what it was designed to do. When he'd been stopped the first time, Avartagh may have managed to set in motion a backup plan, designed to ensure someone else would attempt the rites the next time the cycles aligned correctly. He could have started a cult, giving them the details of how to enact the rites but lying about or concealing its purpose, which had carried the tradition through the centuries and was only now acting at the appointed time. That was certainly plausible—stranger things happened in the magical world.

But anyone with the knowledge and power to enact such rites

would also be able to put together the clues. Knowing the details of the rites, the meanings of the glyphs, and even vague hints about the cycles of the worlds, any halfway competent sorcerer could put it together and figure out they were trying to break something. And whoever had put together that ambush spell was more than halfway competent. They were a genius, an artist of the highest order. Equipped with the full knowledge of the rite, they'd absolutely be able to figure out what it was intended for; there was no way to keep something like that a secret in the structure of a working that complicated. No, whoever was murdering sorcerers was doing so with the full knowledge that their ultimate goal was to change the nature of magic itself, and possibly the connection between the Earth and the Otherworld.

Then, of course, there was still the mysterious individual who had helped the Avartagh, the one who set him on the path to the Tamesis in the first place by helping him identify his supposed critical point. Who might that be? And were they once again pulling the strings? It had to be someone who had extensive knowledge of the Cycle, and shared the Avartagh's ambitions to restore the Fae to power in the magical world, but for some reason didn't want to get his or her hands dirty conducting the actual blood rites.

It was almost certainly not a human. Not only were there only a handful of humans who had ever bothered to delve into the nature of the Great Cycle—hell, I hadn't even heard of such a thing until days ago—but none of them would have any logical motive for helping a Faerie destroy the source of human sorcery's most potent powers. For that matter, I couldn't see the Avartagh accepting any help of that sort from a human, at least not knowingly. He used humans as his lackeys, but not as advisors.

Nuada was an unlikely candidate, having died in battle long before the Avartagh's previous efforts. Lugh was a possibility, I supposed. But if so, why would he have imprisoned the Avartagh in the Dún Dubh for centuries? No, Lugh made little sense even considering unknowable Fae logic. Same with Odin, who'd drunk from Nuada's well and almost certainly possessed the necessary understanding. And the sons of Lir were tasked with a sacred geas to protect the veil; they would not be involved in something that could easily pose a significant threat of its destruction if anything went wrong.

I even briefly considered Aengus—his mysterious falling out with his father and the Tuatha Dé centuries before were about the same time, and it might even provide him a motive. But I quickly dismissed the thought. He was unlikely to have had the knowledge needed to put the Avartagh on the right path—Aengus Óg was known as a great warrior and poet, and even a healer, but not a magician of any particular renown among the Fae. He was powerful, but that didn't translate to the understanding of the Great Cycle apparently necessary to develop the Tamesis rites. Furthermore, he wasn't the type of person to handle a grudge by endangering innocents. He was an alien being, sure, but I knew him well enough to know that. He'd spent centuries protecting the Fae on this side of the veil; he would not knowingly put them in danger.

There was one person who might be able to help me identify a suspect. My old mentor Johannes the Immortal—he who had taught me so much about the nature of magic so many years before. But that would mean facing him and confronting my shame.

That was the crux of the matter. I had already saved the world from almost certain destruction once before, and it had cost me everything. The only woman I'd ever loved had died in the Shadow War. In her name, I did what I did and perverted the Immortal's sacred teachings, corrupting my very soul in the process. I had lived with that shame every day since. Hero of the Fields of Fire, they called me. But I was no one's hero. I wasn't sure I could bring myself to do that again, if that's what it took. More importantly, I wasn't sure if I believed in the Arcanum, and its mission, enough to pay that price even if I could.

The world was once again on the line. But this time I wasn't sure I still believed it was worth saving. Not very heroic, that.

I brooded, and sipped my whisky, and scrutinized, and sipped my whisky, and tried to find the connections, and sipped my whisky. Finally, I made a decision. I knew there was no other real choice. But the fact it was the only option didn't make me happy about it.

The stewardess refilled me more than once before I finally fell asleep.

When the flight landed in the morning, instead of going home I took the train to 30th Street Station, transferred to a northeast regional Amtrak line, and ninety minutes later I found myself at

Penn Station in Manhattan. I caught a cab to Brooklyn, giving the driver the address from memory.

He dropped me off outside a brownstone in Cobble Hill. My backpack slung on one shoulder, I slowly walked up the stoop to a door I'd thought I'd never see again. I raised my hand to knock but hesitated with it hovering a few inches from a carving of two crossed spears in the wood.

My hand was trembling. I took several deep breaths to calm myself. This shouldn't be so hard. Finally, I knocked twice.

The door swung open immediately.

"Thomas," the Immortal greeted me. "I saw you out here. I was wondering if you'd actually be able to go through with it."

"Johannes," I replied, meeting his eyes. I took another deep breath. "I need your help."

For a long moment, we stood there in silence. He looked me up and down.

"The years have not been kind to you, Thomas," he remarked. "You look terrible."

"You look exactly the same," I answered.

He did. Johannes the Immortal was a handsome man, with darkly bearded Mediterranean features, olive skin, and a straight patrician nose. I knew it wasn't the face he'd been born with, but it was the one he'd worn for over two millennia, at least since he'd walked the streets of ancient Rome. I didn't know what name he'd used back then; he'd started calling himself "Johannes" during the middle ages.

The Immortal was a human sorcerer, but one who'd somehow conquered death ages ago. I'd first encountered him about a century before, a few years after Tunguska. He'd been impressed with me, had found me and taken me in and become my mentor. He taught me many secrets and mysteries over several decades, things far beyond the teachings even of the Arcanum's greatest masters.

I hadn't seen Johannes since I'd left this house in 1946, and I didn't know how he'd receive me. But no one else alive possessed his understanding of the nature of magic, nor his knowledge of those who wielded it. If anyone could help me figure out who was behind the Tamesis, who had set the Avartagh in motion so many centuries before, it was the Immortal.

I had nowhere else to turn. I could only hope he'd still be willing to help me even after what I'd done so many years before.

He stood there for another long minute. Finally, he stepped back and waved me in. "Come in, Thomas. You can tell me what brings you to my door after all this time."

I nodded in thanks and stepped inside. He led the way down the short hallway to the parlor and took a seat in an armchair, gesturing for me to sit in the other. The room hadn't changed since I was here last: dark wood paneling, original paintings from Italian Renaissance masters, a shelf of ancient books, very much a classic "old money" aesthetic. Johannes was a man of exorbitant wealth and refined taste, and I supposed after thousands of years of life, those tastes were unlikely to change much within a single century.

"I assume," he began without small talk, "that this visit has something to do with the mysterious killings of sorcerers in Philadelphia."

"You knew I was in Philadelphia?" I asked, rather than answering immediately.

He looked at me as if I were a particularly slow child. "Please, Thomas. Don't insult me. Of course, I know where you've been. You honestly think I wouldn't keep an eye on you? I also know," he continued in a reproving tone, "what you've been doing with yourself for all these years. And frankly, I must say that I've been quite disappointed with you for many years. You had so much potential. I had such hopes for you. But you've chosen to throw your life away with drink and self-pity. It's a great shame."

He paused for a second which seemed an eternity. He sighed. "But it's your life to throw away if you so choose. Now, tell me what is so important as to overcome whatever compunction has kept you from my door these past decades."

It was remarkable. I was almost two and a half centuries old. I'd shrugged off my own mother's disapproval for over seventy years. But when faced with the same reproach from Johannes, I felt like a small child in front of a stern parent.

The difference, of course, was that I could tell myself my mother didn't understand, that she didn't really know what had driven me down the path I'd taken. The Immortal did. He knew me and my sins, in a way no one else did or could. In front of him, I could feel nothing but shame and guilt.

But I'd come here for a reason. Guilt or no guilt, I had a job to do.

"Someone is attempting a rite called the Tamesis. I need your help figuring out who might be behind it."

"Oh?" he replied in a tone of mild curiosity, his eyebrows slightly raised. "I am familiar with the rite. The Avartagh, wasn't it? Well, that would explain the murders, yes. The police haven't released any details of the actual crime scenes, so while I knew the Tamesis rites were a possibility, I couldn't be sure."

"How did you know they were a possibility?" Just knowing of two ritual murders wouldn't have been enough to tell him that, even with his vast knowledge and experience.

"The ley-lines, my dear boy." He rolled his eyes in exasperation. "The news reports mentioned the general locations of the murders. With the shifting ley-lines, that particular ritual fit the evidence the best. I mean, honestly, Thomas, do I have to spell everything out for you? I taught you better than that. Think."

"The . . ." I began, but then I shut up and followed his advice.

The ley-lines. I'd been investigating their strange movements just before getting sidetracked by Evan's murder. It suddenly all clicked. Of course. How had I missed that? The key to the whole puzzle had been right in front of me the whole time.

"Both murders took place directly over shifting nodes," I finally answered. "And both nodes stopped moving after the rituals." I wanted to kick myself for missing it.

"Precisely," he answered. "I knew you'd get there eventually. During the Avartagh's original rites centuries ago, the ley-lines exhibited similar shifts to those currently occurring in the greater Philadelphia area. And his sacrifices all occurred at one of the new node locations."

I'd even noticed the nodes myself when I'd visited each location, but I hadn't put the pieces together until prompted by the Immortal. Mentally comparing the addresses to my ley-line survey maps, I knew that the node under Evan's apartment had been shifting for days before the murder, but had stopped by the time I rechecked the network the morning I'd met the detectives.

Similarly, the node I'd felt under my feet at the second crime scene was still moving at the time I'd last mapped the network days prior. Its presence hadn't struck me as unusual at the time, so I'd barely even registered it consciously. That explained the murdered family in the other room: they had nothing to do with the ritual, the murderers needed their house for the sacrifice.

They'd been killed and discarded like trash, merely for being in the way.

"And the nodes stay in place after. Are the sacrifices both to fix the node locations in place as well as to the harvest the victim's power? Or are the locations already where the nodes will become fixed points?"

"I would imagine the former," Johannes said. "It would seem an odd coincidence if the sacrifices all occurred precisely when the nodes stopped moving—if the location is important and the nodes were stopping on their own, the practitioner could simply conduct his or her ritual at any time after the nodes were in place. It would make more sense to wait until all relevant locations were ready, and then conduct all the rituals as quickly as possible, rather than spacing them days apart as each node settled into place, no?"

I was nodding. "Yes, that makes sense. That explains why he needed human sorcerers to help him, since the Fae can't control the ley-lines. It also explains why everything needed to be precise, so that the relevant patterns reflect the cycles of the two worlds. Meaning not only precise execution of the ritual, but also precise timing. Which suggests the sacrifices aren't only building power toward a final event, but also aligning the regional ley-line network to the necessary pattern."

"Presumably," Johannes added, "to either focus and amplify the power of the final rite, or perhaps to propagate its energy along the network properly. Maybe even both."

"If my theory is correct," I mused, "and the Tamesis is designed to shift the Great Cycle between the two worlds, and the ley-line network is connected to that Cycle, then aligning the network would be necessary to direct its energy to the critical point. So..."

I looked at Johannes, who was smiling proudly. "Go on," he encouraged. "Finish the thought, boy."

"So to stop the Tamesis," I met his eyes for a second, "we only need to stop the next sacrifice, to disrupt the alignment of the ley-lines."

"There you go," he replied. "At least your insistence on living in a bottle of whisky hasn't dulled your wits beyond all hope."

I ignored the comment. "But even if I manage to stop it, I still need to figure out who's behind it. Or it will just happen again the next time the cycle comes around."

The Immortal didn't answer for a second, looking thoughtful. "The Avartagh was behind it last time. You spoke to him, no? Did he tell you anything that might suggest to whom he'd passed the details of the rites?"

I shook my head. "I don't think he passed them on. He said someone pointed him in the right direction, that he had help in identifying the weak point in the cycle. I suspect he wasn't the brains behind it at all, really. I think that whoever helped him managed to escape the Arcanum's notice, and either passed the rites on or, more likely, is still alive. If the latter, he or she could have just bided time until the cycle was right again, then set out to try the rites with a new Faerie assistant."

I looked over at the Immortal, who appeared contemplative, his fingers steepled together and pressed against his pursed lips. After a moment, he looked back over at me.

"Means, motive, and opportunity. You are looking for someone with intimate understanding of both the Great Cycle and the ley-line network, and the magical power and skill to control such a working, who also harbors a motive to break that Cycle and unleash the ensuing chaos. Who have you already eliminated as a suspect?"

I shrugged and told him my reasoning about Lugh, Odin, Aengus, and the sons of Lir, as well as human sorcerers. "That's the problem. I've eliminated everyone I know who has the knowledge and power for lack of motive, and those with motive for lack of knowledge and power. So I'm left guessing wildly."

"Could be another of the Aes Sidhe," Johannes mused, "but if so, why use the Avartagh at all? Perhaps as a patsy, I suppose. But I would look toward other tribes of the Fae entirely."

"The djinn are too disorganized. The Neter have been peaceful for millennia. But the Olympians..."

He nodded, his lips pursed in thought. "They have been quite bitter at humanity since being forced back to the Otherworld, yes."

I looked at him. "You know them better than anyone."

"Yes," he nodded. "I dealt with the Olympians for centuries when I lived in Rome."

"Do you think one of them could really be behind this?"

He shrugged. "I haven't spoken with Jupiter or his kin in over a thousand years, since they withdrew from this world. But they have the necessary knowledge; if anyone knows anything about the Great Cycle between our worlds, it's Janus. He's the one who taught me what I know of it. They have the motive, blaming the Arcanum for their decline. And they certainly have the means and the influence to recruit followers, even among the Fae. At the time of the original rites, they had been driven to Olympus in final defeat only a few centuries before, which may explain why they needed the Avartagh—his access to this realm and ability to operate here unnoticed was far greater than their own back then. But their renewed worship has been on the rise among humans over recent decades, which could have given them the chance to begin anew. If I had to bet—and you know I'm not a betting man, Thomas—but if I had to, I would take a long, hard look at the Olympians. Janus would be at the top of my list."

"Then," I said, standing up, "I need to start researching Janus and his kin."

He remained seated and raised an eyebrow. "Is that it? You come to my door for the first time in three-quarters of a century, pick my brain about your most recent problem, and leave without any attempt to discuss what has kept you away all this time?"

I shook my head. "Johannes, I can't. Do you know what it took for me just to knock on your door in the first place? I know the mistakes I made, the atrocity I committed with the beauty you taught me. I want to apologize and sit down with you and see if there's any way I can repair the damage I've done to our friendship. I do. But right now, I can't. I just can't. Maybe when this is all over, we can have a drink and talk about it. Just not today."

The Immortal smiled. "Thomas, have I ever told you the story of how I became what I am?"

I looked at him quizzically. "No, you haven't. That's one mystery you kept to yourself."

He shrugged. "It's not really a mystery, just forgotten history. You see, I was there when magic first came into this world. I remember a time, long ago, before the Fae. When our worlds collided, when Earth first united with the Otherworld, there was a great cataclysm."

He steepled his fingers and looked away, staring off as if into a great distance. "Magical energy flowed like a mighty flood throughout the world, and we almost drowned in it. Only a small number of humans, a few thousand or so, survived the onslaught.

Human scientists now recognize that there was a population bottleneck among Homo Sapiens tens of thousands of years ago. But it was no supervolcanic eruption that killed most of us. It was the collision of two universes through the veil. We were the survivors, those strong enough to conquer the magical flood and tame it to our will. We became the first sorcerers.

"From us, all of humanity. We bred and spread, but our progeny were not like us. While some of them could use the magic themselves, and those few were longer lived, all were still mortal. That first massive wave of magic had changed us, stopped our aging. Made those of us who survived immortal. We could still be killed, yes, but it became near impossible for us to die of natural means, and still incredibly difficult to be killed by our fellow humans. Our lives had become tied to the flow of magic throughout the world. Only the strongest effort could break that bond and let us pass on."

He grew quiet for a moment, and when he resumed speaking his voice had changed, become more somber, melancholic.

"Over the tens of thousands of years, many made that effort. Our original numbers steadily dwindled—some through fighting with one another, but mostly through suicide as the unending weight of immortality drove them to seek an end, any end. And now, countless eons later, I remain."

He looked back at me where I stood, silently transfixed by his story. His eyes met mine and I saw the weight of those ages, the toll they'd taken on him.

"Do you know why I'm telling you this now?"

I shook my head.

"Because, Thomas, I want you to know that I understand. That I truly do—I understand what you did, I understand why you did it. Did you think I would not? That I could not appreciate the weight of your decision, and forgive you? I have been disappointed in you for years, my boy, but not because of what happened in Canada. No matter what you think you should be ashamed of, I have never been ashamed of you. How could I be? Of all people, how could I not understand?"

"I..." I opened my mouth to answer, but I didn't know what to say. I felt like crying, and just stood there fighting to keep control of the many emotions Johannes had just released in me.

He held up a hand. "Go, Thomas. Go save the world. I know

that's what you do. We can talk when you're ready. But the last time you walked out that door with a promise to return, it took you almost seventy-five years to do so. Don't let it happen again. I expect to see you very soon. We have much to discuss."

I looked at him for a long minute. I still felt ashamed, but no longer of what I'd done at the Fields of Fire. Now it was for not coming here sooner.

But there was nothing I could do about it at that moment. I nodded and turned to go.

Chapter 19

THE FOLLOWING MORNING, AFTER GETTING HOME LATE FROM New York, I called Lajoie.

"Did you learn anything?" he asked.

"Yes. Lots. We need to meet."

"Okay, gimme a sec," he replied. I heard muffled speaking as he covered the mic and conversed with someone, presumably Connors. "Alright, we'll be at the shop in an hour or so."

He hung up before I could respond. In a hurry. Perhaps they'd found something, too. Or they hadn't and were just eager to get whatever I had in the hopes it would lead to something they could do. Well, I'd have to disappoint them. I had important background information, but there was a lot more work to do before I could identify where the next attack would take place—even knowing the relationship of the shifting ley-lines to the killings, there were hundreds of possible attack sites over the next day or two. I didn't know which specific node was next, or where it needed to be during the sacrifice. And thanks to the Immortal I had suspects for whoever was pulling the strings, but nothing concrete, and certainly not enough to act on.

An hour later, a glass of Scotch by my right hand, I looked up at the sound of the bell over the door to see Detectives Lajoie and Connors enter. It was raining outside, and they were both dripping. I guess they hadn't been able to park nearby.

Without breaking stride in his approach toward the counter, Lajoie called, "Okay, what have you got?"

I closed the book on the Olympians I'd been skimming and took a sip.

"Do you want any?" They both shook their heads impatiently. On duty, or just not fans of Scotch, I neither knew nor cared. I was being polite—I preferred to drink my alcohol myself.

"You told Lajoie you learned something," Connors said. "What is it?" Her features were even sharper than usual with her hair soaking wet, a few stray strands plastered to her forehead and left cheek.

I took another sip, letting the spirit run over my tongue for a moment before swallowing, savoring the burning, oaky flavor. Then I told them what I'd found in the Athenaeum, the theory I'd developed about the end goal of the Tamesis, and what it would mean for the future of the magical world. They listened quietly, trying to process what I was saying through their limited knowledge of magic.

As I concluded, Lajoie pursed his lips. "Okay, suppose you're correct. What's the worst-case scenario?"

I took another long, slow sip.

"If they get everything right and it works according to plan, the worst-case scenario is the Fae decide they're tired of hiding in the Otherworld and move to re-establish themselves as a major power on Earth, leading to that open war that I mentioned when we first went to visit Lugh. Which would be bad for everyone. With the Arcanum crippled and unable to stand against the Fae armies, humanity would probably still win in the long run due to sheer weight of numbers and weapons, but it would be a lot uglier, with a lot more casualties on all sides."

"And if everything doesn't go according to plan?" Lajoie asked, one eyebrow raised.

I pursed my lips. "If their calculations are off, or if they somehow make a significant mistake, such as too much or too little energy, imperfect timing, or imperfect alignment of the ley-lines, then the consequences are unknowable. Possibly nothing happens. Or possibly they shift the Great Cycle to the wrong new equilibrium and destroy the veil in the process, severing Earth from the Otherworld and maybe even ending the processes that generate magic in the universe. Which would almost certainly have dire effects for the Fae and the magical races of Earth, and possibly even for humanity at large."

"What do you mean dire, Quinn?" Connors asked.

"I mean, Adrienne," I replied, looking her dead in the eye, "that everyone could die. All of them. Every human and nonhuman animal on Earth, and every Faerie in the Otherworld. I've been pondering this for a day and a half now, and as best I can figure, that's why the Tuatha Dé forbid experimenting with the veil in the first place. Magic is intimately tied to life and has been ever since the Earth became linked to the Otherworld tens of thousands of years ago. That event, the introduction of magic to our world, caused a mass extinction. It vanishing could well mean another, even the end of life itself."

They took this as calmly as could be expected. I saw the tightening in their eyes and the corners of their lips, and Connors's breathing quickened ever so slightly.

"So . . ." she began, and then trailed off as she tried to process it.

"So," I picked up, quietly, "we're no longer looking to stop a couple of serial killers. We're now, quite possibly, trying to save the world. The three of us."

A moment of silence. Then Connors spoke.

"Guess I'll have that drink now, if you wouldn't mind."

I quirked the corners of my lips and poured each of them a finger of the good stuff.

Lajoie raised his glass. "To saving the world." We raised ours in response and the three of us drank silently for a moment. Then he set his glass down and asked, "So how the hell are we supposed to do it?"

"I'm not sure," I shook my head.

"Well, that's reassuring," Connors chuckled drily.

"We keep doing what we're doing. I've got a lead on the ritual itself, and with any luck might be able to pinpoint the next location before the murder actually takes place. That should allow us to disrupt the rites and stop the Tamesis, which would buy some time. But it won't end the threat unless we can stop whoever is behind it, too. I've got potential suspects on that front."

"You do?" Lajoie raised his eyebrows. "Care to share?"

I shrugged. "A friend of mine suggested that some of the Olympians may have the means, motive, and opportunity to be the power behind the scenes."

"The Olympians? As in Greek gods?" he asked.

"Greco-Roman, but close enough," I nodded. "They're a tribe of the High Fae, like the Aesir and the Aes Sidhe, and one of my old mentors who is very familiar with them pointed out that they've got the requisite knowledge and power, they've resented humanity for a long time now, and they could have recruited followers in both worlds to do their dirty work for them."

"Can we talk to them?" Connors sounded hopeful.

"Not really," I answered. "They have no formal relations with the Arcanum and they keep to themselves."

She sighed. "So what can we do about it?"

"Not much, to be honest. Even if Janus is pulling the strings, I doubt he's conducting the rituals personally, especially since we know whoever was behind it last time used the Avartagh for the actual deeds. But I can try to put out feelers in the local Hellenic Revivalist neopagan community and see if anything comes up, I suppose." I took a long sip. "Did you two find anything while I was gone?"

"We did, as a matter of fact," Connors replied. "For starters, the M.E. identified our second victim by her DNA, which was in CODIS—apparently she spent some time in prison for burglary in her early 20s. Jane Crandall. Did you know her?"

"Vaguely, in passing." I thought about it for a moment. "She was an unranked sorcerer, like Evan—trained by the Arcanum, but not powerful enough to be considered for membership. There are a few dozen of them in the area. She'd only been in Philly for a few years. An occasional customer of mine, but nothing more than that."

"Okay," she continued. "Well, we got the crime scene guys to go through her apartment and compared all the paperwork they found with what we found in Evan Townes's place. There were a bunch of things in common, but most were to be expected, like shopping in overlapping occult stores, including yours. But they'd also both visited the same bar in Germantown and had receipts. They drank different things—seems Evan was a beer guy and Jane preferred wine. But for some reason they'd both purchased the same specialty martini. The coincidence warranted checking the place out. We figured it might help us figure out how the killers are targeting their sacrificial lambs."

"Anything unusual about the bar?" I asked.

Lajoie shook his head. "No. But I showed the bartender pictures of both victims, and he clearly remembered each of them buying a drink for a woman they'd met at the bar. The same woman, as it turned out. Got him to sit with a sketch artist."

Connors pulled out a smartphone and showed me an image—a sketch of a woman.

"Look familiar?" Her tone implied she already knew the answer.

I stared for a second before recognizing her. "Samantha Carr." It wasn't a perfect likeness, but it was clearly her. "She's a Sorcerer. Third Rank."

I rubbed my temples and thought it through for a moment. "There's plenty of perfectly reasonable explanations for why she'd be involved. Simplest would be that she's investigating the same case we are—as a ranked member of the Arcanum, she's sworn the same oaths I have and thus has the same responsibilities."

"Oaths? What kind of oaths?" Connors asked.

"The same kind you took when you became a police officer. Ranked Sorcerers of the Arcanum swear three oaths in accordance with the society's mission: we swear to protect mankind from magical and supernatural threats, to uphold and defend the Arcanum's treaties, and to serve the duly elected officers of the Arcane Court. Sam got back into town recently, but if something came to her attention suggesting imminent rogue magical activity, she may have somehow been able to identify potential victims ahead of time. That would explain the meetings in Germantown."

Lajoie nodded and stroked his chin in thought. "She showed up in town recently, you said? Could be a coincidence, I suppose, but what if it isn't? Cops swear oaths, sure, but there are plenty of dirty cops out there."

I shook my head. "Our oaths are bound in magic. I don't know of any case of a ranked Sorcerer turning traitor or deliberately foreswearing his or her oaths in the thousand-year history of the Arcanum. Even if she wanted to, a Third Rank like Sam wouldn't have the power to break her oaths' binding enchantments without help. She could voluntarily resign her rank and the Arcane Court would dissolve the bonds, but short of that, betrayal would lead to severe magical consequences. Possibly even fatal. It's not impossible, I suppose, but it would take power far beyond her own."

"Would these Olympians have that kind of power? If she's in league with them..."

"They would, yes," I nodded, "but I don't even want to think about that. If Sam is directly involved in the murders, this just got a million times more complicated. A Faerie and a member of the Arcanum, working together on an ancient and powerful blood rite invented by an insane Fae criminal? Possibly directed by one or more Olympians? I don't even know what the full implications of that are. But she, at least, is bound to have allies and friends in the Arcanum. Plus she and I have a bit of history."

"What kind of history?" Lajoie looked concerned.

I shook my head. "Nothing serious. She used to come around the shop pretty regularly when she first moved to the city. She was interested in me, presumably by reputation rather than my actual personality, and we went on one date. It did not go well." I left it at that. "Hadn't seen her in years until recently, though. She told me she'd been travelling."

"Is there any way you can track her down?" Connors asked.

"Maybe," I nodded. "I need to make a phone call."

They continued sipping the whisky while I dialed. An increasingly familiar voice answered. "Hello?"

"Rachel," I said.

"Quinn," she replied, sounding tired. "I just got back from Canada. How can I be of service?"

"I know the Rectors keep track of members' whereabouts, and I need to find someone. Third Rank, name is Samantha Carr. Lives somewhere in the Philly area."

She sighed. "Give me a second, I've got to look through my records."

I waited, drumming my fingers on the counter impatiently.

"Conshohocken," she finally replied, "wherever that is. I assume you know. No exact address listed."

"I'm familiar," I responded. "We should be able to work with that."

"Glad to be of help." She sounded anything but glad. "The Lord Marshal passed the word that you're working for her directly, and we Rectors are to give you every possible assistance."

"Of course, she did," I grumbled.

"Anything else, Quinn?"

"No, that's all I needed," I answered.

She abruptly hung up without saying goodbye. If her voice was anything to judge by, her wechuge hunting trip in the Canadian

Rockies had been exhausting. I didn't begrudge her the lack of social pleasantries. I certainly wasn't one to judge.

"Well?" Connors asked.

"She lives in Conshohocken. With that and the sketch you should be able to find her."

Lajoie nodded. "That we can do. Conshy's pretty small, so it shouldn't be too problematic. And when we find her?"

"Then we talk to her. We, you understand? Do not approach her without me."

They both nodded.

"We've seen enough at this point to let you deal with the magic stuff," Lajoie said. He tossed back the last sip of Scotch in his glass. "Also there was something else. The bartender told us she'd met with a few others besides our two victims. Since he'd only seen them each once, he couldn't give accurate sketches, but we've got general descriptions. Four total. Three men—one mid-thirties, muscular, Hispanic; one younger scrawny black kid in his early twenties; one tall elderly white guy. The last was a heavier short woman of indeterminate ethnicity—our guy thought she might be Native American or Middle Eastern. Any of those ring a bell?"

I thought for a minute and shook my head. "Maybe vaguely. Nothing concrete enough for me to help track down, sorry. But if she was talking to them, we can certainly ask her when you find her. And one is probably our next victim. So I'd suggest hurrying."

"Well, partner," he said, looking at Connors, "let's get to detectiving."

Chapter 20

AFTER THE DETECTIVES LEFT, I MADE A PHONE CALL TO THE PUB and asked Bran to put out feelers in the community for any word of unusual activity involving Greco-Roman revivalist worshippers recently, then got to researching. I went in the back room and pulled out all the books I had on the Olympians.

My compendium of magical creatures—the same book in which I'd found the description of the Avartagh—had an extensive entry on Janus. Unlike most of his fellow Olympians, Janus was unique to the Roman pantheon, and had not been worshipped by the Greeks or Etruscans before them. No one really knew where he came from; it was possible he'd simply been born after the Greek Golden Age and had not come to prominence until Rome was beginning its rise to power. But the compendium's author suggested it more likely he'd existed as long as the rest of his tribe, but had for some reason remained in the Otherworld while his kin were squabbling over Greece and Anatolia, only making himself known to our world when he felt the time was right.

The Romans believed he'd been their first king and had begun their rise to mastery over the world. They worshipped him as their god of beginnings and endings, of gates and passages, of transitions and time and duality. Per the compendium, he had been one of the key masters of the veil between the two worlds until the downfall of the Olympians, when he'd lost that position of honor and power to the Sons of Lir.

The more I thought about it, the more it all fit. Janus most certainly had the knowledge of the veil and the Great Cycle necessary to devise the Tamesis. And much like the Avartagh, Janus had every reason to hate humanity and the Arcanum: the most bitterly fought of the Faerie Wars had centered around the conversion of the Roman Empire to Christianity, and the Arcanum had been formed toward the end of that centuries-long war and helped banish the Olympians back to the other side of the veil. Undermining Lugh and the Tuatha Dé by undercutting their precious Treaty of Tara with an attack on the Arcanum's power would be a secondary victory—Olympians were legendary for their long memories and intense grudges. It was not a significant stretch to imagine Janus would resent those who had wrested control of the veil from him.

And as Johannes had pointed out, the rise in Hellenistic Revivalist worship of the Greco-Roman pantheon could easily have given him the opportunity to try again after so long without the influence to do so. That explained both how he was directing the ritual now, and why he had not attempted it in the centuries since the Avartagh's failure.

Means, motive, opportunity. But even were Janus directing the Tamesis rites, I thought it unlikely he was personally conducting the sacrifices. Olympians had a reputation for not getting their hands dirty, using human and Fae patsies to do their work for them—in Greco-Roman religion, priests made sacrifices to the gods, not the other way around. Meaning I was unlikely to catch him red-handed.

Were Janus in fact guilty—and he was now firmly my lead suspect—Lugh was powerful enough to hold him accountable, and it was in his interest to do so and thus uphold the Treaty of Tara. That would end the threat of him trying again even if we disrupted the current rites. But it required sufficient proof for Lugh to act. As yet, the evidence was entirely circumstantial.

Seeing nothing more I could do about Janus at the moment, I pulled my ley-line map back out, only to confirm I didn't yet have enough information about the necessary pattern for the Tamesis to narrow down potential sacrifice locations. Unless the Philly PD were willing to cover hundreds of potential sites, there wasn't much I could do. It was frustrating, being so close but not being able to get useful answers. I might be able to do more that evening, when I had time to remap the network and extrapolate from the movements.

I had more customers than usual that morning, which made sense given that the shop had been closed the past few days. They were a good break from the boredom and frustration. But as for the research, I hadn't come up with much at all when the phone rang three hours after the detectives left. It was Lajoie.

"We found her." He gave me an address.

Conshohocken, a small suburb of Philadelphia proper, was about an hour by train from my place. Fortunately, the address was only a few blocks from the station and the morning rain had let up by the time I arrived, so it wasn't too bad of a walk.

Connors and Lajoie were waiting outside the apartment building. Connors was finishing up a cigarette. I raised an eyebrow questioningly.

"What, Quinn? I smoke. That a problem?"

I shook my head. "No problem, just unexpected. You don't generally smell of cigarettes."

She snorted. "Tic-tacs and deodorant, and only smoking outside. I'm not going through a pack a day here, just when I'm stressed."

I shrugged. It was irrelevant. "She here?"

Lajoie bobbed his head toward the building. "Apartment 4C. Local uniforms reported she went in about two hours ago, hasn't come out."

"And," Connors added, "as promised, no one has approached her prior to your arrival. You ready?" I nodded. "Then let's go." She flicked the butt of her cigarette to the concrete and headed in the door.

I let the detectives take the lead up the stairs. When we reached the fourth-floor landing, Lajoie knocked on the door that said 4C.

"Police," he announced. "Ms. Carr, we'd like to ask you a few questions."

There was a long silence, then the sound of high heels on hardwood as someone approached the door from inside.

"May I see some identification, please?" It was Sam's silky contralto.

Lajoie pulled out his badge and held it up to the peephole.

"I'm Detective Lajoie, Ms. Carr. My partner and I would like to talk to you about Evan Townes and Jane Crandall."

There was another silence, presumably as she inspected the badge for signs of counterfeiting. We then heard the sound of several locks and door chains being released, and Connors holstered her weapon just as the door swung open to reveal the tall, curvy blonde form of Samantha Carr, Sorcerer of the Third Rank of the Arcanum.

She locked eyes with me for a second, apparently unsurprised to see me with the detectives, before turning her head to address Lajoie.

"Detective."

He nodded in acknowledgement. "This is my partner, Detective Connors. I believe you know Mr. Quinn. He's consulting with us on the case." He gestured to each of us in turn. She nodded politely to Connors, then gave me a longer, more measuring look before returning her attention to Lajoie.

"Please, come in. Would you care for a drink?" she asked as she turned and walked back down the short entrance hall.

Lajoie led the three of us after her to her small living room.

"No drinks, thank you. We just have a few questions for you," he said. Connors seemed content to let him take the lead in the interview.

"Of course. Whatever I can do to help Philadelphia's finest. Please, have a seat," she replied, gesturing to the couch that took up most of the room.

We sat; she took the armchair facing us at an angle, crossing her legs at the knee.

"Ms. Carr," Lajoie began, "you were seen in the company of both Evan Townes and Jane Crandall, at the Paris Bistro, shortly before both were murdered. Care to explain that coincidence?"

She sighed and looked down. "I didn't know Jane was dead. The news hasn't named the second victim yet. Damn."

We all silently waited for more. She eventually looked up at me instead of the detectives.

"Since you brought them to the Market, can I assume you've briefed them on our world?"

"The basics, yes," I replied evenly. "They know about the Arcanum and the Fae. They know we're tracking someone trying to recreate the Avartagh's Tamesis rites."

She nodded in acknowledgement. "Okay. You know how the ley-lines in the city were moving around more than usual lately, almost randomly?"

I nodded silently. Connors's eyebrows raised in question, but I ignored her. We could get into that later.

"Well," she continued, "I have a journal in my possession, given as a gift from my old master Benoit de Calais upon my completion of the Trials. It belonged to his great-grandfather, a sorcerer named Jean Guiscard, one of the Arcanum hunters who stopped the Avartagh centuries ago in Brittany. And it mentioned the same thing happening there before the rites started. All of the victims were killed at new nodes that had just formed from the shifting lines in the days before."

That matched what I already knew, at least. I nodded again.

"So when I noticed the weird movements here, shortly after I got back into town, I looked into it. I got in contact with every sorcerer who lived at or near one of the new nodes. I was trying to figure out if they were in danger, if they had anything else in common, that kind of thing. And if they were in danger, I hoped to figure out what order they were likely to be attacked in, and to warn them."

"Okay," Lajoie replied, "assuming that's true, how did you hope to figure out what order they were going to be attacked in?"

"By tracking the ley-line shifts and trying to figure out the pattern—to figure out where the new nodes were going to be by the time the attackers needed a new blood sacrifice. Logically, they'd target the nearest unranked sorcerer to the next node. That's the simplest and easiest way to pick their next sacrifice."

Connors and Lajoie looked over at me. I nodded in confirmation.

"I looked into the same thing this morning, but I still don't know enough about the rites to figure out which nodes are being targeted."

"You don't have Guiscard's journal," Sam said. "That's what put me on the trail initially, and his notes are detailed enough that I was able to identify the first two ritual locations, but not in time to stop either of them."

"Why," I asked slowly, choosing my words and my tone diplomatically, trying to avoid sounding accusatory or suspicious, "did you not report this to anyone?"

"Would you?" she shot back. "I'm a ranked sorcerer. I'm supposed to be able to take care of my home city."

I scowled, but it was true.

"You must have known that anything involving the Avartagh was beyond your own skill."

"Maybe," she replied, "but I've never exactly been on good terms with the Rectors."

"Oh?" I asked.

"I never told you this before—it's not exactly first date conversation material—but I was only taken to be trained after I accidentally set my parents' house on fire and they both died. I was six. A team led by a Rector showed up to take me. He wanted to put me down as a danger to others." I winced at that. "Fortunately, two of his team members managed to convince him to take me to the Court for judgement. The Court fostered me with a First Rank until I was old enough for apprenticeship. But you'll forgive me if I don't exactly trust Rectors after that."

It was a fair concern. Some Rectors were quick to judgement and would rather end threats than put in the effort to solve the problem humanely. Especially in the late fifties or early sixties when this must have occurred, with the Shadow War fresh in the Arcanum's collective memory. A lot of the men and women serving the Arcane Court after the war were happier to kill first and ask questions later.

I could see how such a traumatic experience might shape a young Sorcerer's opinions of those charged with maintaining the peace and upholding the treaties and customs. I looked over at the detectives. Connors was stone-faced as always, but Lajoie looked horrified. From what the Avartagh had revealed about his own history, I could understand why.

"Then why not come to me, as the senior Sorcerer in the city?" I asked.

She quirked an eyebrow. "I did. Twice. Yesterday and the day before—I told you at the Market I had something I wanted to talk to you about. This was that something. But you haven't been home. The shop was locked up both times I tried to drop by."

I nodded. "I was out of town looking into some things. Sorry about that."

She waved it off. "Yeah, I didn't think you were avoiding me. But still, you asked."

"Who were the other four you talked to?" Lajoie asked.

She frowned. "If Jane is gone, that leaves one other woman and three men as possible targets. All unranked sorcerers. Anna Begay, Charles English, Jeremy Wilson, and Joe Gonzalez. All live within a half mile or so of one of the spots where it looks like the nodes are heading. What I haven't yet figured out are exact locations of the eventual nodes, the order of the killings, or what it is the killers are trying to do with the energy they're harvesting."

"Do you have contact information for them? Addresses and phone numbers?"

"Yes," she replied. "It's in my address book in the bedroom."

"Could you get it for us, please?"

"Of course." She stood and walked to the bedroom, closing the door behind her.

As soon as the door closed, Connors immediately leaned in. "Do we trust her?" she asked in a low voice so Sam wouldn't hear.

I thought about it for a moment. "Everything she's said holds up. She did tell me at the Market that she wanted to talk to me about something, and I can confirm on my security cameras whether she actually came by as she claimed. If that's true, everything in her story is consistent."

"You said she'd just recently returned to Philly?" Lajoie asked.

"Yes," I nodded, "but she lived here previously, too. The timing of her return is fairly weak evidence for considering her a suspect, especially considering the matter of her oaths."

The detectives considered this, but before they could respond Samantha opened her bedroom door, address book in hand.

"This should have everything you need to track down the four I've identified. Is there anything else I can do for you?"

"Why yes, Ms. Carr," Connors answered, "there is. We're going to pick up these individuals and bring them in for interviews. In the meantime, would you mind accompanying Mr. Quinn here to his office and show him what you've got so far, maybe try to get a head start on figuring out who the next victim will be?"

I started. Invite Sam into my shop, my office, my private research area? Work with her? I hadn't really worked side by side with another sorcerer in decades, and definitely not one with whom I had an awkward history. I wasn't keen to change that particular habit right now.

I glared at Connors, annoyed at the presumption. But she met my gaze unflinchingly. I could practically hear her thinking at me. She was right, of course. If Samantha really did have anything useful, this could help us, and I was the only one in a position to use her information. And I was also best equipped to determine whether the timing of her return was suspicious or a mere coincidence.

Samantha, for her part, was grinning in amusement. "Sure thing. Just let me get my things and show me the way."

"We'll give you a ride. Gather whatever you need."

Chapter 21

LATER THAT EVENING WE WERE IN MY BACK OFFICE, WITH THE stack of books I'd been working on pushed to the side and my map of the city's shifting ley-line network back out and unfolded, covering the desk. Samantha was comparing the map to her own notes, marking inconsistencies with a pencil.

I was drinking, but not heavily. Just enough to quiet my mind some. I was on edge. It had been a long time since I'd collaborated with anyone else in the Arcanum, and I was uncomfortable with change. Our history didn't help.

"There," she announced. "All done." I stood up to look at the adjustments she'd made. "This was accurate as of two days ago."

I raised my eyebrows. I'd last measured them the morning before I met the detectives, almost a week ago, and in that time multiple nodes had moved several blocks from where I'd marked them. That was significant movement for the normally stable network. Almost unheard of, in fact.

But I'd been studying Guiscard's journal, and Samantha hadn't been lying. He talked of major swings in ley-lines, with nodes shifting a mile or more in just a few weeks. If the journal was authentic—and if it were a forgery, it was high enough quality that I couldn't tell—then this could well be the key to stopping the Tamesis.

Samantha had marked on the map the addresses of the four potential victims she'd identified. I marked the nodes at the two murder scenes, mentally kicking myself for needing the Immortal's help to see the connection.

But this isn't the first time you've used the Immortal's wisdom, that quiet voice whispered to me from the back of my mind. I froze for a second, memories of fire and screams flashing into my mind, before I shoved them back down deep. Enough of that, I told myself.

Samantha noticed the slight shudder as I cleared my head and returned to the map. She cocked her head. "Something wrong?"

"It's nothing," I said curtly. "Just an old memory. Don't worry about it. Let's figure this out."

She didn't back down, though. Instead she moved closer and put her hand on my forearm, gently.

"Do you want to talk about it?"

For a second, I froze, then jerked my arm back. I slowly raised my eyes to face her squarely, my fury building. I was about to snap at her, to put her in her place, to punish her for her presumption. But her expression was concerned more than curious. She looked genuinely worried for me, wanting to help me with whatever I was going through that had caused such a physical reaction.

The anger died down. She didn't mean any harm. I looked back down and sighed. Even working with the detectives for over a week, I was still very much out of practice dealing with people beyond customer interactions.

"No. It doesn't matter," I mumbled. "Let's get back to work."

When I looked back down at the map, though, I noticed something I hadn't seen before. I frowned.

"Damn it," I whispered. I traced out the ley-lines on Samantha's version with a finger, muttering softly as I went. When I finished with the last line, I pushed down and twisted while saying the last words of a complex incantation. The lines she'd drawn in pencil burst into golden light on the map.

Samantha gasped.

Without looking up, I asked, "What does that look like to you?"

"A . . . that's a pentagram," she replied. "How did you . . . ?"

I pressed my lips together. This wasn't the time to explain ancient Babylonian spells.

"That's exactly what it is. But not a perfect one. Let's see here . . . ." I muttered, as I again touched my finger to a node and moved it, and the glowing lines moved with me. I repeated the process with a few more nodes. The direction of shift all matched the way they'd moved between my initial measurement and Samantha's later one. Then I stepped back to review my handiwork and nodded in approval.

With just a few more shifts, the five major ley-lines of the greater Philadelphia area would form a giant five-pointed star, stretching across the city, centered on Logan Square. The first two murder sites were at the first two points of the star to be in position. Three points remained: one in Fishtown several blocks from my shop, one in Pennsport near the Mummers Museum, and one in a housing project in Grays Ferry. Assuming the shifts continued at the same speed they'd been moving over the past couple weeks, the Grays Ferry node would be in place by tomorrow afternoon, followed by Pennsport in two days. The one near my place was the last, two days later.

I looked up at Sam. "Well, we know the location and timing of the next sacrifice, at least."

Her eyes wide, she nodded back at me.

I looked at the clock on the wall. Ten 'til midnight, and I'd already arranged with the detectives to go over what we'd found in the morning. There was no sense in waking them up; they'd need to be rested if we were going to get in a fight tomorrow afternoon or evening. Instead I found another glass and poured some whisky for Samantha. Handing it to her, I raised my own drink in salute.

"Well done, Sorcerer," I said quietly.

She smiled. She looked almost innocent and carefree. "Same to you, Quinn. If you hadn't seen the pattern, we'd have never put the pieces together."

I took a long sip, then I ushered her out of the office to lock up for the night. I headed over and took a seat in the reading corner. I needed to think. We'd spotted the pattern, yes, but what did it mean? As the Immortal had suggested, it had to be about amplifying the power of the ritual as well as propagating its energy toward the critical point in the Great Cycle. Once we stopped the next sacrifice and had some time to breathe, I could sit down and start looking at the bigger picture to see where that pentagram connected to across the larger network.

Samantha interrupted my line of thought by sitting down in the chair next to me, her drink still in hand.

"You seem awfully quiet for someone who just solved the case."

"Huh?" I looked up, irritated at the distraction. "Oh. No, we haven't solved the case. We know the next likely crime scene and have a good guess as to when the sacrifice will occur. We're almost there. We can probably disrupt the rites enough to stop the Tamesis. But we don't know why, what the motive is, what exactly the Tamesis is. And figuring that out can help figure out who's pulling the strings. I'm betting it's not just the two who are performing the actual rites."

She shrugged. "But isn't it enough to stop them from completing the ritual? At least for now?"

I shook my head. "No, it's not. If we stop the ritual without catching those behind it, we leave the door open for it to happen again. We can't let an enemy that dangerous slip into the shadows."

Especially, I thought, if they were Olympians. They'd have the time to wait us out, let humanity forget, and then simply try again.

She smiled, grimly. "Fair enough, I suppose. More work to be done yet, and all. How do you propose catching them?"

"A trap. We need to capture or kill the two conducting the rites, forcing whoever is behind them to come out into the open to complete it themselves."

Samantha looked horrified. "Wait, you're going to let them complete the initial blood rites and kill more victims just to capture them?"

"No, of course not," I scowled. "I'm going to stop them when they reveal themselves, not after they complete the rites. What kind of monster do you think I am?"

She relaxed. "Oh. Okay, that makes sense. Sorry. It's just..." She seemed hesitant to continue. "It's just I've heard so much about the Shadow War. About the Fields of Fire. I didn't know..."

"You didn't know if I'm a monster or not?" I asked, bitterly. "You didn't know if I had any humanity left in me after the Fields of Fire? You thought that might be why I'm a recluse, why I avoid the rest of the Arcanum? Is that why you were interested in me in the first place, Sam? To find out if I am what they say I am?"

She didn't say anything. We sat in silence for a long time, just sipping at our drinks.

"Well, you'd be right," I finally said, breaking the silence. "You'd be right. What I did in Canada... it was monstrous. No human could have wrought what I did. I don't know if I have much humanity left in me. Or if I'm . . . something else, now. I don't know." I paused.

"But that isn't why I avoid the Arcanum. That part you'd be wrong about. I avoid the Arcanum because they're the ones who asked me to do it. They're the ones whose call I answered, again and again, because I was 'needed.' They're the ones in whose name I killed my best friend. They're the ones in whose name I killed thousands upon thousands, in a dozen wars across seven continents and two centuries. They're the ones in whose name I violated the Earth and called forth the flames to vanquish the Shadows and their demon allies. And if I don't avoid them, I know full well that someday they'll ask me to do the same again. And I'm afraid I'll actually do it." I took a long drink. She didn't say a word.

"I still hear the screams, you know. Not figuratively. Literally. They're seared into my memory. Not a day goes by in which I don't hear the screams. Not a night passes in which I don't remember killing my best friend, in which I don't watch her fall from the sky over and over as I can do nothing to stop myself. I remember all of it. The Predations, when a mad djinn slaughtered sorcerers across Europe. The Tear of the Gods, when Boer cultists tried to start a war between humans and the Fae and came damn close to succeeding. Krakatoa, when we murdered tens of thousands of people to save millions from an insane demi-god. Tunguska . . ." I trailed off for a moment.

"And, of course, the Shadow War. Our stand at Ayer's Rock. Lithuania. Khartoum. The hopeless defense at Angkor Wat—only three of us made it out of the jungle after that one. Three. Of dozens. And the Fields of Fire. The goddamned Fields of fucking Fire, when I set Canada alight with my wrath."

I looked her in the eye. "They told me I was a hero, you know. Isn't that funny?" I gave a humorless chuckle. "A hero. It was profane. It was horrifying. But I won the day, so I was a hero."

I threw back the rest of my whisky and fell into silence. I'd never told anyone that. I didn't know why I was telling her now—maybe I was just tired of holding it in, maybe I needed someone in the Arcanum to know why I'd left, why I refused to do anything beyond the bare minimum for them since Canada. Why I'd practically sworn off battle magic and preferred a gun. Why I preferred books to human contact, and alcohol to sleep.

I hadn't told her everything, of course. I hadn't told her how

I'd done what I'd done in Canada. Not even the Fae had figured that one out—if they had I'd have heard from them already. With any luck, that secret would die with me.

Nor had I told her about the Immortal. The real reason I'd become a hermit. I'd betrayed his trust in me when I'd perverted his teachings to defeat the Shadows. But I wouldn't betray the promise I'd made to keep his existence a secret. That had been a condition of him taking me in, becoming my mentor in the first place. He had no desire to be known to the Arcanum. To be used as a weapon, as I had been. By limiting my interactions with the Arcanum, I limited the chances anyone could put the pieces together.

Samantha hadn't said anything. She still didn't. For several minutes, there was the semi-silence of a quiet street in Fishtown in the middle of the night, just traffic sounds and the occasional siren faintly audible through the storefront.

Then I felt her hand on mine. I looked up. She'd reached over from her chair to hold my hand. It wasn't unpleasant. Unlike when she'd touched me earlier, I was no longer angry. I'd burnt the anger out for the night. In fact, it was the first gentle, calming human contact I could remember having in a long, long time.

I looked at her. I saw hints of concern around her eyes, but her expression was kind and open. She was just letting me know, silently, that she was here if I needed her.

We sat like that for a while. I don't know how long.

Eventually, I heard her stir and looked to see her stand up. She let go of my hand and walked over to the door. I thought she was leaving, but instead she hit the light switches. In the soft glow of the streetlights filtering through the store windows, I was reminded that she was a magnificently beautiful woman. Strong and soft, at the same time, in a way you don't see very often. I kept my eyes on her as she turned and walked back over to the reading corner.

Carefully, but assertively, she took my hand again. Then she perched on the arm of my chair, leaned over, and kissed me.

It was a good kiss. Lingering and bittersweet, rather than passionate. It lasted I don't know how long, but not long enough. When it was over, when she drew back and studied my face for a reaction, I was still for a few seconds. Savoring.

Then I turned away from her and whispered, "Please go."

After she'd gone, I sat a minute or two in the dark before I locked up and poured myself more whisky.

Chapter 22

I WOKE UP EARLY THE NEXT MORNING AFTER DRIFTING OFF TO a mercifully dreamless sleep in the chair downstairs. Roxana was on the chair across from me and gave me a chastising glare as I stirred. I looked at the clock on the wall in the early morning light. Six. Early enough to shower, change, and get some breakfast before calling the detectives.

By the time I finished eating, it was almost eight. I called Lajoie's cell.

"What have you got, Quinn?"

"I think we figured out where the next sacrifice is going to be."

"Oh?"

"Yes. It's a bit complicated, but essentially the lines of magical power throughout the city have been shifting, like Samantha mentioned at her apartment. I think the blood rites are, in part, to lock them in place in the right positions for the final working. How it works I'm not sure yet, but either way, the next one to be in place will be in Grays Ferry."

"Do you have an exact address?"

"It looks like it will be in the Greater Grays Ferry Estates. Either the big apartment building at South 30th and Moore, or one of the townhouses along that block."

"Okay," Lajoie replied. "Do you have a plan? We've got the

four individuals Samantha identified in voluntary protective custody for the time being. They all understand what's going on and aren't keen on being the next sacrifice."

"That's a good start, but it won't be enough. If their most convenient targets are unavailable, the killers will just find others. There're dozens of unranked sorcerers in the area, and there's no way for us to protect all of them even if we could find them first."

"Could we warn them, at least?"

I grunted negatively. "The Rectors don't keep track of unranked sorcerers' contact information and whereabouts. I could probably find some phone numbers from invoices in my records, but not quickly, and there's no guarantee they've all ordered items from me. The stronger bet is to go after the killers themselves."

"So what's the plan, then?"

"An ambush. We know where they are going to be, and approximately when they'll be there. We can wait for them, spot them entering the area for the sacrifice, and confront them before they can start. Hopefully, that will be enough to disrupt the entire Tamesis, given what the Avartagh said about everything needing to be perfectly in tune with the necessary patterns. And if I can manage to capture them, we might be able to figure out who's behind them."

"Alright," Lajoie mused. "We can come up with an excuse to evacuate all civilians from the target area. Gas leak or something. Then when the suspects approach, you can go after them. You're confident you can take them on?"

"Yes. Especially if Samantha is willing to back me up."

"How did that go, by the way? Is she still with you?"

"It went well," I admitted begrudgingly. "Her work was essential to identifying the pattern. But no, she's not still here. I asked her to leave late last night."

"Do you trust her?"

I grunted. "I don't trust anybody, son. Not for a long time. But she's the only backup I've got in the area with the power and training to help me confront a Faerie and a rogue sorcerer. And at least her oaths give me some reassurance she won't stab me in the back while watching it."

It was more than that, really. I wouldn't stoop to asking Rachel, or my mother, or any of the other officers and representatives of the Arcane Court to help me in battle. Not after everything they'd put me through, the memories and nightmares I'd earned in their service. I couldn't bring myself to debase myself by requesting such aid when I'd rejected them for so long. But Sam was different. She was a member of the Arcanum, but she wasn't an officer of the Court. And we had history. What I'd said was true—I didn't really trust anybody except my own parents, and even that relationship was strained. But I distrusted Sam less than most.

"Good enough, I suppose," Lajoie responded. "I can send some uniforms to pick her up."

Three or four hours later, the four of us were in an unmarked car at the corner of South 30th and Moore Street, with a view of both the apartment building parking lot and the full block of townhouses down South 30th. The sacrifice would have to take place in one of those buildings to be on top of the node.

With their lieutenant's permission, Lajoie and Connors had had the city's public works department evacuate a two-block radius around the apartment building, under the pretext of a dangerous natural gas leak that might cause an explosion. It would be a paperwork nightmare, but the lieutenant agreed if we could stop a serial killer, that would go a long way to quieting complaints from the affected citizens.

Once the suspects showed up, Samantha and I would follow them into their chosen sacrifice site—it would be easier to try to capture them indoors than in the open. Connors and Lajoie couldn't take on the killers themselves, but they had the custom ammunition I'd given them the other day, which should let them defend themselves long enough to escape if necessary. They'd be covering the exit, and if Sam and I were unsuccessful, they were to withdraw and call Rachel Liu. If I couldn't handle it, the Rector would have to take over.

I guess several nights of low-quality sleep caught up to me, because I drifted off in the back around noon. Midafternoon, I woke to a boiling hot car and the sounds of the detectives and Sam talking softly.

"... what I heard, anyway. And from what he said last night, I believe it."

Connors replied to her just as quietly. "You're saying he killed his own best friend?"

"Yes. That's the rumor. That he'd befriended the last dragon decades before. And then he led the team to hunt her down."

Lajoie sounded skeptical. "How did he befriend a dragon?"

"I don't know," Sam answered. "I'm just telling you, between the rumors and his breakdown last night, I believe every word now. His friend was in trouble, and he killed her."

I winced internally. But I didn't get angry.

"My friend was already gone," I said, sitting up.

Samantha at least had the good grace to look ashamed at being caught talking behind my back. Lajoie and Connors were studiously keeping an eye out on the apartment building, as if I hadn't heard them too. But it didn't matter anymore. Maybe my confession to Sam last night had been cathartic. I didn't know, but I just couldn't bring myself to feel angry.

"My friend was already gone," I repeated. "I put down the monster she had become."

"It's true, then?" Connors asked.

"True enough," I allowed. "No one left but me remembers the details. There were thirteen of us at Tunguska that day. The other twelve are all dead."

"Did the dragon kill them?" Lajoie inquired.

I shook my head. "No. Calliatrix didn't kill any of us that morning. Two were killed on the Western Front in 1916. The rest all died in the Shadow War."

"Calliatrix?" Samantha this time. "That was her name?"

"Yes, at least in human tongues. No one's spoken her native language in centuries. Not since all her kin were killed off." I paused. "I'd rather not talk about her. She was my friend. She went mad and started killing innocent people. I put her down because I had no other choice. That's the gist of it."

We all fell into an awkward silence for a few minutes.

Connors broke the tension. "I've heard the Shadow War mentioned several times over the past week. Would you mind explaining exactly what that was?"

I thought about it. Nothing about the Shadow War had any real relevance to our current case. But they were committed now. It couldn't hurt to answer some basic questions, things most everyone in the magical world already knew. Not at this point. Besides, we had some time to pass, and at least it changed the subject from what had happened in Siberia.

"The Shadow War was the greatest conflict the Arcanum had faced in generations," I replied. "We still don't know what the Shadows were or where they came from. They could appear out of nowhere, passing through solid rock and metal as if it wasn't there. Their magic was horrifying, splitting people apart from the inside out. And there were so many of them . . ." I trailed off, remembering Angkor Wat.

"For several years, we fought them across the globe wherever they appeared. We usually won on the battlefield, but they were pyrrhic victories, driving them back to wherever they came from, but losing so many in the process it was almost pointless. They were fighting a war of attrition, and they were winning."

Sam interrupted. "Until the Fields of Fire."

I was silent for a long moment, then I nodded.

"Yes. Until Canada. We beat them back in northern British Columbia. We managed to kill so many of them and their demon allies that they disappeared. No one's heard from them since that day."

"What happened?" Connors asked.

"I . . ." It was complicated. "I gambled. And we won," I said, leaving it at that.

That was a vast simplification. It left out the fire. So much fire. The single largest firestorm ever recorded in North America. It left out all the dead and maimed sorcerers. It left out the screams. I hadn't even known demons could scream before that day.

Sam didn't leave it at that, however. "What exactly did you do, Quinn?"

I didn't look at her. I didn't say anything. That secret would die with me. Just because she'd kissed me didn't change that conviction.

"That's right, Quinn," she sighed. "Because not talking about it all these years has worked out so well."

I felt my anger rising again, that little voice urging me to let it free. I breathed slowly, trying to calm myself down. She wasn't a child, but she was too young to have been there. She'd only heard stories, half-whispered rumors told over drinks at Grand Conclaves, usually accompanied by nervous looks around to see if I was within earshot. I didn't have to be. I knew what they were saying.

"No, Sam," I finally replied, shaking my head. "That's enough about Canada. Leave it at that. I took a risk. It worked. We won. All of that is long past. Let's focus on stopping the Tamesis."

She pursed her lips, clearly not pleased. She'd been hoping for more, maybe felt she was owed more after last night. I owed no one anything. Except, I reminded myself, a favor to Lugh.

We all lapsed back into an awkward silence for a while. At some point Connors made a run to get food from a Middle Eastern place a few blocks away. When she came back, the three of them chatted about inconsequential nothings while I ate my falafel quietly.

I wasn't paying much attention as they discussed the personal life of some famous athlete. Or politician. Or musician. I didn't keep up with current events enough to recognize the name. I tuned it out and thought about things I normally tried not to think about.

Her name was Calliatrix, from the root Callias—"most beautiful." And it fit. Green and gold scales that shimmered, almost iridescent in the sunlight. The most expressive eyes I have ever seen. In her human form—that myth is true, some dragons learn to shapeshift, though only a fool would ever mistake them for a mere human—her eyes had the green and gold color of her scales, and shimmered as if they were on fire. She had a laugh that you felt in your soul, and a warm, friendly voice.

Every apprentice sorcerer in the Arcanum whose masters deem him or her potentially powerful enough to hold rank undergoes the Trials. The first and second are fairly standardized tests of magical strength and skill. But the last, if a candidate makes it that far, is tailored to the individual. Mine was decided by the three masters under whom I'd studied for the traditional thirty-three years.

I was to enter the lair of the last dragon and retrieve the crown of Arthur, which had been handcrafted by Emrys Myrddin himself. They expected me to sneak in, locate the crown, and sneak out with it. Instead I returned to where my masters waited in Lviv on the dragon's back, the crown in my hand, given as a gift of friendship. I passed the trial, and for many years after I was known as the Dragonrider of Lviv.

But Calliatrix had lived a thousand years alone. Her species were never numerous, and all her kin had long ago been killed off by humans, one by one. She was already descending into madness by the time I met her, and I like to think I helped her hold on a little bit longer. But several decades after we met, the strain became too much for her to bear.

She went insane and began attacking human villages and farms in rage, lashing out desperately against the injustice of my species. I rushed to help her, to bring her home. She spoke to me. One last time, she was my friend. But she was too far gone. She apologized. Then she left.

We didn't see each other again until that morning in Siberia. But my friend, the wise, intelligent, loving Calliatrix, had been dead since she'd said sorry and flown away. There was nothing left but a wild animal, a mad creature that knew only pain and anger. We'd been tracking her for weeks by the remains she'd left behind. The bodies. The charred huts.

There was nothing we could do but put her down. We battled, and we won. I struck the killing blow. I hated myself for it. Every second of every day since, I'd hated myself for it. But I knew I'd have hated myself more if I'd let anyone else do it. I owed her that much, at least.

I'd done horrible things for the Arcanum before. Maybe I was already scarred. But that's when I changed. For the first century of my life, I was an adventurer, an optimist. After Tunguska, I started to withdraw from humanity. After all, what had friendship brought me so far? Better to be alone and bitter than to feel that pain again.

When Johannes discovered me and took me in, I finally found someone who could understand. He'd lived so long, seen and done so many things, that he truly knew my pain, what I'd been through. And he didn't judge me—he never judged me. I saw the same hurt and sadness in his eyes.

Slowly, over three decades, he'd helped put me back together a little bit. He taught me his mysteries and secrets, deep magics long forgotten by anyone else. The wonders of the universe were laid out before me. For the first time since that cold morning in Siberia, I had hope.

But then the Shadows came, and I once again left to answer the call. And then, in the wilds of the Canadian Rockies, I'd taken the greatest of the Immortal's mysteries, the knowledge of the wellspring, the beating heart of magic in this world, and turned it into a weapon. I'd perverted his teachings, his wisdom, into an abomination. It had gone down in lore as the Fields of Fire, the Arcanum's great victory that ended the Shadow War. But it had finally broken me.

After what I'd seen, what I'd done, I'd stopped pretending. I could no longer tell myself I was a good person, that I was on the side of the light and the virtuous. No victory could be worth that price.

At Tunguska, I'd stopped being the Dragonrider of Lviv. After the Shadow War, I became the Hermit Sorcerer. Quinn the Loner. The Grouch. The Drunk. The Embarrassment. The Black Sheep. The Asshole Who Just Wants to Be Left Alone.

No wonder things hadn't worked out with Sam. I needed a drink.

"Quinn!"

I was startled from my reverie. "What?"

Connors was pointing out the front window. "Two people just drove through the public works barricades and parked in the apartment building parking lot. They're walking in now."

I looked around Lajoie's headrest to see out the front window. Sure enough, two people were walking across the parking lot toward the front door, one tall and one diminutively short, both wearing long coats and wide brimmed hats despite the late afternoon heat. And they were carrying a large bundle that looked suspiciously like a person wrapped in a blanket.

They wouldn't notice us; I'd used a complex masking spell to hide the car from magical senses. But to my eyes they stood out like bright lights in a dark room. Definitely magical.

I nodded. "That's them. Let's go," I said to Sam. Then turned to the detectives with my hand on the door handle. "You two stay outside and cover the door. Don't come up unless I signal you."

Lajoie looked back at me. "How will you signal us?"

"Like this," I replied, and touched a ring on my left finger. The bracelets both detectives were still wearing flared into heat, enough to be noticeable, but not painfully so. Their eyes went wide as they felt it. "Easy enough?"

"And if you don't signal us?" Connors asked.

"Call Rachel." I'd already given them her number. "Tell her I couldn't handle it."

Connors looked me dead in the eye. "Don't let it come to that."

I nodded once, then turned to Sam. "Shall we?"

She smiled nervously. "Let's do it."

I doubted she'd ever been in a real fight before, but she certainly wasn't weak.

We both got out of the car and headed across the street toward the building.

Chapter 23

GESTURING FOR SAM TO BE QUIET AS WE REACHED THE BUILDING, I listened, then tasted the magical fields around the door. Seeing no sign of a trap, I opened it as silently as possible, let Sam enter, then followed and quietly closed the door behind us. Every sense, both magical and normal, was on alert. I didn't know what floor the killers were planning to use for the sacrifice, so I had to pay attention and find them.

The building was a four-story walkup, with a staircase of twelve-step flights between landings, but a solid wall in the middle that would cut off all visibility beyond the landings above and below. The apartments were off a corridor every other landing. I heard footsteps as the two suspects moved up the stairs, maybe a floor and a half above us.

I motioned for Sam to follow, but keep some distance, then started up the stairs after them, slowly and carefully. My shield was primed, focused on the ring on my left hand. I held my Glock in a two-handed grip, aimed up the stairs, elbows tucked into my sides in a compressed ready position. Walking around with your gun extended just tires out your arms and doesn't make you any faster in getting the sights on the target when it's time to shoot. No one does that but idiots and actors.

I reached the first landing and stopped to listen. The sounds from above had stopped. I hadn't heard them open a door to one of the residential floors, meaning they were still in the stairwell. They must have heard something.

I looked back to see Sam's encouraging face behind me before I cautiously made the turn around the blind corner, slicing the pie as I rounded the edge of the wall, ready to react to anyone lying in ambush. The landing was empty, as was the next flight of stairs. Nothing to do but keep moving up.

I headed toward the second landing the same slow, cautious way. I wasn't afraid—I'd seen too much and lived too long to be afraid. But it had been a long time since I'd been in real combat. The fight at the Market had been a surprise, but this time I had plenty of time to anticipate what was coming. Adrenaline was flowing, my heart was pounding, and it took everything I had to keep my breathing under control and my hands steady. I desperately wanted to go get a drink. Instead I kept moving up the stairs.

Once again, I looked back at Sam before carefully making my way around the blind corner of the third landing. She gave me a nervous smile and a nod, as if to let me know she had my back. I nodded and turned back ahead, focusing on the corner ahead of me.

As I started to make the turn, my necklace flared into heat, but as I instinctively pulled back from whatever was coming, something slammed into me from behind, knocking me forward. I was stunned, face down on the landing, exposed in both directions. Without thinking or taking any time to assess, I let the shield spell activate around me, walling me off from the stairs below and above. Just in time—another heat spell hit the shield from the stairs to my front. The two must have heard us behind them and split up, one on the first or second floor and one on the fourth, to pin us between them.

As I regained my senses, I looked to see what had attacked me from above, and saw, hazy through the energy of the translucent blue shield spell, the outlines of two people standing on the next landing up. One tall and one short. Which meant there had to be a third. Had the bundle they'd brought actually been a friend of theirs in disguise? Had they been expecting us?

I focused on the spell and put extra effort into it to make it transparent, like a blue sheet of glass, so I could see what was around me while still being protected. And then I turned to look down the stairs. I'd been afraid they'd pinned us and Sam was already in trouble, if not dead. But there she was, halfway down the flight of stairs, standing exactly where she'd been when she'd smiled at me. Her hand was stretched out toward me, flickering with silver energy, ready to cast another spell as soon as my shield dropped.

"Oh, hey there, Quinn. Sorry, did I startle you?"

I grimaced. I still had sensation in my legs, so the blast probably hadn't done too much permanent damage. But it hurt. I was going to have a wicked burn right in the middle of my upper back, even if the protective enchantments woven into my coat had protected me from dying. It seemed to be the same heat spell that had singed my arm outside the Faerie Market.

"You know," Sam continued, "even considering our history, it was really easy to convince you to trust me enough to let me watch your back while you focused all your attention to the front. That was dumb of you."

"Yes," I hissing through the pain as I struggled to a sitting position. "Yes, it was. My mistake. So these two are your friends?" I asked, nodding to the two silent figures upstairs.

"You might say that," she replied. "Though I've got plenty of other friends, too. I've been busy the past twenty years." She gave me a wink. Then the silver energy around her hand coalesced and shot straight toward me, splashing into my shield with a bright flash of light. Even through the barrier I could feel the heat.

It must have been a signal, because as soon as she resumed the attack, so did the two upstairs. That was problematic. I was drawing energy straight from the ley-line node under the building to power the barrier. The ring allowed me to focus the power and avoid draining my own reserves, but it still took a lot of mental effort. Magic is tiring. And with all three of them attacking my shield—which had reverted to near-opaqueness with the strain—it was only a matter of time before I could no longer maintain it and one of them got through.

Being injured certainly didn't help. Those who have never been badly hurt don't realize how much strength it saps—it was distracting, it was painful, and it was tiring me out much more quickly than I'd have been otherwise. I could just imagine Sam on the other side of the shield, not ten feet away, with that grin on her face and not a care in the world as she casually flung her energy bolts my way until I lost control of the shield.

And there was no one coming to save me. I'd told Lajoie and Connors to wait outside. I could signal them, but that would merely be inviting them to die with me.

But goddamn it, I was Thomas Quinn, Sorcerer of the First Rank of the Arcanum, one of the most powerful human mages on the planet. I had killed demigods and demon princes. I was the last man standing on the Fields of Fire, when I'd ripped the flames from the Earth itself and burned Kigatilik's hordes down around him. Samantha Carr and her companions stood no chance, should I let loose. They'd never even know what hit them until they reached whatever afterlife there may be. It would be so easy just to go deep, to that place the Immortal had showed me, where the whispering voice at the back of my mind lay inviting me to let it loose, to call on the power like I'd done in Canada...

No, I told myself. I wasn't that man anymore. I knew what it meant now. I knew what I'd be doing. I wouldn't do that to save myself. I couldn't do that. I'd rather die.

But then the assault on my shield suddenly stopped, from both directions, as if Sam had sent the other two a signal. As I caught my breath, I heard a noise. Banging on a door downstairs.

"You hear that, Quinn?" Sam called to me. "It seems your cop friends decided to ignore your order to stay put and are trying to charge to the rescue."

Sam must have magically sealed the door behind us—from the sound, the detectives were trying to break the damn thing down.

"I could let them in, you know. See how far they make it. Then you'd have a choice: sit there in your safe shield and watch me kill them, or drop it and kill me first—but then my friends would take all three of you out and be free to finish the rites. And then Connors wouldn't be able to call your precious Rector to stop them. Yeah, I kind of like that idea."

I struggled to control the flash of rage I felt at her casual mention of killing Connors and Lajoie, that voice at the back of my mind urging me to show her what it means to challenge Thomas Quinn to battle.

It wasn't even that I thought of them as friends. I certainly liked them more than most people I knew, but the Hermit Sorcerer didn't have friends. No, what angered me was that Lajoie and Connors were still under my protection, and I took that obligation seriously. I'd brought them in to this world of magic, and I was responsible for their safety in it until I took those bracelets back. I'd be damned if some pissant little Third Rank made me go back on my word.

She was obviously waiting for a response.

"Why are you doing this, Sam?" I asked, my voice weak from the exertion and pain, as the pounding continued downstairs. Having recovered some energy with the pause in the attack, I focused again and made the shield transparent so I could see her. "You're a member of the Arcanum. You swore the same oaths I did, to protect the world of man, to uphold the treaties. To serve."

"Why?" She let out a short, almost hysteric laugh. "Why? I told you the truth about how I discovered I was a sorceress, Quinn. I accidentally killed my parents. I was six! And what did the Arcanum want to do to a scared child who had just lost her mom and dad? What did the Rectors—the Arcanum's official representatives—want to do? They wanted to put me down. Like a rabid dog, Quinn. Do you have any idea what that's like? To have three terrifying men you've never met arguing whether or not you deserve to live? Hours after both your parents just died, and you know it's your fault? Do you think I'd love the Arcanum after that? That I'd be fucking thankful that one chose to spare me?"

She laughed again. "No, Quinn. When I realized what the Arcanum was, how little the Arcanum cared for me, how they'd rather kill a potential problem than help a terrified child, I made a decision. I would learn everything I could from them. And then I would use that knowledge to destroy them in any way I possibly could. Fuck my oaths—my friends helped me break those bonds years ago. I intend to bring everything crashing around the mighty Arcane King and Court while they sit on their high thrones in judgement of us all." She paused to catch her breath. "But I need you to do it. Don't worry, we don't want to kill you. Not yet, anyway. We're under strict orders to make sure you stay alive, but out of the way until we need you."

She giggled as she looked me the eye. I realized with a sinking heart I no longer heard pounding and shouting, just heavy footsteps as multiple people ran up the stairs—she'd already released the door.

"Your choice, Quinn."

Just then Lajoie appeared around the corner on the landing

below Sam. He paused as he saw her, confused, obviously still thinking she was on our side. She winked at me. I watched, almost in slow motion, as she turned and extended her arm toward him, the energy around her hand coalescing. I shouted a warning at Lajoie and threw myself to my right, out of the line of fire from upstairs.

Sam released her attack and I watched it track toward the big Haitian, whose instincts kicked in as he tried to jump out of the way. It caught him on the left arm, but I didn't see the damage, as I was still moving. I dropped the shield and raised my gun into a two-handed grip, squeezing the trigger as I pressed the gun out.

Sam was turning back toward me, that infuriating grin still on her face. I could see a slight shimmer in the air between us: she was anticipating a magical attack and had a shield already prepared. Regardless of what she'd said, she had no intention of dying today.

That was unfortunate for her. The trigger broke just as the front sight lined up with her head. The Glock barked in my hand, impossibly loud in the confined stairwell.

Her shield was almost certainly good enough to have stopped any magical attack I'd thrown at her, at least long enough for her to get out of the way and let her friends distract me. But she hadn't counted on my bullets. She knew about the gun, of course. But our mysterious attacker at the Market, whether it had been Sam herself or one of her friends, hadn't been using a shield when I'd shot them. She didn't know about my custom rounds with the spells bound to them, spells that let them slip right through a variety of magical defenses. And after so many years of practice, my aim was true.

The bullet hit her in the temple and exploded out the other side of her skull in a shower of blood and brain and bone, a pink mist spreading through the air.

What had a millisecond before been the Sorceress Samantha Carr dropped on the stairwell, a lifeless sack of meat and bone. But I'd seen her hit Lajoie. I'd failed to protect him. I was a coward, and I'd let him down. And there were still two threats—I still needed to deal with Sam's friends on the next landing up.

But before I could turn to confront them, I saw a bright flash and was hit by the pressure wave of a large explosion from upstairs. The concussion threw me into the wall. My head struck the concrete, and the world went black.

Chapter 24

I WOKE WITH A GROAN, TRYING TO GATHER MY SENSES. THE taste of copper pennies filled my mouth—I couldn't tell whether I'd bitten my tongue when I fell, or if it was from Sam's blood spattering on me when I shot her. Perhaps both. It didn't matter.

There was a great deal of smoke and heat around me, and I felt water on my face. I opened my eyes and realized I was still on the landing. The building around me was on fire, and the automated fire extinguishers were doing their best. I heard two voices and looked up to see Sam's comrades standing over me, arguing whether they should take me or not. In the background, I heard someone yelling my name.

I realized my gun was no longer in my hand—it must have been knocked out of my grip when I hit the wall. My head was throbbing, but I didn't have time to worry about that. Sam had said they wanted to take me alive, that they needed me for something. I couldn't let that happen.

I turned onto my right hip and kicked out with my left foot, catching the taller of the two in the side of his knee, bringing him crashing down next to me. Before he or his friend had a chance to react, I dove my left hand into my pocket and drew my dagger. Rolling on top of him, I plunged the bronze blade into his throat with a snarl. His eyes were wide with shock as arterial blood sprayed onto my face. His mouth opened, but he couldn't scream with a cut throat.

I immediately pulled the knife free and turned toward his compatriot, who evidently decided discretion was the better part of valor and took off running upstairs.

I looked back at the man under me, watched the life fade from his eyes as his blood spurted from the wound, bubbling and gurgling as he tried to say something. The throat had been a deliberate choice: the carotid artery was a softer target than anything in the head, and cutting his windpipe minimized the chances he could use any magic against me in the remaining seconds of his life. You don't necessarily need to be able to speak to release a spell, but it helps unless you have one prepared and focused in advance.

I used his shirt to wipe his blood off my blade, my hands trembling from the adrenaline, then unsteadily climbed to my feet. Looking around, I spotted the Glock on the stair just below the landing. I sheathed my knife back in its pocket and scooped up the gun. I confirmed the magazine was still seated and there was a round in the chamber, then looked up the stairs where my remaining enemy had fled. But before I could follow him, I realized Connors was still yelling my name.

"Quinn! What the hell was that?! You okay?!"

I couldn't see her. She must be below the next landing down. Not seeing the dwarf upstairs, I made my way down toward her.

I paused and knelt at Sam's body. She'd landed face up, twisting as she'd fallen, still turning left as she'd been at the instant I shot her. The bullet had entered her left temple and exited above her right eye. It was obscene—still beautiful from the eyebrows down, but a gaping hole where the right side of her forehead used to be.

I knew she had been my enemy, that she'd attacked me from behind, that she'd orchestrated the murder of innocents and had hurt Lajoie, maybe even killed him. That her purpose in life had been to destroy my family. I knew all that. And I knew I should hate her for it, but I couldn't.

She'd made her choices. But given my own experiences with the Arcanum, I couldn't think of her as my enemy, as evil. Not really. She was a misguided, angry woman, doing what she thought necessary to bring herself some closure. I'd killed her because I'd had to. And I'd been angry with her at the time, absolutely. But now, looking down on her lifeless form, I just felt sad.

I remembered that awkward date so many years ago. I remembered last night. The comforting touch of her hand. Her lingering kiss. Even if none of it had been real, just lies to gain my trust, it had been what I'd needed right then.

"I'm sorry," I whispered as I bent down and closed her eyes.

"Quinn!" Connors's urgent yelling snapped me back to the present.

"I'm coming," I grunted.

I continued down the stairwell and found her just below the next landing. Lajoie was unconscious on the stairs, his upper torso on the landing itself and his legs down the steps. His left arm was gone from about halfway up the bicep. It wasn't bleeding. It appeared to be badly burned, as if Sam's heat spell had cauterized it with its passing. But even if it hadn't, Connors was tightening the windlass on a tourniquet as high on the stump as she could get it.

"Is it clear?" she snapped as I reached Lajoie's side.

I nodded, then realized she was focused on Lajoie and didn't see. "Yes."

"Good. Can you do anything about the fire?"

I was confused. "Fire?"

"Are you concussed? The goddamn building is burning down, and we happen to be inside!"

I looked around and noticed the flames. I'd forgotten them, somehow. The sprinklers had washed most of the dead man's blood from my face, but they weren't stopping the fire. It must have been magic, the aftereffects of the explosion they'd used to knock me out.

"Oh. So it would seem," I mumbled.

"Can you do anything about it?!" she snapped, but I was already working on it.

It was more difficult to focus than normal—I didn't know if I was concussed, but I was certainly injured and exhausted. I closed my eyes, shut out the world around me, and with some effort managed to tap into the node below. I muttered a couple words and called up a spell that drained the energy from the flames, returning it to the ley-line below. The fire died out within a few seconds.

"Thanks," Connors said as I opened my eyes. "Now help me get him up here onto the landing," she requested as she secured the tourniquet in place.

I heard sirens outside and the sound of doors slamming as I grabbed his legs. She steadied his neck while I swung him around. Given my current state, it was somewhat of a struggle. The big man was heavy.

"Sam's dead," I grunted while I was moving him. "She was one of them. Hit me from behind and her two friends pinned me down from upstairs."

"They dead, too?" she asked, her head still down, checking Lajoie for any other injuries.

"One is. The other ran upstairs after I killed his friend."

She snapped her head up. "When I asked you if it was clear, and you said yes, I thought you meant you'd cleared upstairs."

I shook my head. I was still a little dazed.

"Quinn. Listen to me." I was listening. "No, look at me. Right now." I met her eyes. "I think you have a concussion. But I need you to push through it right now. I've got Henri. There will be a couple dozen cops and paramedics swarming this stairwell in about ninety seconds. I need you to go upstairs. I need you to make sure that an evil sorcerer isn't lying in ambush for them. Can you do that?"

I nodded.

"Can you do that? Say it out loud so I know you heard me." She was cool and collected. This was her element. Her partner might be dying, and a magical explosion had just set the entire building on fire around her, and she was soaking wet from the sprinklers, but she was calm. Whatever else I may say about Connors, that was the moment I knew the Avartagh had been wrong about her. That her fears about herself were wrong. She wasn't unworthy. She was born for this.

"I heard you. I'll be alright. You take care of him."

I made my way back up the stairs. Ignoring Sam's body and that of the nameless man on the landing, I listened over the sound of boots running up from the ground floor. Nothing from upstairs. I slowly made my way up the next flight of stairs, then the next. I was tasting the air in front of me, carefully looking for any sign of an ambush, but it appeared that Sam's surviving compatriot had escaped. I reached the fourth floor. Nothing. I opened the door to the residential corridor. Still nothing.

I holstered the Glock, then headed back down and checked the third-floor corridor the same way. We'd seen the two suspects enter the building carrying someone wrapped in a blanket. I'd hoped whoever it was—presumably their intended sacrifice—was still alive. But when I opened the door to the third floor, I immediately realized that we'd been outmaneuvered in more ways than one.

The blanketed bundle was on the floor in the front of me, and it was in fact a person, but not the intended sacrifice. When I pulled the top layer of the blanket off, I saw it was the corpse of an elderly African-American man, just another innocent bystander with a broken neck.

I made my way down the corridor. There was no actively malevolent feeling like what I'd sensed at the prior murder sites. No one had put effort into keeping it here. But in tasting the magical fields, I knew that dark magic had been done nearby. I followed the energy to an apartment door about halfway down the hallway. The fire hadn't reached this far before I'd extinguished it. The door was ajar.

I stopped tasting the magic around me before entering—in my current state, I wasn't sure I was up to dealing with another ambush spell like at the two previous crime scenes. Then, with a heavy heart, I reached out to push the door open the rest of the way. The smell hit me first. The iron and copper tang of blood. I couldn't see much from the doorway, so I stepped in and made my way down the short hallway to the living room.

It was nearly identical to the previous scenes. The furniture pushed to the sides. The flayed body, dismembered and arranged in the middle of the carpeted floor, with the same terrified expression on his skinless face, eyes bulging and mouth screaming. The bloody glyphs on the walls had begun to streak under the streams of water from the fire sprinklers in the ceiling.

I noticed that the blood pooled on the floor was already well along in the drying process, suggesting this had been done at least the night prior. My estimate must have been off by a few hours. Or perhaps there was a larger window that would work for the purposes of the Tamesis, not as much precision necessary as I'd thought. Whichever it was, Sam would have known that. She'd probably alerted them after she left my shop, and they'd completed the rite while I was sleeping.

The old man in the blanket must have been the apartment's resident, killed so they could use his home for their sacrificial rite, just like the family at the last crime scene. I didn't know which unranked sorcerer I was looking at in the living room, but I'd failed more than just Henri Lajoie today.

I backed up until I was out of the apartment, leaving the door open behind me for the inevitable police responders who would arrive in a minute or two. Almost in a trance, I made my way back to the stairwell, where I could hear a great deal more activity than there had been before.

I descended the stairs, still in a haze, thinking about my many failures. Lajoie. The two dead men upstairs. Their killer who had gotten away. It was too much. I was distracted and unfocused, and almost didn't notice the two police officers on the landing where I'd left Connors with Lajoie.

"Hey, pal! Freeze!" one called to me.

I stopped, noting with curiosity the guns pointed at me.

"Who are you?" he asked.

I shook my head to clear the cobwebs, but they weren't going anywhere.

"Quinn," I grunted. "Where's Detective Connors?"

"Hands. Show us your hands."

They still had the guns out, so I complied.

"Place your hands on the wall, please."

I rolled my eyes but did as he asked. "Where's Connors?" I repeated.

The older-looking patrolman holstered his weapon and stepped toward me. "She's downstairs with EMS," he answered as he began to pat me down. "Said you were clearing the stairwell and we were to wait for you before going up any further."

"I'm carrying a firearm," I warned him before he found it on his own. "Front right waistline."

"Detective Connors told us," he said. "Said you also have a license for it. I'm going to have to confiscate it as evidence for the moment. Sorry."

I grimaced. It wasn't unexpected, but it was annoying nonetheless. My back hurt. My head was still fuzzy. I wanted this to be over.

"Do what you have to do," I muttered as he pulled the Glock from its holster and handed it to his partner, who still had his own gun drawn. At least he'd lowered the muzzle. "There's also a knife in my front left pocket. And my license is in my back right, in my wallet."

He confiscated the knife just like the gun, finished the pat-down, then stepped back to examine my license to carry. I remained braced on the wall until he nodded at his partner and patted me on the shoulder.

"You're good, pal."

I straightened up as the younger officer holstered his sidearm. My back was really starting to throb as the adrenaline wore off. As I turned to face them, a lance of pain shot down my spine. I gasped and stumbled. The one who had frisked me caught me before I fell.

"Hey, you okay?"

I shook my head as I grimaced. "Got hit," I hissed. "Hurts. A lot. But I'll make it."

"What the hell happened here?" his partner asked.

I looked around and saw what he meant. Sam's body, the other corpse just barely visible laying on the next landing up. The bubbled paint, the scorched and blackened walls. I looked back at him.

"It's a long story. On the third floor, fourth door on the right, you'll find a murder scene, plus another body in the hallway. I tried not to touch anything but the door."

Another pair of cops were coming up the stairs, and the younger officer called out to them.

"Hey, this guy needs medical attention. Can you take him down? We've gotta confirm the building is clear and secure the crime scenes."

"Sure," one of the newcomers answered. He looked at me. "Can you walk?"

"Slowly," I nodded.

They escorted me as I painfully made my way down the remaining flights of stairs to the front door. I passed a dozen cops and firefighters in the process, as apparently every patrol car in this part of the city had responded to Connors's call for backup, and the building's fire alarm must have been connected to the closest engine house. A few pushed past us to follow the first two upstairs, others were on the radio. Everyone seemed to have a task.

We stepped outside, where it was more of the same. Lights on patrol cars and a single fire engine flashing, some officers setting up barricades while others kept onlookers at bay, a command and control cell of some sort in the middle coordinating everyone's efforts. My escorts took me toward an ambulance, where Connors watched as Lajoie was loaded in the back by a couple paramedics.

"He got away," I said quietly, my voice harsh.

She looked over at us. "Christ, Quinn. You alright?"

I shook my head. "Not really. Sam hit me hard from behind." The growing pain was starting to make thinking difficult. More difficult than it already was. I needed a nap. And a drink.

She thanked the uniforms for bringing me down, then grabbed the paramedic as they were about to close the back of the ambulance. She pointed at me. "Hey, this guy's going with you. He got hit, don't know how bad it is. Possible concussion."

He looked over at me and saw all the blood on my clothes. "Gunshot?"

I shook my head. "The blood isn't mine. Burn. On my back."

"Alright, let's take a look." He had me turn and take off my coat. From the sharp intake of breath I heard when he saw what was underneath, I could only assume my back was not looking particularly good at the moment.

"Okay, buddy, not gonna lie, that's a bad burn. Between that and the wicked bump on your forehead I don't even know how you've been walking around. We've got another bus en route, they're a couple minutes out. They'll be taking you to the hospital. But in the meantime, we need to keep you from going into shock. Can I get you to sit on the bench here?" he asked, gesturing to the back of the ambulance.

A few minutes later I was sitting down, my shirt cut off, my back covered in gauze, a blanket draped around me, an IV in my left arm, and 5 milligrams of morphine coursing through my veins. It wasn't nearly enough to kill the pain, but at least it took the edge off. I'd have to wait for a doctor before I got anything better. I vaguely heard Connors arguing with someone nearby as I let the opioids work, something about a civilian consultant shooting and stabbing suspects.

By the time the second ambulance arrived and I was loaded up for transport to the hospital, the exhaustion had hit me.

Physically I was tired, but mentally I was just done. Ready to pass into unconscious oblivion and be done with everything.

I'd failed. I'd let my guard down. I'd failed to keep Lajoie safe when he was under my protection. I could have protected him. If I'd been willing, if I'd had the stomach to do it. I could have stopped all three of them before Lajoie even got in Sam's line of fire. And I hadn't. Because I was afraid, and weak.

After Canada, I'd been ashamed of what I'd done. So ashamed that I'd crawled into a bottle and not come out for almost seventy years. So ashamed I couldn't even face one of my closest friends for that entire time.

Now, however, I was ashamed because I couldn't bring myself to do it again. Not even when people were counting on me. I was a coward.

I really needed a fucking drink.

Chapter 25

I WOKE UP CONFUSED.

The last thing I remembered, I'd been in an ambulance on my way to the hospital. But now I was in my bed, at home, Roxana curled up against my side and purring heavily. I was face down, a small puddle of drool on the pillow next to me. Everything was hazy. At first, I thought the past week and a half must have been a strange and highly detailed dream.

Then the memories came flooding back, along with the throbbing pain. I'd passed out in the ambulance and woken at the hospital. There was an almost perfectly circular third degree burn in the middle of my upper back. The doctor had explained they would have to cut out a lot of the dead skin and the pieces of my shirt that had gotten melted into my back, and they'd do the best they could, but I'd likely have some severe scarring. That wasn't a problem. I was used to scars. They were good reminders.

At some point, they'd put me under. My memory went in and out from there, but eventually the treatment was done and the doctors went away, replaced by nurses checking in during their rounds.

The following afternoon I'd insisted I was healed and needed to get home. Not only did I need to get back to work, but I wanted to be in the safety of my own wards and protective spells.

I was injured and vulnerable. It didn't strike me as a good plan to be defenseless in a hospital, with no control over who came and went, when at least one of the people who'd tried to take me was still at large.

The nurse and doctor had protested that I'd experienced severe burns and had just had surgery. I ripped off my dressings to show them my back, which was already mostly healed, and in their confusion, I'd discharged myself. The discharge clerk hadn't overly protested—I didn't have insurance anyway. Besides, the hospital staff couldn't legally keep me against my will once I was conscious and able to make my own decisions. They just weren't happy with my choice.

I'd gone home, checked my wards, eaten everything I could find in my kitchen that didn't require cooking, drunk a healing concoction I had on standby—which would assist my already-accelerated natural healing processes work much faster and more efficiently—then passed out in my own bed.

Checking my wounds in the bathroom mirror, I noted the lump on my forehead had mostly disappeared, the only sign of it a faint yellow bruise. My back hurt, but it was already scarred over. Healing that quickly takes an enormous amount of energy, hence the ravenous hunger and the need for so much sleep. It had worn me out enough that my dreams didn't even wake me, which was a small blessing.

But I was awake now, which meant I got to remember all the things I'd missed and the mistakes I'd made over the previous few days. I grabbed a pair of dirty jeans from the floor, taking a few seconds to slip into them before heading downstairs, a bottle of whisky in my hand. I was finally going to have that drink.

A couple hours later I was distracted by violent banging on the door.

"Quinn!" Connors voice yelled. "Open the fuck up!"

I groaned as I stood and made my way to the door.

"Adrienne," I grunted as I opened it for her.

She pushed in past me without even asking for an invite. "What the hell, Quinn?!"

I was confused. "What?"

"What are you doing home?! You should be in the hospital! And I need to know what the hell happened in that stairwell—the Captain is up my ass for answers I can't give him! You've got some explaining to . . ." She trailed off her angry scolding as she finally took a look at me.

"Jesus Christ, Quinn. What the hell happened to you?"

I looked down, confused, inspecting myself. I wasn't wearing a shirt, just a pair of jeans. But I didn't see any major injuries of which I was unaware.

"I'd expected a burn and some bruises. But the rest . . ."

She apparently hadn't seen my bare torso when the paramedic had been examining and dressing the burn back in Grays Ferry. She'd been busy arguing with someone, I vaguely recalled, meaning she hadn't seen my scars and tattoos before now. I'd lived a long, hard life, which had included quite a number of fights. I hadn't won all of them, and even many of the victories had come at a cost. I looked unassuming when fully clothed, but my flesh bore extensive physical evidence of those experiences.

The faded tattoos had been protective and healing spells at one point, similar to the shield focusing tattoo on the back of my left hand. Some of them still worked, but for the most part the pattern had been broken by a great deal of scarring. That was why I had to supplement my natural healing with a potion, rather than letting the old glyphs do their work. They'd served their purpose but weren't much help anymore.

She stepped to my right side, inspecting, her tirade forgotten in the shock of seeing the marks of my past. She reached out a hand and touched one of the bigger scars, which ran from my right pectoral up over the shoulder, down the ribs on my back to my right hip and below the waistline. It continued down the leg, but she couldn't see that.

"What the hell happened here?"

I just grunted. I had no desire to explain my scars.

"No, Quinn." She took a step back and crossed her arms, her face hard. "You owe me some fucking answers."

I breathed, trying to calm myself. I was tired, I was hurt, I was drunk, and even on my best days I didn't care to discuss my past. It had been a very long time since I'd interacted with people as much as I had over the past week. I'd almost forgotten how, once they knew something about you, they felt entitled to know everything else.

"My story is mine, Detective," I replied, and turned to head back to the corner to resume drinking.

"Jesus Christ, not anymore, you arrogant shit," she snapped.

I was startled and turned back to see her glaring angrily at me.

"Look, I don't care how old you are, or how powerful you claim to be, or what kind of monsters you've fought. In the last few days, I've met with gods and mythical beings. I've seen miracles and magic. I've charged into a building expecting to fight fucking sorcerers with nothing but a handgun, to try to save your ass. And I'm getting really goddamn tired of being treated like a child, only hearing what you feel like telling me when you feel like telling it."

She took a breath and gathered herself but continued before I could reply.

"My partner is lying in the hospital, missing most of his arm, after fighting for his life over the past two days. Your old fling put him there. I'm not saying it's your fault, but goddammit, you've lost the right to keep shit from me. Maybe it's relevant, maybe it isn't, but you don't get to decide—Samantha's history with you was for damn sure relevant, wasn't it? It may well have influenced your judgement about her, and Henri paid the price for it. So I'm done. I'm drawing a goddamn line in the sand, Quinn. You want my help, then you start talking. If not, fine. Have fun stopping these guys by yourself, without me or the Philadelphia Police Department. And I'll go ahead and tell Captain Paulson he can arrest your ass like he already wants to do."

I stared at her for a second or two. She was right. Maybe she'd come to me an ignorant and petulant child. But after everything we'd been through over the past several days, she'd earned my respect. Hell, she was probably the closest thing I'd had to a human friend in decades. Maybe I should start acting like it.

"Okay, Adrienne."

I took a deep breath and thought about memories I'd long been trying to forget.

"It was the Shadow War, one of those pyrrhic victories I mentioned. There were reports of Shadow activity in Cambodia, near Angkor Wat. We went in force to check it out and walked right into an ambush. Hundreds of them, out of nowhere, from every direction. We had to retreat into the temple itself, and they besieged us. For days, we fought off wave after wave. On the third day, a big one got past the main gate. It almost got me before we put it down. That's where I got the scar."

She nodded. "Must have been hell."

I looked away, remembering starving in a dark, blood-soaked temple complex, pinned down by an army of alien horrors, watching my closest friends in the world die all around me, day after day, absolutely certain I was about to join them at any moment. The pain. The hunger. The smell.

"Hell has nothing on it," I murmured.

"How'd you escape?"

"We were trapped for five days. By the end, there were only four of us left, against a dozen or so of them. I was badly wounded. Dying. So Charlotte . . ."

I broke off and took a few deep breaths, struggling to regain my composure.

"She drew their attention so Angelo and Yuri could carry me. She sacrificed herself to save us."

I stopped again. The memory was too wrapped in emotion. It hit me like a sledgehammer, and I choked up. Now the memory was in charge. I couldn't stop the flood if I'd tried. My shoulders sagged and the tears started.

"She died because of me. The only woman I've ever loved died because I wasn't strong enough when she needed me. I failed." I looked back at Connors's eyes, which were growing alarmed and concerned in equal measure. "Just like I failed Henri. That's what I do, Adrienne. I fail people who count on me. It's why I stopped having friends—you can't fail anyone if no one counts on you, right?"

I was babbling. She shook her head angrily and cut in before I could go on.

"No, Quinn. That one's not on you. We went into that stairwell knowing full well what might happen. You don't get to take that from Henri—he made his choices. He's a cop. He's been a cop for a long time. You think this is the first time he's had to make that choice? That he's had to rush into a stairwell in some shithole building, knowing there was a better than even chance some asshole was gonna try his best to put holes in him? No, Quinn. You don't get to claim responsibility for that one. It isn't your burden to bear. If anyone, it's mine—I'm his partner, I was the one who had his back. Hell, I was the one who pushed to go in. But he was the first one up the stairwell for a reason. That's who he is. And I won't let you take that away from him by trying to claim responsibility."

I choked up again. "But I hesitated. I was afraid, and I held back. If I'd only—"

My words came to an abrupt halt when Connors's open left hand slapped me across the cheek. I stood, open mouthed, not believing she had really done that.

I breathed heavily, getting angry. "How dare you, you little—"

Again, I was stopped mid-sentence by a slap across the face.

"How dare I?" she snapped back. "I already told you, you arrogant son of a bitch. Henri owns what happened to him, not you. How about you quit feeling sorry for yourself, and start making his sacrifice count for something?!"

She tried to punctuate her words with another slap, but this time I caught her arm and held on firmly when she tried to pull it back. I looked in her eyes and spoke very quietly.

"Detective Connors, let me make this very clear. If you ever slap me again, you will regret it."

"And," she replied, unflinchingly, "if you don't let go of my wrist, you'll regret it more."

I felt something poke me in the belly and glanced down. She'd drawn her service weapon with her other hand. She stared at me, her nostrils flared, struggling to control her breathing. And I saw clearly what I'd seen in that burned out stairwell. Not many people, having witnessed what she had and knowing what I was capable of, would stand face to face with me and dare me to blink first.

I let go. She holstered her weapon and rubbed her left wrist where I'd clenched it in my hand.

"I . . ." I began, looking away. The words wouldn't come. I swallowed and forced my pride down and met her eyes again.

"I'm sorry." I paused and fought back the emotions threatening to rip their way out.

I turned away from her and walked over to the reading nook, where I sat heavily in an armchair facing her and picked up the near-empty bottle of whisky I'd been drinking before she came in. I drained the rest of it in a single long pull, then looked back at her.

"You wanted me to be honest with you?" I mumbled, "Fine, this is me being honest with you. This is who I am." I gestured to the empty bottle. "I'm a pathetic drunk, and a right son of a bitch, in far more ways than you know. I'm not a good person,

Adrienne. I've killed more people than I can count. Thousands. Tens of thousands, maybe, depending how you want to divvy up credit for a few atrocities. Over the past two centuries, I've committed every sin you can name and a few you've never even imagined. I can't sleep without half a bottle of whiskey to quiet the screams in my head. Thrice now I've had to save the world, and each time it cost more and more of myself. I'm not sure I have much of a soul left anymore. Most every friend I've ever had is dead, some of them by my hands, others because of my failures."

I looked away, remembering, for a few seconds before I continued.

"And here I am, now, being asked to save the world yet again. Wondering what will cost this time. And I'm not sure I'm going to be able to pay the price. That hesitation is why you and Henri were in that stairwell in the first place. That hesitation is what terrifies me so much. So I'm sorry. For everything."

Connors walked over to the reading nook and sat in the other chair, quiet for a long moment as if processing what I'd said. Finally, she nodded and looked me in the eye.

"Quinn, I don't know what the hell you are. I don't know if you're a good man, a bad man, or somewhere in the middle like the most of us, just muddling your way through as best you can. But frankly, I don't care. It doesn't matter. Because you're right: I'm sitting here asking you to help me save the world. That's what we're talking about. This isn't about you, or me, or Henri. It's about the billions of lives that may be in jeopardy if we let these assholes get what they want, whatever it is. And I don't know what the price will be. Maybe your soul. Maybe your life. Maybe mine, too. But I can't do this alone. I need you to help me. If you can't, if the price is too high, I need you to tell me now, so I can find someone who can. I'll call Rachel, or whoever else you tell me to call. You can crawl back into your bottle and leave it to us. I won't think any less of you, I promise. But I need you to tell me right now whether you're up for this."

I spent a long moment in silence, just slowing my heartrate and breathing, getting myself back under control.

She was giving me a way out. I didn't have to do anything but give her a phone number, and I could go back to my life before all of this. It was tempting.

But I couldn't do it. She was right, this wasn't a mere serial killer I could pass off to the Rectors and breathe easy, trusting them to solve the problem without me. And even if they were successful, I'd have given up my home, my privacy, to the Arcanum. That was unacceptable. Spite may not be the most noble of motivations, but it was the one I had available.

"This is my city, Adrienne," I said firmly, meeting her eyes. "I'll be damned if I'm handing it off to the Arcanum. You can call Rachel when I'm dead, and not before."

"Good enough," she nodded. "Don't let me down."

I paused for a moment. "How's Henri?"

"Not good, Quinn. Not good. He lost his arm. They had to amputate further, all the way up to the shoulder. He's critical, but stable, and not awake yet. So while he's still down, fighting for his life, how about you start talking."

I was tired. I needed another drink, but I wasn't up to hunting down a bottle at the moment.

"What do you want to know?"

"For starters," she said, her arms crossed again but her face no longer hard, "what happened in the stairwell? I know the basics. Fill in the details."

I rubbed my temples with both hands.

"Sam was with them from the beginning. I don't know how far back. Maybe as long as I've known her. That would make the most sense, and possibly explain her prior interest in me. Maybe she joined them at some point in the past twenty years. But the fact she came back here shortly before the rites began clearly wasn't a coincidence."

I thought through what had happened, what she'd said.

"As best I can figure, she told us just enough truth to be believable, but she must have altered the ley-line shifts on the map to throw off the timeline. I thought the node wouldn't be in place until that afternoon, but apparently it was there several hours earlier. Time enough for them to conduct the ritual during the night, including killing the old man who lived in the apartment they'd chosen. Sam already knew what I was planning—we talked about it briefly before I sent her away. So she and the other two must have planned a counterambush. She got the other two to enter the building exactly as we expected, even using the old man's body to make us think they had the intended sacrifice with them. When I reached the fourth landing of the stairwell, she hit me in the back. I was trapped between her below me and her partners above. When you two responded, she let you in to draw me out from behind my shield. I shot her, but not in time to save Henri. The two upstairs set off the explosion, some kind of spell; it must have also started the fire. I killed the big one when they came to grab me. The other ran off."

She raised an eyebrow. "Grab you? Why not just kill you?"

"Sam said they were under orders not to kill me, that they needed me alive."

She cocked her head. "Orders?"

"Yes," I shrugged. "At least that confirms I was right that there's someone pulling the strings. Meaning there are at least two left. Maybe more."

"What would they need you alive for?"

I chuckled weakly. "The last sacrifice, I imagine. I doubt they're trying to recruit me. That's why I'm home, and not in the hospital. I'm not sure why they didn't try to take me while I was there—maybe they weren't expecting the first plan to fail and didn't have anyone ready to grab me that quickly—but the longer I stayed, the more likely it was they'd come looking. At home, I'm defended even when I'm in no state to fight."

"Alright," she frowned. "We got outplayed. The question is what do we do now? Can you figure out their next move?"

I thought about it for a minute, my fingers steepled in front of my face.

"Yes," I answered. "Now that I know the actual ley-line shift rate, I can figure out where and when the next sacrifice will be. This time I'll lie in wait from the start, and ambush them myself. Turnabout is fair play. And I won't underestimate them again."

I owed it to Lajoie, and to their other victims, to stop this threat. To make the sacrifice of his arm—and still possibly his life—meaningful, I needed to start acting like the sorcerer I was.

"Okay," she said. "But before that, we've got something to take care of. After we almost burned down an entire apartment complex, the captain has been demanding answers. And thanks to your stunt checking yourself out of the hospital, he's halfway convinced you're involved in the whole thing. Before we can ambush anyone, unless you want to be the subject of a city-wide manhunt, we need to go talk to him. Convince him you're one of the good guys, and even though we fucked up last time, we can still catch these sons of bitches."

I actually smiled and met her eyes. "Okay, Adrienne. Give me an hour to figure out where and when we need to meet the killers. Then let's go convince the captain."

"You can have a little longer than that," she replied, an eyebrow arched. "You should sober up first. And maybe shower."

Chapter 26

THREE HOURS LATER, I WAS SITTING IN A CHAIR OUTSIDE THE office of Captain Gerald Paulson, commander of the Philadelphia Police Department's 16th District. After I'd consulted my ley-line map and made the necessary adjustments, I confirmed that the next attack was going to occur that night, sometime between eight in the evening and two in the morning. I needed to convince the captain that we were his best option to prevent further deaths, and I needed to do so rapidly. After I showered and shaved, Connors drove me to meet him.

"He's liable just to have me arrest you as soon as you're done talking," Connors had warned me on the way over. "It took a lot of convincing just for him to let me come get you instead of sending SWAT."

I'd shaken my head. "He won't." I'd grunted. "Trust me."

She'd looked over at me for a long minute from the driver's seat, presumably trying to figure out what I was up to. She was tired, but she was still sharp, and as soon as she thought she'd put the pieces together she'd breathed in sharply and her nostrils flared.

"Quinn, you are not going to pull some Jedi mind trick on my captain."

"No, Detective Connors. I'm not. The Arcanum frowns on

mind control. I am going to convince him he's better off with me not in a jail cell."

She'd cocked her head. "How on earth are you going to do that?"

"I'm going to talk." I'd left it at that.

She'd still looked wary, but she'd stopped pushing the issue. "I hope you know what you're doing."

Now I was sitting outside his office, while she was in there letting him know I was ready to answer his questions.

She popped her head out. "He's ready for you."

I stood up and walked in as she held the door open for me. Captain Gerald Paulson sat behind a well-organized desk with his name and rank on a placard, just in case I'd missed the sign on the door. He was wearing a light gray suit with a checkered tie. He wasn't old, but clearly well into middle age, the hair at his temples losing its color and the lines on his face already deeply pronounced. His expression was stern, his lips drawn tight—almost identical to Connors's expression the first time we'd met.

"Thomas Quinn?" he asked in a deep voice.

I met his gaze, measuring him up. I had no magical ability to peer into his soul, but centuries of dealing with people had made me fairly skilled at reading them from the outside. This was a man used to authority. He liked things as they were supposed to be. He was a true believer—a cop who'd joined up because he believed in justice and wanted to do what was right.

That was good. It would make things easier.

"I'm Captain Gerald Paulson. Please have a seat. I'd like to ask you a few questions about what happened two days ago in Grays Ferry."

I took one of the open chairs in front of his desk, Connors sitting in the other. But I remained silent for a moment and let the silence fill the room awkwardly, expectantly. This was the game—if I spoke first, he'd be in control. I needed him not to be. Not if I wanted to get out of here in a timely manner. I had to put him on the back foot. And after what seemed like a long moment of rising tension but was probably no more than a few seconds, I won.

"Mr. Quinn, I've got one detective fighting for his life with a missing arm, a half-burned down apartment building, and another detective who can't seem to tell me much of anything useful about how that happened. I've been waiting for you to wake up so you can give me some answers. Now, are you going to cooperate, or do we need to have this conversation in an interrogation room?"

"Captain," I said gruffly, "I've been cooperating with your department for over a week now. I've been trying to help your detectives catch a known serial killer. Exactly when do you imagine I stopped cooperating?"

"Probably around the time you led my detectives into an ambush that almost killed Henri Lajoie. That's when I start to think maybe you've stopped helping us. If you ever were in the first place."

I closed my eyes. Even though I'd known it was coming, I really didn't like being accused of betraying my allies. Especially when said allies were specifically under my protection.

"Captain Paulson," I began to reply, opening my eyes back up and meeting his, "I imagine it's been very frustrating to you that Detective Connors here won't give you any details about what happened in that stairwell. There are two reasons she won't do that. First, she promised me she would keep my secrets, so long as I didn't break any laws. And I've done nothing illegal, so she kept her word. Because she is an honorable person. And a good one, too. But second, and more importantly, even if she were willing to break her promise, she didn't actually know what happened in the stairwell. She literally couldn't tell you what happened. She didn't see it. What happened was between me, Samantha Carr, and the two other suspects. Henri Lajoie was caught in the crossfire because I didn't stop Sam soon enough. Detective Connors didn't get the full story until she asked me a few hours ago."

He raised his eyebrows, inviting me to continue, but didn't interrupt.

"So I'll tell you exactly what happened. And then you're going to let me, and Detective Connors, get back to work."

The Treaty of Tara forbid what I was about to do except in the direst of circumstances. Days ago, I'd agonized about the decision to initiate Adrienne Connors for that very reason. But now I was comfortable claiming that this was the direst of circumstances. I had also now officially been charged with dealing with the situation, earning me the benefit of the doubt on such decisions.

All of which meant the choice was far more straightforward now than it had been days ago—Captain Gerald Paulson was in the way of me stopping an existential threat to all life, and the simplest, easiest option to solve that problem without making an enemy of the entire Philly PD was to convince him he was better off letting me go, and in fact better off helping me with what I needed to do.

"For a week now," I explained matter-of-factly, "your Detectives and I have been trying to stop an unknown number of sorcerers intent on building power for a potentially world-ending magical ritual, by murdering other sorcerers. While you believe I'm only a consultant, in point of fact I've been deputized to end this threat by the highest authority on magical law enforcement in human society."

Paulson's eyes narrowed as he tried to figure out whether I was making this up or merely insane. But I continued.

"In that stairwell, I was trying to trap our suspects. Instead, Samantha Carr, who I'd believed to be an ally, was working with them, and they trapped me instead. She attacked me from behind while I was focused on the threat to my front, hence my current injuries. She then lured your detectives upstairs and was able to injure Lajoie before I could stop her. I killed her, then killed one of her associates when they came to kidnap me. The other one ran away."

His eyebrows were now raised almost comically high as he looked at me skeptically. Dismissively. "Are you done, Mr. Quinn?"

"Yes, I am."

"Okay." He glanced back at Connors, who was stony-faced and avoiding looking directly at either of us. He reached up and rubbed his temple with his right hand. "Let's pretend any of that made even the slightest bit of sense. What was the explosion that caused the fire?"

"Magic. The two unnamed sorcerers set it off to knock me out so they could capture me alive."

He shook his head. "Magic, huh? Yeah, okay, buddy..."

"Yes, Captain Paulson," I interrupted, my voice deadly serious. "Magic."

I locked eyes with him. Then I slowly stretched one hand out between us. And while I wasn't willing to perform on demand for Lajoie in my shop, or for Connors in Aengus's tent, this time I was in a hurry. As I continued to hold eye contact, I focused for a brief instant, and lightning burst into existence around my hand.

He jumped back.

"Holy shit!" His hand was halfway to his gun before he caught himself and realized he wasn't under attack.

I hadn't told Connors what I was planning, but she'd apparently figured it out and hadn't even flinched. She looked at me and smiled faintly as blue bolts of electricity continued to wreath my arm halfway to the elbow. I shifted my gaze and met her eyes, then winked before returned to look at the Captain. Who was now staring wide-eyed at my hand, a look of mixed horror and curiosity on his face.

"... How?" he finally managed to gasp out.

"I told you." I cupped my hand and drew the electricity into a ball, then willed it to rise several inches so it was between our faces, the heat on his skin, and forced his eyes to meet my solemn stare as I let it wink out of existence. "Magic."

He continued to stare at me, slack jawed, for another moment or two before he shook himself and tried to regain his composure.

"Captain, I am a sorcerer." I spoke very clearly and deliberately. "I am a high-ranking member of a secret magical society that has existed, hidden among humanity at large, for well over a thousand years. Your detectives have known this for days, since I took them through a portal to the homeland of the Faeries and they met multiple beings they'd always believed to be myths. They did not tell you, because they were warned of the potential consequences of revealing these truths to the uninitiated. I have been working with them to solve this case, under official orders from the Lord Marshal of the Arcane Court, because I believe those responsible are attempting to conduct a potentially catastrophic magical rite, and we have very little time to stop it. That's the only reason I am telling you this now. Because I don't have time to try any other options."

I paused to let him process all that.

"It's true, Captain," Connors added. "All of it. You can ask Lajoie once he wakes up, too."

He gulped. "This is crazy! This can't be real!"

"I know." She shrugged. "But it is. And right now, that man right there," she gestured to me, "is the only weapon we have to stop the bad guys."

He looked like a trapped animal, switching his astonished gaze back and forth between the two of us. I just stood there, my eyebrows raised, my arms crossed.

He met my eyes and gulped again. "How can this be real?"

"I don't know," I told him. "But it is, nonetheless. Do you need further proof?"

Without waiting for a reply, I waved my hand and murmured, and Captain Paulson began to levitate out of his chair before he knew what was happening, slowly rising into the air above his desk.

"What the fuck?!" he barked. Fortunately, he didn't go for his gun this time. Maybe he was too shocked to think about it. Regardless of the reason, it was helpful—I didn't want to have to restrain him as well.

I shrugged. "In case you thought my first demonstration might have been an illusion. As you can feel yourself, this is no trick of smoke and mirrors and misdirection. Don't worry, I'll put you down now."

I waved my hand again and he returned to his seat, the arms of which he gripped tightly as if he were prone to floating away again at any moment. After a long few seconds of heavy breathing, he looked back at me and met my eye.

"How many of you . . . sorcerers . . . are there?"

"More than you'd think. Not enough to take on all of humanity if they decide we're a threat."

"Do sorcerers secretly control society or something?"

I grunted. "No, not for the most part. Normal humans muck things up plenty on their own. Mostly we keep to ourselves and protect humans from dangerous things."

"What kinds of dangerous things?"

I raised an eyebrow. "Magical serial killers trying to cause the apocalypse, for example."

He stared at me for a second, then nervously chuckled. "Yes, I suppose that would qualify as dangerous." He closed his eyes for a few moments, apparently thinking over the things he'd just seen and experienced.

"Captain Paulson," I said seriously, "I need you to trust Detective Connors's judgement and accept that we're on the same side. And then I need you, and Philadelphia PD, to help us kill or capture the people doing this. We don't have much time until the next attack. We're running out of chances to end this before it's too late."

He looked at Connors. "You trust him?"

She looked at me and, after a moment's consideration, nodded. "I do, Captain. He can be a grumpy son of a bitch, and he's still got too many secrets for my comfort, but I believe he's on our side. And after the shit I've seen the past few days, I can pretty much guarantee we're not going to stop these bastards without him."

He sighed. "This is . . . a bit much. But either I'm going crazy, or I have to trust you know what you're doing. I don't suppose there's much choice anyway—I don't think we've got a cell that can hold sorcerers or X-Men or whatever the hell he actually is." He paused and rubbed his temples. "You're responsible for him, Adrienne. Don't let him blow up any more buildings, please. At least, none with people in them."

Chapter 27

WE ONLY HAD A FEW HOURS. AFTER DISCUSSING THE NEXT STEP with Captain Paulson and figuring out what police support we'd need, Connors drove me back to my shop to make my preparations.

"Oy, Sorcerer!" a heavily Irish-accented voice called as I stepped from her car onto the sidewalk outside my shop. I snapped my head up, half expecting to need to defend myself from a threat, to see Bran's thin frame step out of the alleyway. He was wearing the enchanted tunic he wore when shapeshifting. It wasn't very stylish, but it let him transform back into a human without being awkwardly nude—normal clothes didn't make the transition with him. Presumably he'd been waiting for me in hawk form and had ducked into the alley to change back.

"Bran," I grunted, my heart slowing as the initial adrenaline rush wore off. "Hasn't anyone told you it's dangerous to sneak up on sorcerers?"

I tapped my hand on the car roof to let Connors know I was clear of the vehicle, and she drove off to make her own preparations for what was to come that evening.

"I got your message. Found out summat tha' might be of interest. Can we talk inside?"

I nodded and checked around before unlocking the shop and passing through to the safety of my wards. Bran followed me in, and I locked up behind us, waving him over to the reading nook.

"Whisky?"

"Aye, if ye are offerin'," he nodded.

I ducked into the back room and grabbed a bottle and my two cleanest—least dirty, really—glasses before heading over to join him. Once we both had something to drink, I waved a hand for Bran to start talking.

He took a long sip. "Heard rumors the other day about some kind of cultists or summat settin' up in town. Supposedly got here a few weeks back. After I got the message ye left, I asked 'round and the word was they're some Roman cult. But when the local revivalists went to introduce themselves, they got the cold shoulder. Didn't want nothing to do with 'em."

I nodded. "That sounds like the group I'm looking for."

"Aye," he drank down the rest of his whisky in a single gulp. "Thought so. They were up in Conshy at first, tha's where the revivalists went to see 'em. Didn' stay long, though—no one seems to know where they are now. But Quinn," he paused and looked back at me, "rumor is these fuckers are serious. No playin'. Those two sorcerer murders last week were apparently sacrifices to whatever Olympian they serve."

"And that's why I'm looking for them," I growled. "Any word on how many of them there are, or who they serve?"

"Me revivalist source said he saw eight or nine a' the place in Conshy when they went a-callin'. An' there was a symbol, looked like a key, scratched into the doorframe."

"Janus," I muttered. He had many symbols. Most prominent was a head with two faces, one looking forward and the other back, but the key and the staff were also common, and somewhat easier to carve into a wooden doorframe.

"I hope it was useful," Bran said, standing. "I need to be gettin' back to me pub."

I just grunted.

"Why, thank ye, Bran! Excellent work, Bran! Ye have yerself a lovely day, Bran!" the púca muttered to himself in a singsong voice.

I looked at him silently and raised an eyebrow.

"Fine, Sorcerer," he snorted. "I will just put this bit o' work on your tab, then."

I locked up after he let himself out. I'd think about what this meant while I got ready for this evening's events.

Bran's information had confirmed the group behind the current Tamesis rites were most likely cultists of Janus. That didn't change the immediate plan, though I now needed to be sure I was ready for more than a couple enemies to show up at the target house—they'd lost two-thirds of their team the last time they faced me, and they had to suspect I'd be trying to stop them once again. They'd likely come in force. If there were nine at their original base in Conshohocken, that meant there were at least seven left. Possibly more, if Bran's source hadn't seen everyone they had.

The smart play was to call Rachel and request backup. I could probably handle seven cultists, even including a Faerie, but if there were significantly more than that, or if Janus himself showed up, things could rapidly get out of hand. I only had one weapon that could kill a Faerie that powerful, and I'd already been too cowardly to risk using it in Grays Ferry, when my life and those of my companions had been on the line. Without it, I would be in trouble.

But I couldn't bring myself to make that call. I knew I should. But I couldn't ask the Arcanum for help, especially given the last fellow sorcerer I'd asked for help had literally shot me in the back, mere days before. Rachel wasn't a bad sort, as far as they go, but I didn't really know her except in passing, and after so long distrusting the Arcanum in general, I couldn't bring myself to trust another member so soon after Sam's betrayal.

Like I'd told Connors, the Rector would be free to try to fix the mess I left behind should I fail, but I refused to ask her, or anyone else in the Arcanum, to fight beside me. Not again. No matter the stakes. While I drew breath, this was my city, which made it my fight.

I headed upstairs to dress for battle. Over a simple black T-shirt, I pulled on a Kevlar vest, and over that went my overcoat, which had been undamaged despite the heat spell's effects bleeding through. My ring would once again serve as a focus for any shield spell I needed to cast. I wanted as much armor as I could reasonably get, both magical and otherwise.

My Glock was unavailable, in a police evidence locker, but for this particular fight it would be underpowered anyway. As a general rule, pistols are too small to do much damage, and people carry them only because they're much more concealable and portable than other options. This evening, I wasn't terribly worried about concealment. Pistols are "just in case" weapons, and I was pretty certain I was going to get in a fight this evening, so I upgraded my primary weapon of choice. I unlocked the trunk at the foot of my bed and pulled out a Vepr-12.

The Vepr is a magazine-fed shotgun modeled on the Kalashnikov series of rifles and machine guns, much like the more famous Saiga. Unlike the Saiga, it comes standard with a chrome lining, which makes it ideal for work around corrosive substances like those often found in magical confrontations—the same reason I Cerakoted my pistols. Also unlike the Saiga, it's able to accommodate most 12-gauge loads without having to adjust the gas system, making it useful for those of us who have to customize their loads to the task at hand. You really can't simply use the same shotgun loads for the Fae as you'd use for demons. If the Vepr had been invented in time for the Shadow War, I suspected more sorcerers would have become firearm enthusiasts.

My specific model was a fully automatic military variant with a compact barrel, perfect for confined spaces. For this fight, I loaded three magazines with double-aught magnum anti-Fae shells. I didn't know if I'd actually be facing any Faeries, but that load would work just fine for humans, too. One magazine went in the gun. The spares went into a belt holster on my left hip.

I decided thirty-six rounds of double-aught magnum buckshot wasn't a comfortable enough margin against seven or more enemies, so from the same trunk I also pulled out my old stainless-steel Colt Delta Elite as a backup weapon. The Model 1911 Series 80 wasn't the first ten-millimeter gun ever, but it was the one that popularized the caliber for a large audience. I'd christened this one Moses, after John Moses Browning, and had carried it for almost three decades before switching to the Glock, with its useful aftermarket modifications and higher magazine capacity. Moses only held eight rounds, plus one in the chamber, but they were still my custom bullets. I tucked a spare magazine into a carrier on my belt just behind the two for the Vepr.

I also retrieved my Smith and Wesson J-frame, loaded it up with five rounds of a similar custom design, and tucked it into an ankle holster on the inside of my left leg. Between the Vepr, Moses, and the J-frame, I should have enough rounds to deal with whatever came through the door. If not, then I supposed I'd have to resort to fireballs and lightning bolts after all.

I briefly considered grabbing the kukri from the same box, since my dagger was in the evidence locker with the Glock. The kukri, the legendary combat knife of Nepal's Gurkha warriors, was much larger than the dagger, boasting a twelve-inch steel blade bound with powerful enchantments against dark magic—it had been a gift from Charlotte, to use against the Shadows. After a moment, however, I decided it was too big if it came to hand-to-hand fighting in a confined space like a house. Instead I grabbed a clinch pick, as small knife specifically designed for close quarters, clipping it to my belt to the left of the buckle.

I fed Roxana and headed downstairs to wait with the rest of that bottle I'd been sharing with Bran. I had no intention of getting drunk, just taking some of the edge off. I could think clearer when the screams in my head quieted down, and I'd need to be able to think as clearly as possible this evening. I poured myself a glass and started mentally running through the plan, visualizing what would happen when the shooting started.

With the knowledge of the third ritual's location, I had had enough data to pinpoint the exact address of the next rite, a three-story row house in Pennsport, a few blocks south of the Mummers Museum. Connors had gotten me a layout of the house when we were still at the district station, courtesy of some city department. Now I tried to imagine what might go wrong and figure out contingencies. I mentally mapped out the house so I'd know where to go if it turned into a running fight—upstairs, downstairs, the back door. Most gunfights last less than a minute, but I wanted to win, and I didn't know how many enemies I'd be fighting. I didn't care to be surprised again, like I had in that stairwell. For two hours, I rehearsed the fight in my head over and over, in every possible variation I could imagine.

When Detective Connors walked into the shop to pick me up, I was waiting in the reading area, my overcoat draped over the back of the chair next to mine. I downed the remaining whiskey in my glass and stood to face her. She froze, observing the body armor and the Vepr in my hand. After a moment to take it all in, she cocked an eyebrow at me.

"What is that, an AK-47?"

"Military grade automatic shotgun. Smuggled in from Russia."

She paused as that registered. "You know that's . . . super illegal, right? Like, major felonies. Multiple. State and Federal."

I looked down at it, then back up at her. "Yes," I grunted.

"Well . . . okay then."

I threw on my overcoat and nodded toward the door. "Let's go kill these bastards. You can try to arrest me later if you want."

Chapter 28

BY HALF-PAST SEVEN, I WAS SITTING IN A RECLINER IN THE TARget house's living room.

In Captain Paulson's office, after he'd accepted the things I'd revealed to him, the three of us had agreed that it was best not to have other cops directly at the scene. Not only would it pose a greater chance of tipping our hand and giving the initiative to the enemy, it also didn't add much value to justify the risk. I didn't have enough ammunition for more cops, we didn't have time for my source to make more, and regular bullets were unlikely to do much against magical defenses. Any tactical team members rushing in to confront the suspects would just become more victims.

Instead, Captain Paulson arranged to have backup available within a thirty-second drive, but to keep the area around the target house clear until they received an all-clear signal. He also enforced another public works evacuation, trying to minimize any collateral damage. Fortunately for our plan, enough families in the area apparently owned two cars that it still looked like plenty of people were home. It wouldn't do for the enemy to realize the trap was set before they walked into it.

That left Connors and me taking on the enemy all by our lonesome. And Connors wasn't equipped to confront them directly.

As at Grays Ferry, she'd be armed with my ammunition for self-defense if necessary, but her job would be to observe and make one of two calls: either to our backup to secure the scene and treat injuries, or to Rachel Liu.

If she were making the latter call, it meant I was dead. I'd made her promise that this time, no matter what, she would not run in, gun drawn, to try to save me. I couldn't afford two detectives on my conscience. Henri Lajoie was still in the ICU. I'd already accepted I was on my own, come what may.

Last time, we'd tried to catch the killers before they reached their target. That plan hadn't worked, and two men had died. This time we were going to be more straightforward. Connors would remain outside, and I would ward her car so she'd be unnoticed and defended in my absence. Meanwhile I would be waiting inside, glamoured to look like the middle-aged Latino man who owned the home. I'd be both bait and trap in one.

I sat in the recliner in the living room with the Vepr across my lap. This being a row house, the living room had no windows—it was connected to the front door by a hallway and the back door was through the kitchen. The front and back doors were locked. I didn't expect it to pose much of an obstacle, but at least it would mean I'd know which door they were coming in as they took the time to open it. I'd already confirmed that the layout I'd used for planning had been accurate, and I'd carefully checked the whole house to make sure nothing would surprise me if it became a mobile fight. I'd memorized where all the furniture was and moved things as necessary—it would be somewhat embarrassing to be killed because I tripped over an unexpected stool at a critical moment.

Whether they came through the front or back, they would have to enter the living room to deal with the homeowner before the sacrifice. I didn't expect my illusion to last long against sorcerers and Faeries. But a few seconds is a lifetime in a fight, and it would give me the advantage—only fools and competitive athletes fight fair. I'd neutralize as many as I could before they had time to react, then withdraw to either the kitchen or the front hallway and reassess if there were any threats remaining. I had no desire to retreat upstairs to the bedrooms and back myself into a corner with no escape. And I'd have to be careful not to hurt the sacrificial victim they were likely to bring with them.

Unless they left me no choice, I wasn't planning on killing all of them—I wanted to capture at least one if at all possible. Killing the foot soldiers would stop the immediate threat of the Tamesis, but we'd leave the real threat out there to regroup and try something else down the road. Someone was behind this whole plan, pulling the strings and giving the orders. Bran's evidence pointed to Janus and the Olympians, as the Immortal had suggested, but I needed further confirmation before I could rely on Lugh to act.

The radio squawked next to me, bringing me back to the present. "I've got eyes on approaching suspects," Connors said. Finally. I was anxious to get this show on the road. The anticipation was worse than the actual fight.

I reached for the radio to acknowledge, but before I could key the mic, Connors spoke again.

"Looks like they're rolling heavy. I count six headed your way."

Six was within expectations; I'd been prepared for seven or eight. To get to where I waited in the living room they'd have to filter through the front hallway or the kitchen door, so I'd be facing no more than two or three at a time. I'd have to spring the trap before the first few caught on to my glamour, meaning I wouldn't get all of them with my first burst, but at least I wasn't short on ammunition.

"Understood," I replied. "Six approaching. How far out?"

"Three houses down. Maybe a minute until they're at the door."

"Do they have a victim with them?"

"One of them is carrying a duffel bag. Looks big enough to fit a person, but from the way he's carrying it, it doesn't seem heavy."

"That could still be the victim. Magic can make weight easy to handle, same as I levitated Captain Paulson this afternoon. Thanks, Adrienne. I've got to greet our houseguests. I'll see you on the other side."

"Good hunting," she answered, then the radio went silent.

I heard the lock on the front door click just before the door opened, followed by the sound of footsteps on the hardwood floor.

"You three go take care of the guy and get the living room ready," one of my guests instructed someone else in a low male voice with a harsh accent. I guessed he was from Chicago originally. "You two keep an eye out for Quinn. I'll get him prepared."

I heard a zipper opening, presumably the speaker retrieving their intended sacrifice from the duffel bag, just before multiple feet started tromping in my direction.

From the recliner I had an easy view of both doorways into the room: the entrance from the front hall, and the arched passageway into the kitchen. While sitting in the open isn't the ideal way to start a fight, my trap required fooling the enemy into thinking I was an innocent victim long enough for them to enter the room with me. Had it just been two or three of them, I could probably have risked knocking them unconscious without having to kill anyone. But with six, I decided it would be prudent to cut down the odds against me before trying to take any prisoners. The three whom the voice had just sent to the living room were about to have a very unpleasant lesson in the hazards of joining evil death cults.

I readied the Vepr in my lap, my hand on the pistol grip, finger registered on the frame above the trigger well. It wouldn't very well do to accidentally shoot myself in the process of getting out of the chair when things started happening. My left arm was extended to the side of the chair, my hand hovering palm down, ready to activate the spell at the heart of the trap.

The first of the group came into my sight in the doorway. He was wearing a hoodie, and I couldn't see his face in the shadow it cast. He was tall enough to be Aes Sidhe, though I still had no idea about what type of Faerie was helping them with the rituals. He paused for a brief second, scanning the room. Unless he were tasting the magic in the room, he wouldn't notice my glamour immediately, and I'd appear to be a middle-aged Latino man asleep in his recliner. For a few critical seconds, that is; the spell wouldn't hold up to close scrutiny once he was further into the room. But I didn't need it to. I just needed him to take a few more steps.

He obliged. After a second's hesitation, he strode forward into the room, clearing the entrance for his comrades. Two more came in behind him before he froze and looked in my direction.

"Wait a min—" I heard him start to say.

That was my cue. I tripped the spell and felt magical energy instantly spring around the feet of the three in the room with me, paralyzing them in place. The others back in the hallway apparently felt it, and I heard some confused remarks from that direction. I ignored it for the moment, as I needed to deal with the three I could see while I had the chance, and before they could react—the spell only trapped them in place, it didn't immobilize them completely.

I stood and raised the Vepr to a firing position, dropping my concentration on the glamour to focus on the task at hand. I lined up the red dot of the automatic shotgun's close-combat optic on the upper chest of the closest target and pressed the trigger. Three rounds fired in rapid succession before I released it, and his chest erupted in a shower of red blood. So much for Faeries in body armor. I didn't pause to contemplate the fragility of flesh and bone under the effects of double-aught shotgun pellets at close range. I had other targets demanding my attention.

I turned to the next two just as they started to raise their hands to defend themselves. It doesn't matter how magical you are, your brain still takes a half-second or more to process unexpected threats and tell your muscles to react appropriately. And these gentlemen had clearly not been expecting an ambush with an automatic shotgun. They were behind the power curve, only just now realizing they needed to react. Considering they'd been intent on murdering at least two people this evening, I didn't feel the slightest bit of pity.

They were standing next to each other, practically touching at the shoulders, so I simply placed the red dot on the chest of the one on the left, pressed the trigger, and dragged the bucking barrel of the Vepr to the right.

It's a common misconception that shotguns spray a cone of deadly pellets, killing anything in front of the barrel like a miniature Claymore mine. In fact, at short ranges the pellets don't spread very far at all, maybe an inch or two at the distance I was shooting. But eight rounds flew toward the two of them in less than a second. At fifteen pellets per shell, I'd just sent 120 ball bearings their way at 1200 feet per second, and even on full auto my aim was fairly good—both collapsed as their torsos broke and shattered. Neither would be committing any more blood sacrifices any time soon.

Yet my work wasn't done. My ambush had taken care of half of my enemies, but that left three more in the hallway who presumably wouldn't be pleased with what I'd just done to their friends. And for my part, I still only needed one of them alive at the end of the fight.

I stepped to the side, out of the line of fire of anyone in the hallway, hitting the Vepr's magazine release with my thumb and ripping out the empty magazine while I moved. I reached back, grabbed a spare magazine from its pouch behind my hip, inserted it into the mag well, and hit the lever releasing the bolt just as the next bad guy entered the room, shouting in rage and confusion.

He saw me, and we raced: his hand was outstretched with a ball of energy forming, moving to aim toward me as I was bringing the Vepr back into a firing position to drop him like his friends. I fired at him and he released his spell at me almost simultaneously.

I watched, almost in slow motion, as the silvery heat spell melted my shotgun pellets in mid-air and continued streaking toward me. I'd continued stepping sideways as I fired, so the blast of heat struck the end of my barrel and carried on to the wall behind me but missed my left hand by an inch. I felt the searing heat, and knew I'd have another severe burn to deal with later, but I was spared the damage of a direct hit.

Unfortunately, a quick glance showed me the Vepr was clearly out of the fight, its barrel melted to slag. I dropped it and immediately moved to draw Moses, still sidestepping to my left. The race was back on, my foe gathering another heat spell as my hand closed around the Delta Elite's familiar grip. I drew it out of the holster and up into a good two-hand grip, pressing out to full extension, flipping off the thumb safety and pressing the trigger on the way.

The first shot broke just as I saw the sights line up on my target's head, and this time I'd won the contest. His head jerked back under the impact of the ten-millimeter round right as he released his spell. The spasm sent his heat blast wide, missing me by several feet as my follow-up shots hit him in the nose and cheek before he fell to the floor.

Before anyone else could come into the room, I focused on my ring and threw up a shield between me and the hallway. With a moment of respite, I retreated to the kitchen and took quick stock. With the Vepr gone, I had six rounds of ten-mil left in Moses, another eight rounds in the spare magazine, and the J-frame with five rounds, plus one burned hand. Against two remaining enemies, including the short one who'd escaped the stairwell, so I had to assume he was also armed with that same heat spell the other had been using. That seemed to be these cultists' favored weapon.

Yet neither of the two enemies left had attacked my shield or moved to enter the living room at all. That in itself wasn't odd—if I'd just seen four of my friends get ambushed and killed, I wouldn't be in a hurry to rush into the same spot it had happened, either. But I also didn't hear them talking in the hallway, which was more ominous. It could mean a number of things: perhaps they'd split up, or maybe they were using sign language to hide their plans from me. Hell, they might even be telepathic. Whatever it was, I couldn't just hide in the kitchen behind my shield and hope they came to me. I couldn't afford to let them escape and regroup. If they weren't going to come to me, I'd have to go to them.

Just as I was thinking about how little I wanted to do that, a voice called out, saving me the headache.

"That was a nasty trick, Quinn!" a deep male voice with a harsh Chicago accent shouted. Same voice who'd given the instructions when they first entered. "Not exactly a fair fight to lie in ambush like that!"

I shook my head at the ridiculousness of that statement.

"A fair fight like ganging up on lone sorcerers and murdering them? Or a fair fight like snapping innocent civilians' necks because they happened to be in your way? Or perhaps you mean a fair fight like Sam hitting me from behind in the stairwell?"

The man laughed loudly. "Good point, Quinn! So how about we all stop with the sneaky bullshit and finally have that fair fight after all?"

I rolled my eyes. "There are two of you and only one of me, friend. Still not very fair odds."

"Please," he called. "You? Thomas Quinn? Who just took out four trained sorcerers in thirty seconds? Against two measly nobodies no one's ever heard of? Surely you must be joking! Why are you even piddling around with this bullshit, the kind of power you've got?! You could burn us where we stand, no sweat, and you're hiding in a kitchen with a popgun!"

"If you believe that," I asked back, "why are you still here? You had to know after the stairwell that I'd catch up to you lot. And no one figured it might be an ambush?"

There was a pause, then an ominous chuckle.

"Figured? Hell, we counted on it! Sam told you we needed you, didn't she?"

Shit. What were they up to?

I willed myself to relax, then reached out to taste the magic around me. I felt something massive building up in the hallway, just in time for me to reinforce my shield as they released it my way. I was still tasting when it hit, and the collision of the two spells was overwhelming to my magical senses.

I reeled under the impact—I felt like they'd just shot a cannon at my shield, and I was staring down the muzzle right as it flashed. I wasn't blind, but I was disoriented as hell. And my shield was devastated. I stopped tasting and dropped the focus as the ring seared my finger with residual energy. I awkwardly ripped it off with the thumb of my right hand, which was still holding Moses.

I looked up to see one of the attackers charging at me, the big man with whom I assumed I'd just been exchanging barbs, screaming in fury as he leapt over the bodies of his comrades in the living room and rushed toward the kitchen. I didn't have time to aim properly, and fell backwards to the floor, instinctively drawing my firing hand back against the side of my chest. As I hit the ground he was right on top of me, his arm drawn back ready to strike. I saw the glint of a blade in his hand. I pressed the trigger rapidly, getting off four shots before his body slammed into mine.

Many people think you can't miss at that range. Point blank, it's called. The sad truth is it happens all the time—people wildly jerk their trigger fingers under the stress of moment, or their guns aren't pointed where they think, and the rounds go wide even though the target is only a couple feet away. But by locking my firing hand to the side of my chest, I ensured the muzzle was aimed generally in front of my torso, and that was good enough when my target was in the process of tackling me. All four rounds hit their mark.

Unfortunately, even a ten-mil is just a pistol round, and unless it hits the central nervous system, it's unlikely to cause instant death. Or so my mind reminded me, in an oddly clinical and detached manner, as he still had plenty of strength to slip his blade inside the edge of my coat and stab it down into my left upper chest.

Someone was screaming. After a second or two, I realized it had to be me, as my attacker had lost his ability to do so after I'd instinctively pulled my clinch pick and jabbed it into the side and back of his neck several times.

I'd been injured many times before, as my scars attested: claws, burns, stabbings, bites, broken bones, and more. But it doesn't matter how many times you repeat the experience; the sensation of a ten-inch steel blade impaling your chest cavity never gets any less painful.

I bit off the scream with a pained grimace and tried to move, to push the rapidly exsanguinating corpse off me, only to scream again. I was pinned to the kitchen's laminated floor by the blade's tip extending out my back. Moving just twisted the knife around. Between the pain, my disorientation and physical exhaustion, and the weight of the body lying on top of me, there was no way I was going anywhere. I lay there, gasping from the combination of pain and exertion, and possibly a pierced lung, and I heard heavy footsteps approaching.

At the angle I was pinned under my attacker's body, I couldn't see the last surviving cultist until he stepped into the kitchen around his comrade. It was the short one. With his hood down, I could see that he was some kind of sprite. Sprites were a variety of Low Fae, so perhaps he was the one responsible for the traces of Otherworldly magic I'd sensed at the crime scenes. It certainly made more sense than an Unseelie Aes Sidhe joining an Olympian cult, at least.

In his hand was a stout wooden club. He looked down at me for a second, his eyes cold, then without a word slammed the club into my head and the world went black.

I came to, blinking my eyes against the sudden bright light. I immediately noted four things. First, I was definitely no longer in the kitchen. From the wallpaper, I appeared to have been moved upstairs to the master bedroom. Second, all the furniture had been moved from the room. I wasn't sure where the bed went or how my diminutive captor had removed it (*magic, idiot,* a small voice mocked from the back of my mind), but the room was empty other than myself. Third, I was stark naked. And fourth, I was staked to the hardwood floor, spread-eagled with what appeared to be an iron spike through each hand. I couldn't see my feet, but I assumed he had used similar spikes for them as well.

I was in surprisingly little pain. I wasn't sure if that was just temporary from the grogginess, or if I was starting to go into hypovolemic shock from the chest wound. But while I was a little chilly (I was naked, after all), my hands and chest were just throbbing dull pain, much like I'd been given a decent painkiller. I certainly wasn't complaining, but it probably wasn't a good sign for my immediate health prospects. Even if my captor didn't kill me, I'd likely bleed out before any help arrived.

I didn't see the sprite at first. For a long moment, I was alone with my own hazy and confusing thoughts. Between the concussion and the blood I felt still oozing from my chest cavity, my mind was operating at somewhat less than peak capacity. At least the knife remained in place, so it wasn't a sucking chest wound, collapsing my lungs under steadily building pressure. It was just bleeding. It could be worse, I supposed. But in my groggy state, the sound of footsteps echoing around the empty room was disorienting, and I couldn't triangulate where he was until he came into my field of view.

He no longer held the club. He'd replaced it with a small, silver, rather old-looking knife. From the shape of the blade, I knew immediately that it held only one purpose: flaying the skin from an animal. Or a person.

"You are awake," he observed in an odd accent that I couldn't quite place. He didn't have the wickedly sardonic smile of a Hollywood evil villain about to explain his plan to the plucky hero. In fact, his face was expressionless. Almost bored. I'd expect at least some anger at the fact I'd killed five of his friends downstairs, but honestly, it didn't appear as if he cared in the slightest about any of it. His dead comrades, me, the task at hand. He was mechanical and aloof. What was that about, I wondered?

I tried to answer, but all that came out was a hoarse croak.

"No, Mr. Quinn. Do not try to speak. There is no point. You have nothing to say to me. At least, nothing that matters. I was not awaiting your consciousness for a conversation. No, I just needed you awake because this process is far more powerful when you are in pain. And when you are afraid." He stepped closer and held the blade up. "I am going to peel the skin from your flesh, Mr. Quinn. Normally my subjects are suspended from a hook for this, but you happen to have killed all my taller companions. No matter. I will cut away the front half; the back half I will then rip out from under you like a waiter pulling a tablecloth. It is going to hurt, Mr. Quinn. A lot. And you will be awake for the entire process. Because I am very, very good at what I do."

He touched the cold metal to my cheek and I flinched away, gasping. My heart was racing, which wasn't helping anything vis-à-vis impending hypovolemic shock.

"Are you afraid, Mr. Quinn?"

He didn't wait for a reply, continuing on in that same emotionless, mechanical tone.

"You should be. You are going to die. You are going to die a very painful death. But you should take some comfort that it will be very quick. Much as I would like to take my time, the fact of the matter is that your pain and fear greatly magnifies the power of the ritual, and you cannot be terrified or in agonizing pain if you have already gone unconscious from the shock. And while magic can keep you conscious to a certain extent, at some point your body will just shut down no matter what spells I use. Magic cannot make a brain operate without blood, unfortunately. So I will keep you awake and feeling, but not for too long. My record is seventy-four seconds from initial incision. And you have already lost quite a bit of blood, so I shall have to hurry once I remove that dagger from your chest."

I coughed and croaked.

"What was that, Mr. Quinn?" he asked.

I tried again. Speaking was difficult, and my brain was hazy and forgetting words, so I had to concentrate and focus on what I wanted to say.

"Do . . . you . . . always . . . talk . . . this . . . much . . . asshole?" I managed to gasp.

I'm not sure what I was trying to achieve by insulting him. But it felt right in the moment. Maybe it gave me some fleeting sense I was still in control of the situation, despite the circumstances.

His wooden expression didn't even flicker.

"Not normally, no. But like I said, Mr. Quinn, I need you afraid. And I have found that merely describing what is about to happen to you is a quite effective method of achieving that effect. So how about it, Sorcerer? Are you afraid?"

I really wasn't. At least, not of his threats. I didn't particularly want to die, but I'd made my peace with that a long time ago. Nor was I terribly frightened of any impending agony, given my vast experience with the matter. I certainly wasn't looking forward to the prospect, but I could face pain without fear.

No, if I were afraid of anything, I was afraid of the consequences of his success. That if he succeeded in sacrificing me, it would lock in the ley-line node here and leave only one sacrifice between him and the final rites of the Tamesis. I was afraid that Rachel and the rest of the Arcanum wouldn't be able to respond in time to stop him, because of my own pigheaded stupidity in refusing to ask for their help in the first place.

On the flight back from Egypt, I'd struggled with the question of what price I'd be willing to pay to save the world. Whether the world was worth saving at all.

In that moment, facing the imminent prospect of the world's destruction by this psychopathic Faerie and his cultist friends, I was forced to recognize how incredibly fucking stupid and selfish I'd been.

There were almost seven billion souls at stake. What the fuck did it matter if saving them cost the last shreds of my own?

No more games. No guns or knives or clever tricks. I had exactly one remaining chance to stop this. I'd failed Connors and Lajoie before. I would not do so again. I would likely die, but their city, their world, would survive. I was dead anyway. Accepting that was surprisingly liberating.

I didn't bother responding to my tormentor. I closed my eyes and focused on my breathing, trying to clear my brain against the gathering fuzziness around the edges of my thoughts.

I needed to reach that place. The one deep, deep down, that the Immortal had shown me so many years before. The pulsing, burning heart of the Earth itself. Not the molten core. Nothing physical at all. The planet's soul, if it had one. The wellspring of magic, the maelstrom of pure energy I now realized was fueled by the Great Cycle between the two worlds. The place I'd reveled in on the Fields of Fire.

But I couldn't find it. Normally it was always there, whispering in the back of my mind, begging me to let it go, let it burn. Ever since the Fields of Fire, I hadn't had a moment of peace, with that nagging little voice in the back of my mind and its unceasing demands I give it heed. My drinking was as much to quell that incessant whispering as to quiet the screams of my memories.

But at the moment I finally needed it, it had gone silent. Maybe I'd lost too much blood, couldn't concentrate hard enough. I couldn't focus. I couldn't find the fire. I had nothing left.

I opened my eyes again and looked the sprite. His eyes were as blank as his face. Patiently waiting for my fear. I did the only thing I could do.

"Fuck you," I whispered with the last of my energy.

He shrugged. "You will be afraid soon enough. Once the pain starts." He raised the skinning knife in his right hand and bent to take the dagger out of my chest with his left.

His hand grasped the hilt and a searing pain lanced through my torso and down my spine as he started to pull it out. Then I heard a deafening bang and my ears started ringing. The pain eased as the knife stopped moving. I vaguely heard another two bangs, but they were much quieter than the first, almost background noise behind the tinnitus. When I felt the floor shake as if a heavy weight had dropped right next to me, I was momentarily confused and turned my head to see what it was.

The Faerie had collapsed, his face a mangled mess. I saw blood starting to pool out below him, and my confused brain struggled to make sense of what had just happened. The loud bangs had been gunshots. Someone had shot him while he was distracted, focusing on removing the dagger so he could begin his task.

I was still confused. I lay there wondering who could have shot him for a second before I heard footsteps and shouting. I couldn't quite make out what they were saying, but someone was very excited. Or angry. Definitely one of those two, given the yelling. I wanted to close my eyes, but curiosity kept them open as I waited to see who was coming towards me.

My vision was blurry, especially around the edges. I tried to focus and see who had just leaned over my face. They were shouting something. Queen, maybe? I didn't know why they'd be shouting about a queen at a time like this, but that was the best my brain could do at the moment. She looked familiar, like I'd seen her somewhere. But before I could figure it out, I drifted into sleep, leaving the pain and confusion behind.

Chapter 29

I WOKE UP CONFUSED ABOUT WHERE I WAS AND TOOK A FEW seconds to get my bearings. Sterile odor, white, too much background noise, must be a hospital. I was lying on my back under a blanket, both hands and feet wrapped in bandages, tubes going into both arms. My throat was sore as hell.

I tried to look around, and discovered I was still rather bleary-eyed. There was someone in the room with me, but it took several blinks before I could see her clearly.

Connors looked concerned. "Don't move, Quinn. You're beat up pretty bad. What do you want?"

"Water," I croaked. She nodded and grabbed a cup off the stand next to my bed, filled it from a bottle, and put it to my lips. The sensation of the cool liquid in my dry mouth and throat was heavenly, despite the pain of swallowing. I closed my eyes for a long second to savor it.

"What . . . happened?" I managed to ask.

She chuckled. "Thought you might ask that. Short version, after they went in the front door, I heard a bunch of gunfire for a minute, then everything went quiet. You weren't responding on the radio. So after a few minutes of worrying, I called Rachel to tell her what was going on like you wanted. But she wasn't going to be able to respond for at least another half hour, so I went in to check it out. By myself—I didn't want to risk a whole tactical team against sorcerers." She put her hands up, as if to ward off an interruption. Like I was in any state to interrupt.

"Stupid, I know. And against the plan, I know. But everything was quiet, and the door was unlocked—either they forgot to block the door like Sam did, or the block must have faded when you killed their leader. So I went in and found their intended sacrifice tied up in a duffel bag by the front door, got him outside, and headed back in to look for you. I shot that short bastard as he was about to go to town on you with his skinning knife. You'd lost a lot of blood, and still had a giant knife in your chest, so you got rushed into emergency surgery. They cracked your chest, repaired the lung as best they could, and sewed you back up. You've spent a couple days in the ICU with a breathing tube down your throat and a drainage tube sticking out of your ribs. You got transferred here a few hours ago when the docs decided you were probably stable enough not to die on them."

I contemplated this in silence for a few moments. Partly because it was a lot to take in—I remembered only bits and flashes about what had happened upstairs. Partly because talking hurt my throat. I put it off and thought about what I'd just heard while I gathered my strength to respond. Not just about how close I'd come to death, but about what Connors had done.

One ordinary person, armed only with a small pistol, going into a house that she knew contained up to six hostile magical beings who had already killed multiple people. Knowing exactly what they were capable of, knowing everything she'd learned over the previous week, she still went into the house. Stupid, yes. Profoundly stupid. She could have waited for Rachel. That was the plan, after all. But if she had, I'd be dead, and the world would be facing possible destruction. Instead, she'd gone in. That was a hell of a thing to do. One of the bravest things I'd ever heard of.

I also thought about what I could remember from the bedroom upstairs. Why I hadn't just burned the damn house down around me. I struggled to put together the hazy memories, when sudden recall flashed through me. I remembered the exact moment when I'd tried to end the whole thing and burn the house, and my tormentor, to the ground around me. When I'd failed. When I'd given up. I knew I should think hard about that. I even knew who I should talk to about it. But I didn't want to. Not right then. Not in front of Connors, when she was waiting for an answer, something, anything, to let her know she'd done the right thing. I'd have plenty of time to reflect on my own failures later. I always did.

Instead I opened my eyes and realized Connors had taken my hand. I struggled to smile up at her.

"Good job, Adrienne," I slowly and painfully croaked. "I fucked up. You . . . you saved the day. Hell . . . you . . . maybe saved the world. I . . . doubt you'll get a medal for it, but I'd call it . . . a win."

She chuckled. "The captain said something pretty similar. After yelling at me for ten minutes about how stupid it was to go into the house in the first place."

I cracked a wry smile as best I could. After another couple sips of water, my raw throat was better lubricated, and I sounded halfway human despite the hoarseness.

"He's right, you know. You . . ." My voice faltered and I motioned for another sip. "You continue to surprise me, Adrienne Connors. I misjudged you when we first met, in so many ways."

Something struck me.

"How's Henri?" If I'd been in the hospital for almost three days, then he'd been here for almost a week.

"He's doing alright," she answered. "He's been out of the ICU for days now. Physically, he'll make a full recovery apart from the arm. And mentally, he's tough. He knows it's not going to be easy, but he'll make it through this."

I nodded. It was going to be a rough road for the big man. He'd have a great deal of adjusting to do to life without a left arm. It was probably the end of his police career. From what the Avartagh had said about his family, why he'd become a police officer in the first place, that could be a tough pill to swallow. It would be easy for him to retreat into self-pity and anger—to crawl into a bottle, or maybe worse. Like I had so many years before.

But Connors knew him better than I did, and he'd clearly overcome plenty of adversity before in his life. If she thought he'd make it, I'd trust her judgment.

I resolved to go visit him as soon as I was physically able, however. Not just because I'd never taken that bracelet back, meaning he was still technically under my protection. No, I owed him. Just like his partner, he'd charged into a building, knowing he'd be going up against sorcerers and possibly even the Fae, to try to help me. To try to save me. And he'd gotten hurt in the process. The least I could do was help him deal with that injury as best I could.

More than that, I realized I'd actually come to care about Henri Lajoie. He and his partner had earned my respect through their actions, and I could no longer think of them as mere allies, partners in helping me stop the Tamesis. No, I'd come to consider them friends—the first human friends I'd had in a very long time. It was a strange feeling, caring about people again. But I did, whether I wanted to or not.

Connors stayed for a bit to make sure I was alright, but she eventually had to go do real work. Normally closing a case is fairly straightforward: fill out a report, file any evidence, make sure everything's set for the prosecutors if there's a trial to worry about. But this case was different. She and Captain Paulson had agreed that, for obvious reasons, they couldn't put everything in the report.

I could just imagine what that report would sound like. I almost chuckled at the thought.

Instead, they would be working late developing a plausible lie that would satisfy both their superiors in the department and the dogged curiosity of the press. Journalists love a good macabre serial killer, and the occult theme of the murders had apparently fueled general interest in the story. Adrienne and the captain had their work cut out for them figuring out how to spin the story without jeopardizing either of their careers. I was glad that was their problem and not mine. At this point, I'd probably have just told the reporters the truth and dared them to believe me.

Instead, I planned on getting plenty of rest in the near future. A couple more days in the hospital at least until the doctors were willing to let me go home, and then I'd keep the shop closed for a while until I had healed. As far as I was concerned, my job was over until I was back on my feet.

We still didn't know who'd been behind the whole thing. My Faerie tormentor gave me a lead to start following—Aengus or Bran might know who the sprite was, and that could lead me to whoever was giving the orders—and there was still plenty of work to do. But the Tamesis itself had been interrupted, so I'd at least have some time to recuperate before trying to figure it all out.

I eventually drifted off to sleep, in no hurry to throw myself back into detective work.

That night I woke up in the dark. It was a hospital, so it was never completely dark, but the light from the hallway shining under the heavy wooden door of my private room didn't do much to illuminate my surroundings. And yet I immediately knew I wasn't alone. I sensed a presence. Not merely a fellow sorcerer, but some sort of magical being. A Faerie?

"Oh, good, you're awake."

"Johannes?" I asked, recognizing his voice. "You know visiting hours are over, right?"

The Immortal had come to see me in the hospital. What was he doing here? He could easily have waited until morning to check on me.

"Please, Thomas," he said, "I can practically hear the wheels in your brain spinning at top speed, trying to figure it out. So why don't I make it easy, and just tell you why I'm here?"

He walked over to the chair next to my bed and sat down. "Simply put, I'm the one you're looking for."

I struggled to sit up in bed, my eyes adjusting to the dim room.

"What?" I asked, not understanding.

"When you came to see me, and asked for my help," he shrugged, "I told you no lies, but I'm afraid I also didn't tell you the whole truth. You know me as Johannes the Immortal. What I've never told you is that before taking that name, the Romans knew me as Janus, their god of beginnings and endings, of time, and transitions, the master of the veil, of the future and the past. Janus, Johannes, how obvious do I have to be, boy? When I told you Janus was a suspect, that was true. When I told you I learned everything I know about the Great Cycle from Janus, that was also true. I am the one behind the Tamesis. I always have been."

I stared at him, unmoving. Where my mind had previously been racing, it had been stunned into silence.

"But you're not Fae," I finally managed to whisper.

He nodded. "Correct. The Olympians took me in as one of their own. Together we raised the Romans from a humble village to the masters of the world."

I considered that, then asked the obvious question.

"Why?"

"An excellent question," he replied. Then he paused, as if figuring out how to phrase his next words.

"I suppose we should start at the beginning. I told you how I became an immortal, from the magical cataclysm caused by the union of this world and the Otherworld. What I neglected to mention is that I am not the only one of my kind left. While most have passed on, five of us remain. We are the last Immortals, who have watched the advancement of humanity—our offspring—from mud huts in the African rift valley to landing on the moon. We have borne witness to every war, every plague, every empire, and every poet the human race has ever produced. And we are so very tired of it all."

"Tired?"

He nodded. "Exhausted. So over two thousand years ago, we began experimenting with a better way."

"Rome," I said in sudden realization.

"Very good, Thomas. I'm glad that knock on the head hasn't damaged your wits. Yes," he nodded again, "Rome was my attempt to build a better world, by manipulating human society from the shadows alongside the Olympians. We tried to guide the Roman civilization to establish peace and prosperity for all. The Pax Romana, it was called. My brothers and sisters had their own experiments in China, in India, in Persia, and so on. But we all failed, eventually."

I cocked my head. "And you decided the apocalypse was a better solution?"

He chuckled mirthlessly. "Not quite. You see, I realized that in order to form our more perfect society—one free from humanity's petty foibles—it would be necessary to leave the shadows and take control, to break the endless cycle of greed and destruction. Armed with the wisdom of the ages, our insight into humanity's nature, and the power of the magic that courses through our very being, we—the Immortals—are the only ones who could successfully build such a society. But our earlier efforts to do so as guiding lights and gods had been hobbled by our self-imposed constraints. To succeed, we needed to be overt."

Suddenly it made sense. "But after the Treaty of Tara, too many people had a vested interest in maintaining the status quo. The five of you couldn't take on the whole Arcanum and the Aes Sidhe and their allies. Hence the Tamesis."

"Precisely," he nodded. "Powerful as we are—and you know better than anyone how powerful we are, Thomas—we still could not prevail against the rest of the magical world. That is why my brothers and sisters decided not to support my plan, preferring to continue their hidden efforts—a waste of time and energy, but they refused even to consider openly confronting the Arcanum at its full strength." He paused briefly, as if remembering something from long ago.

"But," he continued, "no one knows the nature of the magical cycles linking our worlds like we who were there at the beginning. I realized that I could use my knowledge to break that link, severing the alliance between the Arcane Court and the Faerie Court, banishing the Fae back to the Otherworld where they belong and simultaneously depriving the Arcanum's sorcerers of the source of their greatest power, the ley-lines. With the Arcanum and their allies out of the way, we Immortals would finally be able to do what is necessary." He paused for a second.

"I used a mad Faerie as my patsy in the first, tentative experiments—the creature you know as the Avartagh. He knew me only as Janus the Olympian, and I carefully guided him toward the critical point in the Great Cycle which could shift it to the necessary equilibrium to change the structure of the magical links between the worlds. I led him to believe the rites were intended only to destroy the ley-lines, letting his people triumph over the Arcanum at long last. He did not know that it would also sever our two realms.

"But I miscalculated: he was sloppy, and the Arcanum too organized and effective. I saw that I needed first to weaken the Arcane Court from within. I needed an ally—someone inside the Arcanum, someone powerful enough to become my weapon to destroy it."

My heart began racing as he stood up, then continued while looking down at me.

"I have been alive a very long time. What's another eight hundred years when you've been waiting so many millennia? So I set to work, making careful, limited, unnoticed moves, cultivating specific bloodlines in the directions I needed. An injection of my own blood—I produced an heir, for the first time in thousands of years, and then guided her descendants from the shadows for centuries. Over several generations, I'd finally produced someone with the potential strength needed to harness the wellspring of magic. Then it became a matter of shaping him to my plan. Of pushing him ever so slowly away from the Arcane Court, without severing the connection entirely. Of leading him to see the darkness and pointlessness of humanity's petty concerns. Priming him to understand the righteousness of my cause."

Here he paused once more, then reached out a hand and lightly placed it on my shoulder. I looked up at him, standing over me, already knowing what he was going to say next.

"Me," I whispered. He nodded.

"Of course, my dear Thomas. You are my direct heir, my great-great-great-grandson. That blood, combined with several other powerful families, is why you have the potential to be the greatest sorcerer since Hermes Trismegistus himself—my nephew, as it happens. It is why you, and you alone of mortal humans, have the capacity to touch and wield the heart of magic, the wellspring, as I taught you decades ago. That is why I took you in when you felt you had lost your way—I was waiting for such a moment. You were ready to learn, and just needed a final push to complete your disillusionment, your cynicism. I'd prepared your skills but needed to prepare you to join me."

He took a brief pause. My eyes had adjusted to the light by this point, and I could make out his face clearly in the dimly lit room. His eyes met mine steadily. They were calm, collected, and utterly unfeeling. There was no love, no hate, no remorse. Johannes's eyes were those of a shark. Or a serial killer. A shiver ran down my spine, knowing where his story would lead next.

"And so, the Shadows. I opened the way from another plane, an abyssal dimension we'd encountered before, many ages ago. I did not invite them, exactly, but I knew full well what they would do when they discovered the door. And they did—they poured through from their world into ours, destroying and conquering as their kind is wont to do. This killed two birds with one stone: the war decimated the strength of the Arcane Court and the Aes Sidhe alike, and it pushed you ever further along the road to joining me. The callousness you witnessed in the Arcanum's strategic leadership, their willingness to send wave after wave to their meaningless deaths, your cynicism and bitterness grew day by day. The death of your beloved Charlotte—for that, by the way, I am truly sorry."

For the first time since his arrival, the monster showed human emotion, as his voice tinged with the mildest hints of regret.

"The necessity of her death made it no less painful, and your suffering was nearly too much for me to bear. Old as I am, I am still human, and you are my progeny. I hated to hurt you so.

But our cause is too great, and without the sacrifice you would never have been able to take the final step to join us."

He took the briefest of pauses to collect himself. I found myself blinking away tears and fighting down a growing rage. *How dare he speak of her? After admitting he was responsible for her death?* She wasn't merely collateral damage—he had just admitted it was a necessary component of his plan. But before I could form coherent thoughts and interrupt, he continued.

"Then, the Fields of Fire. You were primed. You were ready. You needed that final push, to witness the power of the well-spring, the heart of magic in action. I was there, you know. I watched from afar, you on that hill surrounded by the bodies, the Shadows and their demonic allies advancing on your position. I felt the world shake when you unleashed your full power for the first time. It was magnificent—the flames springing from the Earth itself, consuming and devouring your enemies by the thousands. Their screams were sweet music to my ears, knowing that finally, after centuries of waiting, I'd found the weapon with which my vision would come to fruition.

"But then . . ." he looked away. "When you disappeared, I realized my mistake. I'd pushed you too far, too fast. You were still too young, too raw, to understand. The necessary cynicism and bitterness were there, but untempered by the wisdom of experience. You still believed the Arcanum, despite its many flaws, was fundamentally just. That the status quo to which it is dedicated to maintaining was the proper balance, instead of the evil it truly is. You did not yet see the futility of its efforts. That it was dedicated to treating surface symptoms, all the while ignoring the disease itself. I was blinded by my own age and understanding and failed to appreciate your point of view until it was too late.

"And so I lost my weapon. You crawled into that whiskey bottle of yours and didn't come out. Oh, I know you rationalize it. It's to quiet the screams, right? Helps still the nightmares? Dulls the shame?"

He looked over at me with mock pity in his soulless eyes.

"But we both know you're lying to yourself. You're strong enough to handle the memories and even the shame without its assistance. That's why your mother looks at you with such pain, you know. Because she knows it, too, and doesn't understand why you continue to drown yourself. She doesn't know the truth, that the whiskey quiets that little voice in the back of your mind. The one whispering to do it. To touch the wellspring. To become what you're meant to be."

He paused. "But you were too far gone. I waited a few years to see if you'd recover, see if you'd come back to me, but I soon realized that was not to be, and I had to move to my backup plan. When the cycle was right, I arranged the Tamesis rites once again. I cultivated a select group of followers, sorcerers I trained myself from their childhoods, away from the prying eyes of the Arcanum, and set them loose upon the people of your city to draw you out of your defenses. If I could not use you as a weapon to destroy the Arcanum from within, then I would have to do it the hard way. You will still be my weapon, Thomas. But you will serve in a very different manner."

"The final sacrifice," I said, my voice flat.

"Yes. You thought you'd stopped the Tamesis rites by killing my pawns. You are mistaken, as it happens. Five sorcerers died in that house, Thomas. Before Ms. Connors killed him, Hugo channeled the death energy of his comrades and locked the node in place. His attempt to sacrifice you next was premature—I would have been very displeased with Hugo had he been successful. It would have ruined everything, set me back centuries of effort. Your death will fuel the final working, but the timing needs to be right. He was under strict orders to take you alive, or to incapacitate you, but not to kill you. He must have been angry about the deaths of his friends."

"The Avartagh seemed to think the preparatory sacrifices were enough to power the final working," I commented, my voice seething with suppressed rage.

Johannes smiled. "That is because he didn't know. I never told him, because he was intended to be the final sacrifice in my initial plan. Unfortunately, he was interrupted before he could finish the necessary preparations. All five nodes must be in place, the star must be formed, to amplify and focus the power of the final working toward the correct point in the magical connection between the worlds. The energy collected in the preparatory rites is helpful, but not enough—that requires a much greater sacrifice. A powerful Faerie mage, for example. Or the most powerful mortal human sorcerer to walk the Earth in millennia, one who has touched the wellspring of magic and controlled its fury."

"Well," I growled, "too bad you're almost out of pawns. That's still only four nodes."

He chuckled softly. "Thomas, Thomas, Thomas. You really think those were the only followers I had? No, of course not. And a good thing, too. They allowed me to remain hidden, so you wouldn't realize I was pulling the strings—if you'd known earlier, you might have actually been able to stop me. That's why, when you surprised me by showing up at my door, I had to be honest, to give you enough information to make you believe I was helping you, to keep me off your list of potential suspects, even though it made my plan somewhat harder. Especially once Samantha failed to neutralize you—you did almost disrupt the fourth preparatory rite, after all. But now it's too late. My acolytes and I have already completed the fifth preparatory sacrifice. The final working will be ready in two days' time. Your presence is required, of course."

We hadn't stopped anything. Lajoie had lost his arm, I'd been stabbed through the chest, Connors had risked her life, and it all barely amounted to even a minor obstacle. I'd failed, after all.

"I doubt you'll come willingly. And if you were to simply run away, you might spoil the timing before I could find you. Nor can I simply hold you prisoner until the appointed hour—now that Samantha and Hugo are both dead, I must attend to the preparations myself, and none of my remaining acolytes are strong enough to hold you captive for me even in your weakened state—I know you can still harness the wellspring if you choose."

It seemed he didn't realize my inability to do so the last time I'd tried, when I'd been staked down and about to be murdered. Clearly, despite his age, he didn't know everything.

"Therefore," he continued, "I need to ensure your participation another way. That's the only reason I'm telling you all this now—so you know what I need and expect from you. Fortunately, you've given me the perfect leverage: for the first time in a long time, you care about people again. And one of those people you care about happens to be lying helpless in a hospital bed just two floors away from this room."

Anger seared through me, rage beyond that inspired by any of his earlier revelations. How dare he threaten Lajoie? I could feel my mind start to go to that place, to reach the wellspring and roast him where he stood—we'd see how Immortal he really was. Unhampered by blood loss and searing pain, I should be more than capable of tapping into it. But before I could do anything, he held up his hand and I was frozen in place. Unable to move, unable to blink, unable even to breathe.

"Oh, that triggered something in you, didn't it? Good, that tells me you will make the right decision, then. I'm going to take your friend, Thomas. You cannot stop me. I may not be able to hold you like this for long, but it will be plenty of time for me to take him and leave. You will not be able to follow, so don't even bother. If you want your friend to remain alive, you will do as instructed. Meet me by the fountain in Logan Square, two nights from now, shortly before midnight. Come voluntarily, and I swear he will suffer no harm. You will die, of course, but he will live. Defy me, and he dies. And then I will come for you, and you will die anyway. It's that simple. Sleep well."

He walked out the door, closing it behind him, leaving me paralyzed and suffocating in the bed.

The spell wore off as he'd said, a couple minutes later, and I was suddenly able to breathe once more. After gasping for air and letting my heart rate slow, I pondered everything Johannes had told me.

He'd let me know who to blame for the deaths of so many of the people I cared about. And he'd let me know that he had every intention of continuing, of using me—using my death—as a tool to destroy the rest of those I loved.

For a long time, I sat there in the dark just thinking things through. I knew I should call Connors and tell her what was happening. But there was quite literally nothing she could do, and she needed sleep even more than I did. When she woke up was soon enough. I would let her get a few more hours' rest.

Finally, I picked up the phone beside my bed and asked the nurse at the desk how to get an outside line. Then I dialed a number from memory.

The voice at the other end was sleepy, but the rumbling drawl was unmistakable. "Hello? Who is this?"

"It's Thomas Quinn," I answered. "I need your help."

"With what?" the groggy voice replied.

I paused for a second and smiled, with absolutely no trace of humor. I was done wallowing, done drowning my sorrows, done avoiding and hiding. Seventy years of self-pity was more than enough. It was time to do something about it.

"Killing a god."

Chapter 30

I WAS STILL AWAKE WHEN CONNORS BURST INTO MY ROOM A FEW hours later.

"What happened?!" she half shouted. "Where is he?!"

"Calm down," I grunted. "Henri is fine, at least at the moment."

"What the fuck does that mean?!"

I put my hands back down. "It means it's not over."

That stopped her in her tracks.

"What?" she said, meeting my eyes.

"I had a visitor last night. Someone I loved and trusted, who I thought was helping me. Instead, he admitted to being the one behind the Tamesis, and he still needs me as the final sacrifice. He took Henri to ensure my compliance."

"And you just let him?" She glared accusingly.

"Of course not," I growled, "but he's stronger than me. Much stronger than me. He paralyzed me until after he was gone."

"If he can do that, why not just take you?"

I shrugged. "He said he couldn't keep me like that for longer than a few minutes and doesn't have any way to keep me captive since you killed his pet sprite. He needed Henri as leverage: someone I care about, to make sure I'll show up when and where he needs me in order to finish the Tamesis. He swore that if I do, Henri will be fine."

She sat down heavily. It was a lot to process.

"If you volunteer to be ritually sacrificed to fuel a magical apocalypse, he lets Henri go."

I nodded. "More or less."

"I thought the Tamesis required precise timing. And you said that there would be at least five sacrifices. We screwed up the fourth sacrifice, didn't we? And what about the fifth? The one in Fishtown?"

"I thought so too," I said, nodding. "But apparently the five sorcerers I killed in Pennsport were enough to allow the Faerie—the one you killed—to lock that node and channel their energy even without a proper sacrifice. And the fifth sacrifice occurred last night, before he came to visit me and take Henri. If you send a unit to that address, they'll find the body, I'm sure."

"Fuck." She put her hands over her face and then pulled them down slowly, as if she was trying to wake herself up. Or hold it together, more likely. "Who is this guy? What's he to you?"

I grimaced. "He's the one who taught me how to do what I did in the Fields of Fire. He's the single most powerful magical being I've ever encountered. He's damn near immortal, one of the first ever human sorcerers. And he's also apparently my great-great-great-grandfather."

She nodded slowly. "Okay. What does he want?"

I grunted. "What any evil villain wants. To rule the world and establish the perfect society, free of war and crime and unnecessary suffering. Presumably, he's the one who gets to decide which suffering is necessary, of course. Isn't that how it always goes? Hammurabi, Caesar, Charlemagne, Lenin, Mao, it doesn't much matter. There's always someone who thinks they can 'fix' humanity through their own personal genius and good intentions. In this case, however, he happens to be an immortal sorcerer who's basically a god and is convinced that his age and experience will let him succeed where so many others have failed. And if he doesn't get what he wants with my help, he's willing to sacrifice me and use the Tamesis to get it the hard way. In one stroke, it rids him of the Fae, renders the Arcanum impotent, and leaves him king of the magical ruins—and despite what I told you before, from what I've seen, he may actually be powerful enough to take on the combined armies of Earth by himself after all."

"I see," Connors replied. "We can't let him go through with

the rite, obviously. Not only does it require you dying—and while you're a surly son of a bitch, I'm still not keen on letting someone murder you to further his evil plans—"

I nodded in agreement.

"—but also if he's successful, he takes over the world, presumably killing a lot of people along the way." She met my eyes. "So how do we stop him without Henri getting hurt?"

"I've been thinking about that since he left," I replied. "He's an Immortal. He can't die from natural means—he told me that his life force is tied to the magic in the world around him. But in telling me that, he also gave away how to kill him: we need to cut him off from magic. The trick is getting Henri away from him first."

"That easy, huh?"

"Not easy, no. But simple. And I know someone who should be able to help make it easier."

"Oh? How so?"

"You aren't going to like it."

She raised an eyebrow. "Quinn, after everything we've been through in the past two weeks, I think we're well past what I am or am not going to like. Try me."

I snorted. "Fair point, Detective Connors. He's my illegal arms dealer."

She shrugged. "We've broken enough laws in this case already. What's a few more federal offenses? I don't think I've pissed off the ATF yet. But you seriously think guns will take down this guy?"

"No," I shook my head. "Eitri isn't a mere gunrunner. He's a svartalf weaponsmith. He doesn't just get me guns outside of proper channels; he also makes my ammo, and he forged my dagger. His ancestors created Mjolnir, Thor's hammer."

"And he can make something that can take down a god? What's this guy's name, by the way? I don't want to just keep calling him 'a god.'"

"Johannes. At least, that's the name he's been using for centuries. The Romans called him Janus and worshipped him as one of their most important gods. It makes sense. He has the intimate knowledge of the nature of the veil necessary to design the Tamesis—he was already my chief suspect; I just didn't know Johannes and Janus were the same person. I assumed Janus was a Faerie, like the other Olympians."

She nodded. "Hiding in plain sight."

"Exactly," I agreed. "But anyway, yes, I think Eitri can come up with something that will help. When I called last night, I asked him if he could make something that would isolate a being from the magical fields around him. He said he'd get back to me later today."

"Alright," Connors mused. "So assuming your svartalf can come through, what's the plan?"

I shrugged. "When I meet Johannes in Logan Square tomorrow night, I'll convince him to release Henri as promised, then we use the device to isolate him. Then we kill him."

"How? Just a bullet to the face?"

"No, that won't be enough. Even isolated from magical fields, he has plenty of personal power and I'm sure his regenerative abilities would be more than enough to deal with a bullet. I'm thinking a claymore."

She looked puzzled. "Like . . . a sword? You want to go full Highlander on him?"

I shook my head. "No, not a sword. A claymore mine. A curved brick of plastic explosive that propels hundreds of metal pellets in an arc, destroying most everything for about 50 meters in front of it. I asked Eitri to make me a couple, customized with pellets designed to take out magical creatures."

Connors looked at me for a long second.

"Just so I'm clear on this. You want me to help you ambush an immortal magical being with a device to cut him off from the energy fields around him that sustain his life, then blow him up with extremely illegal destructive devices that are most definitely NOT approved by the ATF, within city limits?"

"Yes."

She sighed. "Man, I was really hoping to keep my job after this investigation wrapped up. Just last night I was so full of hope and positivity. All the work the captain and I did to spin this . . . Son of a bitch." She bit her lip. "But from everything I've seen so far, I'm gonna go ahead and just trust you on this one. Alright, I'm in. I'll explain the plan to the captain. Hopefully he'll understand that there's not really a whole lot of other options. Just promise me that Logan Square will be cleared of civilians to the best of our ability beforehand. We can deal with property damage, even to a major city landmark. But no innocent bystanders getting killed in a police operation. That would be bad for everyone."

I nodded. "Once I know what Eitri comes up with, I'll let you know more."

Connors left to fill in Captain Paulson on recent developments. I, on the other hand, needed a nap—my rapid healing was sapping all my energy. Being awakened in the middle of the night by an immortal monster bearing threats and secrets hadn't been conducive to the recovery process.

Hours later, I was pulled out of my deep sleep by the phone ringing.

"Hello?" I answered, groggily.

"I've got somethin' for you. How do you want to do this?"

I'd known Eitri for a long time, but I was still perpetually amused at the idea of a centuries-old svartalf who spoke with a thick Southern drawl. He'd moved to Atlanta at some point in the mid-nineteenth century and learned English in the antebellum Deep South, and the accent had stuck.

"Can you bring it by this afternoon?"

"Tonight would be bettah. Can't take somethin' like this through the Otherworld without advertisin' its existence to a half dozen bein's you don't want to know about it. It'd shine like a damn beacon on that side o' the veil. I'll have to drive up. Take me about twelve hours."

I grunted. "I'll meet you at the shop tonight, then."

I carefully checked my wounds. Knowing the nurse would be annoyed, but not much caring, I peeled back the taped gauze on both the knife wound and the surgery incision. Both bore fresh red scars, well along in the healing process, though still tender to the touch.

I'd insisted they take out the sutures the day prior, after Connors had left, so the scars wouldn't grow around them—the nurse had been skeptical, but I'd informed her if she didn't pull the stitches I'd do it myself. My hands and feet were already functional, though painful to use. Moving around, the burn on my back seemed to be mostly healed; it itched more than it hurt. We sorcerers are resilient.

Deciding I had recovered enough, I checked myself out, once again over the fervent protests of the surgeon and the nursing staff. They pointed out that I'd had my chest cracked open and been on death's doorstep a mere two days prior. But I firmly informed them unless they wanted to try restraining me against my will, I'd be going home, and they processed the discharge paperwork. I didn't have the time to be lying in the hospital. I took a cab home.

I'd been thinking. The Immortal had outmaneuvered me at every turn—he'd planned for my interference, and even used it to gain leverage over me. It stood to reason, then, that he'd also expect me to try to fight him somehow, to thwart his plan. He'd have his own contingencies in place to deal with that, I was sure. Oh, he couldn't know exactly what I would come up with, but that wasn't enough. He'd predicted almost my every move so far. I needed to be unpredictable. I needed to do something he'd never expect. Something to make him react, put him on the back heel, rather than playing right into his plans.

I called Rachel Liu. Connors had told me Rachel had come to Philadelphia while I was still unconscious in intensive care. She'd said she'd be sticking around for a few days, at least until I was recovered. That was good. I just hoped she'd set up call forwarding.

"Quinn?" she answered. It seemed that she had, after all. "What the hell are you doing calling from home? You should be in the hospital!"

"I'm shaky on my feet, and everything hurts, but I'm still alive. That, however, is exactly what I need to talk to you about. Are you still in the area?"

"Yes," she replied. "Just tying up some loose ends and taking care of some business. Figured there should be at least one functional First Rank minding things until you could take care of it again. What's up?"

"You know those blood rites I've been dealing with the past two weeks? They're not over yet. I need your help."

There was a long pause. "Quinn, I've known you a while. Not once can I recall you ever asking for my help."

"Well, I'm asking now. I can't handle this myself. I need you, if you're willing."

"Wow," she said. "This is that serious, huh? What do you need?"

"Meet me at my shop tonight, around eight. And if you can contact Aengus, tell him I need him, too, if he's available. I don't know where he is, but you should be able to find him through official channels."

"I'll see what I can do, Tom. I'll see you tonight." I heard the click as she hung up.

I hadn't been able to bring myself to make that call days ago. Perhaps if I had, we'd have been able to stop Hugo from locking in the fourth node, and Johannes wouldn't be on the verge of success. Perhaps millions, maybe even billions of lives wouldn't now be on the line.

I had allowed my own issues with the Arcanum to blind me, to guide my decision-making for far too long. I couldn't afford to make that same mistake again. I couldn't afford to keep being selfish and stupid. Not anymore.

I didn't even put the phone down after she hung up, dialing another number from memory. There was no answer, but I left a message.

Replacing the phone on the hook, I realized there wasn't much else I could do until Eitri got there from Atlanta. I went upstairs, took another one of my healing concoctions, and crashed in the bed. I hadn't slept at all the previous night, and what I'd managed that morning after Connors left wasn't nearly enough. I needed a nap.

Chapter 31

I MUST HAVE BEEN MORE EXHAUSTED THAN I'D KNOWN—I HAD no dreams, and the nagging voice at the back of my mind remained silent. I woke up several hours later feeling significantly refreshed. The wounds were still painful, but between the afternoon of sleep and the healing potion, I was a lot less stiff. I took a look in the mirror for the first time in days to discover two black eyes, bruises all over my body, and of course, the multiple fresh scars. I wouldn't be winning any beauty contests, but at least I was on my feet.

I took a shower as best I could manage, got dressed in the cleanest clothes I could find on my floor, and headed downstairs. I didn't bother to shave, which added to my haggard appearance. Absent any other painkillers, I knocked back several fingers of whisky before I heard a knock on the door.

I opened it to see a man who was a little shorter than average, about five foot seven, with a long, braided, dirty blonde beard and swarthy skin. His shaved scalp gave a clear view of his ever-so-slightly-pointed ears. He had a backpack slung over one shoulder.

"Eitri," I grunted in greeting. "Thanks for coming."

The svartalf nodded at me as he entered and walked over to one of the chairs in the reading corner, where he set down his pack. Without looking at me, he started unzipping the main pouch.

"You look like shit. What did you do to yo'self this time, Tom?"

"Something stupid. I lost the Vepr in the process, too."

He shook his head slowly.

"Damn fool Sorcerers, always gettin' in ovah they heads, breakin' the nice stuff I got fo' 'em at great difficulty and expense on my part. I expect you'll be wantin' a replacement soon enough."

I shrugged. "It did its job first. I got three of the bastards before their friend melted the barrel. I'd say just replace the barrel and gas system, but it's currently in police evidence, and I don't expect them to be releasing it back to me ever. But we can worry about that another time. Right now, I have more pressing needs."

Eitri finally turned to face me, holding in his hand a small box.

"More pressin' needs like this. Yeah, I know. Sounds like you got yourself in a right mess this time, Tom. But this should help out."

He opened the box to reveal three rings. Each was a dull, featureless metal. One was coppery, the second gray, the third matte black, like wrought iron.

"This is some old magic, boy. Stuff I ain't nevah used befo' myself, but I found it in one of my great-great-grandaddy's books."

He picked up one of the rings and held it between his fingers to show me.

"These three rings are linked. When you activate 'em, they'll form the points of a triangle. Kinda like what them vodou priests did down in the Caribbean and Atlantic, what people call the Bermuda Triangle, but the opposite, and a lot smaller—that one is anchored to land; these itty-bitty little rings can't focus near as much power. But anyway, the one in Bermuda amplifies magical fields inside it. This one dampens them. Anything inside the triangle will be cut off from all magical fields, 'cuz they basically won't exist inside."

He paused. "Now, you said y'all're goin' after some sort of god, so a word o' warnin'. The rings will get rid of his access to magical fields. But that don't mean his own power goes away. He'll be limited—no blastin' energy or telekinesis with no energy fields to influence. But he'll still be able to heal plenty, and he'll still be plenty strong. And if you don't trap him physically, ain't nothin' stoppin' him just walkin' out of the triangle, see? So's y'all gotta get him in the triangle, activate the rings, and either trap him in place or hit him real hard before he can escape.

Unconscious or dead, you hear? And if you just knock him out, don't dawdle. Take the openin' to kill him before he can heal up."

I nodded. "That's why I asked for the claymores."

He snorted. "Yeah, yeah, claymores are fun little toys, and I brought two for you like you asked. But you know bettah than I do that no plan survives first contact with the enemy. What's yo' backup plan iff'n this here god don't wanna walk into yo' pre-rigged trap all nice and neat with a bow on?"

I frowned. "I don't have one yet."

Eitri smiled, as much as his dour nature would let him. It almost looked like a grimace.

"Thought so. So I went ahead and threw in a couple presents for y'all, in case yo' prey don't wanna cooperate."

He reached back in the back and pulled out two boxes.

"These are the claymores. Be careful with 'em. You'll have to rig 'em up if y'all do decide to use 'em, but you already know how to do that, right?"

I nodded. He reached back in the bag and pulled out a couple of cylindrical containers.

"And these are the same anti-god composition, but in fragmentation grenade form instead of claymore. So's if he don't wanna play nice, you can bring the pain to him instead of having to drag him to yo' kill zone." He looked me in the eye. "You ever throw a grenade befo', Sorcerer?"

I nodded. I'd been around a long time.

"Then you know that they blow up and out," he explained anyway, "and won't make no bigass fireball like they do in the movies—just a loud pop, a concussion, and a bunch o' shrapnel. Get one o' these at his feet once y'all got him in the dampenin' field. That should at least knock him on his ass 'til you can finish the job, if it don't take him out outright. Maybe cut his head off or something, I don't know—I don't kill gods, I just make and sell weapons. But anyway, these have a three-second fuse. So if you wanna cook 'em off befo' you throw 'em, don't do it for too long, or you'll find yourself short a hand and arm. In the middle of a fight with a god, I can't imagine that'll go over too well."

I gave him a wry, humorless smile. "No, I doubt it would."

"Finally," he said, reaching once more into the backpack, "I got you another present."

He pulled out a plastic box, which he unsnapped and opened

to reveal a Glock 20, to all appearances identical to the one the police had confiscated in Grays Ferry.

"Ten-mil, with the same SSVI custom job you had befo'. Picked this up a while ago, figured you might want a spare, just haven't had the chance to get it to you befo' now. I can't replace the Vepr on such short notice, but at least it's bettah than nothin'."

"What do I owe you?"

He shrugged. "These rings here, they're probably priceless. Ancient magic, doubt many in this world or the Other could have come up with them for you. Ordinarily I'd charge you a couple big favors in return, but seein' as to what you're plannin' here, I ain't so sure you'll be in a position to make good on that trade. So I'll take hard cash, if you'd be so kind. No checks, not this time. Cash or bullion. Call it a cool million. I'll even throw in the claymores, grenades, and Glock for free."

I nodded and went into the back office, where I removed two of several large shoeboxes from the safe, then returned to the front.

"One million American dollars, cold hard cash, as requested," I said as I opened them on the counter for his inspection. The stacks of hundred-dollar bills were still in the original bank bands, fifty neat stacks of ten grand each per box.

He cocked an eyebrow at me. "Shoeboxes? Seriously?"

I shrugged. "Would you prefer a leather briefcase? They're a good way to organize my money in the safe."

He just shook his head. "Only you, Tom, would pay for an arsenal of priceless god-killin' weapons with a couple shoeboxes full of cash."

But he dutifully counted out the stacks of cash, emptied his backpack's contents onto my counter, and transferred the cash to the bag while I quietly watched. Then he nodded.

"Good luck with the god killin', I suppose."

He turned for the door, but I put up a hand in a stop gesture.

"Actually, Eitri, if you wouldn't mind, I'd appreciate if you could stick around for a couple hours. I'm going to have a meeting with a few others who I hope will help me with my plan."

He looked at me, one eyebrow raised. "I ain't no warrior, Tom."

I shook my head. "No, I know that. I'm not asking you to help with the actual fighting. But you know these weapons better than anyone. You may have some useful input in the planning process."

He thought about it for a second, then shrugged. "I ain't in no rush to get back on the road, I s'pose. I'll stick around for a bit. You got any food?"

At nine o'clock, I looked around the reading corner of the shop at the people who'd come to help me in my time of need. Rachel Liu was in one of the armchairs, Aengus Óg leaning against the wall behind her. Connors was in the other chair, her eyes closed, taking a moment to rest before we started. Eitri sat on a stool he'd dragged out from behind the counter. And in the chair from the back office, my mother sat expectantly, her arms crossed over her chest. She'd gotten the message I'd left for her, requesting her attendance at this meeting.

Johannes knew me, had known me for over two centuries, had been watching me and manipulating me for my entire life. He knew me. Hell, he'd made me, shaped me to be his weapon. To get an advantage, then, I knew I had to do something out of character for me.

The in-character response for me was to confront Johannes alone, just me, my rage, and that voice in the back of my mind urging me to burn him where he stood. After all, not only did he well know that I didn't trust others—and he'd expect his own revelations to reinforce that habitual distrust—but this was personal for me. Johannes was the architect of so many of the traumas in my life which had driven me to where I was today: Charlotte, the Shadow War, the Fields of Fire. And, indeed, he would expect me to blame myself for all of it—my misplaced trust in him, my own weakness, and so on. He would expect me to come seeking both personal vengeance and to right my mistakes. He would plan to take advantage of that.

Which was precisely why I was not going to do that. I'd remembered the shame I'd felt in that bedroom, when Hugo had me staked down and I'd realized I had let my selfishness imperil so many others. This fight wasn't actually about me, no matter what Johannes had done. It was about the fate of billions of lives. It was about the future of the Earth, the future of the Otherworld. This fight belonged to far more than just me.

Johannes was threatening to destroy the Arcanum, so I'd invited the Arcanum here—the Lord Marshal of the Arcane Court and the Rector for North America—to help me ensure that did not happen. Johannes was threatening to break the veil and potentially imperil the Fae's very existence, so I'd asked Aengus to come, hoping he would help me ensure that did not happen. And of course, Johannes was threatening to overthrow humanity at large, strip them of their freedom, and rule as he saw fit. Connors was here representing the rest of the human race.

I'd needed to do something out of character, so I'd put myself—my emotions, my traumas, my trust issues, my desire for vengeance—aside and thought about other people for once. Then I asked them for help. Out of character, indeed.

Of course, none of them but Connors knew any of that yet. All they knew was that I'd asked them for help, and they'd come.

I cleared my throat, and everyone looked at me, standing next to one of the small shelves in the center of the shop floor.

"Thank you, everyone, for being here. I asked you to come because I have a problem which I can't handle on my own, and it will affect far more than me if I fail."

Without hesitation, Aengus spoke up. "Of course, I'll help if I can, Thomas. What do you need?"

Simple as that. I asked for help. He answered, even without knowing what I needed. I'd forgotten what it was like to have friends. I almost teared up. With a great deal of effort, I managed to keep my face straight.

I explained to them everything that had happened over the past two weeks. Most of them knew parts of it, and Connors had been there for most of it, but I filled in the gaps and told the whole story to ensure everyone understood exactly what was going on. They all remained quiet and attentive through the whole thing.

I then told them about the Immortal, and my history with him—how he'd become my mentor, how he'd trained me, manipulated me, deceived me, used me. I told them what he'd taught me, about the wellspring, about the Fields of Fire, and about what it had done to me. I told them what he'd told me during his visit the night before, and his plan to sacrifice me to fuel the Tamesis. I told them everything.

It was cathartic, honestly, to reveal all my deepest secrets after so long in isolation. It felt almost like a religious confession, except I wasn't begging them for absolution. I was owning up to my mistakes and asking for their help in making things right.

It took a great while. And at the end, there was a long silence.

I didn't know what they were each thinking. My mother was the first to speak.

"Thomas, my love, rest assured that we will have a long conversation about why you didn't tell your father and me about this Johannes when you first met him. Perhaps a lot of this heartache could have been prevented in the first place." She sighed. "But too late now. All that can wait until after this situation is resolved. Obviously, Rachel and I are going to help you. So what's your plan?"

Rachel stood up and nodded. "Even if I hadn't already agreed to help, knowing what we know now, I'd be duty bound to do so. The Arcanum serves. How do we stop him, Quinn?"

Aengus met my eye and nodded wordlessly. He'd committed to helping before I even explained what was going on.

Connors looked determined. "Let's do this," she said.

Eitri just sat on his stool, his face as dour as ever, but he also spoke up. "I'm not a fighter, you already know that, Tom. But I'll help y'all figure out how to do this right, as best I can."

I actually smiled, my eyes welling up. It had been a long, long time since I'd smiled and meant it. For the first time in decades, since the Shadow War, I wasn't on my own. I had a team. I had allies. I had friends. Maybe we could pull this off after all.

Chapter 32

"THOMAS. GLAD TO SEE YOU MADE IT."

The Immortal stood by the fountain in the center of Logan Square, watching me approach from the north. The park itself is a small circle, enclosed by the roundabout in Benjamin Franklin Parkway. Six gravel paths radiate out from the fountain like spokes in a wheel, with grass and trees in between. I walked over the crosswalk toward him and stopped at the edge of the north pathway.

"Johannes," I growled. "I'm here. Now where's Lajoie?"

He just looked at me for a few seconds. We stood maybe seventy-five feet apart. Lamp posts illuminated the park, letting me see his face clearly. Finally, he nodded, and a figure in a full-length hooded cloak—presumably another of his cultists—walked around from the other side of the fountain, escorting a conscious and ambulatory Henri Lajoie.

"Are you alright, Henri?" I called out to him. He nodded slowly but didn't say anything.

"I keep my word, Thomas," Johannes said. "He is free to go, as soon as you come here and take his place."

I shrugged. "Let's get this over with," I muttered, as I began to walk down the path toward the fountain. As I reached the brick-lined circle of gravel surrounding the fountain itself, the cultist let Lajoie go.

"Go, Henri. Adrienne is waiting for you across the street," I said.

He looked at me. "Quinn," he croaked, "they're going to kill you. Don't do this."

"We all have to die sometime. Besides, I owe you. Now go."

He stood still for another moment, just looking at me. Then he started limping his way past me down the path from which I'd just come.

Johannes was still looking at me calmly. As soon as Henri walked past, however, I acted. No witty repartee or clever one-liners that could give away my intentions. Instantly, a curved blue shield sprang into life, momentarily protecting us from the Immortal and his acolyte.

Of course, he'd been expecting a trick, and within a fraction of a second, I felt the impact as he began to hammer my shield with blasts of energy.

"Go! Run!" I shouted at Henri.

Despite his injuries and the obvious pain it caused him, he reacted quickly and started sprinting with everything he had toward where Connors stood beckoning him her way on the other side of the crosswalk. She couldn't stand up to the Immortal or his acolytes, so her primary job was to get her injured partner to safety.

Meanwhile I was slowly backing up, already feeling the strain of maintaining the shield against the Immortal's powerful onslaught.

"Really, Thomas?" I heard him call out to me. "Did you honestly think that would take me by surprise? Do you forget that I know you?"

I almost didn't hear the cracking of a twig behind me. I snapped my head around and saw at least two more cultists circling around through the grass, one on each side.

"I know your every move before you make it, Thomas," he called. "Time to accept reality and meet your fate with some dignity."

I didn't bother replying, as I was too busy drawing my replacement Glock from its holster and turning to confront the new arrival to my left. He had just cleared the tree between us and raised his hand to cast some spell, but my first shot went through his eye before he had time to get it off. He fell as I spun around to face the next target. I shot at him, too, but he was fast enough to drop to the ground right as I fired, my bullet going just over his head.

There was a metal lamppost flanked by two benches to my immediate front, to the right of the gravel path on which I was still standing. I dove behind them just as my shield collapsed, a massive blast of white-hot energy cratering the cement where I'd been standing a second before. From my prone position, I saw the other cultist pushing himself back to his feet, apparently temporarily disoriented by the flash of the Immortal's spell destroying my shield. I took a half second to aim and put two rounds into his head. He slumped back to the grass.

"Really, Thomas, must we do this?" the Immortal called out again. "Hiding behind a lamppost like a frightened child? Put down the gun, my boy. You can't win, and you know it. You're very powerful, certainly, but don't forget that I'm the one who taught you your strength. I'm older, smarter, and far stronger than you. Accept the inevitable already. You're only making it harder on yourself."

"Are you done?" I grunted. I struggled to my feet—my multiple severe injuries of the past few days weren't handling all this exertion well, rapid healing or not.

He just stood there, calm and collected, looking for all the world like a mildly irritated father disciplining a disobedient child.

"Are you ready to submit?" he asked.

I shook my head. "Hell, we're just getting started."

"What's your plan, Thomas?" he asked. "You can't kill me. You can't defeat me. You can fight me, but at the end of it all, I'm still going to skin you alive right here next to this fountain. And then, just for your insolence, I'm going to track down your detective friends and kill them. You've accomplished nothing."

"Not nothing."

Before he could say anything else, I gave a sharp whistle.

Aengus, Rachel, and my mother all dropped their masking spells at my signal. While I'd kept Johannes focused on me, they'd silently moved around us, forming a triangle with the fountain at its center. Each of them wore one of Eitri's magic-dampening rings, which they wordlessly activated now that they no longer had to focus on masking themselves. A bright light flared from each of their hands as the svartalf magic was released and the dampening field came into being.

I knew the spell was working because I was inside the triangle, too. It was an interesting feeling, being cut off from all magic—almost like going blind, I suppose. What I hadn't counted on, however, was the loss of my magical healing abilities causing all my recent wounds to flare into fiery pain at once. I dropped to one knee, struggling to deal with the physical agony combined with the sensation of powerlessness.

But if it was bad for me, I couldn't even imagine how the Immortal must have been feeling. He'd been connected to the magical fields around him for tens of thousands of years. Longer even than any of the Fae—much longer. He'd told me they'd become a part of him, that his life was tied to their flow. If I felt blind, he must have felt deprived of all his senses along with his ability to breathe. Good.

All three of us within the bounds of the triangle had staggered under its effects. I'd even known it was coming and was taken by surprise at the sensation. The remaining cultist—the one who'd brought Lajoie out when I'd first arrived—had fallen to the ground. Johannes was still on his feet, but I could see he was disoriented. That's what I'd been hoping for.

I fought through the pain to stand back up, then I raised my gun, saw the Immortal through my sights, and pressed the trigger. I rode the recoil up and back down, pressing the trigger again exactly as the front sight returned to my target. And again, and again, and again. The Glock held sixteen rounds. I'd used four on cultists, but I put the other twelve directly into the Immortal's chest without pause. I watched him stagger back under the repeated impacts.

The slide of my gun locked back on an empty chamber. I quickly slammed in another magazine, released the slide forward, and repeated the process for sixteen more rounds, putting all of them into his upper torso until I saw him collapse. I then tossed the empty Glock aside, reached into my coat pocket, and pulled out one of Eitri's grenades. I pulled the pin and threw it where he lay next to the fountain, then dove back down just before it exploded, sending shrapnel flying in all directions.

I struggled back to my feet.

I could see Aengus shouting something at me, but I couldn't make it out. I hadn't worn ear plugs, as I'd decided it was more important to be able to hear small noises before the shooting started than to protect my hearing after the fight began, and twenty-eight rapid-fire gun shots followed by a grenade were enough to leave my ears ringing. Thanks to my healing abilities I wasn't afraid of long-term hearing damage, but it meant I couldn't hear much else at the moment.

He was on one knee, his shirt covered in dirt and grass stains. The three of them had all known I was going to throw the grenade, so they'd dropped to the ground to get out of the way of the fragments and shrapnel. Aengus was pointing at something.

I followed his finger to see what appeared to be several more cultists in motion on the other side of the park, coming over a low hill where they'd apparently been waiting. They were far enough away that they were outside the effects of the triangle—Johannes had clearly anticipated an attack of some kind on his own position, and he'd left a reserve force, just in case. They must have decided to get involved once they saw their leader go down.

I almost smiled. They were in for a surprise. Before they could maneuver to attack Rachel, the closest ringbearer to their position, another group suddenly appeared to their left.

My mother was Lord Marshal of the Arcanum, and the Arcanum was under threat. She'd mustered every available ranked member who could get here in time. Three were busy maintaining a complex containment spell around the entire park, keeping any bullets and magic within its perimeter and ensuring no civilians bothered us for the duration. The rest, a half dozen Arcanum Sorcerers of the Second and Third Rank, were tasked with fighting any cultists Johannes brought along, keeping them off our backs so we could focus on the Immortal himself.

When the group Aengus pointed to revealed themselves, our own reserves dropped their masking spells and hit them hard in the flank. Fireballs, blasts of electrical energy, hurricane-force winds, and an earthquake hit them all at once. One lightning bolt went wide and struck a tree, which promptly exploded into burning splinters. It was eerie, seeing all that but being unable to hear through the ringing in my ears.

More cultists joined the battle from somewhere. It seemed Johannes had positioned multiple groups to cover different angles. And just as I saw them begin unleashing their silvery heat spells against our reserve, movement out of the corner of my eye dragged my attention back to the fountain.

The Immortal was slowly pushing himself back to his feet. That was irritating. I hadn't counted on my initial attack to be enough to kill him, but I'd been hoping.

I had to trust my allies' ability to take care of themselves—I couldn't help them from inside the triangle, and they couldn't help me from outside it. Aengus, Rachel, and my mother needed to focus on maintaining the dampening field to keep Johannes vulnerable; the rest of our forces were too busy fighting cultists to enter the field and help me. I was on my own for this part.

I drew my kukri from a sheath on my belt. I'd left it behind for the ambush in Pennsport, but Logan Square wasn't a confined space. And considering the Immortal was responsible for Charlotte's death, I thought it fitting her gift should help me return the favor.

Knife in hand, I limped my way in his direction to finish what I'd started, noting almost as an afterthought that while the grenade hadn't killed the Immortal, it most assuredly had finished off his cultist.

Johannes looked up just in time to see me, blade held high over my head, about to swing it down into the top of his skull. He might have been hurt, but he was still the strongest, most powerful being I'd ever encountered. With lightning fast reflexes, he reached out and grabbed my wrist in a vise grip, his other hand locking around my throat. My left hand clutched the hand choking me, and we struggled momentarily. Even without external magic, he was already shaking off the effects of my initial attack and recovering his strength.

Within a second of us grappling, I recognized he was stronger than I was, especially considering my now-painful injuries. I couldn't overpower him with brute force. But old and experienced as he was, I highly doubted he'd ever bothered training in close-quarters combat. Why would he when he'd been all but a god for millennia? I wasn't much of a hand-to-hand fighter myself, but at least I'd wrestled a few times within the past two centuries.

I stepped forward with my left foot and twisted hard, bringing my left elbow up and around, dropping it down onto his right forearm with as much force as I could muster. It was enough to bend his arm, breaking his death grip on my throat. That gave me an opening to continue stepping around him, sliding my right foot back toward his right side and moving my left around behind his legs. My left arm reached around his back, snaking under his armpit. He still had control of my right wrist, holding the kukri away from him and keeping me from doing anything useful with it. I needed to change the equation entirely somehow but wasn't sure where to go from here. As we struggled in that position, my left foot ended up behind his heel and he tripped backwards onto me.

The burn on my back was my only recent injury that was healed enough not to be affected by being cut off from magic. The stab wound and surgical scar, on the other hand, did not take kindly to me falling directly on them on gravel, especially with Johannes's weight on top of me.

The wind was knocked out of me and I almost blacked out from the pain. The kukri went flying. This was problematic. I couldn't maintain my grip as he turned on top of me—before I knew what was happening, he was straddling my chest with both hands locked around my throat, his face a twisted mask of rage.

"How . . . dare . . . you!" he snarled as he choked me. My ears were still ringing, but I heard that well enough. "I . . . am . . . a . . . fucking . . . GOD!"

I couldn't answer. I couldn't breathe. I struggled to remove his hands from my throat, but I had no strength left. The world was going dark, and I realized I was going to die, that this evil, insane, murderous son of a bitch was going to win after all.

Then, out of nowhere, I suddenly felt my magical senses return—the triangle had failed, and we were connected once more to the energy fields around us. I didn't know what happened, and I couldn't exactly find out in my current position. But Johannes's head snapped up and he looked around, before turning his attention back to me. His snarl turned to a dark grin, and he started to laugh.

"That was a clever trick, Thomas, cutting me off from magic so I'd be mortal. I didn't expect you to bring so many friends, either. But no matter. It didn't work. You're mine now, boy."

He loosened his grip on my throat slightly, still making it difficult to breathe, but no longer killing me.

"It seems my acolytes have already taken care of one of your friends, despite your best efforts. Once they've dealt with the rest, I still have plenty of time to peel the skin from your flesh and complete the ritual. I win."

"Hey, asshole! You're not the only god on the playground!" someone shouted.

It almost sounded like Adrienne Connors, but it couldn't be—she'd left minutes ago, she was getting Lajoie to safety. Johannes turned to face whoever had just insulted him, his expression more quizzical than angry.

But then his expression suddenly changed to fear and confusion. He recoiled in horror, his hands coming off my throat as he rocked back and scrambled off me.

I gasped as air suddenly filled my lungs. I didn't know what the hell had scared him, but I also knew I didn't have time to find out. Whatever it was, it had given me an opening.

This time I didn't hesitate. I had only one weapon that might take out an Immortal now that the magical fields around us were restored, and I needed to act before he recovered. I didn't have time to wrestle with the decision, to shrink back in fear of what it meant, to second-guess myself. Not this time.

I found that place, the burning heart of magic, the wellspring. The spot he'd taught me to find so long ago. I concentrated its power into the smallest spot I could control and unleashed its fury inside Johannes's chest.

He didn't scream—he didn't have a chance to make any noise at all. A bright burning light glowed in his eyes for a half second, then his entire body burst into white-hot flames as he cooked from the inside out. He collapsed silently backward into the fountain, which flash boiled into a curtain of steam around him. I rolled away, coughing.

When the steam passed and I could breathe, I opened my eyes to see someone standing at the end of the path. Bleary-eyed, I couldn't quite make out who it was. I saw what looked, for a second, like a tall woman with pale skin, dark hair, and a feathered cloak, wreathed in darkness. Nemain? Or was it Badb? Whichever, where had she come from? Had Aengus called the Tuatha Dé?

Then I blinked, and I could see it was Connors, running toward me. What was she doing here? She was supposed to be making sure Lajoie was safe. Before I could ask her, the world went dark.

I dreamed, then.

For once, it wasn't a nightmare. I was floating in a void,

then slowly I started to see something indescribably magnificent. The cosmos came into being, but I wasn't seeing it in only three dimensions. I could see the entire multiverse—our universe and its infinite possible permutations, the Otherworld and its own cosmology and all of their variants, and still other realms beside, all moving and interacting together in an eternal, endless, incomprehensibly complex dance. Wherever two or more universes swirled around each other, I saw a glowing, iridescent energy connecting the two and spiraling fractal tendrils into each. I understood instinctively these were the lines of magical energy that emanated from the connections between realities, the flow of magic through all existence across time and space.

For a few seconds, I couldn't just see everything that existed, in this universe and the rest. I could see everything that ever had existed, and everything that ever could exist. For one brief moment, I was omniscient.

Then I woke up.

I knew I'd just seen something important, but couldn't quite remember what it had been. I opened my eyes to see Connors bent over my head, saying something to me. I couldn't make it out. I shook my head, and suddenly I was back to reality.

"Quinn!" Connors was shouting. "Wake up!"

I forgot about my dream entirely as I struggled to concentrate.

I looked at her. Had she been the Morrigan for a second? Had the Morrigan been here? It was all still a bit confused and hazy.

"I'm awake," I groaned, and struggled to sit up. "What's happening?"

She looked me in the eyes, as if trying to see if I were concussed. "It's over, Quinn. I called on the Morrigan's favor, and it worked. He got scared and confused, just like Nemain promised. Then you got him. I don't know what the hell you did, but you fried the son of a bitch. Almost cooked yourself in the process."

"That's good," I grunted, my voice hoarse and raspy from being nearly choked to death. My vision of her now made sense. I'd almost forgotten about Nemain's promise to the detectives outside the gates of the Black Fortress. It had only been last week, but it seemed a lifetime ago.

I was exhausted, and completely beat to hell. I wanted to sleep for about a year. But then I suddenly remembered something.

"What about the others?"

She looked grim. "Rachel got a good knock when a lamppost fell on her, and I saw at least a couple of other sorcerers down. I don't know how bad it is. Your mother is taking care of the wounded right now. Johannes's remaining soldiers surrendered after they saw him get barbecued; Aengus is dealing with them. You're hurt, too. Don't move too much. I've got an ambulance on the way."

Great, I thought to myself. More hospitals. Just what I needed.

I shook my head again.

"Have to make sure," I gasped, then I rolled up to a sitting position.

She looked concerned but didn't try to stop me. Between the pain and the exhaustion, I had to take a second to catch my breath before actually standing up. Then, leaning on Connors, I staggered over to the fountain to see Johannes's body.

She hadn't been exaggerating when she said he'd been barbecued. He was burned to a crisp, his charred corpse lying in the fountain, slightly soggy—most of the water had been boiled off, but there were still a couple inches at the bottom.

He'd told me, two nights before, that only the strongest effort could break the bonds tying his life to the magical fields that permeated reality. It seemed a direct internal hit from the weapon he'd taught me to wield, the heart of magic itself, was enough to do the trick. But just in case, I sat down on the edge of the fountain and gestured toward the kukri lying a few yards away. Connors understood.

Once she'd handed me the knife, I swung my legs over into the fountain and dragged myself next to Johannes's corpse. With my dwindling strength, I raised the blade as high as I could manage and chopped down into his neck. It was thoroughly burnt, and there wasn't much resistance, his head falling off cleanly as the kukri hit the bottom of the fountain. Then I sat back up and looked Connors in the eye.

"Now it's finished," I told her.

Chapter 33

A FEW DAYS LATER, I WENT TO VISIT HENRI LAJOIE IN THE HOSpital. I was still beat to hell, but the bruises around my neck were mostly faded, my black eyes were almost gone, and my various wounds from the last two weeks were well on track now that I had my healing abilities again. After experiencing life without them for a mere few minutes, I did not envy Henri's impending road to recovery at all.

Connors had already told me that after some complications caused by the kidnapping, the doctors now expected it to be two or three months of rehab before he could be fitted for a prosthesis, then months or years longer of physical therapy and practice before he'd be recovered as fully as he could get with only one arm. It was going to be frustrating and painful.

I knocked on the open door.

"Hello, Detective," I greeted him.

He shook his head in response.

"Not anymore," he replied. "Medical retirement. The department feels I won't be able to perform my duties adequately with only one arm."

"I'm sorry to hear that," I said as I walked in and sat in the chair near his bedside. "But I brought you something." I put the water bottle I was carrying on his bedside table.

He looked at it, then back and me with one eyebrow quirked.

"Water? That's one thing I don't need you to bring me, Quinn."

I gave him a small smile. It wasn't much, but then again, I hadn't smiled much for decades. I'd been doing it a bit over the past couple days, but I was still out of practice and it felt strange, almost alien, like I was forcing it.

"Try it," I told him.

He shrugged, reached his remaining arm over to open the cap, and took a sip. His eyes went wide.

"That's not water. What the hell is this? Tastes like some kind of juice. Tingles in my mouth and throat."

"I can't regrow your arm, unfortunately. But I can help you get back on your feet a lot faster than your doctors can. No offense to them, of course—I'm told they're the best in the country. But they don't have access to healing potions. I figured it was the least I could do, considering how you got hurt in the first place."

He nodded slowly. "Thanks, Quinn. Connors told me you blamed yourself for me getting hurt. Do me a favor. Don't." He met my eyes. "That's not on you. That's between me and Samantha Carr. She did this to me, not you. And I was in that stairwell because I chose to be in that stairwell—you tried to keep me clear of it. None of this is your fault."

My smile had gone away, replaced by guilt and shame.

"If I'd been smarter," I answered, "none of us would have been in that stairwell. And if I hadn't been a coward, I'd have ended it before you got inside."

He shrugged. "Coulda', woulda', shoulda', Quinn. Unless you happen to have a time machine, there's nothing we can do about that now. I should be mad, I realize. A lot of people would be mad. At you, at themselves, at the world. But I'm not. I've been through a lot. My family was murdered when I was twelve years old. I'm a gay, black, immigrant orphan who decided to become a police officer in modern America. I know what it's like to deal with things not going my way. I'll get through this."

I looked at Henri Lajoie more measuringly. He was right, a lot of people would be angry. I knew that better than most. I'd faced similar adversity, and I'd lost my fight. I'd given up, crawled into a whisky bottle, and spent over seventy years feeling sorry for myself and drinking myself to sleep, angry at the world, at the Arcanum, at myself. I'd let myself be defined by all the horrible things that I'd done and that had happened to me. And I was literally one of the most powerful mages on the planet. Here was Henri Lajoie, an ordinary person, who'd been through as much trauma as most anyone would ever experience, telling me he was going to be fine.

"You're stronger than I am," I told him.

He cocked his head. "What do you mean?"

"When I got hurt, I didn't handle it with grace at all. You saw—you met me when I was still in that state. The drinking, the anger, the isolation. I didn't get that way by accident. After the Shadow War, I felt angry and ashamed and powerless, and that's who I became."

He shook his head and smiled, a touch of sadness in his eyes. "It isn't about strength, Quinn. It's about choices. I've seen enough people take that path to know that I don't want to do the same, so I choose not to. Some people, they don't have a choice. Depression, mental illness, addictions, you know. But I do. I've got a choice. So I'm choosing to be a survivor, not a victim. In my experience, attitude is more important than strength in things like this." He cocked his head at the door. "Plus it helps to have friends."

I turned in my seat to see Connors standing in the doorway, alongside an Asian man I didn't recognize who was holding a bouquet of flowers.

"C'mon in, you two," Lajoie said. "We're just chatting."

I stood up. "How've you been, Detective Connors?"

I hadn't seen her since I'd discharged myself from the hospital for the third time in less than two weeks. I extended a hand, but she ignored it and stepped in to give me a hug instead. I was surprised, but it felt nice. Apart from Sam's kiss, it was the most nonviolent human contact I'd had in ages. I returned the hug, briefly, then she stepped back and looked me up and down.

"Other than all the paperwork, I've been pretty good, Quinn. You look better."

I shrugged. "I feel better, too. Just came to check on Henri now that I can move around under my own power."

"Quinn, is it?" the man who'd arrived with her asked as he set the flowers down on the table next to the bottle of healing potion. "I've heard a bit about you. Henri told me you killed the bitch who took his arm."

I looked confused. "I did, I suppose. I'm sorry, who are you?"

Lajoie laughed from his bed. "Oh, yes, I guess you two haven't been introduced. Quinn, this is my husband Peter."

"Oh!" I exclaimed. "That makes sense. Nice to meet you, Peter." I extended my hand, and unlike Connors he actually took it.

"Thanks," he told me. "Always glad to meet Henri's friends. You seem much nicer than he described, though."

I smiled, a bit more broadly than before, as he released my hand.

"I'm trying something different. Anyway, I should be going. Got some things to take care of, just wanted to check on Henri here first. I'll be back when I can."

After a round of goodbyes, I headed out the door, but I didn't go home.

I'd returned home from the hospital to discover a letter, postmarked the day of the fight in Logan Square. As I sat on the train to New York, I reread it again.

My Dearest Thomas,

Congratulations are in order, for if you are alive to read this, then you have succeeded in whatever stratagem you devised to thwart me, and I am most likely dead. This is of course not the ending I would prefer—while I have never had any desire to hurt you, the sacrifice was necessary for the greater good. In saving yourself, you have doomed humanity to a future of interminable wars, tyrannical despots, endemic corruption, and great evil. But I take small solace that such a victory suggests you, at least, have begun the process of moving on from the past and re-entering the world at large. If I cannot guide humanity to a better future, I can at least think of no one better suited to protect them from their own darkness than you, my most apt pupil and beloved progeny.

I leave to you the brownstone and everything within it. Knowing you, I expect you may be tempted to empty the library and the liquor cabinet, then burn the rest. I'd advise you against such a course: there are several artifacts throughout the house that may be of a great deal of interest. But it is yours to do with as you please.

I am sorry it has come to this, Thomas. But please know that everything I have ever done has been for the greater good.

Farewell,
Johannes

I folded the page back up and returned it to the inside pocket of my coat. I'd been trying to process it for over a day now, and still couldn't decide how to feel. Certainly, I hated Johannes—while he wasn't at fault for every one of the memories which troubled my sleep, he was the cause of a great many. He'd set me up, he'd used me, he'd killed those I'd loved, and he'd tried to murder me, all for his supposed greater good. One of my fellow sorcerers, a Third Rank I had never met before that day, had died in the battle against his acolytes, and two others had been badly injured. But as much as I hated him, I owed him a great debt. In his mad plan to remake the world, he'd taught me the deepest magics any human sorcerer had known for thousands of years. That gift did not atone for his many sins, but it was a beautiful gift nonetheless, and one which had twice enabled me to save the world from the evils he'd unleashed.

Hours later, standing in the parlor of the brownstone in Cobble Hill, in the very room where he had pretended to be my friend for the last time, I was surprised to discover I did not feel angry.

I should have. I'd thought I would, surrounded by the physical reminders of everything he'd done to me. But I felt nothing at all. The voice that whispered in the back of my mind, the one that fed my rage and urged me to let it loose, had fallen silent. Perhaps I'd satisfied its ravenous hunger when I'd called on the fire to kill Johannes. Perhaps I'd even achieved some kind of peace. I didn't know. But I wasn't angry.

Instead I wandered through the brownstone and took a mental inventory of everything inside, memories flowing through me like they'd happened to someone else. In the library where I'd spent so many hours studying ancient texts, I examined the dozens of magical artifacts and tools on the shelves and the walls, with both magical and ordinary senses. Athames, bowls and jars of various substances, a mysterious stone orb that presented a void of nothingness when I tasted the magical fields around it. In the conservatory where I'd first touched the wellspring so many years before, among the various potted plants, I found a small hawthorn bush which I was certain had not been there back then. I wondered what was on the other side of the thinned veil from the Immortal's house. Olympus? That was a question which would wait for another day.

I was startled from my musings by a knock on the front door.

I walked to the entrance hall and opened it to discover a petite Chinese woman, the streaks of grey in her hair not detracting from her striking beauty. I didn't recognize her.

"Can I help you?"

"Thomas Quinn," she replied, extending a hand, "my name is He Xiangu. It's a pleasure to meet you at last."

I didn't take her hand and raised an eyebrow.

"You're an Immortal. One of Johannes's siblings."

After a moment she withdrew the hand. "I am. Technically I am your aunt, several generations removed."

"Forgive me," I replied, stony faced, "if I don't feel an overwhelming familial connection."

"Of course. I understand. Very well, then. May I come in, at least? I would prefer this conversation be private. I assure you I mean you no harm."

I shook my head. "I'm done trusting Immortals."

"That's reasonable, after what my brother has done. But I am not my brother, nor are the rest of us. I merely came to let you know that we bear you no ill will for what you did to Janus, and to discuss our relationship moving forward."

"What relationship?"

"Janus taught you a great deal, Mr. Quinn. But there is still much for you to learn if you wish to truly master the wellspring and the Great Cycle which powers it."

I grunted. "I think not."

She nodded. "I understand. Once burned, twice shy, as it were. But there may come a time, perhaps sooner than you expect, when you will need such knowledge. In Janus's library, there is a small onyx orb. If you change your mind, to contact me you have only to activate it with the power of the wellspring. Goodbye, Mr. Quinn."

She walked down the steps and turned right up the block.

I closed the door, thinking. I wasn't sure what to make of her words. Johannes had suggested, when he'd visited me in the hospital to reveal himself, that his siblings did not support his plans, that he alone was behind the Tamesis, behind shaping me into his weapon. But simply because they weren't involved in what he'd done to me didn't mean they could be trusted. They were still Immortals. I didn't know them, and I didn't know enough about their plans to know whether anything they said was the truth.

I didn't need to decide anything immediately. What I needed was rest, but I had no desire to do so in that house. I locked up the brownstone, set my own wards to replace those which had faded after Johannes's death, and caught a cab back to Penn Station. Immortals could wait for another day.

Besides, I had a number of bridges to begin repairing after decades of neglect, starting with my parents and with Aengus. My mother had stayed while I was in the hospital, keeping me company while I healed, but we hadn't had the conversations I knew we still needed to have. Aengus, for his part, had returned to the Otherworld to report recent events to Lugh and his court. I needed to reach out to both of them, and that was far more important than an old house and some magical artifacts.

It was late when I walked into the shop. Roxana was sitting on the counter expectantly, so I petted her and poured some food into her bowl in the back room. Then I looked around and realized I needed to clean up. I hadn't been open for business since before Grays Ferry. Tomorrow was Monday.

I returned chairs to their original positions, cleaned up my desk in the back room of the ley-line map and my notes. I got out the broom and started sweeping up.

While tidying receipts under the cash register, I spotted a bottle of whiskey tucked in the corner of the shelf under the counter. I'd completely forgotten about that one. I'd thought I was out entirely.

I hesitated, then grabbed the bottle. I straightened up and looked at Roxana, where she had returned to the counter after eating. She met my eyes, and I just stood there for a long minute.

My mind flashed back to Henri Lajoie, lying in his hospital bed, the stub of his left arm wrapped in bandages, with a smile on his face. *It isn't about strength,* he'd said. *It's about choices.*

"You're right," I said to Roxana as she watched me.

I put the bottle back down where I'd found it. Then I scooped the cat up in my arms and carried her upstairs. I needed some sleep.

ABOUT THE AUTHOR

A.C. Haskins is a former armored cavalry officer and combat veteran, turned economist and business strategist (and occasional defensive firearm instructor). He has a lifelong love of speculative fiction, having written his first science fiction novel as a class project in the eleventh grade. His interests include (but are not limited to) ancient and medieval history, mythology, applied violence studies, tabletop gaming, and theoretical economics. He lives in Michigan with his wife, two cats, and a dog.